I0831826

ALSO BY K. PATRICK CONNER

Dying Words

Kingdom Road

Blood Moon

Westbound

a novel by

K. Patrick Conner

NaCl Press San Francisco 2022

 Published in the United States by NaCl Press, San Francisco.

ISBN 978-0-9856312-2-2

This is a work of fiction. Names, characters, places and incidents either are the product of the author's imagination or are used fictitiously. Any resemblance to actual persons, living or dead, is entirely coincidental.

For Christine

Westbound

CHAPTER ONE

WITH HIS LEATHER SATCHEL in his lap, Elliott Madison gazed out the window of the northbound bus, amused, as always, by the ritual lunacy playing out on Polk Street. Through the smudged glass, he looked out at a uniformed meter maid standing beside her motorized cart, waving her ticket book at the outraged driver of a delivery van double-parked in front of a Korean restaurant, while a woman in a tight black dress and stiletto heels burst out the door of a nail salon, reaching up to catch her platinum white wig as she fled down the sidewalk. All Elliott could do was shake his head. For nearly forty-five minutes, he'd been looking out upon the daily bedlam, ever since he boarded the bus at the Civic Center. The 19 Polk was running so far behind schedule that he'd been tempted to get off and flag a cab. But he reminded himself that he was in no particular hurry. It had been a productive day at the library, and he liked to think of himself as a patient man, even when at the mercy of the city's maddening public transportation system.

When the bus finally crossed Broadway at the foot of Russian

Hill, he rose from his seat behind the back doors, gripping the overhead railing as he waited for the bus to pull over to the curb. As the doors folded back, he stepped down onto the sidewalk and started up the block. In his brown corduroy coat and gray felt hat, his satchel in his left hand, he was walking gingerly, his lower back stiff and tender. Several years ago, his doctor had sent him to a neurologist, who put him through a battery of diagnostic tests and determined the discomfort was caused by a herniated disc putting pressure on his sciatic nerve roots. The neurologist recommended an injection of steroids to relieve the pressure, but Elliott was hesitant. He had a lifelong aversion to needles, and the thought of having one inserted into his lower back was disconcerting, to say the least. So for now, he adhered to a pain-suppressing regimen that consisted primarily of daily doses of ibuprofen, augmented by the occasional glass of bourbon. He would submit himself to the steroid injection only when the drugs and liquor lost their efficacy, only as a last concession to his age.

At the corner, he turned onto Vallejo Street and started up the hill, the street lined with three-story apartment buildings, Edwardians mostly, painted blue and white and gray, their bay windows looming above the sidewalk. The gray shingle building he had inherited from his father was just across Larkin. He walked past the gingko planted in front of the building, across the sidewalk covered with the bright yellow leaves the tree shed every autumn, then climbed the marble steps and let himself in through the metal grate across the front porch. As the grate closed behind him, he crossed the porch and unlocked his door. After picking up the mail the carrier had slipped through the slot at the bottom of the door, he started up the two flights of stairs that led to the flat he had lived in for the past forty years.

Waiting for him at the top of the stairs was his granddaughter's dog, a small black mutt of indiscernible breed, its left ear folded over as if he'd been sleeping on it.

"Hello, Hank."

At the sound of his name, the dog turned and trotted down the hall, his tail whipping back and forth, leading Elliott to the back door with a sense of purpose if not urgency. Elliott opened the door, and Hank hustled through it, heading down the back stairs to conduct his business. As Elliott closed the door, he reminded himself that he needed to clean up the yard. It was a chore that by all rights should have been performed by his granddaughter, who had brought Hank home as a puppy three years ago, pleading with him to let her keep him, promising to attend to his every need. Elliott had agreed – but reluctantly. He could not say he was surprised to discover Alissa's commitment to Hank's care was aspirational, at best.

After tossing the mail onto the hutch beside the kitchen door, he noticed that the dishes he'd left in the sink that morning were no longer there. He knew Alissa hadn't washed them. It was only when he saw the dishwasher was on its dry cycle that he remembered his housecleaner had come that day. And that was always cause for concern. After taking off his hat and draping his coat over the back of one of the chairs at the table, he made his way into the living room to conduct a quick inventory and assess the damage. He proceeded directly to the fireplace. It was only a month ago that his housekeeper had managed to knock the daguerreotypes of his great-grandparents off the mantel, the glass over the portrait of his great-grandfather cracking when it landed on the tile hearth. Elliott had had every intention of admonishing her, of reminding her just how much those daguerreotypes meant to him, but when she returned two weeks later and he saw how badly she felt about what she'd done, he found himself consoling her instead.

For as long as Elliott could remember, the daguerreotypes had resided there on the mantel, the wooden case propped open to display the two portraits mounted in oval frames. They had been taken in San Francisco in the James Ford studio on Clay Street on July 26, 1863. Photographed in the prime of his life, his great-grandfather

– William Henry Madison – was a formidable, intensely serious man with dark eyes, a pronounced forehead, and robust mutton-chop sideburns. In a black frock coat and a white linen shirt with a cravat tied into a bow at the collar, he was sitting stiffly upright, unmistakably aware of the solemn image he was projecting for posterity. Elliott's great-grandmother – Amelia Snyder Madison – was wearing a dress with a high ruffled collar, her long brown hair spun up onto the top of her head with a few errant strands brushing her slender neck. She had high cheekbones, smooth white skin, and a modest smile. Not yet thirty years old, she was uncommonly poised, her dark eyes beholding the camera, entirely unafraid in the sudden burst of flash powder.

Although his great-grandfather died in 1864, his great-grandmother lived well into her nineties, and on those occasions when Elliott and his father drove up to visit her on the family ranch, his father told him about their remarkable lives – his great-grandfather's terrifying voyage around Cape Horn and his grim travails in the Sierra gold fields, his great-grandmother's heartbreaking journey across the continent on the California Trail, the homestead they developed into a prosperous sheep ranch. Elliott had listened, absolutely rapt, absorbing every word. He had carried those stories with him all his life, clutching them as if they were memories of his own. And yet, it was not until he retired from the *San Francisco Chronicle*, where he had worked as an editor for more than thirty years, that he had finally resolved to write a book about his great-grandparents to insure they received their proper recognition as two of Mendocino County's early pioneers.

HE HAD DECIDED to prepare a pot of clam chowder that evening. Although his granddaughter was a vegetarian, at least philosophically, she was nonetheless willing to eat clam chowder. In her view, the mollusks didn't count, even as fish, and she was always willing to set her ethical concerns aside when it came to bacon. As he began cutting the bacon into pieces and sautéing them in a cast-iron skillet, he had no idea where Alissa was or what she might be doing, much less when she might come home. But that was nothing new. She would call when she wanted to call. She would make an appearance when the mood struck her. With regard to his granddaughter's plans, he lived in a state of sustained ignorance, and he saw no reason to believe that might change in the foreseeable future. She had just turned twenty-three, and there were days still when he found it hard to believe that she had been living with him for the past nine years.

As he diced the onion on the cutting board, he imagined Alissa was with her bandmates, Martin and Walter, her two closest friends. To be perfectly honest, Elliott didn't care for their music. Why his granddaughter wanted to become a drummer in a heavy metal power trio was beyond his comprehension. As a young girl, she had reluctantly consented to sit for lessons on the piano in the living room. But upon entering high school, she declared the piano lessons were over and announced that she intended to play the drums. Ignoring his own best judgment, he purchased a five-piece drum kit for her and had it set up in the garage, and that's where she and her bandmates practiced. He had no one to blame but himself for the ghastly din that rocked the building three or four nights a week. They called themselves The Sores.

When the bacon was slightly browned, he tossed the diced onion into the skillet, sautéing it until the pieces were soft and translucent before scraping the bacon and onion into the pot of clam juice and vegetable broth. As he stirred the pot with a long wooden spoon, he realized how tired he was. It had been a long day at the library, reviewing what he hoped would be a final draft of his book about his great-grandparents, nearly fifteen years after his research began with the cache of letters and journals in the drawers of his great-grandmother's secretary, now standing beside the fireplace in the living room.

He had read through his great-grandfather's journals first, poring over them assiduously, page by page, taking meticulous notes. They were nothing less than a biographer's dream. The entries in his journals are precise and unambiguous, recorded by date, typically offering a concise summation of the events of the day, and yet other entries included longer meditations on his great-grandfather's broader ambitions and intentions. William Madison was articulate and insightful and intended for his journals to be read. He was not the kind of man to forsake the opportunity to influence his legacy. He regarded himself as one of that rare breed of men who define their time as much as their time defines them, and even in a life that would be cruelly cut short, that would, in Elliott's humble opinion, clearly prove to be true.

He had spent that afternoon reviewing the section of his manuscript that concerned his great-grandfather's passage around Cape Horn, a voyage that began in Charleston, South Carolina, where Madison had been born on October 3, 1819. His family had lived there since the early 1700s, residing in a brick three-story mansion complete with two tiered piazzas from which to stand in the evening breeze and gaze out at the bay. Madison had been a sickly child who suffered from severe asthma that largely confined him to bed for the first four years of his life, but he gradually outgrew his health problems, nurtured by a nanny who cared for him as if he were a child of her own. He excelled in school, and at the age of seventeen enrolled at South Carolina College in Columbia. He later earned a degree in law. At the urging of his father, a federal judge, he joined a law firm in Charleston that represented some of the most prominent men in the city, and for the next several years, he practiced law with distinction, resolving disputes among the city fathers in service of the title and authority of the Southern aristocracy.

But like the rest of the nation, Madison was intrigued by the initial reports of the discovery of gold in California. Although he had become engaged to a woman whose father owned one of the largest cotton gins in the state, with each new report from the gold fields, the greater Madison felt the temptation to join the thousands of men who had already left to seek their fortunes. Finally, he could resist that temptation no longer. A month before he was to be married, he broke off the engagement, resigned from the law firm and booked passage to California. His father pleaded with him to reconsider, but on May 17, 1851, Madison bid his family farewell, then boarded a ship named the *Cordelia* and sailed out of Charleston harbor.

With its two white pine masts towering 120 feet above the deck, the 320-ton brigantine promised to be a swift seaworthy vessel, and the consortium of New York investors that owned the *Cordelia* advertised that the passage around Cape Horn to San Francisco would take no more than four months. Elliott had studied the route the *Cordelia* would take, charting it on maps in the library, and he'd found it counterintuitive, to say the least, that to travel by sea to California often meant initially sailing east across the Atlantic. But that was the course selected by the captain, who wanted to avoid the heavy winds and strong equatorial currents that ran through the islands of the Caribbean. Instead, the *Cordelia* sailed up the Eastern Seaboard, stopping in New York and Boston before riding the Gulf Stream across the northern Atlantic.

His great-grandfather had never been out to sea for any length of time, and he and many of the other passengers became violently ill when the ship ran into a series of squalls shortly after sailing out of Boston Harbor. But Madison soon gained his sea legs and spent as little time as possible in the poorly lit, unventilated quarters below deck. He preferred standing on the foredeck and gazing out at the slate gray horizon, which is where he was on the morning of June 18, when he heard the cry from the crow's nest that land had been spotted off the port bow.

Later that evening, he recorded that sighting in his journal, and Elliott had quoted him directly in his manuscript:

"The Azores were almost impossible to make out against the

horizon, but by late afternoon we could see the emerald green peaks rising out of the sea. The sight of the islands occasioned great excitement among the passengers and crew alike, for it meant we had successfully completed the first leg of our voyage."

After taking on water and supplies at Ponta Delgada, the *Cordelia* set a course to the south, picking up the trade winds, and soon the ship crossed the Tropic of Cancer and sailed down the west coast of Africa. Under a cloudless sky, the *Cordelia* glided effortlessly across the ocean, leaning away from the warming winds, skating across the waves as they sailed past the Cape Verde Islands and then bore down on the northeast coast of South America. They spotted Cape Sao Roque on the morning of June 29, and for the next six days, they made their way down the east coast of the continent, arriving at Rio de Janeiro on July 5.

The Baia de Guanabara was a magnificent natural harbor, surrounded by soaring granite monoliths with darkly forested ridges receding into the distance, and after nearly two months aboard the *Cordelia*, Madison and the other passengers were anxious to set foot on solid ground. The following morning, they climbed into the whaleboats and were taken ashore. Madison spent the day wandering through the city, admiring its decadent colonial architecture, walking its cobblestone streets and through its waterfront plazas and sun-drenched gardens. The steady fare of salt pork, hard bread and beans aboard the *Cordelia* had left him craving the simple pleasure of fresh fruit, so he indulged himself in the open markets, savoring the guavas, bananas and oranges. But he was anxious to resume the voyage to San Francisco.

"Nearly two months have passed since we sailed out of Charleston, and we are not even halfway to California," he wrote. "The voyage around Cape Horn is certainly going to take longer than the four months the owners of the ship advertised, which is a source of great frustration for us all."

Elliott could certainly understand that frustration. His great-grandfather was anxious to begin a new life, eager to seek his fate in the gold fields, and Elliott had to appreciate his quiet optimism and sense of anticipation. But with the benefit of hindsight, having read his great-grandfather's journals, Elliott also knew that his great-grandfather had no idea what awaited him, the ordeal he and his fellow passengers would soon go through.

WHEN THE CLAM CHOWDER was ready, Elliott ladled it into a bowl and carried it over to the table. It was only as he set the bowl down that he realized he had forgotten to pick up some oyster crackers. He walked over to the cabinet above the counter to see if he might still have some from the last time he made the chowder, but he knew, even as he reached for the cabinet door, that he didn't. Alissa loved oyster crackers. She ate them by the handful straight from the bag. He quickly scanned the shelves, but no, as he suspected, there weren't any crackers. He hoped Alissa wouldn't be disappointed. He knew she wouldn't hesitate to let him know if she was.

He returned to the table and sat down, dipping his spoon into the chowder for a taste. As he raised the spoon to his mouth, he was surprised to hear the door at the bottom of the stairs creak open. He paused and listened to the soft thump of Alissa's black high-top sneakers on the carpeted treads, relieved not to hear any other footsteps. He didn't particularly care for it when Alissa brought her friends home. It made him uncomfortable to think what they might be doing behind her closed bedroom door.

As she appeared in the kitchen doorway, he said, "You're home uncommonly early."

"So?" she asked, as if it were an accusation.

She bent down and scooped Hank into her arms, the dog pawing at the air as she nuzzled his belly. She was wearing a pair of ragged blue jeans, ripped across her thighs as if she'd been caught in barbed wire, a black leather jacket adorned with chains. Her dyed-green hair rose from her scalp in spikes. Her bloodshot eyes were crudely outlined with dark mascara, her eyelids smeared with green eye shadow. Elliott dearly wished his daughter Claire was here to discuss these matters of dress and comportment, but he also knew that Alissa had stopped listening to her mother years ago.

"I assumed you'd be out with the boys, that's all," he said.

"Martin has a cold sore on his bottom lip," she said. "It's disgusting."

"I'm sorry to hear that," Elliott said.

"And Walter's in trouble for scratching his father's car with his scooter."

"I see."

Elliott pointed at the bowl on the table in front of him.

"Clam chowder," he said. "Shall I fix you a bowl?"

"I'm not hungry."

"Are you sure?" he asked. "It's not bad, if I do say so myself."

"No, thanks," she said.

She leaned down and set the dog on the floor, then took off her jacket and dropped into the chair across from him, looking on as Hank sauntered over to his water bowl.

"Has he been fed?" she asked, watching the dog slurping water with his long tongue.

"He most certainly has," Elliott said. "And I must say his digestive system seems to be functioning properly, judging by the scale and volume of his deposits in the backyard."

"Don't be gross," she said.

"Prodigious, actually, for a dog his size."

She turned to him, a stainless steel ring through her lower lip, a galaxy of stars tattooed on her neck. He wondered if she was under the influence of alcohol or marijuana. It always worried him to think his granddaughter might be intoxicated.

"I'll clean up the yard this weekend," she said.

"You'll forgive me if I don't hold my breath," he said.

"And what is that supposed to mean?" she asked indignantly.

But Elliott didn't want to argue. He was glad Alissa was home. She was often out well into the night, well into the morning, and he found it difficult to sleep when he didn't know where she was. He tried not to worry about her; he tried to prevent his mind from indulging his darkest fears. But she felt no obligation to tell him where she was going or when she might return. And he knew better than to ask, just as he knew better than to call her on her cell phone. He certainly knew better than to let himself fall asleep in front of the television in the living room, where she might find him when she came home and think he was waiting up for her. He had to remind himself, constantly, that she was an adult, responsible for her own decisions, however ill-considered they often were.

"It just means that I'll do it," Elliott said. "That's all."

She rose from the chair and picked up her jacket.

"Are you sure you won't have a bowl of chowder?" he asked.

"Maybe tomorrow," she said.

"Tomorrow, then," Elliott said, as if exacting a promise. "I'll try to remember to pick up some oyster crackers."

But she had already turned and walked out of the kitchen, trailed down the hall by her dog.

WHEN HE FINISHED EATING, he carried the empty bowl over to the sink, then poured himself a glass of bourbon and returned to the table. As he sat down and took a sip, he could envision the *Cordelia* sailing down the coast into the South Atlantic, the ocean clapping against the ship's sturdy hull, the sails ruffling in the wind; he could see his great-grandfather standing at the gunwale, watching as an exotic new world revealed itself to him, league by league. At times they were escorted by as many as a dozen dolphins, flashing through the water alongside the ship, then bursting through the surface and arcing across the waves. Later, when they reached the colder southern waters, great blue whales rose from the depths of the ocean, spouting more than twenty feet into the air, waving their huge flukes before crashing back into the water. The days were cooled by the occasional thunderstorms that arose in the afternoons. As the storms broke apart, sunlight slanted down into the ocean.

But Madison and many of the other passengers had become increasingly concerned about the health of the captain, a former whaler named Joshua Pitts, a skeletal old man lured out of retirement by the sudden demand for passage from the great cities of the East to California.

"The captain does not look well. He suffers from a violent cough that shakes the whole of his body and leaves him gasping for air. He remains in his cabin for days at a time. His first mate, a swarthy Hungarian named Spielman, has all but taken command of the ship and has proven himself to be a brutal tyrant who makes no attempt to conceal his contempt for the young seamen he commands, many of them having signed on for the voyage to California because they couldn't afford to purchase a ticket of their own."

The weather began to turn after the *Cordelia* passed the mouth of Rio de la Plata. The mornings were cold and gray, the afternoons blustery. The days grew shorter and the nights longer. Above the southern horizon, they could see the Magellanic Clouds, the mysterious clusters of stars named for the Portuguese navigator who died attempting to sail around the world. The Southern Cross seemed to grow closer every night. Far to the west, they glimpsed the Patagonian coastline, the high cliffs crowned with blue-green forest, a dark plume of smoke trailing across the sky, its origin unknown.

But soon the winds drove the ship hard to the east, beyond sight of land.

"After determining their longitude with his chronometer, the captain ordered Spielman to take down the mainsails and replace them with older sails stored below deck. I did not understand the purpose of the captain's order until it was explained to me that the captain didn't want the weather we would soon encounter to tear the newer mainsails apart. It was an explanation I found, in a word, ominous."

Five days later, the *Cordelia* entered the Strait de la Maire and charted a course through the uninhabited islands at the tip of the continent. The ship tacked to the north and south in the face of the heavy headwinds, heaving through the rolling ocean, rising to the crest of one wave before plunging into the deep trough below. The ocean seemed to grow angrier by the hour, the huge waves breaking over the deck. The sky darkened nearly to black, and the wind raged, as violent, Madison observed, as the hurricanes that periodically savaged the South Carolina coast.

Madison was forced to spend virtually all of his time below deck. There was no fire to warm their quarters. The whale oil lamps suspended from the ceiling were barely able to push their light into the darkness, making it virtually impossible to distinguish night from day. Many of the passengers had fallen sick again, and there was nothing that could be done for them. As the *Cordelia* pitched from side to side, all Madison and the other passengers could do was cling to their berths.

"I am not a religious man," Madison wrote. "But as I lie in my berth, listening to the quiet prayers of those who fear we are about to be lost, I envy the solace they find in appealing to their God for deliverance."

For the next eight days, the sky was clear and white, and midday on August 17, they heard the cry that land had been spotted off the starboard bow. All but the deathly ill climbed out of their berths and made their way onto the deck to look out upon the dark face of Cape Horn. The sighting cheered the assembled passengers, including Madison.

"I could not but hope the worst of the voyage was behind us."

But the following day, the winds abruptly picked up again and a wall of dark clouds appeared to the west. The gale came upon them quickly. The wind howled and shrieked. As the ship plunged through the heaving ocean, the old sails began to tear apart. Hail raked down, rattling the deck and clogging the scuppers through which the water on the deck sluiced back into the ocean. The masts swung wildly across the sky, the hull groaning as if the ship might break apart. One seaman was washed overboard by the waves pounding the deck. Another, high in the rigging, lost his grip and vanished into the ocean.

The gale lasted three days before it blew itself out. Finally, they could see land on the eastern horizon. The captain emerged from his cabin, his eyes blood red and his face a pallid gray. The quarter-master had to steady him as he raised his looking glass and studied the faint blue streak of land. When Spielman turned and called out to the helmsman to set a new course to the northwest, they realized that they had finally reached the Pacific.

"We felt an immense relief at having rounded the horn," Madison wrote. "But I did not permit myself to participate in the extemporaneous celebration. We still face, even under the very best conditions, another eight weeks at sea before we arrive in San Francisco. Then, and only then, shall I celebrate."

ELLIOTT ROSE from the table and walked down the hall to his bedroom. His blue-and-black robe hung from a hook on the back of the closet door. After putting it on and loosely tying the sash, he made his way into the living room, where he sat at his great-grandmother's secretary. In the right hand drawer was the first of his great-grandfather's journals. The leather-bound volume was in poor condition, the result of its age and the difficult circumstances it had been compelled to endure. Secured with a thin strap, the cover had been embossed with his great-grandfather's initials, but the spine had torn years ago, releasing the pages from their binding. As far as Elliott was concerned, the journal was more than a record of his great-grandfather's voyage around Cape Horn. It was also an artifact, in and of itself, and he treated it, as well as his great-grandfather's subsequent journals, with reverence as much as appreciation. It had taken him a fair amount of time to learn to read his great-grandfather's handwriting, filling every unlined page with his cramped script, but by the time the *Cordelia* was sailing up the Chilean coast, Elliott could read the handwriting as easily as if it were his own.

After ten days, the ship put in at Valparaiso to repair the storm-damaged spars on the foremast and to replace the shredded sails with those they had stored away. While the passengers were ashore, the crew smoked the ship to kill the rats, lighting piles of sulfur in large iron kettles deep in the hold, the heavy yellow smoke seeping out of every seam of the ship and then drifting across the harbor. That evening, after the smoke had dissipated, the crew gathered up no less than six barrels of dead rats, which they then hoisted onto the gunwale and dumped into the bay.

They spent four days in Valparaiso, leaving on September 15, and as the trade winds carried them north across the dark blue waters of the Pacific, Madison and the other passengers hoped their long voyage was nearing its destination. But those hopes evaporated less than two weeks later, when the ship stalled in the equatorial doldrums, the wind dying out and the ocean falling still, its glassy surface reflecting the white-hot sky. After nearly five months at sea, the passengers and the crew were exhausted, and the suffocating heat sapped what little strength they had left. All they could do was wait for the wind to return. The hours crawled past. Each day seemed an eternity.

"I have come to hate the ocean," Madison wrote. "I hate its vile moods and insidious currents, its sinister collusion with the wind and rain. I can only wonder when, if ever, this agonizing voyage will end."

Mercifully, three days later, with the *Cordelia* lying two hundred miles southeast of the Sandwich Islands, the air began to awaken, a breath of wind whispered across the water. When Madison looked up, he saw that others had noticed it, too.

"I rose to my feet and walked over to the gunwale to look down at the water. We could see the ripples spreading across the surface, receding from the hull of the ship. We could feel the air beginning to stir. When I looked up, I saw that the mainsails had begun to slough ever so slightly. By nightfall, the wind began to gather, and the ship, moaning in the darkness, began to move. It seemed nothing less than a miracle. Perhaps we will soon be delivered from this equatorial purgatory."

By the following afternoon, the ship was in full sail, and Madison resumed his favored position on the foredeck. The air was clean and fresh, and the *Cordelia* sailed effortlessly northward, drawing closer to California by the day. Finally, on November 4, they heard the call they had all been waiting for.

"As the coastline appeared in the distance, we erupted in cheers, shaking hands and clapping each other on the back, knowing that our long ordeal would soon be over."

They sailed up the coast for the next week, the golden hills and high dark cliffs easy to behold off the starboard bow, and on November 12, they spotted the Farallon Islands, just outside the entrance to San Francisco Bay. But it was late in the afternoon, and a dense fog folded over them, sealing out the remaining daylight. They had no choice but to wait until the following morning to risk the treacherous waters at the narrow mouth of the bay.

That night, the passengers chased their disappointment with whiskey liberated from the galley, and Madison saw no reason not to participate. In their quarters below deck, he and his fellow passengers drank and sang well into the night. It was the priest who suggested they bring the captain down for a final toast. Before anyone could discourage them, two of the passengers rushed up onto the deck and pounded on the door of the captain's cabin, shouting for him to let them in. When Madison heard them breaking down the cabin door, he and several other men climbed up to the deck to see what they meant to do.

The captain had already been dragged out of his cabin. Curled into a fetal position, his stiff emaciated body lay motionless on the deck. There was no way to tell when he had died, but no one particularly cared. It was proposed that they bury the captain at sea, and with Spielman watching, one of the seamen grabbed the captain's ankles and another took him by the wrists. With the passengers and crew loudly cheering them on, they swung the captain over the gunwale and into the darkness. His body scarcely made a sound as it splashed through the surface.

That was enough for Madison. He turned and started back down to his berth. As far as he was concerned, the celebration was over.

"In the morning, we will sail into San Francisco Bay. Nearly six months have passed since we left Charleston, considerably longer than I had anticipated. But I have made it to California, and that is all that matters now."

As Elliott closed the journal, he still found it hard to believe that his great-grandfather had survived the voyage around Cape Horn. Passengers on so many other ships had not been so fortunate. And yet, the entries in his journal betrayed no fear or despair, even as he and his fellow passengers huddled below deck during the heaviest storms, no sign of regret that he had forsaken a life of comfort and prosperity in Charleston to risk his life in his rush to get to California. They revealed instead his courage and resiliency, his intensity of purpose and clarity of vision, traits that would serve him well in the years to come.

Even so, as Elliott returned the journal to the drawer of the secretary, he wished his great-grandfather had still been alive when he and his father drove up to the ranch in Anderson Valley all those years ago. There was so much he would have liked to ask him, so much he still didn't know about either of his great-grandparents, so much he understood now that he would never know.

HE ROSE FROM THE SECRETARY and returned to the kitchen and poured himself a glass of water. After taking a sip, he walked over to the hutch and picked up the mail, then he sat at the table and began casually flipping through it, discarding the flyers and solicitations, setting aside the bills to be paid later. It was then that he noticed the small white envelope addressed to him – a letter from one Phoebe Crighton. The return address was New York City, the postmark September 25, 2005. He had never heard of Ms. Crighton. He had no idea why she might be writing to him.

With his fingertip, he tore open the end of the envelope and withdrew a letter, written in a looping hand on lined purple stationery, purple morning glories illustrating the margins.

Dear Mr. Madison,

I am writing to you at the suggestion of Lila Dumas, director of the Anderson Valley Historical Society. I am researching the life of my great-grandmother's uncle. His name was Benjamin Harrigan, and he fought with the 128th New York Volunteer Infantry Regiment during the Civil War. After the war, he moved west to California, to Mendocino County, specifically, where he worked on your family's ranch in Anderson Valley. Would you, by chance, have any information about him? I would be most grateful to hear from you.

Sincerely,

Phoebe Crighton

After quickly reading the letter a second time, Elliott folded it up and slipped it back into the envelope. He was not pleased, frankly. In fact, he was more than a little irritated. Yes, Lila had been an immense help to him during the course of his research. It was true that he could never have completed his manuscript without her assistance. But she had no right to give his address to a perfect stranger. There was no way to know who this woman might be. For all he knew, Ms. Crighton, if that was her real name, could be crazy. It was entirely possible that she might be a con artist, preying on the elderly, and he would think that Lila, not a day under eighty herself, would be sensitive to his concern. As he rose from the table, he vowed to discuss the matter with her at his earliest convenience.

But no, he had no information about Ms. Crighton's great-grandmother's uncle. He had never heard of Benjamin Harrigan. It was possible, of course, that Harrigan had worked on his great-grandparents' ranch. Over the years, scores of men had been employed by his family. His father told him once that by his account, no less than sixteen languages had been spoken on the ranch at one time or another, from the language spoken by the indigenous Pomo to Boontling, a quaint dialect comprised of cryptic phrases and ancient references still shared by an aging and ever-dwindling number of valley residents. But Elliott knew nothing about Benjamin Harrigan. He had nothing to tell Ms. Crighton. He would write back to her, of course, for he knew all too well the frustration of an unanswered inquiry. But he was sorry. He could not help her.

CHAPTER TWO

WITH LITTLE SUNLIGHT during the day, the small bedroom above the stairs was always cold and dark, so Elliott reached over and turned on the lamp beside his desk. He set his cup of coffee beside the writing pad, then slipped on his yellow sweater, buttoning it across his chest before sitting down and turning on his stereo receiver, tuned to the city's classical station. He listened for a moment to determine what was playing – Rachmaninoff, his Piano Concerto No. 2 – then sat back in his chair and took a sip of coffee. This was his study, his private sanctum. This is where he wrote his manuscript, the first draft scrawled out on white legal pads, the ensuing drafts and revisions typed into his Apple laptop.

He lifted the screen of the laptop and pressed the power button to turn it on. As he waited for the computer to boot up, he opened the upper right drawer of his desk and withdrew a sheet of his personal stationery, ordered when he began his research with the hope that it would confer a sense of formality and authority to his correspondence. He slipped the sheet into his printer tray and then turned his attention back to his laptop. His letter to Ms. Crighton would be concise and to the point. He saw no reason to engage in any unnecessary pleasantries.

FROM THE DESK OF ELLIOTT MADISON
SAN FRANCISCO, CALIFORNIA

October 2, 2005

Dear Ms. Crighton,

I am in receipt of your letter of September 25, 2005. In response to your inquiry, yes, it is within the realm of possibility that your great-grandmother's uncle worked on my family's ranch in Anderson Valley. Unfortunately, the name Benjamin Harrigan is not familiar to me. I am sorry I cannot be of more assistance, but I wish you all the very best in your research.

Sincerely,
Elliott Madison

After reading the letter again, examining it for typographical errors and misspellings, Elliott printed it out and signed it, then folded the letter neatly in thirds and slipped it into an envelope. He addressed the envelope to Ms. Crighton, then rose from his desk and started down the hall, tucking the letter into his coat pocket as he paused to glance into Alissa's bedroom. The floor was covered with piles of clothes and her high-topped sneakers. Her leather jacket was draped over the lip of the aquarium once inhabited by two lacy angelfish. Curled up beneath a mound of blankets with Hank nestled against her chest, she was still asleep, of course, having stayed out until nearly three in the morning. As Elliott started down the stairs, he knew it was entirely possible that she would still be sleeping when he returned from the library that afternoon.

He let himself out of the building, then made his way down the hill to Polk Street, walking past the stainless steel water bowl in front of the pet supply store and the crates of produce stacked in front of Real Foods market, past the heavyset security guard outside the drug store, flicking a cigarette butt into the gutter. As he approached Broadway, he saw that traffic had stopped in both directions – an old man with a long gray beard and a wooden staff was shuffling through the intersection, wholly indifferent to the angry blare of car horns, a deranged prophet who looked to have wandered into the city, trailed by a congregation of aged pit bulls.

When the old man finally stepped up onto the far sidewalk, Elliott crossed the street to the mailbox on the opposite corner. He withdrew the letter from his coat and dropped it into the mail slot, letting it loudly bang shut as he walked over to the bus stop. As he sat down to wait for the 19 Polk, he was relieved to have concluded his correspondence with Ms. Crighton. He had answered her inquiry to the best of his knowledge, and he truly did wish her well in her quest to learn more about her great-grandmother's uncle.

HE REACHED UP and removed his hat, then let himself into All-Star Donuts and Burgers, a four-table coffee shop on the bottom floor of the Balboa Hotel. On his way to the library, he liked to drop in for a quick cup of coffee and a glazed donut, fortifying himself in anticipation of the day's work in the stacks. He walked past the glass case filled with trays of donuts, past the tables arranged along the front windows, where an old man in a gray peacoat was hunched over a plate of charred toast and a woman in a pink full-body leotard was staring down at a pair of eggs fried sunny-side up. At the end of the counter, Elliott placed his satchel on the floor, hiking his hip up onto a stool as the cook flipped the potatoes and onions sizzling on the flat-top grill, a burst of steam rising up into the hood of the overhead fan.

The lone waitress walked down to him, a middle-age Vietnamese woman with her glossy black hair in a long ponytail. She knew what he wanted, what he always ordered. She asked as a matter of courtesy.

"A cup of coffee and a glazed donut, Mr. Elliott?"

"Please," he said.

She walked down to the coffee pot and filled one of the white porcelain mugs, then carried the mug back to him and placed it on the counter.

"Thanks much," he said.

As he picked up the container of cream and poured a generous dollop into his coffee, she brought his donut on a small plate.

"Excellent," he said.

He picked up the donut and took a large bite, licking the sugary glaze from his fingertips before washing it down with a sip of coffee. He was looking forward to working on his manuscript today, taking what he anticipated to be a last look at the chapter about his great-grandfather's experiences in the Sierra gold fields. He had studied those entries in his journal carefully, plotting out those months day by day, beginning with his arrival in San Francisco. Through his research, Elliott liked to think he knew well the city his great-grandfather found when the *Cordelia* passed through the dark cliffs that loom above the mouth of the bay. The muddy streets were fronted by hastily constructed boarding houses and raucous saloons, the new central square framed by hotels, gambling halls, and billiard parlors. Tents and shanties clung to the hills above the sheltered cove and pushed back into the sand dunes to the west, while scores of ships lay abandoned in the bay, their bare masts tilting skyward, just beyond the wharves that had been constructed on pilings driven deep into the bay mud.

It was the Central Wharf, extending some 2,000 feet into the bay, that his great-grandfather stepped down onto on November 13, 1851.

"The afternoon was cool, chilled by fitful gusts of wind. My legs were weak, and my joints sore. I took each step tentatively, worried

I might lose my balance as I walked across the broad timbers of the wharf. I stepped down lightly onto the street and then made my way up to Portsmouth Square. The streets were crowded with people from every corner of the world, their voices spilling out of every doorway I passed. Above the customs house, an American flag snapped in the wind. Somewhere a band was playing, which lent a brassy score to the pandemonium."

Before striking out for the gold fields, Madison spent several days in the city, speaking with a number of people and finding a general consensus that many of the rivers and creeks in the southern Sierra were quickly being worked out, surrendering most of their surface gold to the thousands of men who had overrun their banks.

"I intend to take my chances on my own claim, and even though an untold number of men have also rushed up into the canyons in the northern Sierra, there is still a sense that it is possible for a man to strike pay dirt there, either working alone or throwing in with a small company of men willing to work together and share the profits. So that is where I intend to go."

As Elliott took a bite of his donut, he remembered finding the map of the gold fields his great-grandfather had purchased at Cook's Periodical Depot tucked inside the back cover of his journal. He remembered gingerly unfolding the map and spreading it out on the table in the kitchen. It was a magnificent work of art, even in its distressed condition. He needed a magnifying glass to fully appreciate the map's fine detail, illustrating the rivers and creeks that ran down from the Sierra into the Sacramento and San Joaquin rivers, locating the towns that arose, often overnight, to serve the miners congregating there, noting, even, a number of their unnamed camps. His great-grandfather was most interested, of course, in the Feather River and the two branches – the East Fork and the West Fork – drawn on the map.

"The proprietor at Cook's told me that it was his understanding that the East Fork and the West Fork were not the only branches of the Feather River, that there were several other significant tributaries that were not on the map, and that, of course, was exactly what I was looking for."

The following morning, Madison boarded a side-wheel steamship named the *Nicolette*. Its boiler whistling, the steamer pulled away from the Central Wharf at daybreak and headed up the long northern arm of the bay, plowing through the muddy currents of the Sacramento River. It was well after dark when his great-grandfather finally saw the lights of Sacramento. After waiting for the deckhands to tie the *Nicolette* up, Madison and the other passengers climbed the side of the levee and then made their way into the city, their breath rising before them in the cold air.

The streets were lined with mercantiles and warehouses, hotels and boarding houses, saloons and gambling halls, but Sacramento nonetheless seemed a dismal city, a foul stench lifting from the refuse that had been dumped onto the puddled streets and churned into an ankle-deep slurry by the pack trains and freight wagons. Madison walked up the plank sidewalk, past the horses tied along the rails and the men huddling in the shadows between the buildings, calling out to him as they extended their empty hands and cups. He heard gunshots, three sharp reports in rapid succession. A woman screamed as a black horse galloped up the street.

When he reached the Adams Hotel, he pushed in through the door of the saloon operating on the bottom floor, crowded with men forcing their way up to the bar, where they paid for their liquor with gold pinched from leather pouches and weighed on crude scales.

"It was the first time I had seen gold in its natural state, and I was surprised how casually it was dispensed there and at the tables where men were playing cards. The silver coin I placed on the bar to buy a glass of whiskey marked me as a recent arrival, but the bartender, I should say, did not hesitate to accept it."

For the rest of the evening, Madison allowed himself to warm up, sipping whiskey while admiring the soaring voice of a woman in a long black dress singing beside an upright piano. Accompanied by a pianist wearing a black felt derby, she had clearly been classically trained, a soprano rising above the clamor of the men playing Monte at the tables. As Madison listened to her sing, he couldn't help but wonder what had brought her here to perform before such a churlish indifferent audience, so far from the grand concert halls on the East Coast.

"Still, I was grateful for what was likely to be my last taste of the civilized world for the foreseeable future."

It was nearly midnight when he climbed the stairs to the second floor of the hotel, where dozens of cots had been arranged along the walls and in a double-row through the center of the open room. As many as fifty or sixty men were sleeping or trying to read in the scant light of the oil lamps. As Madison stretched out on his cot, he could hear two men quarreling across the room – suddenly, a swift flurry of blows before they crashed onto one of the cots and then were pulled apart and shoved away from each other. Madison closed his eyes. All he wanted was silence, a few hours of untroubled sleep, and then he would be on his way.

At dawn, he was awakened by the stirring of the other men, pulling on their coats and shoving their feet into their boots. He dressed and made his way down to Front Street, where he walked along the levee until he found one of the shallow-draft steamers heading up the Feather River. The deck of the ship was packed bow to stern with supplies bound for Marysville and the mining camps beyond. He found a place to sit on a wooden crate filled with tins of sardines, and as the steamer pulled away from the bank, into the dense fog that coiled upon the surface of the river, he pulled up the collar of his coat and sat back to escape the cold.

Late that afternoon, the ship arrived in Marysville, a thriving commercial center from which stage lines, caravans of freight wagons, and pack trains delivered food and supplies to the ephemeral towns and mining camps along the tributaries of the Feather and Yuba rivers. As Madison walked up from the landing, the streets were thick with teamsters and their braying mules. At a mercantile near the town's central plaza, he purchased a pick and a shovel and a large tin pan, a dark wool blanket and a cast iron pot, salt pork, flour, dried apples, and coffee. That night, he bedded down in a boarding house across the plaza.

"Tonight, as I lie on my cot, my mind races, anticipating all that lies ahead. In the morning I shall set out for a town called Hamilton, a settlement so small that it cannot be found on the map I purchased in San Francisco. I feel as if I have reached the rim of the known world."

It was a journal entry that Elliott had read over and over, so eloquent in its simplicity and yet suggesting so much more. His great-grandfather truly had reached the far perimeter of the world he knew, and he was poised now to cross into the province of the unknown. He was seeking gold, certainly, hoping to stake himself to a new life on his own terms, but after studying his journals, Elliott had come to believe that his great-grandfather's quest was deeply personal as well, as if in leaving Charleston, he had also gone in search of himself, hoping to learn who he was and who he might become.

WHEN HE FINISHED EATING his donut and drinking his cup of coffee, Elliott slipped a five-dollar bill under his plate and walked out of the coffee shop. With his satchel in his left hand, he made his way down Hyde Street. It was a warm autumn day, uncommonly still with a gold-tinted sky – earthquake weather, it was called by those who had lived in San Francisco long enough to remember. And Elliott certainly did remember the last major quake to strike the city. These strange balmy days always gave him a sense of uneasy anticipation, reminding him that another earthquake could strike at any moment, perhaps of even greater intensity and duration than those terrible fifteen seconds when it felt like the world was breaking apart.

And it was, in fact, on a day very much like this when Elliott's own world imploded, when his wife Evelyn abruptly informed him that their marriage was over. They had been married for twenty-eight years, virtually inseparable from the day they met at the university in Berkeley. After two years in the Navy at the end of World War II, assigned to a minesweeper clearing shipping lanes in the South Pacific, he was a student in the school of journalism, while she was working toward a degree in the English department. They were married in a simple ceremony in Tilden Park and moved into a house on Euclid Avenue above the rose garden. He often thought those might very well have been the happiest days of his life. He and Evelyn took long hikes in the East Bay hills and sat on the grass during outdoor performances at the Greek Theater, invited their fellow writers and journalists over for pasta and cheap red wine, lit scented candles in the bedroom windows and made love late into the night.

When he finished his graduate work and was hired as an assistant city editor at the *Chronicle*, they moved into San Francisco and rented a two-bedroom apartment in the Richmond district. There they embarked on a mission to sample the chow mein and egg rolls at every Chinese restaurant west of Arguello Boulevard, rode their bicycles through Golden Gate Park and down the Coast Highway, adopted an orange tom who appeared in their backyard one rainy night, naming him Blake for Evelyn's favorite English poet. While he ran a team of reporters covering the municipal, superior, and federal courts, Evelyn tutored aspiring young writers at San Francisco State and wrote poetry, eventually finding a small press in Massachusetts to publish a chapbook of her work.

He would never forget how elated they were the day they learned that she was pregnant, how they celebrated that night by driving out to the ruins of the Sutro mansion on the cliff above Ocean

Beach, drinking champagne while watching the sun sink into the Pacific. Although it was a difficult pregnancy, their daughter Claire was perfectly healthy, a deliriously happy child who was speaking in complete sentences at eighteen months. And when Elliott's father passed away, the three of them moved into the upper flat in the building he had left them on Vallejo Street.

But when Claire departed to attend the University of Colorado, the flat suddenly seemed empty and quiet, a void, he would later realize, they unintentionally filled with their careers. He had become the deputy city editor largely responsible for the desk's enterprise reporting and then had been promoted to city editor, which meant he often found himself staying late in his office, reading the stories budgeted to run the next morning. Evelyn, meanwhile, had taken a full-time position teaching creative writing at City College, where she spent her days in the classroom or meeting with students in her office, often working late on her poetry or reading her students' papers. He could feel the distance growing between them, but on those few occasions when he tried to talk to her, she told him there was nothing to say, bristling at his suggestion they see a marriage counselor.

One evening, Elliott drove out to the Bamboo Garden in the Richmond District, a Chinese restaurant where, as far as they could determine, they had eaten the night Claire was conceived. He ordered Evelyn's favorite dishes – garlic eggplant and wonton soup, asparagus with shrimp and mu shu chicken, sweet and sour pork. Carrying the bag of takeout, he called out to her as he climbed the stairs leading up to the flat. He set the bag on the kitchen table and waited for her to join him. As she stood in the doorway, he began lifting out the cartons, introducing each dish with a flourish, hoping they would remind her of better times. But when she began crying, he realized the problems with their marriage ran far deeper than he thought. And yet he never imagined that she might have found someone else.

It was on a warm October day like this that she confessed she had fallen in love with a documentary filmmaker named Gregorio Rosales, who was working on a project about Dolores Huerta.

"I don't understand," was all Elliott could say.

"There's nothing to understand," she said. "I'm moving out this weekend."

"Can't we talk about this?"

"There's nothing to talk about, Elliott. My decision is final. I've made up my mind."

Sitting at the kitchen table, Elliott simply stared at her, trying to comprehend what she was telling him.

"What about Claire?" he managed to ask.

"I've already spoken to her," Evelyn said. "I called her last night."

"And how did she take it?"

"She's upset, as you might expect. But she understands."

"Well, I don't understand," Elliott said.

"Please, Elliott – don't make this any more difficult than it has to be."

"I don't have any say in this?" he asked.

"There's nothing to say, Elliott. The marriage is over."

That Saturday afternoon, he stood back and watched as the movers she'd hired carried out her clothes and boxes of books, a set of fine china handed down from her grandmother, an antique chair and a chest of drawers imported from Japan. From the front steps, he looked on as she climbed into the cab of a rented pickup, and then with a final glance back at him, she was gone.

When he returned to the flat, he drank the last two fingers of bourbon in a bottle of Early Times, but it wasn't enough, so he grabbed his coat and hat and walked over the hill into North Beach, making his way down Columbus Avenue to La Rocca's Corner. He stepped up to the bar and ordered a glass of bourbon, determined to drink until he drowned his pain. Shortly after midnight, he toppled off his stool, slumping to the floor and striking the bridge of his nose on the foot rail. The bartender helped him sit up and packed his nose with paper cocktail napkins to stanch the bleeding, then called a cab to take him home. The driver had to help him up the porch steps. He crawled up the stairs to his flat and fell asleep on the bathroom floor, only to awaken with two black eyes.

Six months later, the marriage came to an inglorious end in his lawyer's office, the signing of the final divorce papers as anticlimactic as it was depressing. He spoke with Evelyn rarely after the divorce was finalized. He saw her even less frequently, especially after she and Rosales moved north to St. Helena in the wine country. But with Claire still binding them together, they managed, over time, to develop a relationship that was amicable if not warm. She sent him notices when she was going to be reading her poetry, and when her third chapbook was published, he attended her book party at City Lights. It pleased him when she signed his copy, "For Elliott, with enduring love, Evelyn."

But five years ago, Evelyn and Rosales moved to Mexico City. Although Claire had flown down to visit them several times, Elliott hadn't seen Evelyn since. He still thought about her, of course, especially on days like these, when the temperature rose up into the seventies and eighties and the sky took on a soft golden hue. He liked to remember those grand days when they lived in Berkeley, when they were so impossibly young, when anything seemed within their reach, their lives rolling out before them like the cool blue Pacific. And yet those days seemed so distant now, so long ago, as if they had been lived by someone else.

HE WALKED down to the library, passing through the main entrance and then down a series of steps leading into the soaring six-story atrium. He crossed through the sunlight filtering down from the skylights and climbed the open stairs leading up to the second floor, then the two flights of stairs to the third floor. After walking past the reference desk, he entered the musty stacks, emerging from the long rows of shelves along the library's north wall. This was where he liked to sit when he was researching his project, reading the histories and biographies that provided a broader context for the entries in his great-grandfather's journals, reading about the masses who rushed into the Sierra, the stories of those who realized their dreams of unimaginable wealth and the stories of those who lost everything, including, in some cases, their lives. Although his research was largely finished now, he still came to the library nearly every day, even if he really didn't need to, now that he was merely reviewing his manuscript and making last revisions. It gave him a sense of purpose, as if he needed a reason to leave the flat.

He made his way down the wall until he found an empty desk beneath one of the windows. As he took off his hat, he saw that Delilah was sitting at the adjacent desk. She was wearing a purple velour dress with long strands of glass beads hanging from her neck, silver bracelets around both wrists. Her long red hair fell to her shoulders, her eyes slits above her pitted cheeks. He'd been told that Delilah might not be her real name. She was said to have fled a bad marriage in Houston and had taken the Greyhound west, assuming a new identity when she arrived here in the city. All Elliott knew for certain was that she liked to come to the library when she grew tired of sitting alone in her room in one of the nearby residence hotels. She liked to listen to jazz cassettes on her Walkman, her right foot quietly tapping the carpeted floor.

When she saw Elliott taking off his coat, she smiled at him.

"Coltrane," she whispered, as if to let him in on her secret.

With a discrete nod, Elliott sat down and opened his satchel, withdrawing his manuscript and returning to his great-grandfather as he packed up his gear and walked out of the boarding house in Marysville. Beneath a high gray ceiling of clouds, a pack train consisting of perhaps twenty sullen mules was heading northward out of town. With his gear rolled into the blanket, pick and shovel over his shoulder, Madison fell in behind them. The stages and freight wagons had worn deep ruts into the road, puddled with water or slick with mud. Several times he slipped, at one point landing hard on his left knee. He walked for hours, stopping only occasionally to adjust his gear or to look up at the foreboding Sierra, stepping aside to let the wagons and the men on horseback pass by, exchanging nods with the men plodding down the road in exhaustion and defeat, like foot soldiers returning from a theater of war.

He arrived in Hamilton just after nightfall. On a broad bend in the Feather River, the town consisted of a single hotel, two saloons, a general store and a blacksmith shop, surrounded by tents and crude shacks dispersed across the grassy foothills. Madison was exhausted, unaccustomed to such sustained physical exertion, and the months aboard the *Cordelia* had made him only weaker.

"My feet are sore and raw, my knees and ankles weak, and my shoulders ache. I don't believe I could have walked another mile."

He spent the night at the hotel, then started up the road again in the morning. It was noticeably cooler than the day before, and he moved slowly, working out the stiffness in his legs and shoulders. Gradually, the river began to swing around to the east. With each hour, the road grew more difficult, passing through the gullies and ravines between the hills, climbing into the oak woodland, the river rushing hard through the channel it had carved into the basalt plateau. That afternoon, he reached a town called Long's Bar, where the Feather roared out the mouth of its narrow canyon, the forested ridges of the Sierra looming above its furious discharge. It was a significantly larger community than Hamilton, supporting more than twenty stores and trading posts and a sprawling canvas-covered hotel called the Batavia.

"After dinner, I asked one of the owners of the Batavia about the upper reaches of the river. Pursuant to that conversation, I am particularly intrigued by the West Branch of the North Fork, which is said to pass through a remote gorge deep in the mountains. It is my understanding that few men have risked working that branch of the river, and so that is where I intend to go."

Shortly before noon the next day, he reached the confluence of the North Fork and the Middle Fork. From there, he followed the ridge above the North Fork, the sparsely traveled road steadily gaining altitude. As the day wore on, it was increasingly clear that he was leaving the most heavily worked sections of the river behind. The mining camps were growing successively smaller, and the wagon ruts were not nearly as deep as they had been below.

The ruts ended at a camp that looked to be occupied by no more than a handful of men, their bedrolls and blankets scattered across the ground, their heavy wool coats hanging from the stubs of branches broken off the trunks of the pines. A soot-blackened pot sat on the rocks that enclosed a fire pit, a last few coals from that morning's fire still smoldering in a bed of ashes. Covered with black flies, strips of venison hung from a rope strung between two of the pines, while wood ants swarmed over the last few potatoes in a gunnysack. The rank odor of unburied human waste hung in the air.

Leaving the camp behind, Madison pressed on, trying to follow a trail all but obscured by a thick mat of leaves and pine needles, searching for the occasional boot print to confirm he was still on the right path, waving through the cobwebs that hung like curtains between the pines, snapping off the low branches and tossing them aside. When he heard a low growl, he froze, his heart beating quickly in his chest – a mountain lion crouched no more than twenty yards away. He was afraid to move, caught in the intense glare of the great cat's eyes. But after a tense moment, the mountain lion ambled away, disappearing into the forest.

Finally, just before dusk, he reached the West Branch as it emptied into the North Fork. With darkness nearly upon him, he found a place to camp in the forest above the river. He gathered wood for a fire, and soon flames were darting through the steam hissing out of the wet bark. Sitting beside the fire, he quietly chewed on a piece of smoked beef. If he had any lingering doubts about his decision to leave Charleston, he put them to rest in his journal.

"As I stare into the flames, I cannot help but think about the life I left behind. I could not have shed the trappings of my past more completely. I have reduced my existence to its elemental core. Never have I been more certain that I made the right decision in leaving Charleston. Never have I felt more alive."

When he woke in the morning, the sky was low and dark, threatening rain. He started up the path as it led into the thick forest, stopping to catch his breath whenever he emerged from the woods and could stand on the edge of the canyon and look down upon the river surging through the boulders below. He could see why this branch of the river had been scarcely worked. It was precisely what he was looking for.

With only deer tracks to guide him, it took several hours to find a way down the side of the ridge. Above the canyon wall, the ground was soft and loose, forcing him to kick the edges of his boots into the soil to gain purchase. He grabbed the stunted pines and clung to the manzanita, lowering himself down the precipitous slope, at times skidding from one outcropping of rock to another. The deeper he descended, the steeper the canyon walls became. As he crept along the canyon wall, he leaned back into the cold granite, forcing himself to avert his eyes from the torrent of water below. At one point, a rock rolled out from beneath his right foot, but he caught himself and watched as it landed on a bench of granite, kicked up once, and then disappeared into the churning water.

When he finally reached the bottom of the canyon, he gave himself a few minutes to rest, then began making his way up the river. He scrambled through the boulders and across the talus slopes, climbing over the downed pines and leaping across the slivers of streams that painted the canyon walls. And then it began to rain. It fell lightly at first, scarcely heavier than the mist that rose above the river, but soon the rain was coming down hard, blown in all directions by the wind gusting up the canyon. Lightning cracked across the blackened sky. Thunder detonated immediately afterward, so loud he flinched. And yet, he could smell wood smoke.

He pushed ahead, fighting through the low-hanging limbs of the pines and struggling through the dense brush, the smell of smoke growing stronger as he made his way upriver. And then on a gravel bar above the river, he spotted a makeshift lean-to, a sheet of canvas stretched between the pines, the rain sluicing off the sagging canvas, pouring onto the sandy ground. A thin plume of smoke rose from a stacked-rock fire pit, pinesap crackling in the flames.

"Hello!" he called out.

He waited for a moment, then shouted out once more.

"I say, is anyone there?"

Finally, a corner of the canvas folded back, and a man with long black hair stepped out into the rain.

"Who goes there?" he shouted.

Sitting back in his chair, Elliott had to smile. Even now, he could only marvel at that chance encounter on the West Branch, described at length in his great-grandfather's journal. The man's name was Ames Snyder, of course, and the meeting of those two men on December 6, 1851, would prove to be one of the single most important events in his family's history.

A farmer from Lee County, Iowa, Snyder had spent the summer working a claim on the South Fork of the Yuba River, but he'd had little success there, so he'd headed north, eventually locating what he believed to be a promising stretch of the West Branch just below the gravel bar, a narrow pool fifteen to twenty yards in length. His plan was to dig a channel parallel to the pool, and when the water dropped in the summer, divert the river into the channel so he could work the sand and gravel in the exposed riverbed. It was an ambitious plan, more work than any one man could undertake alone. He was looking for a partner to help him carry it out.

And so a partnership was formed, a common enterprise that

would serve their mutual interests well. But even more importantly, it was a convergence of paths that would ultimately bring Elliott's great-grandparents together in Anderson Valley, the kind of serendipitous moment that can only be fully appreciated in the context of the long arcs of their lives. He would never forget the day he came across that entry in his great-grandfather's journal, squinting down at his handwriting and instantly recognizing the name Snyder, his great-grandmother's maiden name. He would never forget the thrill of that moment, the realization that he had just made a discovery of his own, no less valuable to him than the flakes of gold his great-grandfather and his new partner would soon disinter from the bottom of the West Branch.

CHAPTER THREE

AS THE 19 POLK pulled away from the curb, Elliott reached up for the overhead handrail and started down the aisle. Slowly, the bus made its way up the street, crawling from red light to red light, the narrow two lanes choked with idling taxis, double-parked delivery vans, and men unloading bobtail trucks. As he dropped into a seat beside an elderly woman anxiously guarding the plastic bags of produce at her feet, he glimpsed a bike messenger streaking along the right side of the bus, his long blond hair sailing out behind him as he leaned over the handlebars – suddenly he was cartwheeling through the air, vaulted over the thrust-open door of a parked green Volkswagen, landing on his back on the trunk of an old Buick. As the bus slowly rolled past, Elliott looked on as the bike messenger lifted his head and pushed up onto his elbows, glancing around as if to determine what had just happened to him. Elliott had seen it before, of course, more often than he could remember. He liked to think he had seen it all on Polk Street. Nothing surprised him anymore.

As the bus returned him to Russian Hill, he wondered if Alissa had gotten out of bed yet. Rarely did she rise before late afternoon anymore, and it worried him, honestly. He liked to remember his granddaughter as a curious intelligent child who loved to dress up with a silver tiara, cardboard wings, and glitter on her shoes, who reached for his hand when they walked up to Swensen's to buy peppermint ice cream. He liked to remember the girl he took to Golden Gate Park, where they rented pedal boats at Stow Lake and plowed through the gray-green water, looking for ducks and turtles as they passed in front of the waterfall, the girl who could run all day on the soccer field and who decorated her bedroom mirror with the blue ribbons she'd won in age-group swimming competitions.

But when his daughter's marriage collapsed, she and Alissa moved into the flat on Vallejo with him, and almost immediately Alissa began retreating into herself, withdrawing from her mother and, to a lesser degree, from him, her metamorphosis into a moody teenager so rapid he scarcely noticed the transformation until it was all but complete. Claire, who had been so close to Alissa, couldn't understand why she could no longer communicate with her, and their abrupt estrangement threw all of their lives into chaos. There were shouting matches and screaming fits, slammed doors and silences that seemed to lengthen every day. By the time Claire remarried and moved to Los Angeles, she and Alissa were scarcely speaking, communicating in terse exchanges only when absolutely necessary.

Her departure left Elliott in sole possession of a sulking eighteen-year-old who had barely managed to graduate from high school. She seemed depressed, supremely bored. Although she enrolled at City College, she never showed up for her classes. Later, she found a job as a part-time barista at a coffeehouse in North Beach, but she was quickly dismissed for failing to show up on time for her shifts. In an open display of defiance, she made no attempt to conceal her drinking and smoking marijuana, habits she had picked up in high school. The few friends she brought home were tattooed skateboarders and pimply video game players. Her only sustained interest was her music, the heavy metal rock she and her bandmates played at a deafening volume in the garage – slashing guitars, thumping bass and pounding drums, the lyrics, at least those he could understand, at once menacing, nihilistic, and vaguely satanic. He often felt powerless in her presence, utterly without influence. There were days when he felt like he was living with a stranger, a young woman he might have known in another lifetime.

But he would buy oyster crackers for her, for the bowl of clam chowder he hoped she would eat when he got home. Rising from his seat as the bus crossed Broadway, he stepped down onto the sidewalk and walked up to Real Foods. He passed through the crates of tomatoes and avocados and oranges stacked on the sidewalk and then entered the market, making his way through the produce bins to the aisles of dry goods. He scanned the shelves quickly, finding crackers of all kinds, many of them made from grains he'd never heard of, before he finally spotted a bag of New England oyster crackers. He reached for the bag, wondering how long it had been sitting there on the shelf, turning the bag over in his hands in search of a sell-by date. When he didn't find one, he carried the crackers up to the checkout counter.

He recognized the cashier, of course, a slim young man standing beside the cash register in a red-and-yellow tie-dyed undershirt, his brown hair falling to his shoulders, a wisp of a mustache across his upper lip.

"Hello, Cuba."

Cuba closed the cash register drawer.

"Hello, Mr. Madison."

"You wouldn't happen to know how long these crackers have been sitting on the shelf, would you?"

Cuba took the bag from him and examined it quickly, then shrugged the question off.

"I'm sure they're fine," he said.

"They could have been sitting there for years," Elliott said.

"Would you like to talk to the manager?"

Elliott could have laughed. The question was ridiculous. No, he didn't want to talk to the manager. Without a sell-by date, there was nothing the manager could tell him, either. He had no choice but to take his chances and buy the crackers.

"Just ring them up," he said, reaching for his wallet.

"I'm sure they're fine," Cuba assured him.

"I'll let you know," Elliott said.

AS HE CLIMBED the stairs leading up to his flat, he was gratified to hear water running in the shower. It pleased him to think that Alissa would have noticed the water draining quickly out of the tub. He had spent nearly an hour that morning unclogging the drain, using the end of a metal coat hanger to pull up clumps of her soapy green hair. When the water in the tub no longer rose to her ankles, she would realize what he had done for her. Which is not to suggest she would say anything. Expressions of gratitude or appreciation did not come naturally to her. But she would know that he was looking out for her, whether she wanted him to or not, and, as far as Elliott was concerned, that was all that mattered.

At the top of the stairs, he was greeted by Hank. He let the dog out the back door, watching for a moment as he hustled down the stairs, then he made his way into the kitchen, where he tossed the bag of crackers onto the counter and took the bowl of clam chowder out of the refrigerator. As he poured the chowder into a saucepan and placed it on the stove, he could hear Alissa turn off the shower, the pipes shuddering in the wall. He hoped she was hungry.

He was pouring himself a glass of bourbon when she entered the kitchen, wrapped in a white terrycloth robe, a towel around her neck, her hair damp and uncombed.

"I bet you thought I would forget," he said.

She looked at him, puzzled.

"Forget what?"

He pointed at the bag of oyster crackers.

"I told you I'd pick some up."

Unimpressed, she walked over and poured herself a glass of the bourbon.

"If you say so," she said.

He watched her take a sip. She looked at him, as if to dare him to comment.

"I'm an adult," she said. "I'm legal."

And that was true. She was of a legal age to drink alcohol. He could not deny it. But as he turned back to the stove and stirred the chowder, he could only imagine what Claire would think of her daughter beginning her day with a stiff drink, even if it was nearly five o'clock in the evening. And, for the record, he did not necessarily disagree with her. But he also knew there was nothing to be gained by making an issue of it, as Claire surely would have.

"Have you talked to your mother lately?" he asked.

She sat at the table, crossing her right leg over her left.

"What's that supposed to mean?"

"I was just asking."

"Why would I want to talk to my mother?"

"I was just wondering how long it's been since you last spoke to her," he said.

"I don't know. I don't remember. She calls all the time. She's always leaving messages on the answering machine."

"Do you ever call her back?"

"Why do you even care?" she asked, looking at him as if the conversation had soured in her mouth.

"You need a relationship with your mother," he said.

"She's the one who moved to L.A."

And that silenced him. He couldn't argue with that.

When the chowder began to boil around the edge of the saucepan, he ladled it into two clear glass bowls and then carried the bowls over to the table, setting one in front of Alissa and one for himself across from her. After giving her a spoon, he started to sit down but caught himself and grabbed the bag of oyster crackers.

"Almost forgot," he said.

He watched as Alissa reached for the bag of crackers and shook a few onto the thick surface of the chowder, then picked up her spoon and took a taste.

"Well?" he asked.

Her mouth wrinkled.

"The crackers are mushy," she said.

Elliott shook several of the crackers into his own bowl, then raised a spoonful to his mouth. She was right – the crackers were old, just as he had feared they might be. He was tempted to get up and spit them into the sink, but instead, he gamely swallowed, silently resolving to have a word with Cuba at the next opportunity.

"So where were you all day?" Alissa asked, as if she didn't know.

"The library," he said.

"I might have guessed."

"Surely you don't disapprove."

"I don't even know what you do down there," she said.

But of course she did.

"You know I've been working on a project about my great-grandparents – about your great-great-great-grandparents."

"This was like a hundred years ago, right?"

"Or more."

"So who cares about them?"

"I care," Elliott said. "And my hope is that some day you'll care, too."

"Not likely."

"Well, that's my hope, anyway."

She shook her head at him, as if she thought he was a fool. He would state the obvious anyway.

"It's important to know who you are, where you come from,"

he said.

"Not to me," she said.

But her indifference did not faze him. He had grown accustomed to her insouciant attitude. He knew better than to take it personally.

"Well, we'll see," he said. "You might surprise yourself."

AS ELLIOTT PLACED the last of the chowder in the refrigerator, he could hear Alissa walking down the stairs and letting herself out of the flat, without, of course, a word about where she was going or when he might expect her to return. That was nothing new. That was who his granddaughter was. She would do what she wanted, when she wanted to do it. She would come home when she came home and not a moment before. And, Elliott reminded himself, worrying about her served no useful purpose. If only it were that simple.

After rinsing off the dishes and placing them in the dishwasher, he made his way into the living room and sat in the gray club chair. As he lifted his feet onto the ottoman, he looked across the room to the daguerreotypes of his great-grandparents. In the wooden case that preserved their portraits, their presence on the mantel always gave him comfort, as if they were not merely his ancestors but oracles, their presence silently informing his thinking, shaping his interpretation of their journals and letters, guiding his hand as he wrote the stories of their lives.

He leaned down and opened his satchel and lifted out the folder containing his manuscript, placing it on his lap and thumbing back to the long winter of 1851-52, when his great-grandfather and his new partner began digging the channel they hoped to divert the West Branch into that summer. It was cold miserable work, prying up the larger rocks and rolling them out of the way, using the materials they excavated to construct a berm above the section of the riverbed they wanted to expose. The sun rarely reached the bottom of the canyon, and the winter storms often lasted for days, driving them to the shelter of the lean-to. Madison was not accustomed to such intense physical labor, but he gradually grew stronger and took no little pride in his newfound ability to perform hard labor for days on end. Still, the digging of the channel was requiring more time than he and Snyder had expected.

In March, two young boys from Mexico walked into their camp, and when Madison and Snyder learned they were looking for work, they promptly hired them. The older boy was named Mateo, the younger brother Hector. Mateo loved to talk. When he wasn't talking, he was singing. When he wasn't singing, he was mimicking the scrub jays and the starlings, the crows and finches. Hector, no more than fourteen years old, was a mute.

"They are tireless workers, no matter how long the day," Madison wrote in his journal. "If this enterprise is to succeed, it will be largely due to their sustained labors. We are fortunate to have them."

The West Branch ran high all spring before finally beginning to drop in early April, but it wasn't until the full heat of summer arrived that they began work on the dam that would divert the river into the new channel. As the river dropped, the chute the water passed through above the stretch of river they wanted to work was no more than twelve feet across, but the force of the water concentrated as it rushed past the two large boulders at the head of the pool. They worked several large wedges of granite over to the mouth of the chute to establish the base of the dam and then used smaller rocks to raise the dam and fill the gaps. Gradually, the water rose and began to spill into the new channel, but still the dam leaked, the volume of water sufficient to prevent them from working the riverbed below.

"Ames made the decision to cut up the canvas lean-to in order to make sandbags, and we saw immediate results. With each sandbag we put in place, more water flowed into the channel and less passed through the dam. Finally, the water in the riverbed was reduced to a manageable flow, easily directed into a shallow trench."

On July 23, 1852, they began to work below the dam, digging into the sand and gravel, hauling the excavated materials over to the crude cradle that Ames had constructed. The device fascinated Madison. He had never seen anything like it. He watched as Snyder dumped the sand and gravel into the riddle, a perforated plank that collected the gravel and allowed the sand to pass through the holes and land in a narrow trough below. And then with a steady rocking motion that gave the cradle its name, he used the water in the trench to wash away the sand in the trough, leaving the heavier flakes of gold behind the wooden riffles.

They approached the riverbed methodically, working along the base of the south wall of the canyon, where Snyder expected to find the richer deposits. But the gravel there was deeper than they anticipated, and their initial results were disappointing. Still, they persevered, working from dawn to dusk seven days a week.

"A group of men from Minnesota have been working directly above us, and their good fortune has reaffirmed our belief that the West Branch will yield as much gold as the other northern rivers. But it has also caused us to worry that we might have selected a poor section of the river to work."

By late August, they were working nearly five feet below the top of the dam, the water seeping through it reaching nearly to their knees. With each day, they grew increasingly aware that they were in a race against the early autumn rains. Although the afternoons were still hot, the days were getting shorter, and there was an unmistakable chill in the morning air. Finally, in September, they began to see the kind of yield they had been hoping for.

"With each shovelful of sand and gravel, we began to find significant quantities of gold in the cradle's trough. Our work has taken on a new urgency. We are working as hard and fast as we can."

The first storm arrived in early October. Ominous iron-gray clouds gathered overhead. Lightning cracked above the canyon, the thunder rumbling in several counts later, just as the first heavy raindrops began to crater in the sand. As the clouds cast the canyon into darkness, they gathered up their tools and carried them up to their camp. From beneath what remained of the tarp, they watched the rain pour down for nearly three hours before the storm began to abate, the far wall of the canyon turning blood red in the sunlight angling through the separating clouds.

The West Branch rose nearly two feet during the night. As day broke, they looked down upon the water cascading over the top of the dam.

"There was nothing we could do but wait for the river to drop again. We knew we had already done well, better than we had any right to expect. At the same time, we hadn't finished working the riverbed beneath the dam, and we didn't want to walk away to forever wonder if we had left the richest deposits unturned."

They waited two days for the river to drop before they walked back down to examine the dam. It seemed to have weathered the storm without significant damage, so they returned to the riverbed, determined to work until the next storm moved in, constantly watching the dam to make sure it held. It never occurred to them that the berm might give out.

But late on the afternoon of October 29, the berm collapsed just below the dam. As the river surged through the crumbling rock and gravel, flooding into the riverbed, Madison and Snyder scrambled up the bank. Hector made it, too, but the swirling current caught Mateo by the legs and dragged him down, pulling him beneath the surface. Shouting his name, they ran down the bank, scrambling through the rocks at the foot of the canyon wall, checking every chute and fall amid the fractured granite, dashing through the riffles and shallows. Finally, Madison spotted the boy floating facedown, caught in an eddy at the mouth of a narrow pool.

"I see him!" he shouted. "He's here!"

He jumped into the pool and pulled up Mateo's head, rolling him onto his back and then dragging him over to the sandy bank.

He dropped to his knees and began pumping the boy's chest with both hands, pressing down hard to expel the water from his lungs. When the boy failed to draw a breath, he pumped his chest even harder, so hard he feared he might crack the boy's ribs. But he could see in Mateo's still eyes that it was too late. When Snyder finally arrived, Madison simply shook his head. There was nothing to say.

With Hector looking on, they carried Mateo back to their camp and gently laid him on the ground. As they began wrapping his body in a blanket, Hector released a sudden anguished cry. Madison spun around as the boy fled, disappearing into the pines.

"Hector! Wait!"

He started after him, spotting him as he ran down the river, but in the fading light, he knew that he would never be able to catch up to him. When he returned to the camp, Snyder was waiting for him.

"No, he's gone," Madison said.

They dug a grave there in the clearing above the river, and then as night fell, working silently in the firelight, they lowered Mateo into it and shoveled the sand and gravel over him. When they finished, they formed a cross on the surface of the grave with pieces of white granite.

That night, it began to rain, a light drizzle initially, then growing heavier, the water pouring off the canvas tarp. They huddled around the hissing fire, trying to ward off the cold. At the first light of day, they began packing up the camp. It was then that Madison noticed Hector, watching them from the edge of the pines, his wet black hair smeared across his face.

"Are you all right?" Madison asked him.

When the boy only stared at him, Madison tossed him a piece of dried venison.

"Come on," Madison said. "Come with us."

When they finished packing, they began climbing out of the canyon, pulling themselves up by the shallow roots of the pines and the smooth red limbs of the manzanita, their boots slipping on the slick granite. When they finally reached the crest of the ridge, they looked back down into the canyon and could see the river running high with the storm surge, pouring over the top of their dam, as if to wash away all evidence of the months they had spent there, any trace of what they had found and what they had lost.

Elliott lifted his eyes from his manuscript. It had not been easy reading the journal entries his great-grandfather had written in the aftermath of Mateo's drowning. Stricken with guilt and remorse, his great-grandfather wrote about Mateo as if he had lost his own son. And yet, for Elliott, those grief-stricken journal entries also served to reveal the depth of his great-grandfather's character, the nature of the man himself.

"We should never have returned to work below the dam," his great-grandfather wrote. "We took a calculated risk, and I will regret it for the rest of my life. I will never forget this fine young man, and I will never forgive myself for his death."

CHAPTER FOUR

SITTING AT HIS DESK, Elliott leaned back in his chair and looked up at the topographical map of the California Trail and all its variants, tracing the routes taken by westbound emigrants. It was a sequence of maps, actually, that he had carefully taped together. Pinned to the wall of his study, the crude assemblage was nearly six feet long, the specific route taken by his great-grandmother's party illuminated with a fluorescent green marking pen with dozens of sites marked where the party had rested or camped. It still amazed Elliott to think that his great-grandmother had crossed the continent when she was just eighteen years old, walking alongside the wagons constructed by her father and brother for more than two thousand miles. It was, by any measure, an extraordinary journey, no less daunting and arduous than his great-grandfather's voyage around Cape Horn.

The chapter of his manuscript concerning his great-grandmother's journey west was based primarily on the letters she wrote to her cousin Emily, supported, of course, by his own extensive research.

Like his great-grandfather's journals, those letters had resided in his great-grandmother's secretary for years. They were dry and brittle and disintegrating along the edges. Several had become damp at some point, and the ink had dissolved into stains. He had read the letters over and over, more times than he could count, taking detailed notes, weighing every word and turn of the phrase, reading them aloud as if that might reveal some nuance he missed on the page. His great-grandmother had written the letters in moments stolen from the obligations of the day, effectively recording her journey in chronological installments, and he had selected excerpts for his manuscript, just as he had quoted liberally from his great-grandfather's journals.

The chapter began with her father's return to Lee County, Iowa, where for nearly four years, she and her brother Zachary had lived with their cousins on their aunt and uncle's farm, left there by their father after their mother died during the cholera epidemic of 1849. She had been stricken without warning, violently voiding her bowels and vomiting long after her stomach had been emptied, burning with fever and trembling with cold. They prayed it was a severe case of influenza, but they knew the epidemic had come up the Mississippi on the riverboats, and as she lay in bed, writhing and delirious, there could be no doubt that it was cholera. She lasted through that night, but by morning her skin had begun to blue and her hands had curled into claws. They lost her just after noon the following day. Her father was devastated by the sudden death of his wife. After laying her to rest in a grave at the back of the farm, he rode off in mourning, his destination unknown, promising only that he would come back for them.

For Amelia and her brother, life with their cousins was a dismal existence. Their uncle was a dim suspicious man who rarely spoke. Their aunt was a stern, intensely religious woman who led the family in prayer every morning and warned them about the dire prophecies of the Bible every evening. At night, Amelia often lay awake in the bed she shared with Emily, biting her lip to conceal her crying, trying to imagine where her father might be. She prayed that he would write to her, but no letter ever arrived. She hated him for abandoning them, but she lived for the day when she might see him again.

She had just turned seventeen when one afternoon in November 1853 she saw the silhouette of a man on horseback approaching through a lightly falling snow. She desperately wanted to believe it was her father, but she was also cautious, having deceived herself many times before. She walked out to the road and stood at the gate, watching as the solitary figure rode toward her, occasionally disappearing as the road through the gently rolling hills dipped out of view. Finally, he raised his hand.

"Father!"

As she ran down the road, he swung down from his horse and spread his arms wide. As he swept her off the ground, she threw her arms around his neck as if to never let go.

"I knew you would come back! I knew it!"

That night at the table, he told them that he had been to California, his long black hair coiled upon his shoulders, a dense black beard concealing his face, all but his dark eyes, glistening in the light of the tallow candles. He told them about the year he'd spent in the Sierra, searching for gold on the Yuba River and then on the West Branch of the Feather. He told them he had found a partner there, a man named William Madison, and he told them about the tragic death of one of the boys they had hired to help them.

He told them that after climbing out of the canyon, he and his partner and the dead boy's brother made their way down to Marysville, where they bought a wagon and several horses and then set out across the great Central Valley, making their way around the meandering sloughs and channels of the delta and the marshes on the northern perimeter of the bay, then north through the grass-covered hills to Sonoma. Their intention was to acquire land, but they were aware that most of the richest land in the state had already been doled out by the Spanish and then by the Mexican governors, vast land grants comprising tens of thousands of acres. When they arrived in Sonoma, they were advised to speak with a man named Cyrus Alexander, an early settler who knew the unclaimed land to the north as well as anyone.

They met with Alexander at his ranch in the Russian River Valley. Over a dinner of boiled mutton, he told them that most of the land along the river had already been taken and more settlers were arriving every day. He told them about the ranchos to the north, the Sanel and the Yokayo, and Rancho Tomales and Rancho Albion on the coast. But between the Pacific and the Russian River, the Coast Range was almost entirely unoccupied, other than by the Pomo, who had lived there for thousands of years. Alexander told them specifically about a long narrow valley the Pomo called Tabootah. To the best of his knowledge, only a single family had settled there, a man named Walter Anderson and his wife and sons, and so that is where they decided to go.

They headed up the road leading to the northern ranchos until they saw wagon tracks splitting off to the west. They assumed the tracks had been left by Anderson's wagons, and for the next three days, they followed them through the grassy meadows and stands of oak and madrone, through the manzanita and chaparral and over a series of densely forested ridges, along a trickling creek until they emerged from the woods and rode out into the valley that Alexander had told them about. Tule elk and black-tailed deer wandered freely across the valley floor, grazing on the waist-high meadow grass and wild oats. A bald eagle soared above as a covey of quail flew up out of the grass and scattered before them. The ridge above the creek was cloaked with ponderosa pine and Douglas fir and towering groves of coastal redwoods. The hills receding into the distance were covered with live oak and black oak and red-barked madrone. They knew this was the land they were looking for.

After staking out two adjacent claims along the creek, they set about building a cabin to get them through the winter. On the ridge above the creek, they cut down the tall straight firs they would use to build the cabin, chaining the logs to the horses to drag them down to the cabin site. There, they squared the logs before pulling them up skids and dropping them into place, and when the walls were up, they installed a simple roof with logs they ripped in half with a whipsaw. With the cabin to shelter them from the rains, they cleared enough land for a large garden, turning the soil with their picks and shovels and planting potatoes and onions in long raised rows. They built a corral for the horses, a shed for their saddles and tools, a smokehouse to cure the deer they shot and the salmon they speared in the creek. And when spring finally arrived, her father saddled his horse and bid his partner goodbye and began the long journey back to Iowa, returning for anyone who wanted to join him in that secluded valley in the Coast Range.

Amelia was overjoyed. It was quickly decided that she and Zachary, as well as Charlotte Carver, soon to be Zachary's bride, would return to California with her father. His plan was to leave in late April to make it to St. Joseph by early May. There, they would wait until the grass on the plains was tall enough to support the oxen, and then they would set out across the continent. The journey would take four months, perhaps even longer.

In December, they bought the running gear for two wagons in Fort Madison. Her father and Zachary constructed the maple wagon boxes themselves, building false bottoms that they divided into storage compartments and then arching green hickory bows above the beds. With Charlotte's help, Amelia sewed the heavy canvas wagon tops, lining the insides with pockets and then waterproofing the canvas with linseed oil before her father and Zachary stretched it over the bows. The wagons would be pulled by six oxen each, yoked in pairs to the long tongues attached to the front axles.

As winter began to break, they started loading the wagons. Amelia was astounded by the amount of food purchased by her father. They laid in sacks of flour and cornmeal, bacon packed in bran to keep it from spoiling, coffee and sugar and bushels of dried fruit. For the first time, she began to sense not only how far they intended to travel, but also the distance that would lie between her and Emily. Realizing it was entirely possible they might never see each other again, they vowed to write to each other for the rest of their lives.

THREE WEEKS after leaving Lee County, they arrived in St. Joseph, where hundreds of people were biding their time in their tents and wagons, waiting to cross the Missouri River, still running high from the heavy spring rains. Nearly two weeks passed before the scows and steam ferry could risk the dangerous currents. Finally, a great cheer went up, and the first wagons started down the bank to the landing. Amelia watched as the scows and steam ferry began carrying the settlers and their wagons and livestock to the opposite shore. With each crossing, the line of wagons on the bank above the river crept forward.

"I was terrified," she wrote in her first letter to Emily. "The closer we got to the landing, the faster the river seemed to run. And of course we had heard the stories of the scows that had capsized and the men and women who had drowned."

But there was no turning back and no other way to cross the river. Her father gave a shout, and the oxen lumbered down the road to the landing. At the crack of his whip, they lunged forward and pulled the wagon onto the ferry. Amelia leapt aboard and then turned and looked back at St. Joseph, and suddenly the city seemed to be moving away from her. She spun around and hurried to the prow of the ferry as it plowed through the churning currents, swaying from side to side, its boiler shrieking. By the time they reached the middle of the river, her fear had all but vanished.

"When we reached the far shore, I asked Father if I could return with him to help bring Zachary's wagon across. He smiled at my newfound courage, but he nonetheless declined my offer. I was disappointed, of course, but he wanted me to watch over our wagon until he got back."

They camped that first night on the west bank of the river, where dozens of wagons were forming themselves into companies for mutual protection and support. They agreed to join a company led by a farmer from Tennessee named Eleazor McCaleb, whose family alone comprised six of the twenty-eight wagons in the party. They left the next morning at dawn, the trail still soft from the recent rains, the iron-rimmed wagon wheels sinking into the muddy ruts left by the companies ahead of them. But they struggled onward, and when they reached a gentle rise above the river, the immense grassland lay before them, spreading gently toward the distant horizon.

Elliott liked to envision his great-grandmother walking along the side of the wagon as the company rolled westward. He could see her scanning the treeless plain, spotting the occasional antelope or deer, looking up at the great white clouds tumbling overhead. He imagined her falling into the rhythm of the trail, comforted by the steady footfall of the oxen and the low moan of the wagons, so young and innocent, a girl enraptured by the new world she was traveling through.

At the end of every day, McCaleb would signal for the company to halt, and in the waning hours of daylight, they would pull the wagons into an outward-facing circle, forming a corral for the oxen, while their cattle and sheep, as well as the hobbled horses, grazed on the open grassland. Amelia and Charlotte would prepare dinner, cooking over wood fires, if any wood could be found, dried chips of manure if not. Afterward, the men would rotate onto sentry duty for three-hour shifts. Whenever her father was assigned to the night's watch, Amelia would lie awake on her blanket beneath their wagon, listening to the nickering of the horses and the barking coyotes, waiting for him to return. Only then, as he stretched out beside her, would she fall asleep.

A little more than a week out of St. Joseph, they reached the junction with the trail from Independence and joined the column of wagons heading up the valley drained by the Little Blue River. The valley was green and lush, the trees along the river filled with songbirds bursting into flight as the wagons rolled past. As they headed north, the days passed quickly, marked by afternoon showers and blinding sunsets.

They left the Little Blue as it turned to the west, climbing up out of the valley and making their way across a broad stretch of sandy hills, eventually reaching the promontory from which they would catch their first glimpse of the Platte River.

"Father told us we would reach the Platte River today, but we were not prepared for what we saw. It is a river of shallow channels and sandbars, the color of gold as it spreads across the vast plain. The river is far larger than I had anticipated. For the first time, I began to understand that even with Father's description of the trail that lies ahead, it is a land that cannot be imagined before it is seen."

The next day, they started up the Platte. As they passed Fort Kearney near the head of Grand Island, the trail was firm and the grade almost imperceptible, an easy haul for the oxen. A low range of sandy hills rose to the left of the trail, the river on their right. The days were warm, and a breeze came up in the evenings and stirred the heavy air.

Elliott couldn't be sure exactly where they saw the buffalo. His great-grandmother's letters do not include specific dates, other than the dates they were posted. His best estimate is that they were several days out of Fort Kearney, perhaps even a week, when McCaleb abruptly signaled for the company to halt. When Amelia asked her father why they were stopping, he pointed to the buffalo on a bluff above the trail, their broad hunched shoulders covered with dark hair, their shaggy beards nearly touching the ground. As he reached for his rifle, the buffalo began stampeding down the bluff, hundreds if not thousands of them rushing toward the Platte and plunging into the water. By the time the last of the herd reached the river, the first buffalo were standing on the opposite bank, barely visible in the distance. A last few buffalo straggled down the hill behind the herd, and the men in the company took down several of them.

"Father helped dress the buffalo out. The hides were tough and difficult to cut, but we cooked the thick steaks that night. The meat was dark and rich, unlike anything I had ever tasted, in its own way as strange and unfamiliar as the prairie itself."

In the morning, they returned to the trail, traveling for much of the next few days three or four wagons across to reduce the amount of dust the trailing wagons would have to endure. Late one morning, they reached the maze of shifting channels and newly formed islands that marked the confluence of the North and South Forks of the Platte. There they headed up the South Fork, reaching the Upper Ford two days later. They could see the wagon ruts leading down to the edge of the river, still running high with the late snowmelt.

"At Father's suggestion, the men blocked up the wagon beds to give the wagons a higher clearance, and then they took the wagons across one at a time. The oxen wanted no part of it. Under the whip, they stumbled reluctantly down the bank into the river, dragging the wagons behind. The wheels immediately sank into the soft river bottom, and the men had to wade into the water and help turn the wheels by hand. We spent an entire day fording the wagons and herding the cattle to the opposite bank."

After crossing the South Fork, they climbed a sharp incline to the top of a flat plateau, then followed the trail to the northwest. After two days, they reached the rim of the plateau, where the trail pitched down the steepest descent the company had so far encountered, the floor of Ash Hollow nearly a half-mile below. The only way to descend was to detach all but the lead oxen from the wagons, chain the rear wheels to the wagon boxes so they couldn't turn, and then lower the wagons individually with ropes. It was a slow but terrifying descent, the consequences of a broken rope all too obvious. But they managed to get the wagons down safely, and the next morning, they started down the hollow, through the ash and cedar and the thickets of gooseberries.

At the mouth of the hollow, a series of springs gushed from the bare canyon walls.

"The water was cold and clear, the sweetest water I have ever tasted and such a welcome change from the warm silty Platte," Amelia wrote. "We drank until we couldn't drink anymore."

Beyond Ash Hollow, the trail began a steady gradual climb. While the days were long and hot, approaching the summer solstice, the nights grew increasingly cool at the higher elevation. Soon a range of hills appeared to the south, breaking the listless horizon, and then they could see Courthouse Rock looming above the plains, its sheer face marking their progress.

"We had been looking for Courthouse Rock for several days, and when we finally saw it, it seemed so close, so near. But we soon learned that nothing is as close as it appears on the open plains. We didn't reach it for two more days."

That afternoon they could see clouds beginning to gather to the west, dark at the base, pure white as they boiled up into the sky. When they heard the thunder rumbling in the distance, the men hurried to form the wagons into a circle, but before they could drive the oxen into the corral formed by the wagons, the storm's dark shadow was upon them. The temperature abruptly dropped, and lightning cracked across the sky. When the thunder clapped immediately afterward, the terrified cattle bolted, fleeing back down the trail. Suddenly, the wind came up, the heavy gusts upending wagons and blowing their possessions across the plain. The hailstorm raged for nearly two hours before it began to relent. By then, night had fallen. There was nothing they could do but wait for daybreak.

In the morning, they saw that seven of the wagons had been

overturned by the storm, the wind shredding the canvas tops of several others, including her brother's wagon. The company lost two days righting the wagons, collecting their scattered belongings and rounding up the cattle and oxen. But by the following morning, the sun poured down through the freshly washed sky, and the company returned to the trail.

In the week after the storm, the company made its way past the unearthly spire of Chimney Rock and the striated face of Scott's Bluff, passing through the arid badlands on the trail worn into the sandstone by the companies that had traveled there before them. Finally, far across the dusty plain, beyond the scattered wagons and Indian encampments, they spotted Fort Laramie on a bluff above the Laramie River, its fortified walls rising above the outlying fields and corrals, its flag snapping in the wind as if to assert the fort's territorial imperative upon the wilderness that surrounded it.

"Emily, I cannot tell you how excited we were to see Fort Laramie. It was the first outpost of civilization we had seen since Fort Kearney. Mr. McCaleb decreed that we would rest at the fort for three days, time enough to acquire more provisions and make repairs to the wagons. Not a voice was heard in opposition."

The company crossed the river on a bridge recently constructed by the soldiers and then stopped in a meadow to the west of the fort. Dozens of companies had camped there before them, preparing for the next leg of the trail. The meadow was littered with the remains of broken-down wagons, cannibalized for anything of value. Her father and Zachary stripped the canvas from one of the wagons, and after a few alterations stretched it over the bows on Zachary's, replacing the canvas that had been torn during the hailstorm. On both wagons, the iron rims had loosened on the wheels, the wood contracting as it dried out on the trail, so her father and Zachary drove thin shims under the rims, taking care not to work the wheels out of round.

That afternoon, Amelia and Charlotte crossed the meadow to

a small creek where they washed clothes, a luxury they had rarely allowed themselves on the trail. After spreading the wet clothing on the brush to dry in the sun, Amelia sat on a rock and placed her feet in the icy water, soaking out the soreness from the trail, and it was there, with snow-covered Mt. Laramie behind her, that she finished her first letter to Emily.

"We have traveled more than six hundred miles," she wrote. "Father is satisfied with our progress. He says we couldn't have traveled much faster without unduly punishing the oxen. But he also cautions that crossing the plains, with its solid trail, ample grass and available water, is the easiest leg of the journey. We soon shall see what the future holds for us."

ELLIOTT LIKED TO VIEW his manuscript as the logical culmination of his long career as a journalist, his crowning achievement as a researcher and writer in his own right. He wanted to believe the years he had spent in the newsroom had prepared him well for such an ambitious project. For more than three decades, he had worked closely with his reporters, particularly on their long investigative stories and multipart series. It was deeply rewarding work, helping guide their research and develop their reporting strategies, supervising the meticulous accumulation of facts, counseling them as they methodically constructed their stories. He had always insisted his reporters adhere to the highest standards of the profession, and he had made every effort to produce his own manuscript in strict compliance with those same core principles.

And he had learned long ago the value of primary documents, their indisputable provenance and authority. He knew just how fortunate he was to have discovered his great-grandfather's journals and his great-grandmother's letters in the drawers of the secretary. As he sat at his desk, listening to Brahm's Violin Sonata in D Minor, he understood what treasures had fallen into his hands.

His great-grandmother's letter about that first leg of the journey, mailed from Fort Laramie on June 28, 1854, is nothing less than a joy to behold, a letter filled with wonder and awe, written by a young girl swept up in the momentum of a grand adventure. And yet, her second letter, posted at Fort Hall seven weeks later, would reveal an ominous shift in tone. It is subtle, but it is also unmistakable. Elliott had noticed the change the first time he read the letter aloud. His great-grandmother was no longer an innocent teenage girl. Rather, the letter had been written by a young woman clearly affected by all she that she had endured and witnessed. She had come to understand the gravity of their journey, the inherent danger and risk, the chances they took every day on the trail. She understood the journey they had embarked upon was no longer an adventure but an ordeal from which all they could reasonably ask was to survive.

After leaving Fort Laramie, the company headed west into the Black Hills. The trail led through a series of ridges and ravines with a few isolated cedars and pines clinging to the desiccated hills. The plateaus were barren except for the sparse dry grass, sagebrush, and prickly pear. Every afternoon, the wind rose, gusting in from the west. Thunderclouds rolled overhead, and lightning flashed in the far-off mountains. But it rained only occasionally, sudden flurries of heavy raindrops.

By Elliott's calculations, the company was about a week out of Fort Laramie when they reached the North Fork of the Platte River. The river there was wide and too deep to ford, but a man from one of the companies ahead offered to sell them the raft his company had used to ferry their wagons across the river. He had purchased the raft from a party ahead of them, and he was asking the same price his party had paid for it. If McCaleb's company bought the raft, they could use it to cross the river and then sell it to one of the following companies and recoup their costs. It sounded like a reasonable offer, and McCaleb told the man he had a deal.

The raft consisted of three large logs that had been ripped in half and then hollowed out, the logs then lashed together with rope with thick planks laid across them. The wagon owned by a minister named Prentice Jacobs was the first to be ferried across the river. After his wagon was secured to the raft, the Reverend Jacobs and three other men climbed aboard. Using long wooden poles, they pushed the raft away from the shore and then began negotiating the subtle currents. From the shore, Amelia nervously watched until the wagon was safely delivered to the far bank.

Shortly after noon, they loaded a wagon owned by a blacksmith named Luther Pearson onto the raft.

"As the raft pulled away, Mr. Pearson turned and waved at all of us on the shore. After waving back at him, I began helping Zachary and Charlotte prepare for the crossing. But when I heard the men shouting, I knew something was wrong."

In the middle of the river, a corner of the raft had caught a large snag. Pearson and the other men were trying to free the raft, but the snag began to roll in the current, its branches rising up out of the water. The raft tilted into the current, the wagon listing to the side as the upriver planks dipped beneath the surface. Pearson and two other men hacked at the snag with axes, but they had to draw back when their weight caused the edge of the raft to dip even deeper. Suddenly the wagon shifted, the ropes securing it to the planks snapping taut as the current pushed harder against the side of the raft. With the raft about to capsize, the men leapt into the water, all but Pearson, who was still chopping at the snag when the back of the wagon broke free, toppling over and then crashing into the river on top of him.

"When the raft washed up on a shallow sandbar, Father and several other men pulled Mr. Pearson out from beneath the wagon. But it was too late. All of us watching from the bank knew that Mr. Pearson had drowned."

After crossing all the wagons and laying Pearson to rest, the company moved solemnly up the trail. When the North Fork turned to the south and entered a narrow impassable canyon, the trail led across a desolate windswept plain. They decided to travel as much as possible in the early morning, then rest through the afternoon in the shelter of the dry gullies that scoured the plain before returning to the trail at sunset, their progress illuminated only by starlight.

Eventually, they reached the Sweetwater River, a quick-running tributary of the North Fork, the gray granite dome of Independence Rock visible to the west. The Sweetwater's valley offered good grass and easy passage, and the company resumed traveling by day. When they reached the summit of South Pass, the unassuming spine of the continent, the company halted to appreciate what they had accomplished, and to remember, Reverend Jacobs reminded them all, the price they had paid to get there. Two-and-a-half months had passed since they left St. Joseph. They had traveled approximately nine hundred miles. The Atlantic lay behind them, the ocean of their past. Now all rivers led to the Pacific, the ocean of their future.

The company made good progress on the gradual descent from the pass, making camp near Pacific Spring, then reaching the Little Sandy River the following afternoon. The Little Sandy was cold and clear. The company rested there for several hours and then pressed on to the Big Sandy, arriving just after nightfall. Only a few of the wagons troubled to build a fire and make dinner. The others simply prepared their bedrolls and fell into an exhausted sleep.

The company rested there a day, preparing to cross a long stretch of desert by cutting as much grass for the oxen as they could carry in the wagons and filling every cask and barrel with water. They set out the following morning, and by noon the sun had blanched the sky, the heat shimmering on the bleached white soil. There was no shade, not even the promise of water. They drank sparingly from their canteens, their perspiration evaporating instantly, salt crystallizing on their skin as the ground burned through the soles of their boots. A hot wind came up in the afternoon, making their progress even harder, and one of their oxen gave out beneath the pitiless sky.

"We lost one of our oxen today," Amelia wrote. "It sank to its knees in the burning sand and could go no farther. Father released the poor animal from its yoke and then remained behind as we moved on. As soon as we were out of sight, we heard the gunshot, and we knew that Father had put the ox out of its misery."

They stopped late that night to rest the animals and give them the grass they had cut at Big Sandy, then they returned to the trail at daybreak, still heading due west. Late that afternoon, they could see the hills above the Green River, but as the company pressed on, the hills remained on the horizon, the distance masked by a series of unseen ravines. Finally, the men at the front of the column of wagons gave a shout, seeing the river at the bottom of the valley below, winding through the band of trees growing along its banks. As they started down the trail, they struggled to hold back the anxious oxen, sensing the presence of the river. Several of the wagons found it necessary to release their oxen, but Amelia's father and Zachary managed to guide their wagons down to the valley floor before letting the oxen bolt for the water.

At daybreak, they began ferrying the wagons across the Green. The water was high and the current swift, but the Mormons who had come up from the Great Salt Lake to guide the flatboats knew the river well, and by mid afternoon, all the wagons had crossed.

They spent the next week traversing a series of forested ridges. The weather was mild, and the fragrance of the pines and fir sweetened the air. There was water in the creeks at the bottoms of the ravines and game in the forests. Zachary took a buck near Ham's Fork, and that night they ate venison and cobbler made with chokecherries gathered by Charlotte.

They had initially intended to take the Hudspeth Cutoff, which would bypass Fort Hall and save three or four days on the trail. But several members of the company wanted to purchase supplies at the fort or needed to exchange their oxen. Others said they wanted the rest, and still others simply craved a taste of civilization. So they proceeded north, heading up the Bear River Valley, passing through Soda Springs, where the cutoff led to the west.

They arrived at Fort Hall on August 11, 1854. On the south bank of the Snake River, near its confluence with the Blackfoot, the fort had served for years as an important way station for emigrants on their way to both Oregon and California. But when the trail to California bypassed the fort, only those bound for Oregon or in need of supplies or help stopped there. And as the traffic declined, the fort slid inexorably into disrepair. In her second letter, Amelia wrote that everyone in the company was disappointed when they first saw the fort.

"Its whitewashed adobe walls seemed to slump in the heat, its flag limp under the relentless glare of the sun. But we have traveled some five hundred miles beyond Fort Laramie. After three months on the trail, we are more than half the way to California. But the oxen are wearing down, and so are we, and Father has made it clear that the hardest days are yet to come."

ELLIOTT COULD FEEL himself being watched, a pair of eyes behind him. When he turned around, he saw Hank in the door of his study, lying on the hardwood floor, his long chin on his fore-paws. Quietly, the dog began to whimper. Elliott knew what he wanted, what he always wanted.

As he rose from his chair, Hank leapt up and began trotting down the hall, proceeding directly to the back porch, where he sat beneath his leash, hanging from a wooden peg on the wall. It was Alissa's responsibility to take Hank out for the occasional walk, of course, but the task had proven to be largely incompatible with her nocturnal lifestyle, which meant the responsibility had fallen to Elliott, just as he knew it would when he agreed to let her bring the dog home. But he didn't mind, particularly. He enjoyed taking

Hank up to the small park at the top of the hill. He welcomed the fresh air and the chance to stretch his legs, always an invigorating break from work on his manuscript.

He crossed the porch and took down the leash.

"Now hold still," he said.

When the leash was secure, he grabbed his coat and hat and walked the dog down the stairs and out onto the street. Hank knew exactly where they were going. Straining against the leash, he led Elliott up the sidewalk, across Jones and then around the concrete wall at the end of the street. They walked up the narrow ramp on the right, the sidewalk leading through the manicured gardens that lined the street to the cloistered brown-shingled mansions at the summit of the hill. The park was just beyond a low concrete balustrade, little more than a small patch of grass enclosed by a hedge of thorny pyracantha.

Elliott leaned down and unclipped the leash.

"There you go," he said.

He watched as Hank dashed across the grass, barking at the robins feasting on the fermenting orange berries, leaping up at the birds as they burst into startled flight. Elliott loved this quiet sanctuary above the steps leading down to North Beach, its sweeping views of the glass-and-granite high-rises downtown, the rust-streaked cargo ships plowing across the blue-gray bay in the distance. He had been coming here for years, ever since his father passed away and he and Evelyn moved into the flat with their daughter Claire, spreading blankets on the grass for sunny afternoon picnics, blowing soapy bubbles off her fingertips and watching them sail away on the breeze.

And when Alissa was a young girl, Claire would bring her here, too. One day, they found a newborn starling that had fallen out of its nest, a ball of black fluff with a tiny yellow beak, certain to die within hours if left alone. Alissa begged Claire to let her bring the starling home, and Claire finally acquiesced. With Claire's help,

Alissa fashioned a nest for the baby bird in her bedroom, shredded newspaper in a cardboard shoebox placed on an electric heating pad. She fed it tiny bits of cat food on the end of a twig and filled a mayonnaise jar lid with water and arranged it at the end of the box. She named the starling Mandy for reasons no one could understand, and she could only explain with a shrug of the shoulders.

But soon the starling began attempting to fly, extending its feathery wings and hopping around in the box. So they carried the box up to the park and knelt on the grass, and Alissa gently scooped up the starling, cupping it in her hands until it leapt up and flew away, swiftly disappearing into the dense foliage below the park. For days afterward, Alissa demanded to be taken up to the park to look for her starling. There were days when she came home thrilled, sure she had seen Mandy, other days when she returned to their apartment crushed with disappointment.

One night, as Claire was putting her to bed, Alissa asked if the starling might have died. Claire sat down beside her and told her that there was a plan for every living being, even if it wasn't always easy to know what that plan might be. They might not know where Mandy was, but now they knew that she had always been destined to save the newborn starling and give it flight. The thought provided great comfort, and Alissa drifted off to sleep, and as Elliott watched Hank ripping the grass with his paws, the thought gave him comfort, too, if only he could know what Alissa's plan held for her in the days to come.

When he felt his cell phone vibrate, he withdrew it from his coat pocket and saw that Claire was calling.

"Now this is an unexpected pleasure," he said.

"Hello, Dad. How are you?"

"I'm fine," he said. "Hank and I are enjoying a splendid afternoon up here at the park."

"You're walking Hank?" she asked.

"I am," Elliott said.

"Isn't that Alissa's job?"

Elliott knew where this was going, where his conversations with Claire often went.

"Technically, yes," he said.

"What do you mean – technically?" she asked. "I thought the only reason you let her bring that dog home was to teach her a little responsibility."

"Well, yes, that's true," he conceded.

"So how is she going to learn this responsibility if you're out walking the dog for her?"

It all made Elliott weary.

"So is this why you called – to scold me for walking the dog?"

"I called because I wanted to hear how Alissa is doing," she said. "I don't know how many messages I've left on the answering machine, telling her to call me."

"Well, she seems to be doing fine – no different, no changes."

"Which means she's sleeping all day and staying out all night, drinking and smoking pot and playing that awful music."

"Pretty much," Elliott admitted.

"I'm worried about her. I really am."

"Yes, I understand," he said. "I worry about her, too. But I think she's doing all right."

"You have more confidence in her than I do," she said.

He wasn't going to argue.

"That's probably true," he said.

"Will you tell her to call me, please?"

"Of course," he said. "But that doesn't mean she will."

"I know better than to hold my breath."

Elliott allowed himself a smile.

"It's good to hear from you, Claire. It's always good to hear your voice. You need to call me more often."

But his daughter had already turned off her phone.

He slipped the phone back into his coat pocket. It was all something of a mystery to him, to be perfectly honest. He had never understood why Alissa had become so sullen and brooding. He didn't know why Claire's relationship with her daughter had deteriorated to the extent that they were barely speaking to each other. It was tempting to attribute the animus between them to the disintegration of Claire's marriage. And it was certainly true that her ex-husband, a freelance magazine writer who was often gone for days, if not weeks, at a time, and then sequestered himself in the upstairs office he rented in North Beach, had been little help in raising Alissa. But that seemed too easy, too convenient.

Alissa's issues had initially surfaced in middle school, where she began acting out in class, ignoring or arguing with her teachers, refusing to do her work. Twice while she was in high school, Claire caught her trying to sneak out of the flat in the middle of the night, once trying to sneak back in at dawn. She was sure that Alissa had begun smoking marijuana; she could smell the dank odor on her army fatigue jacket. She was also sure that Alissa had begun drinking, her suspicions confirmed the night they received a call from General Hospital, where Alissa was in the emergency room, having passed out at the house of a friend after drinking nearly a fifth of Southern Comfort.

And yet the outbursts of anger and the raging arguments, the long deathly silences, didn't begin until Alissa's senior year of high school. By then, Claire had divorced her husband and was seeing Albert Nakuro, a commercial photographer based in Los Angeles. He seemed liked a decent man, three years younger than Claire, tall and lanky with a long black ponytail. On those occasions when he was in the city, Claire seemed genuinely content in the relationship. But Alissa, for her part, dismissed Nakuro without a thought, scarcely uttering a word in his presence, ignoring him as if he were a handyman called to repair a broken appliance.

Elliott found it hard to believe that five years had passed since Alissa graduated from high school and Claire married Nakuro and moved to Los Angeles. He knew it was not an easy decision for his daughter to leave Alissa with him, despite the extent to which their relationship had deteriorated. And yet, now, looking back, Elliott had to believe that Claire had been right. Surely, their relationship couldn't have endured much longer. His daughter had reached the point at which she believed the only way to preserve the possibility that her relationship with Alissa might be salvaged was for her to leave, and as Elliott watched Hank racing around in circles on the grass, he knew all he could do now was hope the damage they had inflicted upon each other had not driven them beyond any chance of reconciliation. All he could do was hope that his daughter and granddaughter would someday find a way to forgive each other.

AFTER NEARLY AN HOUR, Hank trotted over to Elliott and flopped down in front of him, panting heavily, blades of grass stuck to his slobbery muzzle. Elliott attached the leash to his collar, and they walked back down Vallejo to his building. As the porch grate closed behind him, he bent down and released Hank from his leash, then he opened the door to the flat, allowing the dog to race up the stairs, as if to tell Alissa where he'd been.

Elliott picked up the mail the carrier had slipped through the slot at the bottom of the door, then climbed the stairs to the flat. After hanging up the leash, he moved into the kitchen and poured himself a glass of water and looked down at the backyard. In addition to cleaning up Hank's droppings, there was much work to be done in the yard, work that he'd been putting off while he finished his manuscript. And it would not be long before winter arrived. Already the leaves on the Japanese maples were beginning to change color, darkening into deep reds and purples, and the bougainvillea was beginning to lose its papery, bright red flowers. As warm as these October days were, Elliott knew it would not be long before the storm clouds moved in, dark and heavy, pregnant with rain.

He crossed the kitchen and sat at the table and began casually flipping through the thin collection of bills, bank statements, and junk mail. Instantly, a notice from the post office caught his eye – a package had been sent to him, but it couldn't be delivered because postage was due. And then he saw the originating zip code: 10011. New York City.

Phoebe Crighton. It had to be her. There was no one else it could be. She had sent him a package. As Elliott sat back in his chair, he had no idea what it might contain. He had no idea what Ms. Crighton wanted from him now.

CHAPTER FIVE

IN HER TERRYCLOTH ROBE, Alissa sat at the kitchen table, her eyes still inflamed with sleep, her green hair flattened against her scalp. Hank stood on his back legs in front of her, his forepaws on her knees. Elliott watched as Alissa struck a match and lit one of her clove cigarettes, then leaned back and exhaled toward the ceiling, dropping the spent match into a coffee mug.

"Hank and I had a fine time up at the park," he told her.

She looked down at the dog.

"Is that true?" she asked.

As she picked the dog up, he leapt at her face and gave her a quick lick on the cheek before she settled him in her lap, his tongue falling out the side of his mouth to lie across her thigh.

Elliott poured himself a glass of water and carried it over to the table.

"I didn't hear you come in last night," he said.

"It was late – I don't really remember what time it was."

He watched Alissa dig her fingers into the dog's stiff coat, scratching the back of his neck.

"Do you mind if I ask where you were?"

She looked up at him, her eyes filled with hair-thin veins.

"Are you checking up on me?"

"No," he hastened to say.

"Did my mother ask you to check up on me?"

"I was just wondering, that's all," he said. "I didn't mean to pry."

She stared at him, as if trying to decide whether he could be trusted.

"I was at Nigel's," she said.

Elliott didn't know Nigel. He'd never even heard the name.

"Nigel?"

"Walter," she said. "He goes by Nigel now."

"Ah," Elliott said.

She took a drag on her cigarette, exhaling through her nostrils.

"I won't ask what you were doing," Elliott said.

Her face tightened, her eyes narrowing.

"And what's that supposed to mean?"

Elliott tried to wave the question off.

"It just means I don't need to know what's going on between you and Nigel," he said.

"There's nothing going on between me and Nigel. He's our bass player. He's my friend."

"Of course, of course," Elliott said. "I was just wondering where you were."

"Well, now you know," she said, as if to bring the line of inquiry to a close.

He took another sip of water, then rose from the table and emptied the rest of the glass into the sink.

"So, what's on the agenda for today, for what's left of it, anyway?" he asked.

"We're practicing."

"What time?" he asked.

"Nigel and Jeremy are coming over around eight."

"Jeremy?"

"Martin," she said.

Elliott couldn't resist a discrete smile.

"It must be hard to keep all these names straight," he said.

"Not really," she said flatly.

"I hope you're not thinking about changing your name."

"I'm considering it."

"Seriously?" he asked. "What's wrong with Alissa?"

She shrugged while rubbing Hank's ears.

"There's nothing wrong with it," she said. "It's just that I'm tired of it. I've been an Alissa all my life."

"That's true," Elliott said.

"Sometimes I don't feel like an Alissa. Sometimes I feel like someone else."

Elliott didn't know what to make of that, but he could see that she was serious.

"Like who?" he asked. "Who do you feel like?"

She thought for a moment, a toss of her shoulders before taking another drag on her cigarette.

"I don't know," she said. "Cassandra, maybe."

Elliott nodded, turning the name over in his mind.

"Cassandra," he said. "Not bad, not bad."

ELLIOTT WALKED down the hall to his study. After putting on his sweater, he sat at his desk and turned on the stereo receiver – Mahler's Symphony No. 5 – then reached for his manuscript, turning back to his great-grandmother setting out across the Great Basin. After three days at Fort Hall, the company departed shortly before dawn to roll west along the south bank of the Snake River. The sun rose behind them, the first light streaking overhead, chasing the lingering stars. As Amelia walked alongside the wagon, the sun climbed into the ash-colored sky, following them as they made their way along the rim of the canyon. There was no respite. The sun seemed to remain overhead all day, as if to defeat even the possibility of shade.

For three days they followed the Snake, the trail winding through the wiry clumps of sage until they reached the Raft River. There, they headed south, the Raft no more than a meandering stream so late in the summer. But there was good grass along its banks and in the meadows, and the oxen needed it badly. At night, the great beasts lay still on the ground, footsore and exhausted, their ribs protruding through their thick hides, open sores on the backs of their shoulders, worn into their hides by the yokes that chained them to the wagons.

"I don't see how these noble animals will pull us all the way to California, even though our wagons are much lighter than when we left St. Joseph. We have gone through half the provisions we set out with, and we have discarded everything we don't need. Still, we seem to lose more oxen every day. They simply stop and kneel down, unable to take another step, and there is nothing we can do but put an end to their suffering."

When they reached Cassia Creek, the trail turned into its tight canyon. At dusk, they passed two immense granite cones and entered a broad natural amphitheater filled with huge rock formations thrust up violently through the skin of the earth, an unsettling congregation of turrets and columns, domes, spires, and pyramids looming above the wagons. They passed through the long shadows quietly, as if traveling through the ruins of a vanquished metropolis.

After camping by a spring for the night, they started across an open plain, the ruts grinding through the tufted grass and junipers, ascending the barely noticeable grade to Granite Pass. At the summit, they stopped and looked out upon the unforgiving wasteland that awaited them, the truncated buttes and fractured bluffs stretching out before them for as far as they could see. In a weary silence, they began the treacherous descent to Goose Creek.

They lowered the wagons one at a time, locking the wheels and holding the wagons back with ropes, letting them slide down the loose gravel and rock. It was exhausting work, and, late in the afternoon, Arthur Harding's wagon broke free and crashed down the slope, spilling everything he owned before it finally came to rest above the creek. After lowering the other wagons, Amelia's father and several of the other men helped Harding salvage the front half of his wagon, fashioning it into a two-wheeled cart capable of carrying at least some of the possessions he had managed to recover.

The company returned to the trail the next day, weaving through the dark volcanic rock strewn across the valley floor. Eventually, the trail left the creek to follow one of its tributaries to the west. In places, the canyon was barely wide enough for the wagons to pass, but they eventually managed to climb out of the narrow gorge, leaving its water and grass to strike out once again across a dry plain flanked by barren mountains.

"There seems no end to the desolate terrain. With each ridge we cross, another rises in the distance, waiting for us. The trail is lined with broken wagons and the bones of dead oxen scattered by the wolves. It is all Charlotte and I can do to keep pace. It is all we can do to place one foot after the other."

Finally, they reached the Humboldt River. They had been anticipating arriving at its headwaters ever since they left Fort Hall, knowing they would follow the river across the desert for the next three weeks. They could hardly believe what they saw.

"I cannot fully express our disappointment when we arrived at the river's inauspicious headwaters – a dismal sump grown over with reeds and rushes. The warm brackish water moves so slowly through the mud and grass that it is difficult to detect a current. Vultures were tearing apart the rotting carcasses of cattle that had become mired in the mud and could not be pulled out. The stench was inescapable, and so, too, were the clouds of mosquitoes that swarmed through the air, so thick we had to wrap scarves around our faces to keep from inhaling them."

After a restless night, they started down the river, heading slowly down the north bank in the unrelenting heat. The snowcapped Ruby Mountains seemed to dance above the desert floor, reflected in the silvery mirage of a vast lake. Dust devils spun up into the empty sky. The heat rising from the ground scalded their lungs, and the dry air cracked their lips until they began to bleed, so raw it was painful to touch them, even with the tip of the tongue. In places, the dust on the trail was nearly a foot deep. It rose in clouds and engulfed the wagons, caking their faces and clogging their nostrils, stinging their eyes. The sun burned any flesh they dared expose.

By the time they reached the South Fork of the Humboldt, Charlotte could no longer walk for more than a few hours at a time and had to lie in Zachary's wagon. Occasionally the trail was forced away from the river, detouring for miles around the high ridges that stood above the Humboldt's banks. But as they proceeded west, the ridges gradually drew back from the river, the high desert fanning out in all directions. The Humboldt slithered through the sage and greasewood, never more than twenty feet across, rarely more than a foot deep. With each day, the water in the river grew warmer and darker. In some places, the water was nearly black.

"The trail is lined with the graves of those who could make it no farther. Some are marked by simple headstones with names and dates scratched onto the face of the rock. A rare few are dignified with crosses. Most of the dead were merely covered with rocks to prevent the wolves from digging up their bodies, but it is not uncommon to come across the scattered skeletal remains of the disinterred."

Finally they reached Lassen Meadow, where the water was good and the grass abundant. McCaleb decreed they would stay there for two days. Zachary had lost another ox, leaving him with only three, so he and their father decided to cut his wagon in half and fill it with cut grass to sustain the animals on the trail ahead. The half wagon would require just one of the oxen. The other two would be yoked to their father's wagon, which would carry their consolidated possessions and supplies.

"That first night at Lassen Meadow, I lay on my blanket so exhausted I worried I might not be able to rise in the morning. But as I gazed up at the night sky, I reminded myself that we were nearly across the desert. Father said that in a week, perhaps a day or two more, we would reach the Carson River at the base of the Sierra. He warned that these last few days would be the most difficult, but I cannot not believe they could be much harder than what we have already endured."

AFTER RESTING at the meadow, they returned to the trail as it led to the southwest, through a long dry valley between a range of blackened mountains and chalky gray hills. The valley was devoid of any vegetation beyond the ubiquitous sage and greasewood, and progress was slow. The wagons lurched over the exposed rock and plowed through trenches filled with dust, billowing around them like smoke.

Late that afternoon, Reverend Jacob's wagon became stuck, its left rear wheel wedged tightly between two rocks. Amelia's father walked back to help free the wagon, slipping the end of a stout wooden pole beneath the iron-rimmed wheel to pry it up and out of the gap between the rocks. As he worked the pole into position, he instructed Reverend Jacobs to be prepared to start the oxen when he gave a shout. He grabbed the pole with both hands and tested it, making sure the rock would serve as a proper fulcrum, then he glanced over to Reverend Jacobs to make sure he was ready, too. He gripped the pole tightly and then leaned back, pulling down hard to lift the wheel. He gave a shout to Reverend Jacobs. At the crack of his whip, the oxen strained against the weight of the wagon, the wheel riding up from between the two rocks – but as the wagon lunged forward, the pole slipped free, and her father fell, his left leg sliding across the ground just as the wheel dropped down.

His leg snapped, as loud as a clap of the hands.

"Father!"

As the wagon pulled away, he groaned and rolled onto his right side, reaching down and clutching his left leg. Amelia rushed over to him, gasping when she saw that the jagged end of his tibia had punctured the back of his pant leg. Cradling her father's head in her lap, she watched as Zachary slit her father's pant leg and drew the cloth back. The wound was bleeding heavily, so they tied her father's belt around his thigh to serve as a tourniquet and then gently wrapped his leg with pieces of cloth. Carefully, they lifted him onto a blanket spread out across the grass in the half-wagon, but there was little else they could do as he writhed in pain, panting in the heat. They realized they had no choice but to continue down the trail to the Great Meadows.

"Let's pray we find a doctor there," Reverend Jacobs said.

"And what if we don't?" Zachary asked.

Arthur Harding stepped forward.

"I'll ride back to Lassen Meadow and see if I can find a doctor there," he said.

"We'll wait at Great Meadows for two days," McCaleb said. "But then we'll have to move on."

Amelia climbed up onto the plank seat of the wagon and took up the reins. She had driven the wagon only intermittently on the journey west, allowing her father to walk along the trail only long enough to work out the stiffness in his leg muscles and lower back. Now she knew that she would have to drive the wagon the rest of the way.

It took a day and a half to reach the Great Meadows. When they stopped to rest the oxen, she climbed down to check on her father in the half-wagon.

"Father seemed to slip in and out of consciousness," she wrote. "Every time I caught his eye, I gave him water, squeezing a wet cloth onto his lips. But he failed to utter a single word. He was completely disoriented, unaware of what had happened or where he was."

They despaired to find no doctor at the meadows. Amelia removed the blood-soaked cloth around her father's leg to clean the wound. Already the flesh around the protruding bone was turning black, and she could smell the infection.

Finally, Harding arrived with a surgeon from Lassen Meadows. His name was Evans, and he was old and tired with a long gray-streaked beard and trembling hands. When he examined her father's leg, they could see the gangrene had moved up to his knee, nearly reaching the tourniquet around his thigh.

"I'll have to amputate," the doctor said.

Amelia groaned, but Zachary knew the doctor had no choice.

"Do what needs to be done," her brother said.

The doctor opened his bag and removed his scalpel and bone saw. He nodded at Zachary and Reverend Jacobs.

"Hold him down," the doctor said.

But it wasn't necessary. Her father had already lapsed into unconsciousness. The doctor cut away the necrotic tissue, preserving a large flap of skin on the top of the thigh, then he sawed through the bone, dropping the severed leg onto the ground beneath the wagon. He tied off the arteries with thread, then filed down the rough end of the bone so it wouldn't pierce the flap of skin that he then sewed back over the raw stump, leaving a small hole for the leg to drain.

As the doctor prepared to leave, Zachary walked him back to his horse.

"We thank you for coming all this way," he said.

"Let's pray I got here in time," the doctor said.

They rested there overnight. Amelia stayed with her father,

spreading her blanket out beneath the half-wagon, rising to comfort him whenever she heard him stir. He was still disoriented and at times delirious. She listened to his incoherent mutterings, wiping his face with a moist cloth, squeezing his hand and imploring him to hold on. But when he looked up, she couldn't be sure he even recognized her.

As soon as the heat crested the next afternoon, they set out across the desert, traveling all night by the light of the moon. There was no wind, not a sound other than the creaking of the wagons and the slow cadence of the oxen. In the last hours before dawn, the moon sank behind the mountains to the west, and they made their way across the vast alkali flat in almost total darkness, guided only by starlight.

"When I checked on Father, he was lying still on the blanket, his breathing hoarse, summoned from deep in his chest. I could not help but wonder if he knew he had lost his leg, and I dreaded the moment of awakening that awaited him."

When the sky finally began to blue, they were stunned to see the carnage revealed by the daylight. Abandoned wagons were spread out across the desert, the ground littered with chains and tents and tools, books and pans and guns, spindles and china, anything that could be jettisoned to lighten the wagons. But the oxen died anyway, the trail lined with their bloated carcasses. A few of the oxen were still alive, lying on their sides as they pawed the ground with their forelegs, unable to rise. A lone black horse gave a final nudge to a small wooden barrel and then staggered to the ground, too weak even to lift its head.

As they struggled across the desert, Amelia tried not to look at the unspeakable horror that surrounded them, forcing herself to look straight ahead, to focus on the ruts leading across the desert floor. When she stopped to check on her father, he seemed in no discomfort. The bleeding seemed to have stopped, the dressing on his leg black with dried blood. She squeezed a few more drops of water onto his lips, then climbed back into the wagon.

Less than a mile ahead, the trail turned to loose sand. In the intense heat, the oxen stumbled forward, dragging the wagons up a gradual ridge.

"For the first time, I was truly afraid that we were going to perish in the desert. But the remaining oxen saved us. They refused to die – and then, if anything, they seemed to grow stronger, becoming increasingly agitated as they strained against their yokes. It was not until we reached the crest of the ridge and saw the cottonwoods along the banks of the Carson River that we realized they had sensed the water."

Zachary gave a shout, and they drove down from the ridge. When they finally reached the river, Amelia leapt down from the wagon and grabbed one of the empty casks and filled it with the cold clear water, scooping a handful into her own mouth before she hurried the cask back to her father in the half-wagon.

"But Zachary caught me by the arm. I looked up at him, startled by his brusque grip. Only then did I understand. I looked down at Father and cried out his name and threw myself upon him. If Father had to die, dear Emily, I wanted nothing less than to die with him."

AMES SNYDER WAS BURIED in a glade among the cottonwoods on September 21, 1854, the Reverend Jacobs officiating over a simple graveside service, hailing Amelia's father for all he had done to help the company come this far. Amelia was devastated by her father's death, exhausted from the journey across the continent, drained by the debilitating ordeal in the desert. But at dawn the day after her father was laid to rest, she and her brother and Charlotte fell in with the company as it headed southwest, up the Carson River as it ran along the base of the mountains.

After several days, the river forked and the trail turned west, following the west branch of the river into its canyon. For the first few miles, the trail led through the pines that grew down to the edge of the river, and the company passed easily through the forest. But the deeper they pushed into the canyon, the closer the sheer granite walls loomed overhead. Several stretches of the trail were nearly impassable, so tight the wagons could barely scrape past. The oxen struggled, their sore hooves slipping on the granite, staining the rocks with blood from their raw forelegs. The men tried to improve the trail where they could, but at times all they could do was to throw their shoulders against the backs of the wagons and push for all they were worth.

Darkness came early in the canyon. The nights were cold, and Amelia slept beside the fires that Zachary built, staring at the seething coals until her eyes burned and she finally had to look away.

"I did not want to talk to anyone. I had no appetite. I couldn't sleep. At night I laid on my blanket and stared up at the stars and could feel the tears slipping out the corners of my eyes."

After two days, they clawed up out of the canyon, reaching the meadow in the heart of Hope Valley. The river passed quietly through the meadow, through the quaking aspens, their brilliant yellow leaves shivering in the breeze. The air was cool and raised the flesh on their arms, even in the harsh glare of the sun. Shading her eyes, Amelia gazed up the valley and could see the pass they would have to summit.

"For the first time," she wrote, "I can envision the end of this terrible journey."

They started across the valley at daybreak, skirting Red Lake, following the trail along the southern edge of a marsh, intending to camp that night at the base of Carson Pass. The trail leading up to the pass seemed impossibly steep, a long dead pull up the side of the ridge. If the trail itself wasn't evidence that wagons could be taken up such a difficult grade, they might never have attempted it. But they yoked the oxen to the wagons and began the ascent, crawling slowly forward, lashing and shouting at the laboring oxen, the wagons lurching over the logs and stumps and rock that the earlier emigrants had fashioned into a rough trail bed.

Midway up the ridge, the slope abruptly grew even steeper. They had no choice but to stop and double-team the oxen and then take the wagons up the trail one at a time, ever mindful of the wagons from earlier companies that had broken free and now lay in pieces around them. It took all afternoon to ascend the ridge, and from there the trail leveled out, a relatively easy route to the pass. But when they looked out across the forested valley below, they despaired to see a second pass they would have to cross – West Pass, a distant gap amid the sharp white peaks.

They had no choice but to press on. By the time the wagons reached the valley floor, snow had begun to fall, heavy flakes drifting down through the forest. Working in near darkness, they made camp quickly. That night, as they gathered around the fires, they knew that if they were to make it over the pass, they would have to do so tomorrow, even if it was still snowing. They couldn't risk waiting for the weather to clear.

"I wrapped myself in my blankets and huddled before the fire and listened to the men talking about tomorrow. I kept expecting to hear Father's voice, waiting for his sure counsel, and that made me miss him all the more."

She woke at first light as Zachary revived the fire, fanning the still-glowing coals until they broke into flames. Overnight, nearly half a foot of snow had fallen, and it was still coming down, the clouds low and dark, the large flakes floating lazily in the cold air. The camp came alive, and soon they were making their way through the snow-draped woods. When they reached the foot of the pass, they stopped to rest the oxen before the difficult grade ahead, constantly watching the darkening sky. They spoke quietly, exchanging hushed prayers among themselves as they sat and gathered their strength. They rested for nearly an hour before rising to begin the climb.

As they emerged from the shelter of the forest and approached the summit, a fierce wind began to swirl around them. Sitting on the plank seat of the wagon, Amelia squinted down at the tracks through the snow, her head throbbing from the altitude. Nauseous and so weak she thought she might tumble out of the wagon, she felt all but empty, a hollow vessel containing only her grief, her tears burning down her cheeks in the bitter cold. But then she heard Zachary calling out to her. She looked ahead. Standing beside her brother, Reverend Jacobs thrust both arms in the air and lifted his face to the sky. When she looked out across the dark ridges rippling away from them, she realized they had finally reached the summit.

"I turned and looked back down the trail, and I realized that we had made it. We had finally reached California. I knew I should have felt fortunate, grateful even, but the truth, dear Emily, is that I wish we had never left Iowa at all."

It was an excerpt that Elliott could barely bring himself to read, even now, as it appeared in his manuscript. As he rocked back in his chair and looked up at the map on the wall above his desk, he remembered the first time he read his great-grandmother's third letter to her cousin, the anguished recounting of her suffering and despair. Of course he understood the tragic dimension of her journey across the continent, the depth of her loss and sorrow. And yet, in retrospect, all these years later, he also viewed the story of her hellish ordeal as a testament to the resilience of the human spirit and to his great-grandmother's indefatigable will to live.

She and Zachary and Charlotte would make their way down the trail descending from the summit and arrive in Hangtown several weeks later. And from there, they would be directed to Anderson Valley, where she would meet the man who would ultimately become her husband. A new life was dawning before his great-grandmother, even if she couldn't see it at the time. The years that lay before her would not be easy. But she would persevere. She would endure. And she would become the old woman he had known all too briefly as a boy.

WHEN THE SORES began practicing, Elliott grabbed his coat and hat and let himself out of the building, leaving behind the frightful noise emanating from the garage. He made his way down to Polk Street, down the block to Real Foods. As he entered the market, he saw that it was busy, a last rush of people before the store closed for the day. He took his place at the end of the line in front of the counter. There were six people ahead of him, holding their blue plastic baskets filled with groceries. But Elliott didn't mind waiting. A point needed to be made.

In a blue denim shirt with a small red rose embroidered above the pocket, a string of puka shells around his neck, Cuba stood behind the counter, checking out the customers, ringing up each item as he emptied their baskets. Elliott watched as he bagged the groceries, the line slowly inching forward. As Cuba gave the woman in front of Elliott her change, Elliott stepped up to the counter.

"Good evening, Mr. Madison," Cuba said.

But Elliott was not interested in vapid pleasantries. He placed the opened bag of oyster crackers on the counter and stared into Cuba's puzzled eyes.

"Try one," he said.

"What do you mean?" Cuba asked.

"As you may or may not recall, I bought these here yesterday," Elliott said. "Try onc."

Cuba nervously glanced past Elliott to the line of people behind him, then looked down at the bag of crackers. Elliott reached down and shook the bag, several of the crackers spilling onto the counter. Reluctantly, Cuba picked one up and placed it on his tongue.

"You assured me these crackers were fine," Elliott said.

Cuba chewed the cracker quickly and swallowed.

"What's wrong with them?" he asked.

"They're mushy," Elliott said, indignation rising in his voice. "They're stale – they're old. Who knows how long they were sitting on that shclf."

"They taste all right to me," Cuba said.

The discussion prompted the manager of the market to step up beside Cuba, peering at Elliott through his round wire-rim glasses, slipping an ink pen into the pocket of his red-and-gray flannel shirt.

"May I be of assistance?"

"I want a refund," Elliott told him. "I bought these oyster crackers here yesterday, and they're old and stale."

The manager picked up one of the crackers and popped it into his mouth.

"I paid $3.49 for these crackers, which is an outrage in and of itself," Elliott said.

The manager swallowed, then placed his hand on Cuba's shoulder.

"Give Mr. Madison his money back," he said.

With an angry flourish, he swept the spilled crackers off the counter, scattering them across the market floor, then he picked up the bag and looked to Elliott.

"Will that be all?" he asked.

Elliott had to think for a moment, unaccustomed as he was to matters resolving themselves in his favor.

"Yes," he said. "Yes, as a matter of fact, that will be all."

SAVORING HIS MOMENT of triumph and restitution, Elliott strolled out of the market and started up the sidewalk, making his way past the knot of people in front of the hardware store, past the boulangerie at the corner and the old Alhambra Theater with its Moorish turrets and grand marquis, down the street to a Thai restaurant called Lemongrass. He entered the restaurant through the open door, brushing aside the heavy curtain to step into the dining room. An elderly couple was sitting at a table in the front window, stabbing chopsticks into their plates of pad thai, while a pair of young women in light blue pantsuits were laughing over their papaya salads. In the far corner, a man wearing a white shirt and a thin blue tie pinched a piece of shrimp by the tail and raised it to his mouth.

Elliott sat at a table along the wall and looked over to the Buddha residing serenely on the top shelf of an old cabinet, a pair of gilded lions on the shelf below. He could hear the water trickling softly in the small ceramic fountain near the cash register. A moment later, a young waitress in a white blouse and black skirt emerged from the kitchen and approached his table. Her name was May, the daughter of the woman who owned the restaurant.

"Good evening, Mr. Madison," she said. "An order to go?"

"No, I think I'll eat here tonight," he said.

"Would you like a menu?"

"I'll just have the red curry shrimp and a bowl of steamed rice," he said. "And a bottle of beer."

She brought the Singha right away, setting the bottle and a tall glass on the table in front of him.

"Many thanks," he said.

He poured the beer into the glass, watching the foam churn up to the lip, then he took a long swallow. He was not in any hurry to return to the flat, not with The Sores practicing. He ate slowly, spooning the shrimp and curry onto the rice, nursing his beer. When he finished, he decided to order takeout for Alissa and her bandmates. He had no idea if Nigel and Jeremy liked Thai cuisine, but Alissa loved the calamari sautéed with chili sauce, bell peppers, and bamboo shoots. For Nigel and Jeremy, he ordered the pork with mixed vegetables and peanut sauce and the chicken sautéed with broccoli in bean sauce. And if they didn't like it, well, that was fine with Elliott. He would have it tomorrow. Leftover Thai food had always been a guilty pleasure.

Carrying the bag of takeout, he walked back up Vallejo Street. As he approached his building, he was distressed to hear how loud Alissa and her bandmates were playing, even louder, it seemed, than when he left. Fortunately, his closest neighbors were an elderly woman who was virtually deaf and played her television at nearly the same volume and a young Asian couple, both venture capitalists who spent months at a time in Beijing. He didn't blame his other neighbors from calling periodically to complain the deafening racket was degrading their quality of life and very likely depressing property values. He knew they were probably right.

He let himself in through the gate on the side of the building. As he opened the side door to the garage, he was confronted with a blast of sound so intense he had to brace himself before starting down the stairs. At the bottom of the stairs, he watched his granddaughter violently flailing at her drums while Nigel played his bass guitar, his eyes closed as he thumbed the heavy strings, the neck of the instrument nearly as long as he was tall. Jeremy was hunched over his amplifier, extorting ear-splitting electronic feedback through the waist-high speaker, his stringy blond hair falling to the shoulders of his sleeveless undershirt.

Elliott waited for any one of them to notice his presence, and finally Alissa glanced his way, her dyed-green hair spiking in all directions, a sheen of perspiration on her forehead. When she stopped assaulting her drums, Nigel opened his eyes and ceased playing his bass. Jeremy continued for a moment longer before realizing that he was playing alone.

"I don't mean to interrupt," Elliott said. "But I brought some takeout from Lemongrass, in case you get hungry."

He carried the bag over to the workbench in the back of the garage.

"I grabbed some chopsticks and plastic forks and napkins," he told them. "Shall I bring down some plates?"

Alissa rose from her stool and walked over to the workbench.

"We can take it from here," she said.

"Fine," Elliott said. "Enjoy."

He climbed the stairs and made his way along the side of the building, then up the stairs leading to the back porch and into the kitchen. As he draped his coat over one of the chairs, he couldn't help but be amused by the subdued reception to the takeout he'd brought home for the band. Which is not to suggest that he was expecting an expression of appreciation. Alissa and her bandmates hadn't asked for the food. They owed him nothing. But they would eat it all, and in the morning, he would clean up the mess they were sure to leave on the workbench, collecting the empty cartons and carrying them over to the trash bins. And yet, he was glad he'd brought the takeout for the band, and he resolved to do it again in the future with the hope that it might entice them to practice in the garage more often. As loud and appalling as their music was, he would rather have The Sores practicing here than not know where Alissa was, much less what she might be doing.

As he turned to leave the kitchen, he glimpsed the notice from the post office on the hutch. The sight of the yellow slip of paper stopped him, prompting an annoying pang of guilt. No, he hadn't walked down to the post office to pick up the package Ms. Crighton had sent him, despite the fact that he had worked at home all day and could easily have made his way down to North Beach. And it was true that the thought had occurred to him more than once. But he was in no hurry; he felt no obligation. Yes, it was possible that her great-grandmother's uncle had worked on his great-grandparents' ranch. He had already conceded as much in his response to her. But possible was all it was. And, frankly, it made no difference to him either way.

He started down the hall. Perhaps tomorrow he would make his way down to the post office to see what Ms. Crighton had sent him. Perhaps tomorrow he would see what she thought was so important. Or, he told himself, perhaps not.

CHAPTER SIX

WITH A SHARP HISS of its brakes, the 19 Polk pulled into the bus stop behind the library. Elliott got off and walked down to the Grove Street entrance, then passed through the metal detectors and crossed the atrium to take the stairs up to the third floor. As he emerged from the stacks, he began looking for an available desk and quickly spotted a place to work across from Stanley Gilliam, who was slumped down in his chair, dead asleep and snoring like a long-shoreman, his long white hair splashed across his face. Elliott had come to know Stanley well during the course of his research, and so he knew that it was not uncommon for him to drift off for an hour or so while he worked on his science fiction novels. He had written and self-published eleven of the novels, all of them lengthy tomes, his most recent, "Revenge of the Ectoplasm," running more than eight hundred pages. As a gesture of support, Elliott had purchased a copy of the novel, but he'd found it nearly incomprehensible, the product of a mind that careened erratically from thought to thought, no doubt as a result of Stanley's lifelong ingestion of psychotropic drugs. Still, Elliott didn't mind sharing a desk with Stanley, even if he often fell asleep mumbling unintelligibly. He was a pleasant harmless fellow, although he did, on occasion, give off a peculiar oniony odor.

After taking off his coat and hat, Elliott sat down and opened his satchel and lifted out the chapter of his manuscript that focused on those first hard years in Anderson Valley. With virtually no other primary sources available, the chapter was based almost exclusively on his great-grandfather's journal. Most of the entries were succinct and perfunctory, very likely penned after a long day of manual labor. A number of days passed with no entries in his journal at all. And yet, even in their scarcity, those entries reveal just how difficult those first years were.

All that first winter, his great-grandfather and Snyder had discussed their plans for the future, plans they had initially talked through while working on the West Branch. As the rain drummed the roof of the cabin, they sat at the rough plank table and talked at length about the ranch they envisioned – the robust sheep operation and the apple orchard they hoped to bring into production as soon as their labors allowed.

One of his great-grandfather's journal entries spoke directly to the full range of their vision and ambition.

"I am fortunate to have found a partner such as Ames. He is a good and decent man, a farmer by heritage as well as by vocation, and I have no doubt that he will bring this fine land into production as soon as humanly possible. I foresee a partnership in which he will manage our operations here, while I oversee our mutual business interests, procuring the best markets for our wool and apples, as well as investing our profits in other enterprises as opportunities present themselves."

And yet, his great-grandfather also understood that his partner had to return to Iowa to collect his son and daughter.

"I understand why Ames must return to Iowa," he wrote. "He

promised his son and daughter that he would come back for them, and he is a man of his word. I can only look to the future. There is much to be done in anticipation of his return."

That June, shortly after Snyder departed, Madison and Hector rode down to General Vallejo's ranch in Petaluma. It was Snyder's view that the valley was better suited for raising sheep than cattle. Sheep didn't require as much grass and water, which would serve them well in years of scant rain, he reasoned, and the ewes often delivered twin lambs and in some cases triplets, which meant the size of the flock would increase rapidly. For years, California sheep, mostly churros driven north from Mexico, had had a reputation for poor quality wool, but with the recent introduction of significantly better breeds, primarily Spanish merinos, Snyder was confident there would be markets for both the improved gray-white wool and the mutton from the sheep they culled from the herd. So Madison struck a deal with the general to buy seventy merinos, and he and Hector drove them back to the valley and turned them out into the meadow.

That summer, they began clearing land for the orchard, and the entries in his great-grandfather's journal make it clear that progress was slowly won. It was back-breaking work, dropping the heavy limbs of the white oak and black oak and then using the horses to drag the limbs and trunks into a pile near the cabin, there to be cut and split for firewood. It took days to dig out the stumps and for the horses to pull them out of the ground and drag them over to the burn piles.

They saw little of Walter Anderson and his family that first year. For days on end, the plume of smoke rising from their cabin down the valley was the only sign of their presence.

"They are an insular clan, hunters by nature, settlers by circumstance," Madison wrote. "Walter Anderson wants to be left alone, and there is nothing to be gained by approaching him or his sons. They are disinclined to respond, even to a wave of the hand."

And yet they often saw the Pomo walking along the creek or

through the oaks, leaning slightly forward as if to compensate for the weight of the baskets strapped on their backs. They lived in a series of villages scattered throughout the valley, most of the villages comprised of no more than a dozen families living in huts constructed of arched willow saplings covered with brush and slabs of bark torn from the trunks of the redwoods. The village nearest the ranch was called Lemokil, and the Pomo who lived there had constructed a ceremonial house, a large structure built over a circular pit with a hole in the center of its roof to vent the smoke from their ritual fires.

"At night I often hear our neighbors singing and chanting, and I must confess that I find their simple music of whistles, rattles, and log drums comforting. When they left to make their annual summer pilgrimage down the valley to the ocean, I found their absence strangely disquieting."

That first year on the ranch, Madison's sole companion was Hector. They had learned to communicate with their hands and eyes, as well as Madison's primitive Spanish, and Hector did whatever was asked of him without hesitation or complaint. He was an excellent marksman, dropping the black-tailed deer that wandered through the valley with a single rifle shot. Standing on the bank of the creek, he rarely missed as he speared the salmon thrashing their way upstream to spawn. He moved into the meadow grass so stealthily that he could catch the quail with his bare hands, raising his prize high above his head before bringing the birds down and calmly wringing their necks.

"If Hector grieves for his younger brother, he doesn't show it, and yet he has plainly changed. He is older, wiser, seasoned by tragedy, no longer the boy who wandered into our camp on the West Branch."

Late that winter, Madison rode down to the bay to purchase apple saplings at a nursery on the eastern shore. Upon the owner's recommendation, Madison bought eighty saplings: twenty each of the Gravensteins, Baldwins, Winesaps, and Northern Spys, the varieties selected so as to stagger the harvest – the Gravensteins ripening first in late summer, followed by the Baldwins and the Winesaps, and then the Northern Spys in October. Wrapping the saplings in burlap, Madison packed them carefully in the bed of the wagon and then hauled them back to the valley, where he and Hector planted them in long rows, seven paces apart to ensure each tree received ample sunlight, burying the roots just below the bud unions, where the individual cultivars had been grafted onto the root stock.

As difficult as that first year was, it did not go entirely without reward.

"When the saplings produced their first white, five-petal blossoms, I could see not only the fruit of our labors, but the larger beauty of the orchard's precise geometry, imposing order upon the virgin land."

That summer, Madison and Hector began work on a second cabin for Snyder and the family he had returned to Iowa to collect, selecting a site along the streamlet that ran between the two homesteads. In Sonoma, Madison purchased bundles of thick redwood shakes for the new cabin's roof and planks for the floors. He framed in two four-pane windows and hung the door on forged-iron hinges. And every day, as summer faded into fall, Madison found himself looking up to the head of the valley, hoping to see his partner riding into the open meadow. But as the fall deepened and the rains arrived, he saw no one.

"As hard as Hector and I have worked, as much as we have accomplished, it has nonetheless been a year of waiting. I am most anxious for Ames to return."

Finally, on November 17, 1854, Madison saw a pair of wagons making their way down the valley, moving slowly through the dry grass. He gave a shout and waved his hat above his head. When the man walking alongside the half wagon raised his hand in return, Madison immediately started down the path between the cabins, certain the day he had been waiting for had finally arrived. But as the wagons approached, he saw that the man who had waved was far younger than his partner. Sitting in the half wagon was a young woman with her hands clasped beneath her swollen belly, supporting the child she was carrying. The woman in the following wagon wore a long gray dress with a shawl around her shoulders. As they drew near, Madison saw they were gaunt and emaciated, their cheeks hollow and lips bloody and cracked, their eyes retreating deep into their sockets. Their oxen looked as if they couldn't have drawn the wagons another mile, footsore and all but lame, their rib cages bulging beneath their hides, weeping sores on their shoulders.

"We're looking for a man named William Madison," the young man said.

And in that moment, Madison realized who they were, who they had to be.

"Zachary Snyder?"

"Yes, sir."

"Greetings," Madison said. "We've been expecting you, waiting for you."

"I must say we're glad to have found you," Zachary said.

"You must be exhausted."

"Yes, sir, we've come a fair distance," Zachary said.

"Well, come in, then," Madison said. "Come in."

He walked over to the half wagon, and he and Zachary reached up and helped Charlotte down to the ground. For a moment, they had to steady her, as if her legs might give out at any moment. With each of them taking an arm, they helped her into the cabin and sat her down at the table. Madison struck a match and lit the oil lamp, the waving light illuminating the cabin's dark interior – the sacks of flour and beans slumped against the base of the mud-chinked walls, the baskets of potatoes and onions harvested from the garden. As Zachary and Charlotte looked around the cabin, Madison knelt down and lit the wood shavings in the stove. When the fire caught, he stood back up and turned to them.

"It's small, but it should keep you dry," he said, as if to welcome them to their new home.

"It will suit us just fine," Zachary said.

It was only as Madison noticed Amelia standing in the doorway that he realized that he had not seen his partner.

"And may I ask about your father?"

Zachary looked at Madison as if he didn't know what to say.

"I'm sorry, sir. He didn't make it."

"What do you mean?" Madison asked.

"He died crossing the desert," Zachary said. "We buried him along the Carson River."

Madison looked at Zachary as if waiting for more, then he turned to Amelia still standing in the doorway, as if she might shake her head, as if she might tell him no, it wasn't true. But in her weary eyes, he knew that it was.

"Dear God," he said.

AS ELLIOTT GAZED out the library window, he could see his great-grandfather sitting in his cabin the next morning, recording in his journal the terrible news that his partner had died while crossing the desert. He was still in a state of profound disbelief when he walked down to the new cabin to deliver the sides of salmon and strips of venison that he and Hector had cured in the smokehouse, eggs he had collected that morning and a pail of blackberries that Hector had picked along the creek. He found Zachary unloading the wagon, carrying into the cabin the last few possessions they hadn't jettisoned on the trail, while Amelia and Charlotte were washing clothes in a large wooden tub and then hanging the garments out to dry on lines strung among the oaks.

"I was hoping you might have a minute to sit down and talk," Madison said.

"Of course," Zachary said.

They stepped into the cabin, and Madison reached into his coat pocket and withdrew a page torn from his journal. On the page was a hand-drawn map of the upper valley, sketching out the land that he and Snyder had claimed. He spread the map out on the table and with Zachary looking on traced the boundaries of the two adjacent homesteads with his fingertip.

"I don't suppose any land could be worth the price you paid to get here, but I nonetheless hope it meets with your approval," he said.

"My father spoke highly of this valley," Zachary said. "And he was not a man inclined to exaggeration."

"Of course, I'm hoping you'll want to see his plans through," Madison said.

"I'm sure that's what my father would want," Zachary said.

With his thick black hair and dark deep-set eyes, Zachary bore a singular resemblance to his father, so striking, in fact, that in the weeks and months to come, Madison often caught himself addressing him as Ames, a slip of the tongue for which he hastened to apologize. He was a lanky young man, perhaps a little taller than his father, quiet and soft-spoken with his father's even temperament, and while it was true that he did not possess his father's knowledge and experience, it was also true that he had inherited his stamina and determination. As they tended the sheep and worked in the orchard, Madison knew his former partner would be gratified to know that he and his son intended to see their mutual vision fulfilled.

"Zachary even sounds like his father," Madison wrote. "They speak in the same cadence and tones. In a blind test, I would be hard-pressed to distinguish one from the other."

Madison saw Amelia often that winter, but they rarely found occasion to speak at any length, even on Sundays when he and Hector joined them for supper. And yet, in retrospect, it is important to note that those suppers were, in fact, the seminal moments of their relationship. Elliott had studied the evolution of his great-grandparents' relationship carefully, poring over his great-grandfather's entries in his journals and his great-grandmother's letters to her cousin, allowing himself to venture beyond a literal reading of the words, trying to understand what might have gone unstated, attempting to detect what they suggested and what he might reasonably intuit. There could be no doubt that their courtship and marriage were based upon a deep respect and a genuine affection for each other, and if his great-grandparents did not freely express their most intimate thoughts and emotions in his journal entries or her letters to her cousin, subject, as they were, to the conservative social mores of the era, Elliott understood that did not mean they didn't submit to them during the appropriate moments.

His great-grandfather found Amelia to be a highly intelligent young woman, even without the benefit of a formal education, and his references to her in his journals became increasingly frequent in the ensuing months. As spring arrived, he wrote that he often saw her at work in the garden, surrounded by chickens chortling down the rows of tomatoes and onions and corn. One day during lambing season, she told him that she had found two bummer lambs along the creek, rejected by their ewes, so young and weak they could barely stand. Madison laughed when she told him that she intended to nurse them back to health. But she proved him wrong. In a matter of just weeks, the lambs were strong enough to feed on the tender meadow grass. And yet, more than anything, Madison enjoyed watching Amelia care for the bawling infant that Charlotte and Zachary had named Ames, the comfort the child seemed to find in her arms.

"I often find it hard to believe that Amelia is just eighteen years old," he wrote. "She is a lovely girl, poised upon the cusp of womanhood, and modest to the extent that she does not appear to know how truly beautiful she has become."

Elliott found that entry remarkable in its understatement. It was the first indication that his great-grandfather had begun to regard Amelia as more than the daughter of his former partner. Even if not directly stated, his great-grandfather had clearly begun to view Amelia not just as a girl of uncommon intelligence and beauty but also as a prospective bride.

In her letters to her cousin, his great-grandmother also wrote favorably about Madison. Her father had told her about his partner on the long journey across the continent, and she could see that her father's death had come as a terrible blow to him.

"William is older than I had imagined," she wrote. "And yet I find the creases in his brow and the silver in his hair reassuring. I don't know what we would have done if we hadn't found him."

According to his great-grandfather's journal, on July 3, 1855, he and Zachary were setting posts in a fence line, when Madison stopped and straightened up, his hands folded over the end of the shovel handle.

"I wonder if you would have any objection to my paying a call on your sister?" he asked.

Zachary wiped his brow with the back of his right forearm, requiring a moment before he understood what Madison was asking.

"I've got no objection," he said.

"Of course I wouldn't call on her if you think it's inappropriate."

"I expect Amelia will be the judge of that," Zachary said.

"Yes, I suppose she will," Madison said.

That evening, while Amelia and Charlotte were preparing supper, Zachary told his sister about his conversation with Madison. In a letter to her cousin, she wrote that Madison's interest in her caught her completely by surprise. She admired Madison. She was fascinated by his paternal relationship with Hector, and she appreciated the respect with which he treated her brother, deferring to him on many of the matters having to do with the operation of the ranch. But it had never occurred to her that he might call on her socially.

"I told Zachary that I had no idea why William would want to call on me, but of course I will receive him, and I will try not to disappoint him or embarrass us all."

STANLEY WOKE with a start, a sudden gasp as his head jerked up, his eyes bulging as if to burst. Elliott watched as the library seemed to slowly swim into focus for Stanley, sitting back in his chair and gazing down the stacks as if trying to remember where he was, perhaps even who he was.

"What time is it?" he asked.

"A little after two o'clock," Elliott told him.

Stanley took that under advisement, combing out his wiry white beard with his fingertips, then reaching into the pocket of his coat for a bottle of Italian pepperoncini. Every day, Stanley smuggled a jar of pepperoncini into the library, quietly devouring them as he worked on his novels, convinced the peppers ignited the fires of the imagination. Elliott looked on as he twisted the lid off the jar and pinched one of the small green peppers, then tilted his head back and dropped it into his mouth, chewing it industriously before swallowing it down, stem and all. Until recently, he even drank the brine the peppers were pickled in, but he had recently confided to Elliott that he had given the practice up when he began to suspect the brine might be responsible for his frequent nosebleeds.

He raised the jar, offering one of the pepperoncini to Elliott.

"Thanks, but no," Elliott said.

He looked back down at his manuscript, returning specifically to July 18, 1855, the date, according to his great-grandfather's journal, that his courtship of his great-grandmother formally began. It was on that day, a warm Sunday afternoon with a light breeze trailing across the valley floor, that they went for a walk through the young orchard, down the long rows of saplings, eventually sitting on a bench that Madison had fashioned beneath one of the live oaks.

Amelia enjoyed listening to Madison talk about his family in South Carolina and his voyage around Cape Horn, about his experiences with her father on the West Branch and in the valley that first winter. She listened intently, relieved that he was comfortable carrying the conversation. She found him kind and deferential, but he was also intimidating, even if unintentionally so, a man of surpassing confidence and as eloquent as he was wise, a proper gentleman nearly twenty years older, several years older, even, than her father. Still, Amelia was not so young or naïve that she didn't understand his broader intentions.

Madison called on her several more times that summer. One afternoon in early September, they walked down to the creek and then followed the Pomo trail through the cottonwoods and willow that grew along the bank. He told her that soon, perhaps as early as next year, he intended to construct a new house. He pointed to a rise above the open pasture and told her that was where the house would be located. He had already started drawing up the plans. It would be two stories high with a steeply pitched roof, a broad front porch and an upper balcony from which to look out across their land and watch the sun sink beyond the valley to the west. And when he asked Amelia what she thought of his plans, she understood that he intended to build the house for her.

"It will be a magnificent house, of that I'm sure," she said.

She did not resist what she could see to be her fate. On the afternoon of October 7, she was working in the garden when she saw Madison riding down the path between the cabins. He swung down from his horse and draped the reins over the top rail of the fence, then reached up and removed his hat.

"Good afternoon, Amelia. I wonder if I might have a minute of your time?"

"Of course," she said.

He opened the gate and stepped to the side as she passed through it, then he stood before her.

"I've spoken with Zachary, and he has granted me permission to ask for your hand in marriage. You needn't answer now, of course, and please be assured that I shall respect your decision, whatever it might be."

"I am humbled by your proposal," she told him. "I shall give it the most serious consideration."

That night, as she lay in bed, she couldn't sleep, thinking about Madison's proposal. In a letter to Emily, she wrote that she held Madison in the highest regard and was grateful for his attentions. She knew she was fortunate that such a fine man had asked her to be his wife, and she knew he would be a devoted husband. And as she lay on her side in the darkened cabin, she also knew that she could not refuse him. She would become his wife. She would sleep in his bed and bear his children, and if she did not love him now, she would learn to love him. It would only be a matter of time, she was sure.

In the morning, she asked Zachary to tell Madison that she would like to speak with him, and that afternoon he rode down to the cabin.

"Does this suggest that you have made a decision?" he asked.

"William, I would be honored to be your wife."

ON OCTOBER 20, 1855, Madison left for Sonoma, arriving there two days later to meet with a master carpenter named Horace Langer. He showed Langer the meticulous house plans he had drawn up. They spent hours discussing every detail. The plans featured a parlor, library, dining room and kitchen on the ground floor, three bedrooms on the second floor, including the master bedroom with a private balcony. A separate building would be constructed behind the house, complete with a pantry, dairy and a washroom.

"It is a very sound plan," Langer told him. "I would very much like to build it for you."

"Then we have a deal," Madison said.

For the next four days, they painstakingly compiled a list of the materials they would need, and as Madison prepared to leave, Langer said he would arrange for the materials to be delivered by freight wagon no later than March, so construction could begin as soon as possible.

"I shall be waiting," Madison said.

Construction began on March 28, 1856, with Langer overseeing a team of skilled carpenters and stonemasons, common laborers and several young apprentices. Through the summer and fall, the site was a scene of intense activity from daylight to nightfall and then by lantern light, six days a week. It wasn't long before Madison and Amelia could see the house he had designed taking form before them. By November, when the first heavy rains moved in from the Pacific, the house was closed up, and Langer and his team were at work on the finish carpentry inside.

Amelia could only watch as construction proceeded and their wedding day drew near.

"William has declared that the house will be completed in early January, and he has scheduled our wedding for the end of the month. Emily, I so desperately wish that you could be here. I miss you so."

While the workmen finished the house, Amelia and Charlotte worked on her dress for the wedding. Charlotte had brought her wedding dress from Iowa, and she insisted that Amelia be married in it, too. It was a simple, white satin dress and needed only a few minor alterations. But as the hour of her nuptials approached, Amelia grew increasingly anxious.

"The other day while pinning up the hem of the dress, Charlotte told me how lucky I am to be marrying a man like William. And she is right, Emily. I am sure of it. But I must confess that lately I have begun to feel a kind of sadness. I do not understand it, and yet I feel it more acutely every day. When William left this morning to get the minister, I felt like I could barely breathe."

Madison was gone for nearly two weeks, returning with the minister on the evening of January 23, 1857. They entered the house and hung their coats on the wall beside the door, then walked down the hall to the kitchen, where Amelia and Charlotte were preparing supper.

"I'd like to introduce you to the Reverend Taylor," Madison said.

A stout man with long red hair and a thick red beard, the minister stood barely to Madison's shoulder. He squinted at Amelia through the lenses of his silver-rimmed glasses.

"The blushing bride – it is a pleasure indeed to meet you," he said.

"Thank you, Reverend. I'm grateful that you could come all this way."

"I follow the hand of the Lord, wherever He leads me, wherever His work must be done."

"Please, have a seat in the dining room," she said. "Make yourself comfortable. Supper won't be long."

As they ate that night, Reverend Taylor waxed philosophical about the nature of his roaming ministry, telling them he loved nothing more than performing marriages. In his view, baptisms were wasted on the young, and funeral services were lost on the deceased. But marriages were performed upon the living, upon a man and a woman in the prime of their lives, a blessed union in which two lives become one in the name of the Holy Father.

"May I propose a toast?" he said, raising his cup of brandy. "To the bride and groom! May you live long and prosper!"

Amelia did not sleep all night. The next day, she was exhausted, her legs trembling beneath her gown as she and Madison stood before Reverend Taylor in the parlor, a Bible lying open in his hands. Madison slipped a gold wedding band onto her finger, and they turned back to the minister and exchanged their solemn vows.

"In the name of God and by the power vested in me, I now

pronounce you man and wife."

With Zachary and Charlotte, Hector and Reverend Taylor watching, Madison leaned down and kissed his new bride. Her face burned with embarrassment as she looked up at him.

In a letter to Emily, she wrote, "For the first time, I saw how truly handsome William is. I will try with all my heart to become the best wife I can."

That night, Amelia climbed the stairs to the master bedroom. In the light of the oil lamp, she crossed the room and sat on the edge of the bed, her heart beating rapidly in her chest. She could hear Madison ascending the stairs. He knocked once.

"Come in," she said.

He entered the bedroom and walked over to stand before her.

"I could never have dreamed of a more beautiful bride," he said.

"I will remember this day for as long as I live," she said.

Madison leaned down and brushed her cheek with his fingertips, then kissed her forehead.

"It has been a long day," he said. "If you wish, I will gladly sleep downstairs."

"No," she said. "Please sleep here."

"Very well," he said. "Let me give you a few moments, and then I shall be back."

He went back downstairs and poured himself a glass of brandy and carried it into his new library, the walls lined with empty shelves, waiting to be occupied. He thought about Amelia lying in bed.

"I hope Amelia understands that marriage is only the beginning for us," he wrote. "I hope she understands that she will awaken in the morning not merely as my wife but as the companion with whom I intend to spend the rest of my life."

Upstairs, Amelia put on her nightgown and slipped beneath the quilt. As she waited for Madison, she thought about all that lay before her now, the future, the unknowable. It seemed a lifetime since she and Zachary lived with their cousins in Iowa, those endless days of waiting. Never could she have imagined that her life would bring her here to this moment. She wondered what her father would think. How she missed him and wished he could have been here on the day of her marriage. As she listened to Madison climbing the stairs, she understood that she would never be the same. She understood that she had already become someone else.

"Emily, I am sure I will grow to love William. I can only hope that that day comes soon."

CHAPTER SEVEN

AS ELLIOTT PASSED through the stacks, taking a quick break to stretch his legs, he was pleased to see Doris Holbrook was working at the Page Desk. She was a small woman with a limp blue sweater draped over her shoulders, her gray hair clipped back off the sides of her face and a pair of red, dime store reading glasses on the tip of her nose. During the course of his research, Elliott had become well acquainted with Ms. Holbrook. Many of the books he needed to provide a broader context for the entries in his great-grandfather's journals and for his great-grandmother's letters were older books, no longer on the shelves, which meant he had to request them from storage. He would fill out a brief form requesting each book he needed, and after giving the form to Ms. Holbrook, she would rise from her desk to retrieve them.

"I'll only be a moment," she always said.

As he requested the books, Elliott casually explained the purpose of his research and the nature of his project to Ms. Holbrook. She told him she thought it was a noble endeavor, and she was sure his great-grandparents would be proud to know he was so determined to preserve their legacies. Ms. Holbrook's kind remarks affirmed Elliott's regard for her, and as the months passed, he came to know a little bit more about her, learning, for example, that she lived alone in a studio apartment in the Inner Sunset, her only companion a white parakeet named Pauly. It seemed a lonely existence. It made Elliott wonder if she might be interested in getting together.

And yet, he was unsure how to approach her. He certainly didn't want to broach the subject while she was working at the Page Desk, where anyone might overhear their conversation. Instead, he made a point of studying her afternoon work schedule and quickly learned that she took a break every day at 2:30. That was all he needed to know. The following Tuesday, he was discretely waiting for Ms. Holbrook when she slipped out from behind the desk and started down the stairs. He followed her at a distance, making sure she didn't notice him, and when he determined that she was on her way down to the Poet's Café, he held back, watching as she walked up to the counter and ordered a cup of coffee. It was only as she sat down at one of the tables that he permitted himself to enter the cafe.

"What a surprise to find you here," he said, standing beside her table. "May I join you?"

She looked up at him, as if he was the last person she expected to see.

"Hello, Elliott."

"Do you come here often?" he asked, pulling out a chair and sitting down.

"I enjoy a cup of coffee in the afternoon," she said, as if pleased with herself. "I like to think it keeps me sharp, mentally alert."

"I'm sure it does," he said.

"Why do you ask?"

He didn't know, of course. He hadn't intended to ask if she came here every afternoon. He couldn't have cared less.

"Actually, I was wondering if you might be interested in getting together some evening?"

She stared across the table at him, her face as stony as if he'd asked for a pair of her underpants.

"What did you have in mind?"

"I thought perhaps dinner, maybe a movie," he said. "What kind of food do you like?"

"Chinese," she said without hesitation.

"Excellent," he said. "Do you have a restaurant in mind?"

"House of Nanking."

"Perhaps on Friday night?"

And so that Friday, Elliott waited for Ms. Holbrook in front of the House of Nanking, standing on the sidewalk as traffic rushed up Kearny Street, waiting until a yellow cab pulled alongside the curb and Ms. Holbrook pushed the back door open. Elliott helped her out of the cab, and they entered the restaurant and found a table along the wall. Since Ms. Holbrook had selected the restaurant, Elliott allowed her to order their dinner, which, in retrospect, had proven to be an unwise decision. He had no idea Ms. Holbrook liked her Chinese food hot and spicy – the hotter, in fact, the better. He looked on helplessly as she ordered the hot and sour soup, eggplant with chili garlic sauce, kung pao squid, and the Hunan chili fish. Mercifully, the soup was not as hot as it was sour, the eggplant merely numbed his gums, and he was able to avoid most of the fiery red peppers in the squid. But the Hunan chili fish scorched his mouth and then burned down his throat to lie smoldering in the pit of his stomach, the fumes rising up into his nostrils. He tried to douse the flames with a bottle of beer, but to no avail. His eyes watering, there was nothing he could do but smile through clenched teeth, mopping the perspiration from his brow with a napkin while he watched Ms. Holbrook polish off each dish.

When they finished dinner, they caught a cab to the Galaxy Theater on Van Ness, a futuristic four-theater complex constructed of blue-green glass cubes stacked on top of each other. They entered the theater and bought tickets to a French film that Ms. Holbrook wanted to see, but as soon as they found their seats, Elliott excused himself and hustled into the men's room. He was barely able to latch the stall door and drop his trousers before he experienced what could only be described as an exuberant evacuation of his bowels. Sitting in the stall, his face clammy with sweat, he waited until the spasms in his gastrointestinal system finally subsided before quietly rejoining Ms. Holbrook. She didn't so much as glance his way as he sat back down beside her.

As the final credits rolled, they walked out of the theater and hailed a cab to her apartment on Seventh Street in the Sunset. He escorted Ms. Holbrook up to the door of her building. As they stood in the light from the lobby, she coolly informed him that it was not her policy to invite men up to her apartment after a single date. She couldn't have known the relief that policy brought to Elliott, his legs still so weak from the release of his bowels that he worried they might give out beneath him at any moment. She offered him her hand, and he shook it properly, formally concluding the evening.

"Good night, Elliott."

"Good night, Doris. I had a splendid time."

And yes, that evening did make their subsequent interactions at the Page Desk a trifle awkward. But that was fine. They were adults, consenting adults, and, yes, the attraction was still there. Elliott had every intention of asking Doris out again, if not necessarily now, then at least in the near future.

As he approached the Page Desk, Doris looked up at him, dabbing her right nostril with a wad of tissue.

"Hello, Elliott. How may I be of assistance?"

"I just wanted to let you know that you might not be seeing me here much longer."

"Is that so?"

"My manuscript is nearly finished," he said. "I'm merely reviewing it now."

"Congratulations."

"Yes, I'm quite pleased with the final draft."

"Perhaps you'll find a publisher for it," she said.

Elliott had certainly thought about having his manuscript published. The prospect always lifted his spirits.

"Yes, perhaps so," he said.

"Will there be anything else?" she asked.

He watched as she dabbed her nostril with the tissue again, realizing this was his moment, the opportunity to ask if she might be interested in getting together again. But he could feel his will failing, his resolve rapidly draining away.

"I just wanted to let you know why you might not be seeing much of me in the future," he said. "I didn't want you to think I'd fallen off the face of the earth."

"Thank you, Elliott. That's very thoughtful. Now I'll know."

ELLIOTT RETURNED to his desk, where he found Stanley scribbling furiously on his legal pad, the lines of script slanting off in all directions, as if trying to capture the thoughts ricocheting off the walls of his cranium. Elliott sat down across from him and checked his watch. It was shortly after three o'clock, and he didn't intend to work much longer. But he did want to finish reading about those early years in the valley.

For the most part, those early years were good years, difficult, certainly, but years of hope and aspiration nonetheless. His great-grandparents had every reason to believe in the future that lay before them. They wanted children, as many as his great-grandmother might bear. His great-grandfather wanted a son, of course, an heir to assume the family name and manage the operation of the ranch when he grew on in years; his great-grandmother wanted daughters, girls to fill the great house with beauty and compassion. And yet, in her letters to her cousin, she expressed a mounting concern about her inability to become pregnant.

"Emily, I cannot help but wonder if something is wrong," she wrote. "I cannot help but worry that I may be barren."

And so, late that winter, when she finally had reason to believe she was with child, she did not tell Madison right away.

"I confided only in Charlotte. I wanted to be absolutely certain before I told William."

She loved the calm that had descended upon her, the serenity that seemed to carry her through each day, and on those occasions when Madison caught her daydreaming and asked if anything was wrong, she waved him off and told him it was nothing, returning to her quiet reverie. But when her third month passed, she realized the time had finally come to tell him.

That evening after supper, as they sat before the fire in the parlor, she told Madison that she had important news. He looked up and knew exactly what she meant to tell him.

"Could it be true?" he asked.

"Yes, I do believe it is," she said.

He rose from his chair and crossed the room and knelt in front of her.

"I could not be more pleased," he said.

"Nor I," she said.

He reached over to her and passed his hands lightly over her stomach, but she laughed and pushed his hands away.

"It is too early," she said. "There is nothing to feel, not yet."

Madison didn't care.

"It is a boy," he said. "I am sure of it. We will name him Matthew."

"It is a lovely name," she said.

And, yes, that was true – it was a lovely name, as strong and forthright as any son of William Madison would surely be. And yet, in Elliott's view, it was also much more than that. As he looked up from his manuscript, he remembered the day he first read the name his great-grandfather intended to give to his first-born son, immediately recognizing Matthew as the Anglicized name for Mateo, the name of the young boy who drowned on the West Branch. Elliott didn't know when his great-grandfather had resolved to name his firstborn son for Mateo. There was no reference to his decision in his journal. Still, Elliott couldn't believe the name had been selected at random, chosen without deliberation. He had to believe that his great-grandfather wanted to name his son Matthew as an act of remembrance, as if to forever remind himself of Mateo's tragic death.

But three weeks later, Amelia walked out to the garden behind the house, wanting merely to feel the warmth of the spring sun on her shoulders. She let herself in through the gate, the chickens scattering as she made her way through the long rows of ankle-high corn. When she reached the back of the garden, she stopped and looked out upon the fruit trees planted beyond the fence. Suddenly she felt faint. She reached for the top rail of the fence to steady herself but was abruptly seized by wrenching cramps. She doubled over, still clinging to the fence, but she could feel herself reeling, dropping to her hands and knees and rolling onto her right side, the sudden discharge from her womb.

She lay at the base of the fence for several hours, lapsing in and out of consciousness. When she woke that evening, she found herself lying in bed with Madison sitting beside her.

"I'm so sorry," shc said.

"I won't hear of it," he said. "Now you must rest."

SHE DID NOT become pregnant again until late that autumn. This time, she told Madison as soon as she was certain. They were sitting at the table in the kitchen, and she found herself quickly overcome with emotion.

"The words poured out of her like a confession," Madison wrote. "Never have I been so pleased to behold the guilty party."

She felt fine all that winter, resolving to take every precaution, heed every word of advice, accept every offer of assistance. Madison insisted that she remain in bed every morning until the sun rose and that she retire shortly after night fell. When the skies were clear, she sat on the porch and gazed out upon the orchard, breathing in the sweet fragrance of the apple blossoms. When it rained, she sat before the fire in the parlor, a blanket wrapped around her shoulders, another placed over her lap. In the early months of her pregnancy, she was rarely even nauseated, which she took as a promising omen. The only discomfort she felt was a dull pain in the small of her back, which she attributed to the weight she was steadily gaining.

And yet one evening in early May, she noticed that her fingers had become swollen and were difficult to flex. The next day, when Charlotte noticed her rubbing her hands, she confessed that her ankles were swollen, too. Charlotte suggested Amelia sit with her feet raised upon a chair. It made no noticeable difference, but neither of them was overly concerned.

She didn't worry until the headaches began. There was no concealing them from Madison. They forced her to bed, where she lay still for hours, afraid to move for the pain brought by any motion. Charlotte tried to help, sitting with her and placing a cool moist cloth over her eyes. But she then began to have trouble with her vision. Brilliant flashes of light appeared out of nowhere, and there was nothing she could do but cringe and try to turn away from them.

She had just reached her eighth month when her water broke. The contractions came upon her suddenly, lasting through that night and into the next morning. Lying in bed, writhing in pain, there was no relief until midday, when she finally felt the child beginning its descent. Gripping the mattress, she pushed with all her strength. She screamed and screamed again, and abruptly the resistance was gone. She tried to lift herself up, wanting desperately to see her child, but then she fell unconscious.

Charlotte wrapped the child in a blanket and carried it out of the bedroom. Madison was standing at the foot of the stairs. On the bottom step, she stood before him, the bundled child in her arms.

"It's a boy," she told him, lifting the corner of the blanket so he could see his newborn son.

"Glory be," he said.

"It's Amelia you need to be concerned about now," she told him.

Madison climbed the stairs and quietly entered the bedroom, where Amelia lay on her back. He sat on the edge of the bed and drew her hair off her cheek and tucked it behind her ear. He sat with her all that night, eventually falling asleep in the chair beside the bed. She did not regain consciousness until the following afternoon. When she opened her eyes, he kissed her lightly on the forehead, never having known such profound relief.

"May I see my child?" she asked him, her voice so low he had to lean down to hear her.

"Of course," he said.

Charlotte lifted the child from the cradle beside the bed and carried him over to Amelia, placing him on her chest. After a few difficult moments, the child began to nurse, taking her nipple into his wrinkled mouth.

"He's beautiful," she said.

"Yes, he's quite a handsome fellow," Madison said.

And yet, as grateful as Elliott's great-grandparents were that their son was healthy, they knew just how close they had come to losing his great-grandmother. They knew they could never risk another pregnancy. They understood that their dream of a house filled with children would never come to pass. Matthew would be their only child.

AND, OF COURSE, they adored him. Matthew's birth gave new meaning and new purpose to their lives. In her letters to her cousin, Amelia wrote about his blue eyes and downy black hair, about the elemental joy of watching him erupt in delight as she fed him spoonfuls of warm cinnamon applesauce, of feeling his tiny hands wrap themselves around her fingers like the tendrils of a vine, of listening to his ceaseless chattering and sudden trills of laughter. In his journal, Madison documented every milestone in his son's growth: the day he first rose without help to stand, the day he took his first wobbling steps, the day he uttered his first word – "Mama." And he wrote at length about the transformative nature of fatherhood, long meditations about the new lens through which he viewed the world.

"I dare say, the future now belongs to my son."

And as Matthew grew up, so the valley changed around them all. In the years since Madison and his partner arrived in the valley, several dozen families had staked out homesteads along the creeks that ran together to form the Navarro River. At Four Corners, where the road east to Cloverdale intersected the road north to Ukiah, there was now a general store and a blacksmith shop. There was talk of constructing a hotel on the road to the coast. And when Walter Anderson lost his wife and left the valley to live with his daughter in Ukiah, Madison and Amelia had now lived in the valley longer than anyone else.

"It is now our responsibility to welcome the new arrivals to the valley," Amelia wrote. "William has not hesitated to assume that role and neither have I."

Slowly, the apple trees in the orchard matured into production, the harvest increasing each season. They sent the baskets filled with apples by wagon to Cloverdale and then down to the markets in San Francisco, prompting Madison to begin thinking about constructing an apple dryer on the ranch, so they could ship their dried apples to markets as distant as Europe. And every June, Madison, Zachary, and Hector would drive the sheep into the pens in front of the wool barn, where they would shear the bleating ewes and wethers. The fleece were then tossed into long canvas sacks held upright by stilted wooden frames, and when the sacks were full, they were sewn shut and loaded onto wagons, piled three and four sacks high and then lashed down with rope. When all the sheep were sheared, Madison and Zachary would drive the wool wagons through the hills and then down to Petaluma, where the sacks were loaded onto a scow and transported down the river and across the bay to the mill at Black Point in San Francisco.

And with the outbreak of the Civil War, the price of wool soared on the sudden demand for new uniforms and blankets, the war having deprived the Northern textile mills of access to Southern cotton. Suddenly, there was a market for all the wool that Madison and his fellow sheep ranchers could deliver to the mills on the East Coast. Later that year, they gathered in Sacramento to found the California Wool Growers Association.

In his journal, Madison foresaw a larger role for himself in the organization in the years to come.

"It is an honor to be associated with these fine men," he wrote. "I look forward to serving this organization in any way that I can. Given my legal background, several members of the association have approached me about serving in an official capacity, and I have promised to give the matter serious consideration."

During the summer of 1862, after delivering their wool to the mill, Madison spent three weeks in San Francisco. The tawdry boomtown he had passed through on his way to the gold fields had become a flourishing metropolis, and he did not deny himself the pleasures it had to offer. When he returned to the ranch, he asked Amelia to accompany him on his next visit to the city. She was hesitant, as he had anticipated, reluctant to leave young Matthew with Zachary and Charlotte and their children, even for a few weeks. But she could not refuse him.

"I can see how much this means to William, and so I feel as if I must go," she wrote. "But even now, before we depart, I am anxious to return."

Both of his great-grandparents wrote at length about the trip they took to San Francisco the following July. It required little imagination for Elliott to envision them standing on the deck of the steamship they had boarded in Sausalito, passing through a dense bank of fog that had rolled in through the mouth of the bay. Slowly, the fog began to dissipate, and then the air began to fill with light, and suddenly they could see the city, rising before them as if emerging from the depths of the bay. His great-grandmother had never seen anything like it. She could scarcely believe it was real.

"I was delighted that she was so impressed," Madison wrote. "That was exactly how I hoped she would react. That, in many ways, was the purpose of the trip. I wanted her to see the world beyond our ranch in the valley."

After passing through the ships moored in the bay, the steamer tied up along the Jackson Street wharf. Madison stepped down first, then reached back for Amelia, taking her hand as she stepped down onto the heavy timbers. They made their way into the city, walking past whole blocks of new commercial buildings constructed of red brick and granite, past the fashionable hotels and scores of restaurants offering exotic cuisine from every corner of the globe. The muddy streets had been paved with cobblestones, and there were gaslights on the street corners. Carriages and delivery wagons rushed off in all directions. The sidewalks were mobbed with people laughing, arguing, hawking their wares.

They took a room at the five-story International Hotel, where Madison requested a room on the upper floor. While he paid the bellhop, Amelia threw open the window and looked out across the city, glistening beneath the vast white sky.

"I felt as if I had been swept up into the future, leaving the ranch not just miles behind but ages in the past," she wrote to her cousin. "For a moment, I worried that William had taken me to a place from which there would be no return."

For ten days, they indulged themselves in the city's delights and luxuries. They dined at the finest restaurants – Delmonico's, the Sutter, the Lafayette House, feasting on fresh oysters, quail, and salmon. They attended plays at the Metropolitan Theater on Montgomery Street, the Adelphi on Dupont, the Union Theater on Commercial. They took a carriage ride to Russ Gardens, where they spent an afternoon strolling through its grounds. At Anton Roman's bookstore on Montgomery, they ordered several crates of leather-bound volumes for Madison's library at the ranch.

Shortly before they were to return to the ranch, Madison took Amelia to a dressmaker near the hotel. The shop was run by a woman from Paris, who led Amelia into a fitting room in the back and instructed her to undress behind a folding screen and put on a simple chemise with a drawstring neck. When she stepped out from behind the screen, the woman wrapped her in a corset and laced it tightly. A series of petticoats followed before the woman produced a selection of dresses. Amelia chose a dark blue dress with a high ruffled collar, long sleeves and a pleated ankle-length skirt – the very dress she would wear two days later, when she and Madison had their portraits taken in James Ford's studio on Clay Street. Elliott had to smile. Those were the images captured in the daguerreotypes that now reside on the fireplace mantel in the flat on Vallejo Street.

"Emily, when I looked in the mirror, I felt as if I were looking at someone else. I walked out to show William, and when he rose from his chair, I could see how delighted he was. I wanted, above all else, to please him, especially in San Francisco. He loves the city so."

On what was to be their last night in the city, they ate at a restaurant called Winn's Branch, sitting at a table in one of the tall arched windows, the heavy drapes tied back with sashes so they could look out upon the street.

"Tell me, have you enjoyed our stay here?" Madison asked her.

"Of course I have, William. It is a wonderful city."

"You know I would like to spend more time here."

"Yes, I know," she said. "And I dare say you will."

After dinner, they walked arm in arm back to the hotel, and while Amelia retired for the night, Madison sat at the desk in the corner of the room and wrote about their stay in the city.

"I have shown the city to Amelia, and I think it is fair to say that it has impressed her favorably. But she is anxious to return to the ranch to see our son, and I do not fault her for that. We shall be leaving at the first light of day."

The next morning, Amelia woke to find Madison still lying beside her in bed. She found it puzzling that he was still asleep. He always woke early, well before dawn, to prepare for the day ahead. She thought surely he would be up by now, in advance of their return to the ranch. But when she tried to wake him, he didn't stir. In a panic, she fled down the stairs to the desk in the lobby and told the clerk to send for a doctor, then she rushed back to the room and sat beside him on the bed, washing his face with a moist cloth, listening to his labored breathing. When the doctor arrived, he determined that Madison had suffered a stroke. He was immediately taken to St. Mary's Hospital, where for the next two weeks, he lay in bed, slowly regaining consciousness but unable to speak or move his left side. When the doctor told Amelia that little more could be done for him, she knew only that she needed to take him home.

She sent for Zachary. When he arrived, they arranged for Madison to lie on a straw mattress in the bed of the wagon, and then they began the solemn journey back to the valley. When they finally arrived at the ranch, they carried him up to the master bedroom, where in the weeks and months to come, Amelia would care for him, washing him and feeding him, looking into his dark eyes as if she might find him again, searching for the man she had clearly come to love.

"It breaks my heart to see what the stroke has done to him," she wrote to her cousin. "I cannot help but fear that he will never fully recover."

And yet, over the course of the next year, Madison would regain a limited utility of his left arm and leg. Eventually, he regained the ability to walk, albeit with assistance and only for very short distances. But he would never speak again. The stroke left him incapable of communicating other than with a deep growl, a brief nod of the head, a downcast look of disapproval. Every morning, Amelia would help him shuffle out onto the front porch, where he would spend the day sitting in one of the thatched cane chairs, oblivious to the attention of his young son, gazing out into the distance until his head slumped forward and he fell asleep. As the months passed, Amelia found it as difficult to observe Madison asleep on the porch as it had been to look upon him lying in bed. His partial recovery seemed a cruel illusion, raising the false hope that he might someday become himself again. She wondered what Madison understood about his condition, if he recognized the depth of his debilitation. She wondered if he would want to live in this diminished state, imprisoned in the body that had betrayed him. Lying beside him, there were nights when she prayed for his release.

He would gain that deliverance on the chilly afternoon of September 23, 1864, when she walked out onto the porch to wrap a blanket around his shoulders and discovered she couldn't wake him. She instantly understood that he had quietly passed on. She could only assume that he had succumbed to another stroke.

"His suffering is finally over, and for that I am deeply grateful," she wrote. "And yet, I will miss him so."

In her letters, his great-grandmother did not grieve her husband's death. She knew the man she had grown to love had been taken from her the moment he suffered his stroke in San Francisco. She buried him in the cemetery beside the creek that ran through the ranch, a service attended by every man, woman, and child in the valley, their presence that afternoon the fullest reflection of an extraordinary life tragically cut short. Upon his death, the *Mendocino Herald* hailed Madison as "the patriarch of Anderson Valley, a man of vision and foresight who had forsaken a life of privilege and comfort in his native South Carolina to seek a new life on his own terms – and then helped all those who followed to do the same."

As Elliott looked out the library window, he had to wonder what else his great-grandfather might have accomplished had he not been denied his rightful destiny. He certainly would have risen to greater prominence at the wool growers association, and Elliott couldn't help but believe he might have entered the political realm, perhaps as a county supervisor, perhaps as an assemblyman representing the interests of the northwest corner of the state. It was not inconceivable that at some point in his life, his great-grandfather might even have sought a statewide office, perhaps a run for the U.S. Senate.

But instead, at the age of forty-five, William Henry Madison was laid to rest. A slender marble obelisk was placed at the head of his grave, blue irises planted at its base so they might blossom every spring, as if to renew their memory of the great man they had lost.

CHAPTER EIGHT

STOOPED SLIGHTLY FORWARD, Elliott trudged up Vallejo Street, his satchel in his left hand. He didn't feel like cooking that evening and had decided instead to bring home a pizza. Alissa could have a slice or two if she was still at the flat. If she'd already left, she could have the pizza after The Sores' performance that night at a club south of Market. He wondered if she was nervous. She and her bandmates had played in public only a handful of times, their last performance at a memorial service for an acquaintance from high school, a skateboarder who had been struck and killed by a mail truck. He hoped her heart was thumping in her chest, adrenaline surging through her veins. As dreadful as her music was, playing the drums animated his granddaughter like nothing else. He couldn't imagine what her life would be like without it.

As a cable car rattled past, he turned up Hyde Street and walked past the thick white trunks of the ficus trees, then ducked into Za's Pizza, slipping past the two young men sitting at the lone table on the sidewalk. He spotted a seat at the counter and set his satchel on the scoured wooden floor. He would order the same pizza he always ordered – olives, mushrooms and green peppers, adding a generous sprinkling of red pepper flakes. For a moment, he was tempted to order sausage for his half of the pizza, but he could hear Alissa, his ersatz vegetarian, complaining the meat had contaminated the entire pie. It wasn't worth the drama.

He watched the owner slide a pizza into the oven in the back, then slam the upper oven door. Elliott had known Oliver for more than ten years. He was wearing a Resist Authority undershirt and khaki shorts, an apron stained with tomato sauce tied around his waist. When he saw Elliott sitting at the counter, he made his way down to him, perspiration glistening on his forehead as he clapped the flour from his hands.

"The usual?" he asked.

"I'll take it to go," Elliott said. "And pour me a glass of the stout while I wait."

He watched as Oliver raised a glass to the tap behind the counter and tipped the handle back, then shook off the head of foam and placed it on the counter in front of him.

"Thanks," Elliott said.

As Oliver walked back down the counter, Elliott reached for the glass and took a sip of the stout and found himself thinking about the deer camp again. He'd been thinking about those long-ago trips to the deer camp while on the bus returning from the library. Perhaps it was simply the season, the weather, the warm air moving in through the bus window. For years, those long weekends in the woods had been a cherished autumn ritual.

The camp was a good hour north of the ranch. About twenty minutes out of Boonville, there was a gate on the left side of the road to Ukiah. His father had a key to the padlock that secured the gate, and after letting themselves through, they'd drive up the roughly graded road as it led over and across a series of pine-cloaked ridges before they finally arrived at the deer camp, which, truth be told, was little more than a dusty clearing in the pines with a simple plank cabin.

They often met his father's closest friends from childhood at the camp – Tommy Bartlett, Sonny Willis, and the Purdum brothers. When they were young men, they were all avid hunters. The bleached white deer skulls wired to the trunks of the pines that surrounded the fire pit attested to their skills. But over the years, they met at the camp less to hunt than to sit at the table beside the fire pit, drinking beer and playing cribbage and reminiscing in Boontling. Tommy Bartlett was the first of his father's friends to pass away, followed in quick succession by Roy Purdum and then Sonny Willis. When Earl Purdum, the last of the Purdum brothers, died of cancer, Elliott had reason to believe those annual weekends at the deer camp had come to an end. But shortly before his father passed away, he abruptly announced that he wanted to go deer hunting one last time. And even though he had begun displaying the initial symptoms of early onset dementia, Elliott couldn't deny him that final request.

They arrived at the camp shortly before dark. While his father sat at the table, Elliott built a fire and stoked the gas lantern and prepared their sleeping bags on the bedsprings in the cabin. When the camp was set up, he made dinner, placing a cast-iron pot filled with chili on the metal grate over the fire pit. Chili was his father's signature dish, the meal he had always been responsible for bringing when he met his friends at the camp, and they ate it that night as they always ate it – ladled over thick slices of sourdough bread and then buried in chopped onions and grated cheddar cheese, adding a generous dollop of Tabasco sauce to achieve the full affect.

After dinner, they sat around the fire, watched over by the hollow eyes of the deer skulls, pulsing in the firelight. His father was uncommonly lucid that night, telling Elliott stories about the deer they had taken over the years, stories he recalled as clearly and vividly as if they had gone hunting just that afternoon. And he insisted that Elliott go out in the morning and take one last buck. He wanted to hear one last story of the hunt; he wanted one last taste of venison cooked over an open fire. Elliott had never been a particularly serious hunter, but if his father wanted to vicariously experience one last hunt through him, he would give it his best.

He left the camp at daybreak, leaving his father still asleep in the cabin. In the morning chill, his breath rose before him as he hiked down to the creek below the camp and then made his way upstream, scrambling over rocks and fighting through the heavy brush. After less than a mile, he came upon fresh black pellets of deer scat. A few yards farther up the creek bed, he spotted tracks pressed into the wet sand. With his Savage 99 slung over his shoulder, he followed the tracks through the forest all morning and into the afternoon before he finally saw the black-tailed buck through the pines, no more than fifty or sixty yards away. It was a magnificent animal, four or five years old with a four-point rack of antlers, its ears cocked back, listening for any sound, its nose lifted to the breeze moving through the trees.

Elliott slipped the rifle off his shoulder and checked to make sure he had loaded a cartridge into the chamber, then he raised the rifle to his shoulder and squinted down the blue-black barrel, drawing a bead on the base of the buck's thick neck. He couldn't miss. The deer would be dead before it hit the ground. He took a deep breath to steady himself, his index finger slowly squeezing trigger – but at the last second, he stopped himself and lowered the barrel of the rifle, realizing he couldn't do it. He knew how disappointed his father was going to be when he returned to camp, but he couldn't kill that beautiful stag, even for his father.

He didn't make it back to the camp until dusk and was surprised to discover that his father wasn't there. He checked the cabin to see if he had decided to take a nap, but he didn't find him. Stepping back outside, he called out his father's name, and when he got no response, he began to worry. Darkness fell quickly that time of the year. The temperature dropped just as rapidly. He had no idea where his father might have gone. His best guess was that he might have walked down to the creek, where he and his friends used to submerge their beer when all the ice in their coolers had melted. And in the fading daylight, he saw his father's footprints in the sand, leading downstream.

He didn't have to go far to find him. His father was sitting beside a sandy pool, his arms around his knees as he rocked back and forth. He didn't see Elliott or hear him approach. He didn't know Elliott was there until he sat down beside him.

"I thought you'd left me here," his father said.

Elliott draped his arm around his father's shoulders.

"Why would I do that?" he asked him.

His father turned to him, his eyes red and swollen, saliva dangling from the rim of his stubbled jaw.

"Let's get back to camp, shall we?" Elliott said.

He helped his father stand, and with his arm around his waist, they made their way back to the camp. Elliott built a fire and warmed up the remaining chili. After they ate, they put on their heavy coats and stocking caps and sat in their aluminum chairs around the fire, warming the soles of their boots on the rocks that ringed the pit.

"We'll drive home in the morning," Elliott said.

But his father didn't hear him. His head was tilted back, his mouth hanging open as he watched the sparks twist up into the night. When he finally fell asleep in his chair, Elliott carried him into the cabin and put him to bed, as his father must have done for him so many times before, so many years ago.

His father was never the same after that last trip to the deer camp. His memory abandoned him quickly. It wasn't long before he no longer recognized the live-in aide Elliott had hired to care for him. Elliott had no choice but to move him into an assisted living facility with a memory care ward, but that only accelerated his decline. Finally, quietly, his father died while sitting in his wheelchair, listening to his beloved Bach. Taking a last swallow of the stout, Elliott couldn't help but wonder if his own life would unravel as swiftly and irrevocably as his father's. Only time would tell, he supposed. All he knew for certain was that he would be laid to rest in the cemetery in Anderson Valley, buried in the family plot presided over by the obelisk at the head of his great-grandfather's grave.

HE CARRIED THE PIZZA up the stairs and let Hank out the back door and moved into the kitchen. And as he set the box on the table and lifted out a slice, he supposed it was the memory of those trips to deer camp that put him in mind of the summer he'd spent on the ranch with his great-grandmother. He took a bite of the pizza. As he set the slice down on the lid of the box, he found it hard to believe that summer was seventy-two years ago, when he was just six years old and his great-grandmother was ninety-three. But the math cannot be disputed.

His father had driven him up to the ranch in his glassy black Hudson. The Golden Gate Bridge hadn't been constructed yet, so they took the ferry across the bay and then drove north through the hills of Marin and Sonoma. After stopping for lunch in Cloverdale, they headed west on the narrow road through the Coast Range, arriving a long hour later in Anderson Valley. They drove through Boonville and then down the valley for several miles before turning in through the gate and rolling quietly up the road leading into the ranch. He could still hear the gravel popping beneath the Hudson's tires as they drove past the apple orchard and the open pasture, the old red barn with its corrugated sheet metal roof, the sheep pens and shearing sheds, the horse stables and corral.

The ranch house was secluded in a copse of chestnuts, elms, and sycamores, enclosed by a tall hedge of flowering privet. He remembered pushing the car door open and running up the path that led into the cool sanctuary of the garden. His great-grandmother was standing on the porch in her khakis and a blue long-sleeve work shirt buttoned at her wrists, her face dark and creased, her long pewter hair woven into a single braid that lay upon her left shoulder.

"Grandma!" he shouted, running up the steps and throwing his arms around her legs.

"Look at you!" she exclaimed, taking a step back and holding his hands in hers. "Just look how you have grown!"

The summer passed in a blur, every day high adventure. Antonio, the ranch foreman, had two sons his age, Omar and Javier, and together they explored the long cool lanes of the orchard and the far reaches of the pasture, traipsed through the hills behind the ranch and splashed through the creek that ran behind the barn. In the evening, he and his great-grandmother would eat dinner at the table in the dining room, where he would breathlessly tell her about the discoveries of the day – the tiny green frogs they found on the muddy bank of the creek, the blue-belly lizards darting through the stacks of firewood, the mangy feral cats they chased but could never quite catch in the barn. After dinner, he would sit with her on the screened-in porch and listen to the radio, picking up a distant station that played Big Band and swing music. She loved Benny Goodman, Cab Calloway, and Duke Ellington, and yet, the music always seemed to sadden her. He remembered that about his great-grandmother, the pervasive sadness, the air of melancholia, the abiding sense of loss. Her moments of joy she seemed to find just for him.

From the moment he'd arrived at the ranch, he'd pleaded with her to let him ride one of the horses. He was terrified of the great beasts galloping around the corral, but he desperately wanted to ride one. His great-grandmother sensed his trepidation, and she had her own reservations, of course, fearing he might fall off and get hurt. But finally, she relented and instructed Antonio to saddle up a gray mare named Ashes. He would never forget standing beside the mossy green water trough, waiting until Antonio led the saddled mare out of the stable, then hurrying across the corral in the black stitched-leather boots and black cowboy hat his great-grandmother had purchased for him on his birthday.

"Are you ready?" Antonio asked.

When Elliott nodded, Antonio reached down and grabbed him beneath each arm and swung him up into the saddle. Elliott grabbed the saddle horn with both hands, clutching it tightly as Antonio raised the stirrups for him. He couldn't believe how high above the ground he was. He looked down at Antonio and across the corral to his great-grandmother, standing beside the gate. And suddenly Antonio began leading Ashes around the perimeter of the corral. Elliott could still feel the mare moving beneath him, the great lumbering mass between his legs. He had never known anything like it. And when Antonio led him past his great-grandmother, he waved his hat above his head as if he were riding a wild stallion.

Then the mare stopped, and Antonio walked back to him.

"Here," he said, handing him the reins.

Elliott put his hat back on and took the reins in his left hand, still holding onto the saddle horn with his right. But that was not good enough for Antonio.

"Both hands," he said.

Reluctantly, Elliott let go of the saddle horn and gripped the reins with both hands, squeezing the mare's flanks between his legs. When Antonio gave the mare a gentle slap on her haunch, she lunged forward, nearly pitching Elliott out of the saddle.

"Slow down!" he yelled as his hat slipped forward, over his eyes.

But the mare had an idea of her own. She sidled over to the fence and brushed her right flank against the rails, Elliott's knee striking one of the posts so hard his boot fell off. He could feel himself sliding out of the saddle. Dropping the reins, he grabbed the saddle horn and tried to pull himself back up. In desperation, he lunged for the top rail of the fence. But he fell short and tumbled out of the saddle, flipping completely over and landing flat on his back on the ground, a cloud of dust washing over him as the old mare casually walked away.

Antonio hurried over to him.

"That didn't hurt me," Elliott said, pushing up to stand.

He picked up his hat and slapped off the dust. When Antonio handed him his boot, he set it on the ground and stomped his foot down into it. His great-grandmother clapped her hands as he walked over to her.

"You were wonderful – simply wonderful!" she said.

"I'd like to try that again," he told her.

But she laughed and slipped her arm around his shoulders to lead him back to the house.

"That's quite enough for today," she said. "Next summer you can ride all you want, every day. We'll see that you have a horse of your own."

But there would be no more summers at the ranch. Amelia Snyder Madison died that winter at the age of ninety-four. In her obituaries, the *Mendocino County Beacon* called her "the last of that hardy stock of pioneers who settled the valley." The *Ukiah Journal* called her "a woman of courage and vision, who became a prominent rancher in her own right after the death of her husband." It was fair praise, and Elliott certainly appreciated those kind words about the woman who had loomed over his life for so many years. And yet, as generous as those obituaries were, they couldn't possibly tell the full story of his great-grandmother's life. That, of course, was the task he had set for himself

ON THE SIDEWALK in front of his building, Elliott waited for his cab. When he saw it turn onto Vallejo, he raised his right hand and then waited for the cab to pull up in front of him. As he slid across the back seat, the driver turned and looked at him, his eyes slits in his huge pink head.

"The Anarchists Club on Connecticut," Elliott said.

Without a word, the driver tapped the meter, then stepped down hard on the accelerator, the tires barking on the pavement as he turned the cab around and headed south on Hyde Street. Elliott sat back and gazed out the window, wondering what Alissa would think if she spotted him at the club tonight. He had deliberated at length about whether to surreptitiously show up at the club, wanting to demonstrate his support for his granddaughter and yet also afraid to compromise her independence or intrude upon her private world. Ultimately, he'd decided to take the chance. He didn't just want to see her perform, he wanted to see her in her element.

They drove over Nob Hill and then down into the Tenderloin, the driver rolling through stop signs and streaking through intersections as the lights turned red, crossing Market Street as white-hot sparks rained down from the electrical lines above one of the streetcars. The club was in an old two-story warehouse, its stucco façade covered with profane graffiti. As the cab pulled up in front of the club, Elliott tossed a twenty-dollar bill onto the front seat, then pushed the door open and stepped up onto the sidewalk.

A thickset bouncer sat on a stool beside the door, his shoulders bared by his black leather vest, a long black flashlight in his hand.

"Who the fuck are you?" he asked.

Elliott reached up and doffed his hat.

"Elliott Madison," he said. "I've come to see The Sores."

The bouncer studied him for a moment, an amused grin caught in the corner of his mouth.

"No kidding."

"My granddaughter plays the drums."

The bouncer laughed, as if it were a private joke.

"Is there a cover charge?" Elliott asked.

"You can't be serious."

The bouncer waved his flashlight at the door.

"Go on in," he said.

Elliott leaned into the door, pushing into the building, then started up the concrete stairs. At the top of the stairs, he entered the club, where a mob of people were milling around in the dim blue light, all of them in their twenties or thirties, the men in shredded denim and black leather, their heads shaved and nostrils pierced, the women featuring stretch pants, bare midriffs, and plumes of fluorescent hair. Beneath the can lights mounted on the exposed ceiling rafters, a plywood stage had been assembled several feet above the floor. A band had already set up on the stage – a bank of amplifiers and waist-high speakers, a microphone stand at the front of the stage, a drum kit in the back. Elliott hoped the drum kit was Alissa's. It was his understanding that The Sores were the first of three bands scheduled to play, and he certainly hoped that was the case. He despaired to think that he might have to listen to another group before Alissa and her bandmates took the stage.

A bar had been set up in the back of the club. Elliott walked over and took his place in line, fielding the glances cast his way by the club's perplexed clientele, wondering why a man of his advanced age might be in attendance. He offered a genial smile in return, a deferential nod. He was ordering a cup of beer when the band abruptly began to play, a sudden explosion of sound detonating behind him. When he wheeled around, he saw that it was indeed Alissa and her bandmates, furiously assaulting their instruments.

He picked up his beer and worked his way over to stand in the shadows. In the clashing beams of light, The Sores were playing at a deafening volume, far louder than they played in the garage. He watched as Alissa attacked her drums with a vengeance, pounding the snare drum and thrashing the cymbals, stomping on the pedals for the hi-hat and bass drum. Jeremy looked like a man possessed as he extracted each shrieking note from his guitar, jerking violently as Nigel stepped up to the microphone and began screaming incoherently. Elliott could feel the concussive blows of the drums and the heavy thump of the bass; he winced at the fusillade of extortion from Jeremy's guitar. He strained to detect any kind of rhythm or melody, a definable sequence of notes, but the music's discordant elements came upon him too quickly and with such force that it was all he could do to withstand the relentless impact. It sounded, in his view, like a crime against humanity, the end of all sentient life. And yet, when the torrent of sound came to a crashing halt, he saw Alissa lift her head and allow herself a shy smile. That was what he had come to see. That was all the confirmation he needed.

Ultimately, twenty minutes was all he could bear. He staggered out of the club, down the stairs and back out onto the street, opening his mouth and working his jaw, rolling his head around on his neck as if that might alleviate the ringing in his ears. He felt exhausted, pummeled. In the warm night air, he felt as if he'd been running for miles. When he saw a cab, he raised his hand and flagged it down. The driver spotted him at the last instant, slamming on the brakes. Elliott opened the back door and all but collapsed onto the seat.

"Russian Hill – Vallejo Street," he said, his head snapping back as the driver stepped down on the accelerator.

The driver was wearing a maroon beret adorned with military decorations. On the radio, the host of a right-wing talk show was ranting about illegal aliens pouring across the border. All Elliott wanted was silence.

"Would you mind turning that off?" he asked.

With a glance up into the rearview mirror, the driver reached over and turned the radio down, but not off.

"How's that?" he asked.

Elliott closed his eyes, reaching up and pinching the bridge of his nose. He was still trembling slightly, a high-pitched whine in his ears. As the driver drove him back across the city, through the warehouse district and the residence hotels in the Tenderloin, over and across Nob Hill, he tried to relax, to slow his breathing, as if that might subdue the lingering effects of his granddaughter's performance. It seemed a lifetime before the cab pulled over in front of his building.

He got out and walked up the front steps, letting himself into the porch and then climbing the stairs to his flat. After letting Hank out, he shed his coat and hat and poured himself a glass of bourbon, profoundly relieved to be home, relieved to have survived his granddaughter's performance. He was sure Alissa hadn't seen him and that pleased him. He looked forward to telling her that he had gone to see The Sores play. She was certain to be shocked, if not outraged, and he liked that, too. He had learned a little about his granddaughter this evening, and soon she would learn a little more about him.

He raised the glass and took a sip of the bourbon, noticing the red light blinking on the answering machine. He assumed it was yet another message from his daughter, imploring Alissa to call her. He walked over to the hutch and pressed the button to listen. The machine quickly rewound, the cassette snapping to a stop before the message began to play. Initially, all he could hear was the crackle of static, but then a woman's shrill voice called out his name.

"Elliott! Is that you? It's Phoebe!"

He took a step back, the bottom dropping out of his stomach.

"I've got to talk to you!" she all but shouted. "I've got great news! Call me, will you? I'm so excited! The number here is …"

But Elliott didn't care what Ms. Crighton's number was. He reached down and shut the machine off. He had no idea why she had called, why she wanted him to call her. He had no idea what her news might be. As he carried the glass over to the table and pulled out a chair, he remembered that he still hadn't picked up the package she had sent, and perhaps that was what her call was about.

He knew he couldn't procrastinate any longer. Tomorrow morning, he would walk down to the post office and see what Ms. Crighton had sent him. He would pay the postage due. And then, perhaps, he would call her back and hear what her great news was. And then, perhaps, she would leave him alone.

CHAPTER NINE

ELLIOTT WOKE SLOWLY. Lying on his back, he stared up at the cracks in the ceiling for a moment, then rolled onto his side and lifted his head to look at the clock on the nightstand. It was nearly ten o'clock, nearly four hours later than he normally arose. The Sores' performance had clearly taken a toll.

He sat up and swung his legs over the edge of the mattress. With his feet on the hardwood floor, he took a deep breath, then stood up and padded barefoot into the bathroom. After a long shower, he made his way into the kitchen and put on a pot of coffee, but the caffeine had little effect, failing to subdue the dull ache throbbing behind his left eye. So he reached for the bottle of aspirin in the cabinet beside the refrigerator. He shook four of the tablets into the palm of his right hand and was about to pop them into his mouth when the telephone rang.

He looked across the kitchen to the phone on the hutch, listening to it ring once more, and suddenly he knew who it was, who it had to be. He was tempted to let the phone ring. He was tempted to let Ms. Crighton leave another message. She could leave a million messages, for all he cared. But he knew, unfortunately, that that wouldn't work. He had to believe she would just keep calling until he finally answered.

He walked over to the hutch and picked up the receiver.

"Elliott!"

Wincing, he leaned away from the receiver, holding it at arm's length before cautiously returning it to his ear.

"This is Elliott Madison," he said.

"It's Phoebe!"

He closed his eyes, as if it might have been someone else.

"Hello, Ms. Crighton."

"I couldn't wait," she said.

"Wait for what?"

"For you to call me back!"

Elliott pulled out a chair and sat at the table. He leaned forward and massaged his temples.

"What can I do for you, Ms. Crighton?"

"Did you get the package I sent?"

"Well, no – not yet," he confessed.

"That's why I'm calling," she said.

"About the package?"

"I'm coming to California!"

Elliott straightened up in the chair.

"What are you talking about?"

"The day after tomorrow," she said. "I'm coming to San Francisco!"

"Why?" he asked, as if the very thought was preposterous.

"I can't wait," she said. "I've never been there."

"What kind of reason is that?"

"I've made a reservation at the Washington Square Inn. It looks positively darling. I'm looking at my map of San Francisco right now. The inn looks very close to where you live."

Elliott shifted the telephone to his other ear. He knew where the Washington Square Inn was.

"My flight arrives at five in the evening – shall I give you a call when I get in?"

"What for?" he asked, abruptly rising from the chair.

"So we can meet, Elliott. So we can talk. So we can talk about Benjamin and your great-grandparents."

"Honestly, I don't know that there's anything to talk about," he said.

But she wouldn't hear it.

"Whatever time works best for you," she said. "I'm flexible, totally flexible."

Elliott reached up and closed his eyes with his fingertips, understanding that Ms. Crighton was not to be denied.

"All right," he said quietly, conceding defeat. "Call me when you get here."

"I will, Elliott. I will. I can't wait to meet you!"

As he carried the phone back to the hutch, Elliott couldn't believe what had just happened, what he had just consented to do. A woman he didn't know, a woman he'd never even spoken to before today, was flying out from New York City to see him, insinuating herself into his life, insinuating herself into the lives of his great-grandparents. He had no idea what she wanted, what her motives were. He had nothing to tell her. It was ridiculous, absurd, and yet he had agreed to meet with her. All he could do was shake his head. He felt like a perfect fool.

AFTER GETTING DRESSED, Elliott walked back into the kitchen and picked up the notice from the post office. Tucking it into his coat pocket, he let himself out of the flat, then made his way up and over the crest of the hill, down Union Street into the bustling midday chaos in Washington Square.

The post office was directly across from the square, and, as always, it was crowded. Elliott took his place at the end of the line and stood there patiently, listening to the individual dramas playing out at the counter ahead of him: the aging Beat poet in his tie-dyed undershirt, baggy shorts, and Mexican sandals, demanding to know why it takes so long for mail sent manuscript rate to reach the East Coast; the street hustler from Chicago, a silver crucifix nestled in the chest hair spilling out the neck of his silk shirt, insisting that the post office had lost his unemployment check; an old woman in her robe and slippers, believing she was at the water company and trying to pay her bill. The theatrics at the counter left Elliott with nothing but admiration for Arturo, who stood at the counter in his blue postal uniform, calmly weathering the complaints and muttered insults.

Finally, the old woman in her robe turned and shuffled toward the door. Elliott stepped up to the counter.

"Hello, Arturo," he said.

"Good morning, Mr. Madison."

In the years since he retired, Elliott had spent hours at the post office, buying rolls of stamps and looking up zip codes, picking up envelopes too large to be slipped through the mail slot at the bottom of the door to his flat. He frequently conducted his postal affairs with Arturo, who had walked a route on Russian Hill until he slipped on a wet sidewalk one rainy holiday season and blew out a knee.

"I've come for this," he said, handing him the postage due notice.

"I'll be right back," Arturo said.

He disappeared into the back of the post office for only a minute, returning with a thick manila envelope and placing it on the counter.

"Here you go," he said. "That'll be ninety cents."

Elliott reached for his wallet and produced a dollar bill.

"Thanks, Arturo."

Elliott carried the envelope out of the post office, then crossed the street and entered the square, making his way over to a bench across from Sts. Peter and Paul. He was still irritated with Lila for providing his mailing address and phone number to Ms. Crighton. He still couldn't believe she had given his contact information to a total stranger. There was no telling who this Ms. Crighton was, much less what she might have sent him. She seemed harmless, but that was hardly a guarantee.

Using the key to his flat, he tore open the envelope flap, then withdrew a thick sheaf of papers held together with a metal clip. As he placed it on his lap, he saw that it was a xeroxed copy of an old typewritten manuscript titled, "Benjamin Harrigan and the 128th New York Voluntary Infantry Regiment."

A sheet of Ms. Crighton's purple stationery had been clipped to the manuscript's title page, a note written in her loose hand.

Dear Mr. Madison,

This manuscript was written by my great-grandmother Dorothea Smiley. It's about her uncle and the regiment he served in during the Civil War. My great-grandmother was sixteen years old when Benjamin decided to enlist. When he returned three years later, she cared for him during his recuperation from the injuries he suffered on the battlefield and the deprivations he endured as a prisoner of war. I found the manuscript while searching through some boxes in storage, and I thought you might be interested in reading it. I would dearly love to hear what you think when you finish.

Sincerely,
Phoebe Crighton

As he sat back on the bench, Elliott had to laugh. He was entirely at a loss. Yes, it was possible that Harrigan had worked on his family's ranch after the war. He didn't deny it. But no, he didn't know anything about him. And no, he wasn't particularly interested in his experiences during the Civil War.

He had no idea, frankly, why Ms. Crighton was flying out from

New York City, why she wanted to see him. He had nothing to tell her. He certainly wasn't inclined to share what he had learned about his great-grandparents. He hadn't shared his research with anyone, other than with Lila or Doris at the Page Desk. And while it was true that he was close to finishing his manuscript, he still considered it very much a work in progress, and he was not at all prepared to discuss it with a complete stranger.

He lifted the title page and glanced down at the manuscript, his eyes casually drifting down the page, and without any such intention, he found himself reading about the Harrigans, who had immigrated to upstate New York from County Cork in Ireland in the 1830s, settling on forty acres of tillable land outside East Fishkill in Dutchess County. Benjamin was the oldest of seven children, born on May 9, 1841. He was well over six feet tall with broad shoulders, coal black eyes and a dimpled chin. He loved horses and hunting and attended school only during the winter, quitting for good when he was fourteen.

He was twenty years old when he read the newspaper accounts of the Confederate artillery bombarding Fort Sumter in Charleston Bay. He knew little about the secession of the Southern states – Virginia, Georgia, Mississippi, and the other states were only the names of places he had never been. Nor did he have a strong opinion about the abolition of slavery, having known but few Negroes in his life. But in the months to come, he heard about the Union army's costly defeat at Bull Run, the heavy losses at Shiloh, the embarrassing retreat from the Shenandoah Valley, where Union troops had been driven back across the Potomac River. And in the summer of 1862, when Colonel David Cowles, formerly an attorney in the nearby town of Hudson, called for volunteers to form a regiment of infantrymen from Columbia and Dutchess counties, Benjamin informed his parents that he intended to enlist.

Three weeks later, Benjamin and Karl Swensen, a friend from a neighboring farm, took the train to Hudson, where Colonel

Cowles's regiment was training at the fairgrounds. Karl was a year younger, the son of elderly Swedish immigrants, slight of frame with blond hair and blue eyes. He and Benjamin had grown up together, sharing a love of the outdoors and a distaste for the classroom. Although it had been Benjamin's idea to enlist, Karl was quick to join him. As they were about to board the train, Karl's mother pulled Benjamin aside and made him promise to look out for her son. Naturally, he assured her that he would do his best.

When they arrived in Hudson, they saw that hundreds of men had already answered Colonel Cowles's call, and dozens more were arriving every day. Under the watchful eyes of their drill instructors, they began training in the heavy summer heat, marching around the racetrack for hours at a time, heads high, shoulders square, arms along their sides. Soon more than one thousand men had volunteered for the regiment, which was divided into ten companies – four from Columbia County and six from Dutchess County. Benjamin and Karl were assigned to Company H.

On August 30, in a ceremony at the fairgrounds, the women of Hudson presented Colonel Cowles with two hand-sewn flags for the regiment to carry into battle, and five days later, Benjamin and Karl and their fellow infantrymen were formally sworn into service for a three-year tour of duty. The next afternoon, with Colonel Cowles leading the way, they marched out of the fairgrounds and through the city to the steamboat landing on the river, the streets lined with men and women waving and cheering as they paraded past in their new blue uniforms. Bands played, church bells rang, boiler whistles blew. Later that afternoon, they boarded a steamer named the *Oregon*, and shortly after dark, it pulled away from the shore and started down the river.

"As I stood at the rail," Benjamin would later tell his niece, "I knew I was not alone in wondering who among us would return, and who would not."

Elliott looked up from the manuscript and watched a young

man with blond dreadlocks toss a fluorescent green Frisbee across the grass, his golden retriever chasing after it, leaping up to snatch it out of the air. He couldn't believe he was reading about Benjamin Harrigan, much less about the obscure regiment he had served with during the Civil War. And he resented it, to be perfectly honest. He resented the sense of obligation he felt to read the manuscript Ms. Crighton had sent, an obligation he felt all the more acutely now that she was flying out from New York City to see him. She had no right to barge into his life, no right to disrupt his work, and as he slipped the manuscript back into the envelope, he resolved once again to speak to Lila about her egregious lapse in judgment.

But he would read the manuscript, however grudgingly. He would read every last word on every last page, as a courtesy, if nothing else, as a gesture of simple civility. But not this very moment, not here.

WITH THE ENVELOPE under his arm, Elliott rose from the bench and started down Columbus, slipping past the tables arranged in front of the restaurants and cafes, crossing Green Street as the 30 Stockton rolled through the three-way intersection. He walked down the block and entered Molinari Delicatessen, taking a number from the dispenser in front of the cash register and then stepping back to wait his turn, finding a place to stand among the cases of wine and the boxes of dry pasta stacked on the floor, the shelves on the walls lined with jars of olives and peppers, tins of sardines and cans of plum tomatoes, bottles of extra virgin olive oil.

When his number was called, Elliott stepped up to the cold case, chugs of salami hanging overhead.

"Hi, Gino. Let me have a box of the cheese ravioli."

He watched Gino walk back to the glass cooler in the rear of the delicatessen and pick up a box for him.

"And a pint of gravy," Elliott called down to him.

Gino bagged up the box of ravioli and the pint of sauce, then rang up the sale.

"Thanks, Gino," Elliott said. "I'll see you later."

After slipping his wallet back into his pocket, he carried the bag out of the delicatessen and started up the east slope of the hill. He passed through Ina Coolbrith Park, then crossed Taylor Street to climb a series of steep concrete steps, long staggered flights angling through the arching pines and agave. He could feel himself perspiring, sweat trickling down his ribs. Twice, he had to stop to catch his breath. When he finally reached the park at the crest of the hill, the small patch of grass where he liked to bring Hank, he stopped and leaned on the concrete balustrade, breathing heavily, his back tight, his legs loose in his trousers. He had lived in San Francisco all his life, and yet he had never fully adjusted to the city's unforgiving topography. Even after all these years, he was still winded every time he climbed one of the hills.

He gave himself another moment, then made his way down the street to his building, letting himself into the porch and climbing the stairs up to his flat. As he followed Hank down the hall, he glanced into Alissa's bedroom and saw that she was still asleep, still curled up beneath a mound of sheets and comforters. He was not surprised. He'd heard her come in slightly after four in the morning. There was no telling when she might wake up. But it didn't really matter. He'd wait until she rose, and then he'd put a pot of water on the stove to boil. It would only take a few minutes to cook the ravioli and warm up the sauce.

He slid the ravioli into the refrigerator, then took off his coat and poured himself a glass of water. But just as he raised the glass to his mouth, the telephone rang. He looked over to the phone on the hutch, his stomach suddenly clenched, thinking that it might be Ms. Crighton again. It was only as he started across the kitchen that he realized the call was actually on his cell phone.

He lifted his coat from the back of the chair. As he dug the phone out of the interior pocket, he saw that it was his daughter.

"Hello, Claire. How's my baby girl?"

"I'm ready to drive up to the city and strangle her, if you want to know the truth."

Elliott pulled out a chair and sat at the table. He didn't need to ask whom she was talking about.

"Why?" he asked. "What's she done now?"

"That's the problem, exactly," she said. "She hasn't called me back. I mean, how hard is that?"

"She'll call you," he said. "Just give her a little more time."

But he knew his assurance was unlikely to assuage his daughter's frustration.

"I assume she's asleep," she said.

"Yes, that's right."

"I assume she was out all night."

"Actually, she and Nigel and Jeremy performed at a small club last night," he told her.

"Nigel and Jeremy?"

"Walter and Martin," he said. "They go by Nigel and Jeremy now."

"Good Christ."

"Stage names, I believe."

"Just don't tell me Alissa is thinking about changing her name, too."

Elliott was not going to tell his daughter that Alissa was considering calling herself Cassandra, but he was not going to mislead her, either.

"I believe she's giving the matter some thought," he said.

"She told you that?" Claire asked, her voice rising swiftly in alarm.

"She did."

"And what did you say?"

"What could I say?"

"You could have told her that it's a perfectly stupid idea."

Elliott took a long breath, wanting to change the subject.

"Actually, I went and saw her play last night," he said.

"What?" his daughter gasped.

"They played at a small club south of Market," he said.

"You can't be serious!"

"I am, absolutely," he said.

An awkward silence abruptly descended upon them, as if Claire didn't know what else to say or think.

"And how was it?" she asked a long moment later, making no effort to conceal her exasperation. "Did you enjoy yourself? Did you have a good time?"

"Not particularly," he admitted.

"Isn't it enough that you're letting them practice in the garage?"

"They play with great passion, I can tell you that much."

"You're encouraging her, Dad. You're indulging her. You're letting her think that this is all right."

But Elliott didn't want to argue with his daughter. His elbow on the table, he rested his forehead in the palm of his right hand.

"It's not so bad," he said.

"Are you serious?" his daughter all but shouted into the phone. "You support all this? You're defending this nonsense?"

"Not necessarily," he said.

"That's what it sounds like to me."

"I just think we need to let her see where this goes. That's all I'm saying."

"But, we know where this is going, Dad – nowhere. That's where all this is going."

Elliott didn't have anything left to say. And he didn't particularly care to hear anymore from his daughter, either, not when she was in a state like this.

"Listen, Claire, when Alissa gets up, I'll tell her that you called. I'll ask her to call you back."

"Slim chance of that happening," she said.

"You just need to give her some time, some room," he said.

"I can't believe you're taking her side, Dad."

"I'm not taking her side," he said. "I'm not taking anybody's side. I'm just saying she needs a little time to find her way through this."

And finally, his daughter seemed to have talked herself out.

"Is there anything else you want me to tell her?" he asked.

She didn't respond right away, as if she needed time to think. For a moment, he thought she might be crying.

"I'm just worried about her, that's all," she said.

"I understand," he said. "I understand completely."

After saying goodbye, Elliott turned off his cell phone and placed it on the counter. His daughter was wearing him out, as only she could, as she had been for the last forty years. Claire did love Alissa. She always had and always would. But she needed to take a step back, and Elliott didn't understand why she couldn't see that. He had told her as much, but she wouldn't listen. Or perhaps she had heard him and simply rejected his counsel. It made no difference. She was as hardheaded as her daughter, and that, he knew all too well, was the fundamental problem between them – they were too much alike.

AS ELLIOTT RETURNED to the table, his eyes fell on the envelope sent by Ms. Crighton. For a moment, he had almost forgotten about it. For a moment, he had almost forgotten about her. He allowed himself a deep breath, then reached for the envelope and withdrew the manuscript, returning without enthusiasm to Harrigan and his regiment as they arrived at Camp Millington on the southern edge of Baltimore.

There, for the next two months, Benjamin and Karl and the other volunteers would march across the hard red soil, drilling at the company, battalion and regimental levels. It was a dreary routine that began with reveille at five o'clock in the morning and culminated with the playing of taps at nine o'clock at night. Finally, to their immense relief, they boarded a steamship named the *Arago*, and after waiting out an early winter snowstorm, they started down the long arm of Chesapeake Bay.

"Our orders were sealed. We had no idea where we were going. But we didn't care. All that mattered was that our training was finally over."

Under the escort of a man-of-war named the *Augusta*, the *Arago* and three other ships set a course down the Eastern Seaboard, through the Florida Keys and then across the Gulf of Mexico, eventually heading up the Mississippi River to Camp Chalmette, several miles below New Orleans. They endured five miserable weeks there, the camp little more than a field of mud on the edge of a swamp, and then they headed upriver again, arriving at Camp Parapet on February 11, 1863. Conditions there were little improved. The unrelenting rains soaked through their mildewed tents. Mosquitoes swarmed through the air. Scores of men fell ill, stricken by dysentery and yellow fever.

After three months at Camp Parapet, they were called up to participate in the siege of Port Hudson, one of the last Confederate strongholds on the Mississippi. In late May, they boarded a steamship and started up the river. In a drenching rain, Benjamin and Karl and the other men gazed out at the lowland swamps and bayous, the groves of cypress and magnolia and the stands of moss-draped oaks, the silent plantations and the fields of sugar cane and cotton. They reached Springfield Landing that afternoon, and as they stepped down onto the dock, they looked up the river to Port Hudson, located high on the rim of the east bank, some sixty to eighty feet above the shoreline. Before the war, Port Hudson had been little more than a rural Southern hamlet, home to a handful of warehouses storing the sugar cane and cotton grown on the outlying plantations. Now, more than seven thousand Confederate troops occupied the town, and their heavy artillery, mounted above a sharp bend in the river, effectively prevented Union ships from passing below.

When all the men were off the steamer, they fell into formation and marched the eight miles to the staging grounds for the Nineteenth Corps, joining the thirty thousand men under the command of General Nathaniel Banks. They set up camp, and for the next four days, they waited in the sweltering heat for the order to move into position for the assault. On the morning of May 27, they broke camp before dawn and stole through the woods to the edge of a field of young corn. On the far side of the field, beyond the rail fences and a deep ravine, the Confederates had been digging in for months, fortifying their positions and protecting their artillery with sandbags and thick earthen embankments behind scores of downed trees, their branches hacked back and sharpened into spikes. When Benjamin looked up, he could see the sharpshooters high in the cypresses. On a knee, Karl quietly vomited into the grass.

Shortly before daybreak, the Union artillery began bombarding the Confederate positions, the heavy concussions detonating in the darkness and reverberating across the battlefield, shells screeching through the air and exploding in the trees overhead. Early that afternoon, the 128th received the order to charge across the field, led by three hundred former slaves carrying poles and planks that were intended to be used to form bridges to cross the ravine. They burst out of the woods and surged across the field, but as soon as the former slaves reached the first of the fences, the Confederates opened fire. In a panic, they dropped the poles and planks and ran for cover. Behind them, the men of the 128th pressed forward, into the withering gunfire, their battle lines quickly disintegrating into chaos.

Through the drifting smoke, Benjamin and Karl rushed ahead, vaulting the fences and running through the corn, the grapeshot and minie balls whistling past them. But after advancing to within one hundred yards of the Confederate embankments, they dove into a shallow ditch. When Benjamin turned and looked back, he saw two men from the 128th go down behind them, one shot in the right shoulder, the impact dropping him flat on his back, the second man struck in the neck, his hands clutching his throat as he fell face first onto the ground. There was no way to get to them, no way to leave the cover of the ditch. The sharpshooters had them pinned down.

"All we could do was lie there, listening to the men as they lay in the field, hearing their prayers and desperate pleas to be saved or put out of their agony."

Finally, at the first light of day, a temporary truce was called, and Benjamin and Karl climbed out of the ditch and helped recover the dead and wounded splayed across the bloodstained ground, carrying several seriously injured men from their regiment into the plantation buildings that had been converted into hospitals. But twenty-three men from the 128th, including Colonel Cowles, had been killed in the disastrous assault.

"We knew we were lucky to have survived."

FOR WEEKS, the Union artillery pounded Port Hudson, the Confederates periodically returning fire, loading their cannons with any kind of metal they could find – railroad spikes, pieces of scrap iron, broken bayonet blades – the projectiles howling through the air. And as Benjamin and Karl knelt on the edge of the field, they could see the rebels digging in even deeper in anticipation of a second attack.

"We all knew a second assault on the rebels was likely to be as difficult as the first."

On June 14, the 128th rose from their tents and marched down the road leading to the river. In a dense fog, they made their way through the cypress, oak and magnolia, advancing upon the Confederate positions. As they approached their entrenchments, Benjamin dropped to a knee and rested his rifle across the top of a magnolia stump, scanning the embankment for any sign of activity. When he saw something move in the corner of his left eye, he swung his rifle around and fired, but the slug thumped harmlessly into the back of the trench, kicking up a tail of dirt. He pulled his rifle down, reloading as Karl rolled out from behind one of the magnolias, raised his rifle and fired. He dashed across the open ground, seeking the cover of a downed oak. But suddenly his rifle flew up out of his hands and he went down, shot in the upper chest.

Benjamin scrambled over and grabbed him by an arm and the collar of his uniform and pulled him back behind the stump. When he tore open the front of Karl's shirt, he saw that he'd been struck just below his left collarbone. He tore off a piece of Karl's undershirt and stuffed the cloth into the wound, trying to stanch the blood, then he and another man from their regiment lifted Karl up, draping his arms over their shoulders as they dragged him back to the road. With the help of two other men, they hoisted him into the bed of a wagon, and Benjamin climbed up after him. As the wagon lurched forward, he saw that three other men from the 128th were lying there with them, two of the men from Company H. The man on the right had been shot through the left side of his face, the minie ball passing through one cheek and exiting through the other. Beside him, another man was shaking violently, shot in the right knee, clutching the tourniquet cinched around his blood-soaked pant leg. A man Benjamin had never seen before was lying on his back, coughing quietly to himself until blood ran out the corner of his mouth, and then he was still.

When they reached the hospital buildings, the corpsmen loaded the men onto stretchers and carried them over to the rows of wounded lying on the ground. Benjamin followed the corpsmen until they laid Karl down between one soldier who had been seriously burned, his dark red eyes peering out from behind a mask of charred black flesh, and another whose abdomen had been torn open by a piece of shrapnel, his eviscerated intestines in a tangled pile on his chest. One of the attendants knelt down and examined Karl's wound. He promised to get him in to see the surgeons as soon as possible, but as Benjamin looked out across the scores of men lying on the ground, he knew that could mean hours. He lowered his canteen to Karl's mouth and held it there until he took a small swallow, barely enough to moisten his lips.

"Suddenly he couldn't seem to breathe. He gripped my arm and looked up at me, and I begged him to hold on. And when he seemed to give out and sink back into himself, I shouted his name and shook him by the shoulders. But it was not to be."

Benjamin sat with Karl through the night. When the sun rose, the corpsmen came and carried his body over to a wagon filled with corpses. He watched as they swung Karl up into the wagon, then he climbed up and rode with the teamster to the mass graves where they were burying the dead. By the middle of the afternoon, the bodies had been laid out alongside one another at the bottom of a long trench. Benjamin placed Karl's hands upon his chest, his right folded neatly upon his left, then he climbed out and removed his cap as the chaplain asked the Holy Father to welcome the men into his heavenly kingdom. When the chaplain was finished, Benjamin helped the corpsmen fill the trench with the excavated soil, then he started back to camp to rejoin his regiment.

The following day, he wrote a letter to Karl's mother, knowing she would be devastated by the death of her son. Writing had never come easily to him. He spent hours agonizing over every sentence, every word. He told Karl's mother that her son had died bravely in battle, charging the enemy. He told her that Karl's courage on the battlefield brought honor to all the people of Dutchess County. He told her that Karl was admired by every man in Company H.

But he did not tell her that the second assault on Port Hudson had been as disastrous as the first. He didn't want her to think that her son had died in vain.

"I included Karl's unspent pay and a letter he was writing to his mother," Benjamin later told his niece. "But I decided to let Karl take his picture of her to the grave. I hoped she wouldn't mind."

CHAPTER TEN

WHEN ELLIOTT HEARD Alissa turn on the shower, he filled a large stainless steel pot with water, put it on the stove and returned to the table to wait for the water to come to a boil. It would take a few minutes, but he was in no hurry. His granddaughter liked to take long showers, often standing in the old bathtub until the hot water ran out.

He pulled out a chair and picked up the manuscript from Ms. Crighton – Harrigan and his regiment were marching back down the Mississippi, where for the next seven months, Baton Rouge would serve as their base of operations while they paraded up and down the river, searching for bands of rogue Confederates. Their only significant action took place in April, when they were sent up the Red River and engaged the rebels at Monette's Ferry, and after returning to Baton Rouge, they resumed their patrols along the Mississippi. It was hard duty, chasing the enemy through the lowland swamps, but Harrigan and the other men accepted it without complaint and performed it to the best of their abilities.

Early that summer, they learned they were being called up to Virginia, and on July 20, 1864, they boarded a steamship named the *Daniel Webster* and started down the river. Harrigan was as relieved to be leaving the deep South as he was anxious to be heading north and that much closer to home. He and Karl had arrived in Louisiana as raw enlistees, anxiously anticipating their first taste of battle. He was leaving a weary foot soldier, who had witnessed the cruel attrition of war.

"As we passed through the mouth of the Mississippi, we swore we would never forget the men we were leaving behind."

After a nine-day journey up the Eastern Seaboard, they arrived in Chesapeake Bay, aware that only two weeks earlier, the Confederates had brazenly crossed the Potomac River into Maryland, advancing as far as the outskirts of the nation's capital before retreating into the Shenandoah Valley in northern Virginia. The 128th's orders were to join the nearly forty thousand men under the command of General Phillip Sheridan, who had been instructed to put an end to the Confederacy's use of the Shenandoah as a corridor through which they could raid the north and then to lay the valley to waste so the bounty of its rich farmland could no longer be used to sustain the rebel forces.

The Confederates had dug in outside Winchester in the northern valley, a small town on the banks of Abrams Creek as it tumbled through the low-lying hills and the stands of ash, red oak and maples, surrounded by neatly fenced pasture and apple orchards, fields of wheat and corn. At the convergence of several roads, turnpikes and a rail line, the town had already been fought over twice, both bloody Confederate victories, its strategic location vital to control of the valley. When Harrigan and his regiment arrived at Harper's Ferry on the Potomac, they promptly marched south to join Sheridan's forces at their sprawling encampments to the east of Winchester, and for the next five weeks, they engaged the Confederates in almost daily skirmishes, the rebels eventually pulling back behind a defensive perimeter of stone walls and wood rail fences, barricades and trenches.

"Our casualties were few, and little ground was won or lost. But we all knew a major battle lay ahead."

On September 19, Harrigan and his regiment struck their tents in the dead of night and began marching south on the Berryville Pike, quietly passing the shadowed silos and creaking windmills, the great white barns rising up into the moonlight. It was nearly noon before they formed their battle lines at the edge of an open field east of Winchester, and when the signal gun fired, they surged forward, a long undulating wave of blue washing across the valley floor. But the Confederates were waiting for them in a stand of hardwoods, holding their fire until the Union troops were less than one hundred yards away before they fired in unison, a thunderous volley of grapeshot and minie balls. Scores of men fell, slain or seriously injured. Through the haze of smoke, Harrigan could see the Confederates bursting out of the woods, yelling at the tops of their lungs. He dropped to a knee and fired, then turned and fled, running as low to the ground as he could, his rifle in his right hand as he hurdled the bodies of the fallen, the mutilated torsos of his fellow infantrymen.

Finally, he reached a small rise at the edge of the field, where a group of men had stopped and regrouped. He knelt down beside them and reloaded his rifle and fired at the Confederates rushing toward them, and in the furious chaos of battle, they managed to hold their ground until a division of men arrived in support. Reforming their lines, they charged back across the field, this time driving the Confederates back through the woods in which they had initially waited for them, firing on the rebels as they retreated toward Winchester.

As they approached the outskirts of town, they could hear the roar of gunfire and the heavy concussions of the artillery across the valley, and then they could see the Confederates collapsing to the south. With a loud cheer, they charged the rebels positioned behind the stone walls and barricades erected outside the town, but as Harrigan leapt over one of the walls, his left foot landed on a loose rock and rolled out from beneath him. He struggled to his feet, barely able to stand on his twisted ankle. Leaning against the wall, he reached down to help a man pushing up onto his hands and knees at the base of the wall. It was only as the man collapsed that Harrigan saw he had been shot in the face and had lost his lower jaw. He knelt back down beside him, his arm across the man's back as he drew his last breaths, choking on the blood pouring from his throat.

He pulled himself back up and started limping toward Winchester, trailing the battle through the outlying farms, through the bodies, blue and gray, lying along the narrow lanes through the pasture and orchards. By the time he made it into town, nearly an hour later, the last of the Confederates had fled, retreating up the Valley Pike. He walked past the hastily abandoned, red brick storefronts, through the exhausted infantrymen wandering in from the mayhem, the streets filled with teams of terrified horses pulling wagons loaded with the wounded and dying. Corpsmen were frantically lifting the wounded from the wagons and carrying them into a general mercantile pressed into service as a hospital. The dead lay in grotesque contortions beneath the merchandise on display in the front window.

Across the street, an old two-story hotel was burning, flames leaping up into the billowing black smoke. Harrigan flinched, instinctively raising his arm as one of the windows exploded from the heat. In front of the telegraph office, two young soldiers were slumped back against the wall, brothers, perhaps, with their matted red hair. As Harrigan stepped over their outstretched legs, he saw that the larger of the pair had lost his left eye, dangling by its cord on his soot-caked cheek. The other boy was unconscious, blood dripping from his ears onto the shoulders of his uniform. He thought for a moment about stopping, as if he might be able to help them, but he knew there was nothing he could do, and so he walked on, wanting to find his regiment before nightfall.

"The battle had been won. The rebels had been driven back in defeat," he later told his niece. "But to a man, we couldn't help but wonder if it was worth the price we'd paid."

ELLIOTT TOOK the box of ravioli out of the refrigerator and then emptied the pint of sauce into a copper-bottomed saucepan and set it on the stove to warm up. When he heard Alissa turn off the shower, he lowered the ravioli into the boiling water and then waited for them to float to the surface. He was scooping them into a serving dish as Alissa appeared, standing in the kitchen doorway in her robe, a towel wrapped around her neck, her green hair tousled and damp. He wondered how long it had been since his granddaughter last brushed her hair. He wondered if she even owned a hair brush anymore.

She leaned down and dug her fingers into the back of Hank's neck, then sat at the table, stifling a yawn, her eyes still swollen with sleep.

"What are you making?" she asked.

He carried the serving dish over to the table and spooned the ravioli onto her plate.

"I dropped by Molinari's this afternoon," he told her.

She stared down at her plate as if she'd never seen ravioli before.

"I thought you liked ravioli," he said. "You used to."

He dished himself a similar portion and sat down across from her.

"Don't forget the parmesan," he said.

He watched her spoon a little of the cheese onto her ravioli, then reached for the bowl when she finished.

"So how did you sleep?"

She looked across the table to him as if puzzled by his interest.

"You must be exhausted," he said. "You didn't get in until four in the morning."

"You're keeping track?"

"Of course not," he said. "But I couldn't help but hear you come in."

"I was out with Nigel and Jeremy," she said.

"Celebrating after your performance at the Anarchists Club, I assume."

She looked up, as if wondering what he was getting at, then stabbed one of the ravioli with her fork and raised it to her mouth.

"I thought you were very impressive," he said.

She stopped and squinted at him, her eyes flattened into slits.

"What?"

"I was there," he said. "I caught your performance last night, at least part of it."

"You were there last night?" she asked, as if to be sure she'd heard him correctly.

"I was, indeed."

"Why didn't you tell me?" she demanded. "Why didn't you tell me you were coming?"

"Did I need your permission?"

"I had no idea!"

"I'm your grandfather," he calmly reminded her. "And as your grandfather, I have the right to show up in your life from time to time to see how you're doing."

He pointed at her plate with his fork.

"Now keep eating, before the ravioli get cold," he said.

She stared at him, still in disbelief.

"Like I said, I thought you were very impressive," he said.

"And what is that supposed to mean?"

"I've never seen anyone play the drums with such intensity. You were quite something."

"You liked us?"

Elliott shrugged, trying to suppress a smile.

"Now, I didn't say that," he said. "But you were giving it everything you had, and that's all that really matters."

She stared at him, entirely uninterested in his tired bromide, and that was fine. He expected no less as she stabbed another ravioli.

"They're not bad, are they?" he said.

"Just let me know the next time you come to see us, all right?"

"Of course," he said. "But to be perfectly honest, I'm not sure there will be a next time."

"Ever?"

"I wouldn't say never," he said. "But I saw what I needed to see."

He watched as she nibbled the ravioli.

"Maybe one of these days you'll let me take you to the symphony."

"You can't be serious."

"I am, absolutely," he said. "You might like it."

"Ha," she said, dismissing the thought as if it were absurd.

"Well, if you change your mind, just let me know."

"Not a chance."

WHILE ELLIOTT CLEANED UP the kitchen, Alissa got ready to go out for the night. He had no idea what she and Nigel and Jeremy were going to do, and he didn't necessarily want to know. All that mattered was that they weren't going to be practicing in the garage, and for that he was grateful. After the ordeal of The Sores' performance last night, he needed a quiet evening, even if that meant he wouldn't have any idea where Alissa was, much less when she might return.

He was scrubbing the large pot when she returned to the kitchen in her black leather jacket and torn blue jeans, her black high-top sneakers. As always, her eyes were crudely defined with thick lines of mascara, her eyelids green with eye shadow.

"You can leave that," she said. "I'll wash it out when I get home."

Elliott appreciated the thought, knowing the offer was genuine. But he also knew it would expire the instant she walked out the door.

"I'm nearly finished," he said.

"I don't mind."

And he knew she meant that, too.

"I'll tell you what you could do for me," he said.

"What?" she asked warily.

"You could call your mother."

Her mouth wrinkled as if she wanted to spit the thought out.

"Not now, not tonight, maybe tomorrow," he said. "Whenever you can."

"Did she call you today?"

"She did," he admitted.

"What did she want?"

"She's worried about you, that's all."

He expected her to turn away and walk out of the flat. Instead, she lowered herself to a knee and scratched Hank beneath his chin.

"I don't know what she's so worried about," she said.

"Mothers just worry," he said. "They can't help it."

She looked up at him.

"Are you worried about me?"

He wasn't entirely sure how to respond. He decided to concede the obvious.

"Sure, a little," he said. "It's a dangerous world out there."

A laugh escaped her. She kissed Hank on the top of the head, then rose to stand in the doorway.

"I'll see you later," she said.

"Just promise me you'll be careful."

But that was too much, too far.

"Don't be an idiot," she said.

He listened to her walk down the stairs and let herself out of the flat, the steel grate clanging shut behind her. Of course he was worried about her. But he was not as worried about Alissa as he had been. He'd taken a risk in going to see her perform at the Anarchists Club, but it had worked out as well as he could have hoped. He'd seen her in her element, and, honestly, it was not as worrisome as he'd feared.

AFTER PUTTING AWAY the pots, Elliott picked up the manuscript and carried it into the living room. He sat in the club chair and thumbed back to Harrigan as he fell in with his regiment, his ankle wrapped tightly inside his unlaced boot as they drove the Confederates south, pursuing them up the valley for more than twenty miles, back through Middleton and across Cedar Creek. It was after overwhelming the rebels at Fisher's Hill that Sheridan ordered his cavalry to pivot around and sweep back down the valley – burning mills and factories, tearing up railroad tracks and destroying bridges, slaughtering livestock and poisoning wells. And he ordered the 128th and several other regiments to accompany his cavalry, to head north from Harrisonburg and torch virtually everything in their path.

Harrigan and several other men were appalled by the order. They wanted nothing to do with burning farms, the sons of farmers themselves.

"This was not war. This was not what we signed up for. We were soldiers, not arsonists. But those were our orders, and we had no choice but to carry them out."

And so they started down the Valley Pike, setting the fields of wheat and corn on fire and then watching as the long rows of flames spread out across the valley floor, torching every barn, silo, and outbuilding they came upon and then standing back and waiting until the structures were fully engulfed in flames before moving on. Their orders were to spare the private homes, but many burned down anyway, ignited by the sparks and embers swept up by the fires' own winds and blown across the valley, the residents fleeing north down the pike with only what they could quickly load into their wagons, the old, the infirm and the very young, an exodus of refugees from the firestorm.

Slowly, Harrigan and his regiment proceeded north, the dense smoke blacking out the sun, the intense heat scorching their eyes and scalding their throats, heavy flakes of ash drifting down as they passed through Harrison's Cave, Lacey Spring, Sparta. Just outside Tenth Legion, they came upon a small farm owned by a woman named Miller. They piled dry straw against the back wall of her barn and then doused the straw with oil. As they set the pile on fire, she burst out of the house, screaming that her son was inside the barn.

While several men held her back, Harrigan hobbled over to the open barn door, flames already climbing the dry plank walls, thick black smoke streaming from the sharply pitched roof. The boy was sitting on the ground in one of the milking stalls, his arms wrapped around a small black terrier. Harrigan shouted for the boy to come out. When he didn't move, Harrigan ducked beneath the burning beams and started into the barn to get him. But as he approached the long row of stalls, the floor of the hayloft slumped, flaming hay pouring down from above. As the rear wall began to collapse, he spun around and dove back through the curtain of fire, brushing the burning embers from his face and hair as he rolled across the ground. Quickly, the entire structure was ablaze, the flames lunging up into the sky, a great burst of sparks as the roof crashed down.

As Harrigan turned and walked away, he could hear the woman's tortured cries rising above the raging fire.

"I hated General Sheridan for ordering us to burn those farms. And I hated myself for carrying those orders out."

The campaign of terror lasted thirteen days, an eternity for Harrigan as he trudged through the inferno's smouldering remains.

As the 128th camped on the north bank of Cedar Creek, he knew he would never forget the crimes he had been compelled to commit, the incinerated hellscape they left behind. He wondered if he would ever be able to wash the ash from the pores of his skin, the acrid stench of smoke from his hair.

On October 19, he rose before dawn, preparing to go on a routine patrol. The morning was cold and damp, the fog dripping from the white pines and the leaves of the oaks. He pulled on his coat, gingerly sliding his left foot into his boot, the ankle still swollen and wrapped with cloth. Suddenly, he heard gunshots – and then the rebels yelling as they rushed up from the creek, emerging from the fog and charging through their camp, swinging their rifles like clubs, bayonetting men scrambling to their feet.

Harrigan dove out of the way of a huge white horse galloping toward him, scattering fires and collapsing tents, the rider firing at the men fleeing into the woods. When the horse staggered, blood pouring from a bullet wound in its chest, the rider leapt from his saddle. Harrigan raised his rifle to strike him with the stock, but the rider turned in time to deflect the blow with his forearm. He tackled Harrigan around the waist, and they rolled across the ground, through one of the fires before Harrigan managed to slip his arm around the rider's neck. He pulled back as hard as he could, crushing his windpipe. The rider struggled to break free, reaching up and trying to pull Harrigan's arm away, but Harrigan held on as the rider's legs kicked out wildly, his eyes bulging as Harrigan pulled back harder, holding on for as long as he could, long after the rider went limp.

Watching for any sign that the rider might still be alive, Harrigan slowly rose to his feet.

"I never saw the rebel running up behind me, not until it was too late. I raised my arm, but the butt of his rifle caught me above my left eye, and I went down."

HARRIGAN WAS ONE of eighty-two men from the 128th captured at Cedar Creek. As the Union forces retreated to the north, he and the other prisoners were ordered to march south, proceeding up the road in a column two men abreast, prodded constantly with their captors' rifle butts. They marched through the afternoon and into the night. Exhausted and faint from hunger, they finally arrived at the town of Staunton, where they were given a handful of crackers to eat, their first food since they were captured. After a brief rest, they were taken to the train depot and loaded into stock cars, packed in so closely they had to stand. As the train pulled out of the station and began to pick up speed, hay dust swirled through the cars, so thick they could barely breathe.

They arrived in Richmond on the afternoon of October 21 and were paraded through the city to a prison occupying a three-story brick warehouse, formerly the headquarters of a shipping supply company called Libby and Sons. The prison's commanding officer told them negotiations were underway for them to be exchanged for Confederate prisoners. But as the days passed, they realized the prospect of their being exchanged was steadily diminishing, and on November 3, they were once again taken to the rail depot and forced into stock cars. The train left that evening and headed south. They arrived in Salisbury, North Carolina, the following afternoon.

In a drizzling rain, they were marched to a prison that had been established in a former cotton mill.

"As we passed through the main gate, we lost any hope that conditions at Salisbury would be better than at Libby."

The four-story brick mill building loomed above the prison yard, sixteen acres surrounded by a wooden stockade. Armed guards walked along a platform constructed a few feet below the top of the walls, the barrels of their rifles resting against their shoulders. Several feet inside the walls, a narrow trench called the dead line had been dug, and the guards were under a standing order to shoot any prisoner who crossed it. More than ten thousand men had been crowded into the prison, most of the prisoners held in cramped unsanitary quarters inside the mill. Hundreds more huddled in tents staked in the prison yard. Others were left with nothing more than a blanket to wrap around their shoulders as they squatted on the muddy ground.

Harrigan and several other men from his regiment, including three from Company H, managed to obtain a sheet of canvas that they were able to fashion into an open tent capable of sheltering them from the rain. Their only source of heat was the wood brought back every day by a squad of prisoners sent under heavy guard into the nearby forest, and they burned it at night in a shallow pit carved into the ground, edging as close to the flames as they could, seeking its furtive heat to warm their hands and feet. Their daily allotment of food consisted of cornbread containing pieces of husk and cob and a half-pint of watery soup made with rice or beans.

"The only meat we received was said to have been discarded by the slaughterhouse. It compared unfavorably with the rats we caught."

Shortly after arriving at Salisbury, Harrigan fell ill, his initial bouts of vomiting eventually yielding to bloody diarrhea. He rapidly lost weight, his bones surfacing from beneath his skin. He feared he'd been stricken with scurvy or cholera or dysentery, but he refused to be carried into the mill with the other sick prisoners and left to die on the hard plank floors, slowly devoured by lice and maggots. He had seen the bodies of the dead as they were carried out of the mill every morning and stacked like cord wood beside the former mill office, waiting to be delivered to the mass graves.

In mid-November, word reached the prison that President Lincoln had been re-elected. But the excitement generated by the election dissipated several days later when the guards discovered a tunnel that a group of prisoners had been digging for weeks, laboring only at night, discretely scattering the red clay excavated from the tunnel across the dark mud of the yard. The tunnel had nearly reached the prison wall when the guards found it, and when Harrigan and the other men learned that one of their fellow prisoners had told the guards about the tunnel, hoping the information he provided would alleviate his misery, their morale sank even lower.

Not long after the tunnel was discovered, Harrigan heard talk of a prison revolt, a plan to overwhelm the guards during a change of shifts inside the mill. The ill-conceived plan had virtually no prospect of succeeding, but on November 25, a group of prisoners caught fifteen guards by surprise, seizing their rifles and killing nearly all of them. They rushed the gate, intending to break into the arsenal, where they expected to find sufficient weaponry and ammunition to defeat the garrison guarding the prison. But the insurrection collapsed as quickly as it had begun. Only a handful of prisoners made it through the gate before they were shot to death by the other guards, who then turned their rifles on those prisoners who had joined the uprising at the gate. In the aftermath, dozens of prisoners lay dead in the yard, and scores more lay grievously wounded. Later that afternoon, a pair of doctors entered the yard and without ether or chloroform began amputating the arms and legs of the wounded. Their cries could be heard in every corner of the prison.

As winter arrived, Harrigan watched the men without shelter try to ward off the cold by walking through the night, shuffling across the yard, leaning into the wind. Those who stopped and fell asleep often woke to find themselves unable to rise, their clothes and blankets frozen to the icy ground. Still others didn't rise at all. Every morning, the prisoners searched the yard for those who had perished overnight, then stripped off their clothes and boots and sold them to other prisoners. The corpses were then gathered up and slung upon the bodies of the men who had died that night inside the mill, where they remained until the prison gate opened and a wagon was brought in to haul them away. Dozens of men died every day, including two of the men Harrigan huddled with under the sheet of canvas, expiring in their sleep of causes unknown.

For Harrigan, each day was a struggle simply to survive. His arms and legs were covered with ulcerating sores. He could barely walk, even with a cane fashioned from a tree branch brought back by the firewood squad. Many of his teeth had come loose, so he tried not to talk, reserving the use of his mouth for what little food he received. He was unable to sleep for more than a few hours at a time. Between the lack of sustenance and the deprivation of sleep, he drifted in and out of consciousness.

"I could see myself in the faces of the other men. I could see we were all dying."

But then one morning in January, Harrigan and the others heard bloodhounds baying outside the stockade walls, and they quickly realized the dogs had picked up the scent of escaped prisoners. More than one hundred men had managed to tunnel their way out of the prison and then had concealed the tunnel's exit so carefully that it wasn't discovered until the guards took the hounds on their daily rounds. Four days passed before the first of the prisoners were caught and returned to the prison. They explained that they had split into small groups after climbing out of the tunnel and then set off in different directions, hoping the trackers wouldn't be able to pick up all of their trails. With each passing day, the prisoners' hopes rose that at least some of the men might make it back to the Union lines and tell the world about the conditions they were forced to endure.

In early February, Harrigan and the other men began to hear rumors that they would soon be released. But Harrigan had heard such rumors before and refused to believe them. So drawn and wasted he could barely sit up, the tremors in his hands so severe he couldn't lift a cup of water to his lips, he refused to let himself indulge even the faintest hope that their ordeal might be coming to an end. It required all his will to simply get through each day, to resist the delirium and despair that threatened to overcome him.

“I believed my hour was nigh,” he told his niece.

But the day they had all been praying for finally arrived on February 22, 1865. Initially, Harrigan refused to believe it, but late that afternoon, his arms across the shoulders of two men from Company H, his shrunken frame weighing only slightly more than one hundred pounds, Harrigan summoned the strength to walk through the prison gate, bound for Greensborough, North Carolina, where they would board the trains that would take them home.

Of the eighty-two men from the 128th who had been taken prisoner during the battle at Cedar Creek, twenty-five died during the five months they were held in Salisbury prison.

“By the grace of God, I was one of the fortunate who managed to make it home.”

As Elliott lifted his eyes from the manuscript, he could understand why Ms. Crighton wanted to learn more about her great-grandmother’s uncle, why she wanted to track down every last source of information about him. Harrigan was clearly a good and decent man caught up in the horror and insanity of war.

And yet, Elliott still didn’t know why she was flying out from New York tomorrow. And he still couldn’t believe he had agreed to meet with her. He had nothing to tell her, and now he feared that she was going to be gravely disappointed. He realized that he should have simply declined, for her benefit as much as his. He should have found a way to tell her that he was unavailable. But it was far too late for that now.

CHAPTER ELEVEN

ELLIOTT TURNED into the parking lot at Crissy Field, his blue-and-white BMW sedan jostling across the tufted grass. With its sunroof and black leather interior, the BMW was the finest car he had ever owned, a gift from his wife on the occasion of his fiftieth birthday, now nearly thirty years ago. And while he rarely drove the car anymore, now that he was no longer driving to the *Chronicle* office at Fifth and Mission every day, he nonetheless maintained the vehicle in excellent condition, taking it into the shop for regular tune-ups and to the car wash for an annual wax job, caring for the BMW as if to remind himself of better days.

In the back seat, Hank dashed back and forth, leaping from window to window, yipping sharply in anticipation of a walk along the shore of the bay. Elliott shut down the engine and climbed out of the car. As he opened the back door, Hank leapt out and immediately began running in wild circles on the grass. Elliott watched him for a moment, then locked the car and started over to the broad promenade.

"Come on, Hank," he said, slapping his thigh.

It was another uncommonly warm afternoon as they started down the sandy walk along the shoreline. White-headed western gulls glided through the still air, sweeping down at the waves crashing onto the beach. Sunlight glinted off the silvery surface of the tidal lagoon. With Hank trotting ahead, they crossed the bridge over the creek running down into the surf, and when they reached the small grove of pines amid the dunes, they left the promenade and walked down to the shore. The instant Hank saw the other dogs chasing lime green tennis balls flung into the waves by their owners, he bolted ahead, racing across the sand to join them. He loved plunging into the frigid water and then running back and forth across the beach, tumbling across the sand and then shaking himself off, barking in delirious celebration of the day. His joy was such that Elliott tried to bring him here at least once a week.

He found a place to sit beneath the pines, all too aware that Ms. Crighton's plane was due to land in less than two hours. But he was prepared to meet with her, as prepared, at least, as he was going to be. He had enjoyed reading about Harrigan's experiences during the Civil War, more than he had anticipated, frankly. Although he had no evidence to confirm that Harrigan had worked on their ranch, it was also true that he had no evidence to dispute Ms. Crighton's belief that he had. He vowed to meet her with an open mind. He would answer her questions to the extent that he could, and then he would wish Ms. Crighton good luck and tell her goodbye.

HE LET HANK RUN for nearly an hour before he whistled and called the dog's name. Hank wearily trotted back up the beach, and they returned to the parking lot, where Elliott opened the back door of the BMW, so Hank could leap up onto the seat. As Elliott slipped behind the wheel and inserted his key in the ignition, he could hear the dog quietly panting behind him. He didn't have to look to know that Hank was grinning maniacally, his long pink tongue hanging out the side of his mouth.

He drove back to Russian Hill, easing the car into the garage, parking across from Alissa and her bandmates' instruments. He let Hank out of the car, and they walked up the stairs and then along the side of the building. After giving Hank a moment to relieve himself in the yard, they climbed the stairs to the porch. As Elliott entered the kitchen, he could smell the clove cigarette Alissa had been smoking, and then he saw the butt she had stubbed out on a small plate on the table.

He picked up the plate and dumped the ashes and butt into the trash, then made himself a cup of coffee. As he sat at the table, he could hear Alissa walking down the hall. Through the doorway, he watched her lean down and scoop Hank into her arms. She buried her face in the soft hair on his belly, then set him down and joined Elliott at the table.

"Did you have a good time at the beach?" she asked.

"Hank always has a good time at the beach," Elliott said.

"I was asking about you."

"I enjoyed it, too," he said. "It's a good place to think."

"What were you thinking about?"

He started to tell her about Harrigan, about the manuscript Ms. Crighton had sent him, but he knew Alissa couldn't care less about Harrigan and his experiences during the Civil War. His granddaughter had no interest in history, despite his best efforts to pique her curiosity about her own heritage. She was no more interested in the past than she was in the future. She existed exclusively in the moment.

Still, he needed to tell her about his immediate plans.

"I'm meeting a woman at the Washington Square Inn this evening," he said.

Alissa looked across the table, arching her right eyebrow.

"She believes one of her relatives may have worked on our ranch in Anderson Valley."

"Is that true?"

"I have no idea," Elliott said.

"Then why are you meeting her?"

"She's flying out from New York City."

"To meet with you?"

"No, of course not," he protested, though, of course, he had no idea why she was flying out from New York City other than to meet with him.

"Who is she?"

And that really was the question. He knew nothing about Ms. Crighton, nothing but her name, if that really was her name, if that's who she really was.

"I really don't know," he said.

"This sounds weird," Alissa said.

She was right, of course – it was weird. But he had made a commitment, and he intended to honor it.

"I'm going to get ready," he said.

AFTER TAKING A SHOWER, Elliott dressed in his bedroom, putting on a pair of dark gray trousers, a light gray, long-sleeve shirt, and his olive green sweater vest. He examined himself in the full-length mirror mounted on the closet door, adjusting the collar of his shirt as it emerged from the neck of the vest, reaching up and smoothing his thin white hair across his mottled scalp. It amused him to observe that he bore an uncanny resemblance to the former city editor at the *San Francisco Chronicle*. And yet in the lines that radiated from the corners of his eyes and the creases that curled around his mouth, he could see the fifteen years that had passed since he walked out of the newsroom. He found it hard to believe how swiftly the time had passed, and, for the briefest moment, he couldn't help but wonder how many years remained to him.

He sat on the foot of the bed and laced his black wingtips, then stood up and grabbed his corduroy coat and walked out of the room. As he entered the kitchen, he looked up at the clock above the door and saw that it was shortly after seven o'clock. Ms. Crighton's plane would have landed more than two hours ago. She would have taken a cab into the city. Surely, she had checked in at the Washington Square Inn by now. And when the phone on the hutch rang, he knew it had to be her.

"Hello?"

"Elliott?"

"This is Elliott Madison."

"It's Phoebe!"

"Hello, Ms. Crighton."

"I'm here in San Francisco! I'm here at the Washington Square Inn!"

"Congratulations," he said.

"It's very nice, very quaint," she said, her voice falling to a hush, as if letting him in on a secret.

"I'm glad you like it," he said.

"Am I interrupting anything?"

Elliott could have laughed – other than his life, no.

"Not at all," he said.

"I'm so anxious to meet you."

"I thought we might go out for a cup of coffee."

"I would love a cup of coffee, but only if it's no bother," she said.

"What time would you like me to come by?"

"Any time, Elliott. I'm here. I'm ready to go."

"I'll be there shortly," he said.

"Wonderful!"

IN THE FALLING DARKNESS, Elliott made his way down Union Street to Washington Square. He walked along the asphalt path that circled the grass, past the old men nursing half-pints of brandy on the benches beneath the pines, nodding discretely at a woman in a long red coat walking her white standard poodle. The inn was across from the northeast corner of the square, and Elliott knew it to be a respectable establishment. The two-story building with bay windows on the upper floor had been painted a warm brick red, the shutters on the lower windows white above the geraniums in the planter boxes. Elliott paused for a moment at the corner, taking a deep breath as if to compose himself, then he stepped down from the curb and crossed the street.

Supported by two polished brass poles, a blue canvas canopy extended from the front door to the curb. Elliott walked up to the door and reached down to let himself in. Discovering the door was locked, he pressed the button on the wall. A moment later, the door buzzed open, and he stepped into the lobby, filled with antique chairs and tables and a long leather sofa arranged in front of the fireplace.

He crossed the hardwood floor to the desk in the back. The desk clerk was short and squat, his eyes set slightly too close together beneath the single eyebrow that ran across his brow, a pair of reading glasses in the pocket of a gaudy floral print shirt featuring yellow roses against a blue sky.

"Greetings," he said brightly. "How may I help you?"

"I'm calling on Ms. Phoebe Crighton. Could you let her know that Elliott Madison is here?"

"With pleasure," he said, gesturing back to the lobby. "Please, make yourself at home."

Elliott walked over to a high-backed chair in one of the front windows. As he sat down, he looked out at the night descending on the square and wondered how much longer these warm windless evenings would last. He had to believe that it wouldn't be long before the autumn rains arrived, and, honestly, that didn't bother him. He didn't mind the leaden skies and misting rain, the chill in the wind. Of all the seasons, he had come to favor winter. He didn't know when he had come to feel that way, much less why, but winter felt like his natural element now, and he looked forward to its onset.

In a reflection on the glass, he saw a woman descending the staircase behind him.

"Elliott?"

He pushed up from the chair. Standing at the foot of the stairs was a slender woman with long wavy black hair, pale blue eyes behind her silver wire-rim glasses. Her pleated black slacks hung from her narrow waist. A burgundy sweater was draped over her shoulders with the arms casually tied across her light blue blouse. As she crossed the lobby to him, she smiled, her hand extended.

"It's so nice to meet you," she said.

"The pleasure is mine," Elliott said, taking her hand. "Shall we get a cup of coffee?"

"Absolutely," she said.

"I thought we might go to Mario's – Mario's Bohemian Cigar Store, actually. It's a small cafe just across the square."

"Take me anywhere," she said. "Take me anywhere you'd like to go."

Elliott opened the door and then stood to the side to allow Ms. Crighton to step out onto the sidewalk. They started down the block, walking past the post office and the Italian Club, then crossed Union and made their way past Fior d'Italia to the cafe at the corner. As he opened the door and followed her inside, he saw that all the stools along the long wooden bar were occupied, the patrons sipping lattes and nursing bottles of imported Italian beer. But he spotted an empty table in the back and ushered Ms. Crighton past the tables arranged along the yellow wall, beneath the windows looking out upon the square.

He pulled out a chair for Ms. Crighton and then helped her scoot it closer to the table. After taking off his coat, he sat down across from her.

"Oh, I love it, Elliott. Bohemian, indeed."

She closed her eyes and sat back in her chair, taking a deep breath, inhaling the rich aroma of freshly ground coffee beans, focaccia sandwiches heating in the oven. She opened her eyes slowly, as if emerging from a trance.

"Do you come here often?"

"I do," he said. "I've been coming here for years."

He raised his hand to attract the attention of the waitress behind the bar.

"Good evening, Mr. Madison."

"Hello, Melanie."

"What can I get for you?"

He looked across the table to Ms. Crighton.

"May I recommend a cappuccino?"

"That sounds wonderful," she said.

"I'll have one, too," he said.

Elliott watched Melanie walk back to the espresso machine at the end of the bar, then he looked to Ms. Crighton.

"So how was your flight?" he asked.

"Oh, I hate to fly," she said, as if confiding in him.

"It's a long flight from New York," he sympathized.

"I can never sleep on airplanes," she said. "I don't know why."

"Well, you made it here," he said. "That's all that matters."

As Elliott looked across the table to Ms. Crighton, it occurred to him that she didn't look at all like what he'd expected. On the other hand, he hadn't known what to expect. It was difficult to determine how old she was. She was younger than he was, certainly. She looked to be in her late fifties, perhaps even her early sixties, but that was only a guess.

"Lila told me you were a journalist," she said.

Elliott smiled through his teeth. He didn't appreciate Lila discussing his professional life any more than he appreciated her giving out his address and phone number.

"Yes, that's true," he said.

"She said you were an editor."

"I worked at the *Chronicle* for many years, more than I would care to admit," he said.

Ms. Crighton smiled.

"She also told me you could be a little persnickety. But she told me not to take it personally."

"How kind of her," he said.

She reached across the table and patted the back of his right hand.

"Oh, Elliott – Lila adores you. She just thinks you can be a little fussy."

Elliott did not care for the characterization, even if he knew it to be largely true. He was serious. He took his work seriously. And he made no apology for it. But he did not particularly want to talk about himself, not with a woman he'd never even met until a few moments ago.

He leaned back as Melanie brought their cappuccinos, setting them down on the table.

"They look divine," Ms. Crighton said.

Elliott watched as Ms. Crighton picked up the powdered chocolate and sprinkled it onto her cappuccino, tapping the bottom of the container not once but twice, then once more before she raised the cup to her mouth and took a sip, leaving a thin line of foam above her upper lip.

"So tell me why you decided to come to San Francisco, Ms. Crighton."

"I'm just trying to learn what I can about my great-grandmother's uncle," she said. "Lila told me that Benjamin worked on your great-grandparents' ranch. She told me your great-grandmother was still alive when you were a boy, and I thought maybe if I flew out here, you might tell me about her and the ranch."

"Yes, I spent seven weeks at the ranch one summer," he said.

"What was she like?"

Elliott had to resist a smile. He appreciated Ms. Crighton's interest in his great-grandmother, but she could hardly be described in a simple sentence or two.

"I was very young," he said.

"You must have memories. They must be very special."

"Honestly, Ms. Crighton, I'm not sure I understand what you're looking for."

She shrugged.

"I'm not so sure, either," she said.

"I don't mean to disappoint you," Elliott said. "But I don't know anything about your great-grandmother's uncle. He may very well have worked on our ranch, but as I've said, I've never even heard his name. I'm afraid I really don't have anything to tell you. I'm afraid you may have come all this way for nothing."

"Don't be silly, Elliott. It's San Francisco. I love it already!"

MS. CRIGHTON DECIDED she wanted dessert, despite freely admitting that she hadn't had any dinner. Elliott asked if she'd like to see a menu, but she asked instead for his recommendation. He suggested the tiramisu, and when she told him she loved tiramisu, he raised his hand to attract Melanie's attention. She asked if they wanted one fork or two. One, he told her without hesitation.

As Melanie turned away, Ms. Crighton leaned forward, as if to whisper to him.

"So, did you read the manuscript I sent you?" she asked.

"I did, yes," Elliott said.

"Isn't it fascinating?"

That might have been a little further than Elliott would have gone, but he was not going to quibble.

"I read every word," he said.

She reached for her black handbag, hanging by its strap over the back of her chair.

"I want to show you something," she said.

He watched as she dug through her bag, eventually producing a sheet of paper folded in quarters. She spread it out on the table, turning it around so he could see – a xeroxed copy of a photograph of a uniformed Union soldier.

"Harrigan?" he asked as if to be sure.

"Yes."

The image was faint and worn, the thick stock the original had been mounted upon fraying at the edges, the dark stain of a paper clip angling across the upper right-hand corner. But it was a serviceable image, nonetheless. Harrigan's jacket was buttoned tightly to the stunted collar, his cap snug as he stood ramrod straight before the gray canvas backdrop. His eyes were dark beneath the brief bill of his cap, his face thin with hollow cheeks.

"I found it in one of the boxes in storage," she said.

"It's a very fine photograph," Elliott said.

"Isn't he handsome?"

"He's a fine-looking young man."

"It was taken in New Orleans in 1863," she said. "The stamp on the back says it was taken by a photographer named William Leesom. He had a studio on Canal Street."

She picked it up. Her face seemed to soften as she looked at the image of her great-grandmother's long-deceased uncle.

"The original is as thick as a postcard, maybe even thicker," she said.

"It's called a carte de visite," Elliott told her. "They were very popular during that time period."

"It's the only photograph I have of him."

"You should be glad you have a photograph of him at all."

"I'd love to see a photograph of him when he was older," she said. "I'd love to see a photograph of him out here, when he worked for your great-grandmother."

Elliott leaned back in his chair as Melanie arrived with Ms. Crighton's tiramisu, placing it on the table in front of her – along with two forks.

"In case you change your mind," she said.

He watched as Ms. Crighton picked up her fork and cut off a corner of the tiramisu, then raised it to her mouth. She closed her eyes and emitted a soft moan, her shoulders slumping as she dissolved into a state of bliss.

Elliott looked up at Melanie.

"I think we're good," he told her.

Ms. Crighton opened her eyes.

"It's absolutely exquisite," she said.

As Melanie walked away, Ms. Crighton took another bite of the tiramisu.

"So do you know when Mr. Harrigan is supposed to have worked on our ranch?" Elliott asked.

She picked up a paper napkin and wiped the corners of her mouth.

"After the war, Benjamin returned to East Fishkill. He spent almost two years there, recuperating. I don't know the exact date, but he left for California in April 1867. My great-grandmother was heartbroken. She absolutely adored him. He promised to come back, but I don't believe she ever saw him again."

She pushed the tiramisu toward him.

"Are you sure you won't have a bite?" she asked.

He raised his hand to decline.

"I'll never finish it," she said.

"Thanks, but I'm fine," Elliott said.

Ms. Crighton shrugged as if he'd disappointed her, then drew the plate back.

"Do you know how Harrigan got to California?" Elliott asked.

"He booked passage to Panama on a steamship called the *Dakota*. It stopped in Baltimore and New Orleans before it arrived in Aspinall, where he bought a train ticket to Panama City. But he caught malaria there and spent six weeks in bed. When he recovered, he boarded a clipper ship called the *Antonia*, only they ran into a terrible storm off the coast of Mexico. They had to put in at Mazatlan for nearly a week to let it blow over. He didn't arrive in San Francisco until that September."

With her fork, she pointed at the tiramisu.

"Are you sure you won't have even a bite?"

There was no point in resisting further. Elliott picked up the second fork and cut a piece, then lifted it to his mouth.

"Was that so awful?" she asked.

"I'll get over it," he said.

Ms. Crighton smiled as if pleased with herself.

"Benjamin stayed in San Francisco for two months," she said. "He was looking for work, so he went down to the docks where they were unloading lumber, and they told him the mills on the North Coast were always hiring. So he boarded one of the schooners returning to the mills, and in November he hired on with a logging crew that was working along the Big River. He worked on the logging crew for several months before he quit and headed inland, up the Navarro River. He stopped in Boonville and took a room at the hotel. He asked the innkeeper if he knew of any work. It was the innkeeper who told him to go talk to your great-grandmother."

Elliott took another bite of the tiramisu. He didn't particularly care for what he was hearing, but he couldn't dismiss it out of hand.

"I suppose that's possible," he said.

"Benjamin worked for your great-grandmother until he died."

"When was that?"

"In September 1898. I don't know the exact date."

That stopped Elliott.

"That's more than thirty years," he said.

"Yes, I know," she said. "He's buried there in the town cemetery."

Elliott didn't know what to say. It sounded possible, if not entirely plausible. He didn't dispute anything Ms. Crighton had told him.

But thirty years seemed an extraordinarily long time to have worked on his family's ranch. He didn't know what to make of it.

"I really wish I could help you," he said. "I'm sorry I don't have anything to tell you."

She reached over and patted the top of his right hand again.

"Oh, don't worry, Elliott. Don't worry about me. It's such a pleasure to meet you."

WHEN THEY FINISHED the tiramisu, Elliott escorted Ms. Crighton back to the inn. As they walked past the dark pines on the edge of the square, Ms. Crighton reached over and slipped her hand through his arm. The gesture startled Elliott. He certainly wasn't expecting it. But they were not going far. The inn was less than a block away. He supposed Ms. Crighton was simply tired from her long flight across the country and needed an arm to steady herself as they proceeded up the sidewalk. And he was not so rude as to remove her hand, to peel her fingers from his forearm, the sleeve of his corduroy coat.

"Thank you so much for meeting with me, Elliott."

"It was my pleasure," he said.

And that was not entirely untrue. Meeting with Ms. Crighton had not been as disagreeable as he had feared it might be. On the contrary, Ms. Crighton was not without her quirky charm. He was glad she had contacted him about her great-grandmother's uncle. He was glad he had agreed to meet with her. It seemed quite likely that the paths of their ancestors had crossed in the distant past. They would always have that much in common. But it was time to bid Ms. Crighton farewell and then go their separate ways.

At the corner, they waited for a white limousine to roll by before they crossed the street and walked up to the inn. Standing beneath the canopy, Elliott pressed the button beside the door, and the desk clerk buzzed them into the lobby.

"Well, I'm afraid I must say goodbye, Ms. Crighton."

But she didn't appear to be listening.

"How far is Anderson Valley?" she asked.

The question caught him off-guard.

"From here?"

"I'm renting a car and driving up there tomorrow," she said.

"What?"

"I'm meeting with Lila at the historical society tomorrow afternoon," she explained. "I can't wait to meet her. I asked her to see if she could find any other information about Benjamin."

"It's a good two-and-a-half, three-hour drive," Elliott said.

"I want to go to the cemetery, too. I'd like to visit Benjamin's grave."

"You don't even know where the cemetery is," he said.

"I'm sure Lila can give me directions."

Elliott wanted to laugh. The plan was absurd. Ms. Crighton had never been to Anderson Valley. She had never been to Mendocino County. This was her first trip to California. She had no idea where she was going. And it was not an easy drive, especially the narrow two-lane road winding through the Coast Range – and suddenly he felt a sharp pang of despair, realizing what he had to do. Invited or not, Ms. Crighton had become his guest. And by default, he had become her host. He was, at least to some degree, responsible for her, which meant he couldn't let her drive up to Anderson Valley alone. He had no choice. He had to drive Ms. Crighton up to Boonville. He had to take her to her meeting with Lila. He had to take her to the cemetery to find Harrigan's grave.

And he was not particularly thrilled about it.

"We'll leave at nine o'clock," he told her.

"What?"

"Nine o'clock sharp," he said.

"Elliott, are you sure? You don't have to do this, only if you want to. I don't want you to feel like you have to drive me up there."

But he had already turned toward the door.

"Just make sure you're ready to go," he said.

"Don't worry," she called after him. "I'll be ready. We'll have a wonderful time."

AT THE BUS STOP across from Mario's, Elliott caught the 45 Union and took it up the hill. As he stared out the window, he couldn't believe what had just happened, what he had just done to himself. And the fact that he was doing the right thing provided little in the way of consolation. But he couldn't let Ms. Crighton meet with Lila without him. There was no telling what Ms. Crighton might ask about his great-grandparents, or what Lila might tell her, for that matter. The legacy of his great-grandparents was not just his to preserve, it was also his to protect. He allowed himself a tight laugh. Persnickety. Fussy. He might very well say the same about Lila.

He reached up and tugged the cord to let the driver know he wanted to get off at the next stop, then rose from his seat and stood above the back doors. When the bus pulled over to the curb, he stepped down onto the pavement and started down Hyde Street. As he turned onto Vallejo, he was surprised to see the lights were on in his flat. He wondered if Alissa was home, or if she'd forgotten to turn the lights off when she left to go see Nigel and Jeremy.

He opened the steel grate and crossed the porch to the door to his flat. As he climbed the stairs, he could hear the television in the living room. He walked down the hall and found Alissa lying on the sofa, peering out from beneath the hood of her black sweatshirt, a yellow knit comforter wrapped around her legs, clutching Hank with her right arm, curled up on the cushion in front of her. Without her dark mascara and green eye shadow, she reminded him of the schoolgirl who had moved in with him all those years ago. She was watching a cartoon featuring an animated yellow sponge.

"I didn't expect to find you home," he said. "I thought you'd be out with your bandmates."

Without looking up, she said, "Nigel had his wisdom teeth pulled this afternoon, and Jeremy has a migraine."

"Sounds like a rough day for the boys," Elliott said.

"So how was your date?" she asked.

"It was not a date," he quickly corrected her. "I met a woman for a cup of coffee, purely in the context of my research."

"Right."

"I'm serious," he said firmly.

"What was she like?"

Elliott folded his coat over the back of the club chair and then dropped down into it. He wasn't at all sure how to describe Ms. Crighton, other than as a meddlesome intruder who had wheedled herself into his research, and now his life.

"She's unique, I would say. Perhaps a little odd."

"What does that mean?"

"I've agreed to drive her up to Anderson Valley tomorrow."

Alissa abruptly turned to him.

"She has an appointment tomorrow afternoon at the historical society in Boonville," he said as if to explain.

"And you're driving her up there?"

"That's right."

"Why? What are you talking about? How did this happen?"

They were good questions, fair questions. The truth was, he wasn't entirely sure – actually, yes, he did know how this had happened.

"I offered," he said.

"Just like that?"

"I'm afraid so."

Alissa shook her head at him, then turned back to the animated sponge.

"You've lost your mind," she said.

As Elliott pushed up from the chair, he couldn't disagree.

"Maybe so," he said.

CHAPTER TWELVE

ELLIOTT OPENED THE DOOR to the garage, flipped on the light and started down the stairs. He walked past Alissa's drum kit and her bandmates' speakers and amplifiers, over to the tool closet. It had been years since he last visited the cemetery in Anderson Valley, which meant the headstones and grave markers in his family's plot were sure to need attention, and he had to assume that Benjamin Harrigan's grave would be in similar condition, assuming they were able to find it. So he selected the tools he might need to clean them up – a shovel and a rake, a wire brush and a tin pail, a whisk broom and a pair of work gloves – and loaded them into the BMW's trunk. He couldn't say he was looking forward to driving Ms. Crighton up to Anderson Valley, but that was no reason to be unprepared for what they might find.

He closed the trunk and slipped behind the wheel and pulled out of the garage, then drove over the hill to Washington Square. He double-parked in front of the inn and sat there for a moment, waiting for Ms. Crighton. When she didn't appear, he shut down the engine and turned on the emergency lights and walked up to the inn. The clerk buzzed him in, and he crossed the lobby, reaching up and removing his hat, nodding at the middle-age couple in matching pink running suits standing over the banquet table, spreading cream cheese on their toasted bagels. As he approached the desk in the back, the clerk rose from his chair to greet him, wearing yet another floral print shirt, this one featuring orange and blue dahlias.

"Good morning," he said.

"Would you let Ms. Crighton know that Elliott Madison is downstairs?"

"Of course," he said.

He picked up the telephone and dialed her room.

"Good morning, Phoebe. This is Jeffrey at the desk downstairs. You have a visitor."

He listened for a moment.

"I will tell him," he said, returning the receiver to its cradle and turning to Elliott. "Phoebe said she's just about ready. She said you're welcome to come up to her room."

"Thank you, but no," Elliott said without hesitation. "I'll wait for her down here."

"Of course," Jeffrey said.

Elliott walked back into the lobby and sat in the high-backed chair in the front window. With his hat on his left knee, his hands in his lap, he looked out at the street, watching to make sure the ubiquitous meter maids didn't ticket the double-parked BMW. Quickly, he learned that Ms. Crighton was not as close to ready as she had led Jeffrey to believe. Nearly ten minutes passed before he heard her descending the stairs.

"Good morning, Elliott."

He rose from the sofa.

"How do I look?" she asked.

In a pair of neatly pressed khakis, a blue oxford shirt and a dark blue letterman's jacket with gray leather sleeves, she performed a slow pirouette for him.

"You look fine," he said.

"I'm sorry I'm late," she said. "I'm always late. I can't help it. I've always been this way."

"Well, you're ready now," he said.

He motioned toward the door.

"Shall we?"

"Of course," she said.

She turned and waved goodbye to Jeffrey, and they pushed out onto the sidewalk. The instant she saw the BMW, she spun back around to him.

"Is this yours?"

"It is," he said.

He watched as she stepped down from the curb and walked out into the street, moving slowly along the side of the car, inspecting it carefully. She trailed the tip of her index finger along the edge of the trunk and then up the back window, across the roof and down the windshield trim to the hood.

"It's gorgeous, Elliott."

He opened the door for her.

"We've got a long drive ahead of us," he said.

"What year is it?" she asked, taking a step back, still examining it closely.

"1977."

"And in perfect condition – a classic."

"We really should be getting on the road," he said.

"Yes, of course."

She lowered herself into the seat, then looked up at him and smiled.

"You have no idea how much I appreciate your driving me up to Anderson Valley, Elliott. It's going to be a lovely day."

Elliott couldn't bring himself to tell her that he didn't mind.

Instead, he closed her door, then walked around the back of the car and dropped into the driver's seat. As he clasped his seatbelt across his waist, he motioned for Ms. Crighton to do the same.

"You're always on time, and you always wear your seatbelt – I'm learning a lot about you, Elliott. You're proper, and you're cautious, and you're very conservative."

He could not deny it, any of it.

"I'm sorry you find me so obvious."

"Oh, I don't mind," she said. "I find it all rather charming."

ELLIOTT GLANCED into the side view mirror, then turned left onto Filbert Street. They drove past Sts. Peter and Paul and then headed west across the city, skirting the foot of Russian Hill and then driving past the former maritime supply base at Fort Mason, the children flying paper dragons on the Marina Green and the gently swaying masts of the yachts berthed in the city harbor. As they pulled onto Doyle Drive, the elevated viaduct leading to the Golden Gate Bridge, the traffic seemed heavier and faster than the last time Elliott had driven across the bridge. With little warning, the two lanes narrowed to one to permit the traffic from Lombard Street to merge onto the roadway. As Elliott braked and looked to his left, into the oncoming traffic, the driver of the red Chevy Blazer behind them gave a sharp tap of his horn. Puzzled, Elliott looked down at the speedometer and saw they were traveling at thirty-five miles per hour, which, in his considered opinion, was fast enough for Doyle Drive, perhaps too fast, even, as they drove through the Presidio and approached the tollbooths at the southern entrance to the bridge.

With no toll for northbound traffic, the lanes converged to allow those vehicles to pass through and around the unoccupied booths on the far right side of the toll plaza. As the traffic rushed past, Elliott flipped on the turn signal, waited a moment, then merged into the right lane. Suddenly, the open tollbooths were dead ahead.

He hit the brakes as they approached the narrow chute between the two booths on the right, gripping the steering wheel as if bracing for impact – but nothing and then they were making the sweeping right hand turn onto the bridge.

Elliott took a deep breath, then glanced over at Ms. Crighton. She was looking out across the bay, the blue-gray surface gleaming in the morning light. She had rolled the window down slightly, the air moving into the car lifting her loose mass of hair.

"It's so beautiful," she said.

Slightly hunched forward, Elliott looked straight ahead as they passed through the southern tower onto the middle of the span. He hated driving across the bridge. He had always hated it. The lanes were too narrow. There was nothing to prevent the onrushing traffic from careening through the yellow plastic lane markers and crashing head-on into the northbound vehicles. It happened more often than one would expect. He didn't need to remind himself that it was only a matter of time before it happened again.

As they passed through the northern tower, Ms. Crighton pointed at the sign for the vista point on the bluff above the bay.

"Elliott, can we stop – just for a moment? I'd like to take a picture."

As much as Elliott wanted to stay on the road, knowing how far they had to go, he voiced no objection. He took the exit and guided the BMW into the parking lot as a green Volkswagen van was backing out of a parking space. He waited until the van pulled away, then nosed the car into the vacated space. As he turned off the engine, Ms. Crighton opened her door and started to get out, turning back to Elliott when she noticed that he hadn't opened his door.

"Aren't you coming?"

"I've lived in San Francisco all my life," he said. "I have a pretty good idea what it looks like."

But that wasn't good enough for Ms. Crighton.

"I need you to take my picture," she told him.

There was no point in resisting her. He grabbed his hat and climbed out of the car, and they made their way across the parking lot to the edge of the vista point. As they stood at the low stone wall, they looked out across the bay to the far shoreline, the stately mansions in Pacific Heights and the grand apartment buildings on Russian Hill, the towering high-rises of the Financial District in the distance.

"Here," she said, handing him her camera.

He stepped back and peered through the viewfinder until it framed Ms. Crighton against the backdrop of the city.

"Are you ready?" he asked.

As if on cue, she thrust both arms in the air, her hands splayed out in both directions.

"Now!" she shouted.

With a start, he snapped the photograph. As he lowered the camera, Ms. Crighton walked toward him.

"That was a curious pose," he said.

"I was just trying to look happy," she said.

"Of course," Elliott said.

"Now it's your turn."

Elliott could have laughed.

"I'll pass," he said.

"You can't do that."

"I don't like having my picture taken," he informed her.

"That's no reason," she said. "That's silly."

"It's the best I can do."

She shook her head.

"I'm not leaving here without a picture of you, Elliott. You might as well get it over with."

Elliott didn't want to argue with Ms. Crighton. They had a long day ahead. Reluctantly, he walked over to the stone wall and turned back to face her.

She raised the camera and squinted into the viewfinder.

"Action!" she shouted.

"What's that supposed to mean?" he asked.

"It means do something," she said. "You can't just stand there with your hands in your pockets."

Very well. Elliott took his hands out of his trouser pockets and let them rest along his thighs.

"You're not even trying, Elliott."

"Well, this is going to have to do," he told her.

But at that very moment, a gust of wind swept up the face of the bluff. As Elliott reached up and caught his hat, Ms. Crighton snapped the photograph.

"Bravo!" she shouted. "Bravo!"

THEY RETURNED to the BMW and pulled out of the parking lot and began the sharp grade leading up to the Waldo Tunnel. As they approached the tunnel, Elliott couldn't help but notice the car seemed a little sluggish. Glancing up into the rearview mirror, he was distressed to see they were trailing a plume of light blue smoke. He checked the speedometer – fifty-five miles per hour seemed to be all the BMW had. It would have to suffice.

They emerged from the tunnel and coasted down the highway as it led through the wooded hills, the air scented with the heady fragrance of eucalyptus. He could feel Ms. Crighton looking at him.

"Thank you for indulging me," she said.

"Of course," he said.

"I take a lot of photographs wherever I go."

"I'm sure," Elliott said.

And yet, in the corner of his eye, he could see she was still looking at him. He had no idea why. He wondered what she might be thinking, what might be running through her mind, what she might ask him.

"So tell me about yourself, Ms. Crighton," he said, as if to deflect her attention from himself.

The question seemed to amuse her.

"What would you like to know?"

He certainly wasn't going to answer that truthfully.

"Whatever you'd like to tell me," he said. "Whatever you think I should know."

"I was born in New York."

"That's a good place to start," he said. "I didn't know that."

"My father was a jazz musician, a trombone player who drove a cab during the day. He disappeared when I was in the sixth grade. I never saw him again. I have no idea if he's dead or alive."

Elliott glanced over to Ms. Crighton and was relieved to see she had turned away and was staring straight ahead.

"My mother was a chorus girl, a line captain on Broadway until she slipped on the ice in front of our apartment in Brooklyn and tore the ligaments in her right knee. She never danced again."

"I'm sorry to hear that," Elliott said.

"She died of breast cancer when I was a junior in high school. I lived with my grandmother until I enrolled at Columbia."

"Columbia – a very fine university."

"I had a boyfriend from Pittsburgh," she said, smiling to herself, recalling his memory. "His name was Trevor. He was very handsome, and I mean very. We went to Woodstock together. We hitchhiked. But then when we got there, all it did was rain. For two days we sat in the mud, absolutely drenched. We were so far away we could barely hear. We could barely even see the stage. Finally, we gave up and left. I was never so glad to be home in my life."

Elliott smiled in return.

"Yes, I've heard that was quite the gathering," he said.

He peered down into the side view mirror. Traveling in the right lane, he was growing weary of the traffic merging on and off the highway, so he checked the mirror several times in quick succession, waiting for the opportunity to change lanes. When he saw the middle lane was clear, he flipped on the turn signal, counted to three, then made his move. His execution was perfect, and he felt himself relax.

"After I graduated, I moved to Boston and taught elementary school," she said. "That's where I met Michael. He was a medical student, studying to become a plastic surgeon. He told me he wanted to move to Guatemala and open a clinic. He wanted to treat poor children suffering from cleft palates. It sounded so noble, so romantic. I fell madly in love with him."

"I imagine so," Elliott said.

"We were married at his family's summer home in Martha's Vineyard. Our plan was to put away some money, so we could build our clinic in Guatemala. So we moved down to New Haven, where Michael bought into a small practice near the Yale campus. Instead of operating on disfigured children, he performed facelifts on faculty wives."

Elliott was disinclined to pass judgment.

"I understand that can be quite lucrative," he said.

"Quite," she said. "Only we never made it to Guatemala. Instead, I gave birth to two beautiful daughters. I devoted my life to them. I wanted them to have the kind of family that I never had."

"No one can fault you for that," he said.

"Unfortunately, the day my second daughter left for college, Michael informed me that he wanted a divorce. He had already rented an apartment near the campus. The next day he came for his clothes. The marriage was over – just like that."

Elliott glanced over to her. He knew how she must have felt, actually.

"But I got over it," she said, her voice rising as if to the challenge. "I got a job at a nonprofit advertising agency, mostly just answering the phones. Most of our clients were environmental groups. We were trying to save the rainforests. We were trying to save the world."

"There's nothing wrong with that," he said. "A very noble ambition."

"And I started taking art classes at the university. I even sold one of my sketches at a show in an off-campus gallery."

She looked over to him.

"It was a nude," she said.

"Oh, my."

"It was only $50, but I didn't care. I got the name of the man who bought it, and I called him up, and we met for dinner. It was a wonderful evening. Only he was married, and I don't believe in sleeping with married men."

"That certainly seems sensible," Elliott said.

"I have a small studio in Chelsea now," she said. "I go there every morning. I work there every day. I work mostly with acrylics, but lately I've been doing some silk-screening. And then I go back to my apartment. I've lived alone since the girls went off to school."

"Of course," he said.

"Don't get me wrong – I enjoy living alone. I enjoy growing older, don't you?"

"I try not to think about it," Elliott said.

"Really?"

"I'm a few years ahead of you," he said. "More than a few, to be perfectly honest."

"I see life so much clearer now," she said. "I've reached the point where I do what I want, whenever I want to do it. And I don't care what anybody thinks about it, either."

"Good for you," Elliott said.

"I was thinking about going to Europe for a while, maybe renting an apartment in Prague or Vienna or maybe Greece, maybe living on one of the islands. But then I found my great-grandmother's manuscript about Benjamin, and then I contacted Lila, and now here I am."

Elliott couldn't argue with that.

"Yes, you certainly are," he said.

THEY DROVE NORTH, beyond the farthest reach of the bay, through the marsh and wetlands and into the hills covered with gray-green stands of oak and laurel. Traffic was heavy until they passed through Santa Rosa and proceeded up the Russian River Valley. Beneath the dark ridge to the east, the vineyards ran neatly across the rolling valley floor. In the dusty haze, the leaves of the vines had turned purple-red. They could smell the rich ferment of the ripening grapes in the air moving in through Ms. Crighton's window.

At Cloverdale, they pulled off the highway and turned west, the narrow roadway quickly climbing up into the hills, and soon they were winding through the tall pines and fir, the rocky cutbanks crowding the gravel shoulder. When the road began to dip and weave along a shallow creek bed, clusters of mailboxes began to appear along the edge of the blacktop, marking the unpaved roads leading into the isolated ranches and home sites. Finally, they arrived at the upper end of the valley, opening up before them with the forested ridge to the south, grassy hills spreading out to the north.

"Here we are," Elliott said.

"I feel like we've been traveling back in time," Ms. Crighton said.

"I thought that was the point," Elliott said.

The thought seemed to appeal to Ms. Crighton.

"Yes, I suppose it is," she said.

They pulled into Boonville, a town of no more than a thousand residents, rolling quietly past the small plank houses and stucco cottages, trailers with torn screen doors and primer-gray pickups on jack stands. They slowed to a crawl as they passed the weathered storefronts that had congregated along the town's main thoroughfare for as long as Elliott could remember, the country markets and homespun cafes, the open bays of the auto repair shops and real estate offices flying plastic pennants. It was all too familiar. It never seemed to change.

"Are you hungry?" he asked Ms. Crighton. "I was thinking we might have lunch at the hotel."

"That sounds grand," she said.

At the west end of town, he guided the car across the road and parked on the compacted gravel in front of the Boonville Hotel. It was the oldest building in town, a two-story structure with a broad front porch beneath the balcony serving the guest rooms upstairs. Its plank walls had been painted dark red, its double doors a lustrous yellow. A gray cat was perched on the porch railing, looking down as if waiting for them.

As he turned off the engine, Ms. Crighton shed her seatbelt and pushed out of the car. She stood on the sidewalk and looked up at the hotel, then she turned back to Elliott, her camera in hand.

"Are you coming?" she asked.

He was indeed. He grabbed his hat and climbed out of the car. His legs were heavy, his back tight. The three-hour drive had taken more out of him than he thought it would.

As he walked over to Ms. Crighton, she pointed toward the hotel.

"Would you mind standing beside the door?"

"Why?"

"I want to take a picture," she said.

"You've already taken my picture."

"Oh, please, Elliott. Won't you just stand there? Otherwise it will just be a picture of a building."

He wasn't going to argue.

"If you insist," he said.

He walked up the steps and stood beside the door, then reached up and removed his hat, smoothing his hair with his right hand.

"How is this?"

Ms. Crighton raised the camera.

"Perfect," she said.

She took the photograph, then walked up the steps and slipped her hand through his arm. She leaned toward him.

"You're really quite handsome," she said.

They entered the hotel and made their way down the narrow hallway, past the sitting room on the right to the hotel desk, where they were greeted by a young woman in blue jeans and a gray Western shirt with pearl snaps.

"Two for lunch," Elliott told her.

She led them into the dining room and seated them at a table pushed up against the wall, beside the door that opened onto the back deck. In the center of the table was a fluted glass vase containing a small bouquet of yellow chrysanthemums. Ms. Crighton admired the flowers for a moment, then clasped her hands and looked across the table to him.

"This is where it all began, Elliott. This is where Benjamin stopped and asked the innkeeper if he knew of any work. This is where the innkeeper told Benjamin to talk to your great-grandmother."

Elliott couldn't deny it.

"Yes, I suppose that's possible," he said.

Ms. Crighton looked past him to the hotel desk, where that very conversation might have taken place.

"I can't wait to meet Lila," she said. "I'm dying to know what else she might have learned about Benjamin."

CHAPTER THIRTEEN

THE OLD SCHOOLHOUSE was less than a mile west of town. No larger than a country chapel and painted red with its windows trimmed in white, it was a simple one-room structure with a bell on the peak of its roof. For fifty years, grades one through eight were taught at the schoolhouse, kindergarten until the late 1970s, at which point Lila and several others raised the money to renovate the building, so it might serve as the permanent home of the historical society. In the years since he retired, Elliott had driven up to the schoolhouse to meet with Lila more times than he could count, and he would freely admit that their extended discussions about the early settlement of the valley had greatly informed his manuscript. Of course, that hardly excused her cavalier disregard for his personal privacy. Nor, for that matter, did it explain why she was often so willfully annoying, at times almost gleefully so.

As he parked in front of the schoolhouse, he turned to Ms. Crighton.

"Did you and Lila arrange to meet at a specific time?"

"I told her I would see her this afternoon, that's all. Lila said she would be here all day."

They got out of the car and walked across the untrimmed lawn and stepped up onto the low wooden porch. Elliott reached down and turned the doorknob to let them in. But the door was stuck, so he leaned against it with his shoulder and pushed the door into the former classroom, a museum now, filled with a collection of artifacts from an untold number of lives, portraits of the men and women who had settled in the valley over the years, photographs of the orchards they planted and the fields they tilled, the livestock they raised and the timber they cut.

"Hello?" Elliott called out.

But no one answered as they wandered through the cluttered room, Ms. Crighton pausing to inspect a set of blue porcelain dishes in one of the display cases, running a fingertip through the dust that had accumulated on the glass. When Elliott heard the hinges on the back door groan, he called out Lila's name again. A moment later, she emerged from the back porch, now the historical society office.

She stopped the instant she saw them, planting her hands on her hips and grinning broadly, her long white hair falling loosely to her shoulders. The sleeves of her white shirt were rolled up to her elbows. Her blue jeans were nearly threadbare at the knees, a thin black belt cinched around her waist.

"Well look what the dog dragged in," she said.

"Hello, Lila," Elliott said.

Elliott had known Lila for years, long before he began his research. Their families, in fact, had known each other for generations. She had lived in the valley all her life, marrying her high school sweetheart only to lose him in the Korean War. After the war, she taught at the high school until she had to retire to care for her aging parents. It was as she watched their health decline that she began researching her family's history, and, over the years, her interests expanded to include the interwoven stories of many of the early settlers in the valley, including, of course, Elliott's great-grandparents. And so, yes, with her extraordinary biographical knowledge of the valley's history, she had been a great resource for Elliott. But it was also true, he liked to remind himself, that she was not without her own agenda. As director of the historical society, she had asked him to donate his great-grandfather's journals and his great-grandmother's letters to the society when he passed away. He did not appreciate her ghoulish request, but he had promised to consider it.

Lila extended her hand to Ms. Crighton.

"You must be Phoebe."

"How nice to meet you," Ms. Crighton said.

Lila shrugged in Elliott's direction.

"How did you manage to persuade Elliott to bring you up from the city?" she asked. "It's been a while since we were favored with his presence."

"He volunteered," Ms. Crighton said, though, of course, it was not that simple.

"Really?"

Lila looked at him for a moment, then turned back to Ms. Crighton.

"Most folks think he's a cranky old fusspot, but we're rather fond of him."

"You're much too kind, Lila," Elliott said.

She laughed, then motioned for them to follow her into the office. The closed-in porch was crowded with chest-high file cabinets and cardboard boxes stacked against the walls, bookcases overflowing with catalogs, reference books and obscure directories, flat boxes filled with photographs and forlorn family albums she'd rescued at yard sales. Beneath an early map of the upper valley tacked to the office wall, her desk was buried beneath piles of genealogical charts and census records, thick packets of newspaper clippings and court filings copied from microfilm.

"Find a seat," Lila said, gesturing toward the wooden folding chairs leaning against one of the stacks of boxes.

Elliott unfolded one of the chairs for Ms. Crighton and then one for himself. As he sat down, Lila twisted the lid off a large jar of sun tea.

"Would you care for a glass?" she asked Ms. Crighton.

"That would be wonderful," she said.

Elliott didn't have to say anything.

"Did you know that Elliott doesn't care for tea?" Lila asked Ms. Crighton.

"No, I didn't," she said. "Elliott, I'm learning more about you hour by hour."

Lila gave the tea bag a final squeeze before discarding it in the wastebasket beside the desk.

"Actually, I've been meaning to contact you, Elliott. I found something that might interest you."

"And what might that be?" he asked.

Lila pointed at an old leather trunk on the floor beside the back door, its brass corners tarnished nearly to black, its clasp roughly pried open.

"We got this from the old Keegan Ranch," she said.

She poured a glass of the tea and offered it to Ms. Crighton.

"The Keegans came here from Ohio in the late-1860s," she explained to her. "They settled about five miles down the valley and lived there for more than fifty years."

Elliott watched as Lila poured herself a glass of the tea, offering a slice of lemon to Ms. Crighton before dropping a slice into her own glass.

"A couple years ago, a lawyer from San Francisco bought the old Keegan ranch, and this summer, he and his wife found this trunk in the attic and gave it to us."

She picked up a manila envelope and handed it to Elliott.

"Take a look at what I found inside," she said.

Elliott lifted the flap and withdrew a grainy black-and-white photograph of three women in their Sunday dresses, standing beside a horse-drawn carriage in front of the Methodist Church, their faces obscured in shadow beneath the brims of their flowered hats.

Without hesitation, Elliott said, "My great-grandmother is the woman in the middle."

"And the woman on the left is Irma Keegan," Lila said, sitting back in her chair and smiling as if pleased with herself. "Do you recognize the woman on the right, standing beside your great-grandmother?"

Elliott leaned down and studied the photograph carefully. The woman in question was short and stout, her dress billowing out below her ample waist, but it was impossible to make out her face beneath the brim of her hat.

"I have no idea," he said.

"That's your great-grandmother's cousin," Lila said.

"Her cousin Emily?"

"That's right."

He looked back down at the photograph, examining it more closely. He had never seen a photograph of his great-grandmother's cousin, the beloved recipient of her letters from her journey across the continent and the early days at the ranch. He never would have guessed the woman in the photograph was her.

"I'll be damned," he said.

"Their names were written on the back," Lila said, as if to explain how she had identified them.

"She came out from Iowa after my great-grandfather died. She stayed for nearly a year," Elliott said.

"Do you know what became of her?" Lila asked.

"I know she returned to Iowa. I know she died in 1871. But that's all I know," he said, slipping the photograph back into the envelope.

"You may keep it, Elliott."

"Thank you, Lila."

She took a sip of her tea, then reached for another manila envelope.

"But that's not the reason Phoebe came all the way from New York, is it? That's not why you two drove up from the city."

But before she could open the second envelope, Ms. Crighton reached for her handbag.

"I have something to show you," she said.

Elliott looked on as she produced the copy of Harrigan's carte de visite.

"Here he is," she said, showing the photograph to Lila. "This is my great-grandmother's uncle. This was taken in New Orleans during the Civil War."

"A handsome young man," Lila said.

"Yes, he was, wasn't he," Ms. Crighton said.

"I'm sorry to say I wasn't able to learn much about him," Lila said.

She lifted the flap of the second envelope and pulled out several sheets of paper.

"I did find Mr. Harrigan in the 1870 and the 1880 federal censuses," she said, extending xeroxed copies of the handwritten pages to Ms. Crighton, then pointing to the lines she had highlighted with a yellow felt-tip marker. "According to the census forms, he was born in New York."

"That's correct," Ms. Crighton said. "He was born in East Fishkill in Dutchess County."

"His father was born in Ireland."

"That's right, too," Ms. Crighton said. "His father and two uncles immigrated from County Cork."

"And his mother was from Germany."

"She was a Krueger from Hamburg."

"The census lists Mr. Harrigan as a common laborer, living on the Madison ranch with several other men who worked for Elliott's family."

"I believe that's true," Ms. Crighton said. "That's what he wrote in his letters to his niece."

"As far as I can tell, he never married or had any children."

"No, not that I'm aware of," Ms. Crighton said.

Lila took another sip of tea, then returned the glass to the ring it had perspired onto the desktop. She withdrew another sheet of paper from the envelope, a copy of a brief newspaper article.

"I also found a story about Mr. Harrigan's death, published in the *Redwood Journal* on September 12, 1898."

She gave the article to Ms. Crighton, who read it quickly and then sat back in her chair, handing the sheet of paper to Elliott. According to the article, Harrigan had suffered a heart attack while out deer hunting in the woods. Several ranch hands found him the next day, lying on the ground on one of the trails leading through the hills above the river, his dogs still sitting beside him, his horse quietly grazing nearby. They brought his body back to the ranch, and after a funeral performed by Reverend Taylor, he was laid to rest in the cemetery outside town.

Elliott looked over to Ms. Crighton. Tears had gathered in the corners of her eyes.

"I wish I'd been able to learn more about him," Lila said. "But I'm afraid that's all I was able to find, at least for now."

"You don't know how grateful I am for this," Ms. Crighton said.

"At least you know what became of him," Lila said. "At least you know how and where his life came to an end."

WHILE LILA GAVE Ms. Crighton a tour of the historical society museum, providing her a sense of what life in the valley was like during the years her great-grandmother's uncle lived here, Elliott stepped out onto the porch. As he stood at the railing, he looked up into the sprawling oak in front of the schoolhouse. A large black crow perched on one of its limbs, watching him with its yellow eyes as a gray squirrel clawed up the trunk of the tree, pausing for a moment before scurrying up into the upper branches. Elliott breathed in the warm air, inhaling the ripe fragrance of autumn. Although he had been here only last summer, it seemed much longer than that.

He heard Lila and Ms. Crighton emerge from the schoolhouse.

"Well, what do you think?" he asked Ms. Crighton.

"It's very impressive," she said.

"Are you ready to go to the cemetery?"

But she had opened her handbag. As he watched her search through the bag, he knew exactly what she was looking for. His suspicions were confirmed when she produced her camera.

She turned to Lila and asked, "Would you mind taking a picture of Elliott and me?"

"Of course not," Lila said.

"Do we really have to do this?" Elliott asked.

"It will only take a second," Ms. Crighton said.

Lila motioned for them to stand in the shade of the oak.

"Elliott, would you be so kind as to remove your hat?"

As she raised the camera, he reluctantly obliged.

"Closer," she said. "I need you two to stand closer together."

Elliott took a half step toward Ms. Crighton. She reached over and slipped her arm through his and drew herself to him.

"Now smile, and that means you, Elliott."

"Think of something funny," Ms. Crighton said. "Think of the last time you laughed out loud."

"I don't believe anything amuses Elliott any more," Lila said. "Somewhere over the years, he lost his sense of humor."

"Very funny," Elliott said.

"Hold still," Lila said.

Finally, she took the picture. She walked down the porch steps and gave the camera back to Ms. Crighton.

"Thank you, Lila. I just want to remember every minute of this trip."

She took Lila's arm, and they walked across the grass, through the gate to stand beside the BMW.

"How can I ever thank you?" she asked Lila.

"Just let me know whatever else you learn about Mr. Harrigan," she said.

The two women hugged as if they had known each other for years. Elliott opened the car door and waited for Ms. Crighton to lower herself into the passenger's seat.

"Thanks, Lila," he said.

"It's good to see you, you fussy old coot," she said.

Elliott permitted himself a smile.

"It's good to see you, too."

He walked around the front of the car. As he sat behind the steering wheel, Ms. Crighton reached over and touched his arm.

"I like her, Elliott. She's wonderful."

"She's very knowledgeable. She's very dedicated," Elliott said as he turned the key in the ignition.

"And she's very fond of you."

Elliott had no intention of responding to a remark like that.

"Let's go to the cemetery, shall we?"

THEY DROVE back toward town, turning into the entrance to Evergreen Cemetery, the unpaved road leading up into a copse of oaks above a murmuring creek. Elliott parked in the shade. As the engine died out, the cemetery fell quiet, the hush broken only by birdsong. He looked around, through the luminescent dust particles drifting through the sunlight. Plastic flowers and lazy pinwheels adorned the most recent graves. The older headstones were simple and modest, reflecting the lives of the people whose graves they marked. No one else was there. A sense of serenity seemed to settle over them, a world in repose.

"It's beautiful," Ms. Crighton said softly.

"Shall we?" Elliott said.

With his hand at the back of her arm, he led Ms. Crighton through the plots of the first families to settle in the valley, through the tilting headstones and dusty statuary to the tall marble obelisk at the head of his great-grandfather's grave. His family's plot was enclosed by an ankle-high concrete wall that had broken in several places as the ground shifted over the years. Irises grew throughout the plot, spreading from the bulbs first planted by his great-grandmother. Her granite headstone stood beside the obelisk, an ascending angel carved into the stone above her name. The headstones of his grandparents, who died within hours of each other during the 1918 Spanish flu epidemic, were to the left, their names inscribed in the silver-veined marble. The simple grave markers for his mother and father were pressed into the soil directly in front of them. As Elliott took off his hat and leaned down to wave off the dust, it seemed a lifetime since he'd last visited the cemetery.

"I love it here," Ms. Crighton said.

Elliott straightened up and put his hat back on, a light tug on the brim.

"Let's see if we can find Benjamin Harrigan, shall we?"

They began canvassing the older section of the cemetery as carefully and as methodically as they could. But the family plots were not arranged in any specific order, and so they meandered through the slabs of marble and granite, trying to read the names of the deceased, often obscured by patches of gray-green lichen clinging to the surface of the stone. And after a first pass through the old cemetery, they didn't find Harrigan's grave.

Ms. Crighton couldn't conceal her disappointment.

"He has to be here, doesn't he?"

"I don't know where else," Elliott said.

So they took a second pass through the cemetery, and when Elliott found a headstone lying facedown on the ground, he knelt beside it and tried to lift it up, tried to work his fingers underneath the rounded granite top. But the headstone clung tightly to the soil, so he walked back to the car for the shovel and work gloves. When he returned, he slipped the tip of the shovel blade under the top of the headstone and pushed down on the handle, prying the headstone up, then he set the shovel aside and gripped the slab with both hands, a sharp spasm in his lower back as he strained against its dead weight.

"It's Benjamin," Ms. Crighton said. "I know it."

Finally, he heaved the headstone onto its back. But the face of the stone was caked with dirt, and they couldn't make out the name scored into the granite. Elliott tried to brush the dirt away with his gloved hand, but to no avail, so he returned to the car for the wire brush. Kneeling down again, he began removing the dirt. Ms. Crighton shrieked as the stiff bristles revealed their prize: a Union shield containing "Corporal Benjamin Harrigan, 128th New York Voluntary Infantry Regiment, 1841-1898."

"I knew it, Elliott! I could feel it!"

"Well, you were right, Ms. Crighton. Here he is."

As he rose to stand, Ms. Crighton leaned against him. He didn't mind, slipping his arm around her waist, allowing her a moment before he returned to the car. He lifted the tin pail out of the trunk and carried it over to the creek. The bank was grown over with blackberry vines, but he found a place where he could make his way down to the water. Carefully moving the thorny vines out of his way, he laid the pail on its side to collect as much water as he could. But as he lifted the bucket up, one of the vines slipped free and raked his forearm, instantly drawing blood.

"Damn it!" he hissed.

He scrambled back up the bank and carried the bucket over to Harrigan's grave.

"Elliott, you're bleeding."

Ignoring her, he splashed the headstone with water and then scrubbed it with the brush. After rinsing it off with another pail of water, he stood the headstone back up and tamped down the loose soil with his foot to brace it upright. As he stepped back to admire his work, he couldn't help but wonder how long it would be before the headstone toppled over again.

"Do you ever wish you could talk to the dead?" Ms. Crighton asked him.

Elliott looked over to her.

"Yes," he said. "I most certainly do."

WITH MS. CRIGHTON LOOKING ON, Elliott cleaned up the headstones and grave markers in his family's plot, removing the lichen with the wire brush, raking up the leaves shed by the oaks, sweeping away the dust with the whisk broom. When he finished, he gathered up his tools and carried them back to the BMW, then he leaned back against the fender and waited for Ms. Crighton, giving her time alone at Harrigan's grave, watching as she wandered through the cemetery taking photographs. He had to assume that his great-grandmother had paid for Harrigan's headstone. She certainly would have seen to it that a man who had worked on their ranch for more than thirty years was properly laid to rest. For all Elliott knew, she might very well have been the last person to visit his grave.

After taking a final photograph, Ms. Crighton returned to the car.

"Thanks for bringing me here," she said. "I never would have found Benjamin's grave without you."

"We've got a long drive back to the city," Elliott said. "We might as well get started."

He reached for the door handle, but Ms. Crighton stopped him.

"Do we have time to drive by your family's ranch?" she asked.

The request caught Elliott by surprise. He hadn't been back to the ranch in years, not since his last trip to the deer camp, not since his father sold it. But the ranch was only a short distance away. It wouldn't take long to drive there. There was no reason not to agree.

"Sure," he said.

They left the cemetery and headed west down the valley. It was only a matter of minutes before Elliott eased the car off the pavement and parked above the shallow drainage ditch along the side of the road. He climbed out of the car and walked up to the metal gate across the gravel road leading into the ranch. A lock with a heavy gauge chain secured the gate. A sign warned that the ranch was private property and that trespassers would be prosecuted.

Elliott looked out at the vineyard planted by the current owner of the ranch, a real estate developer named Charles Beeman, who had made a fortune selling tract houses in the Southern California suburbs. Beeman and his son owned several wineries in Napa Valley and had purchased their ranch from his father shortly before he passed away. As soon as escrow closed, they hired a team of men with chainsaws to cut the apple orchard down, even though many of the trees were still producing more than a century after they were planted. They then brought in bulldozers to rip the stumps out of the ground and push them into huge burn piles. After plowing the ash into the ground, they planted pinot noir vines, knowing the same climate that made the valley such a fine place to grow apples – warm summer days with evenings chilled by the fog pressing in from the ocean – also made the valley ideal for several varieties of grapes.

Ms. Crighton joined him at the gate.

"I wish we could walk up this road," she said.

So did Elliott. He wanted to see the house that his great-grandfather had built for his great-grandmother one last time. He wanted to remember the summer he'd spent there with her.

"What could it hurt?" he asked.

He walked back up the road a few paces, then down into the

drainage ditch and up the other side. As he stood at the barbed wire fence, he planted his right foot on the bottom strand and pushed it to the ground, then he grabbed the middle strand and lifted it up.

"After you, Ms. Crighton."

She scrambled down the slope of the ditch, ducked beneath the wire and slipped through easily. He was surprised, frankly, how agile she was.

"Isn't this trespassing?" she asked.

"That's precisely what it is."

"What happens if we get caught?"

"We'll be tried and convicted and then sent to prison to serve our sentences," he said.

"That's what I thought," she said, clapping the dirt from her hands.

It was her turn to put her foot on the bottom strand and pull up the middle wire. But Elliott was not as young, nor as agile, as Ms. Crighton. As he slipped through the fence, one of the barbs caught the back of his shirt, tearing it as he rose to his feet.

"Are you all right?" she asked.

Starting up the road, he said, "Follow me, Ms. Crighton."

In the late afternoon shadows, they walked up the road through the vineyard, the rutted gravel leading directly to the work yard and the remains of the old barn, its red plank walls and sun-blackened timbers slumping to the ground, whole sections of the sheet metal roof long since peeled away by the wind. The bunkhouse was gone, and so were the stables. All that remained of the corral and the sheep pens were a few charred wooden posts still standing amid the knee-high grass.

They crossed the work yard and approached the two-story house, surrounded by the ancient sycamores, elms, and chestnuts, following the footpath that led to the tall hedge of privet. Elliott brushed aside the tendrils of white rose that had grown over the narrow trellis, then entered the interior garden. Instantly, he stopped, stunned by what he saw – his great-grandparents' house was in a state of utter ruin. The front door and all the windows on the lower floor were boarded over with sheets of plywood, all the windows on the upper floor broken out with a last few jagged pieces of glass still in the panes. The gable roof had shed most of its thick shakes while the ornate woodwork hung rotting from the eaves. The blue-gray paint had flaked off the shiplap walls. Grown over with wisteria vines, the fireplace leaned away from the side of the house as if about to collapse, a pile of its heavy stones on the ground.

Elliott was outraged. Beeman and his son had no idea what this house had meant to his family, what it meant in the context of the history of the valley.

"I'm so sorry, Elliott."

"They should have just torn it down," he fumed aloud.

"It's a shame," she said.

"It's a desecration."

He took a step toward the house, toward the steps leading up to the front porch, but Ms. Crighton caught his arm.

"We have company, Elliott."

Through the trellis, they could see a blue Ford pickup at the gate. Elliott watched as the driver climbed down from the cab and swung the gate out of the way, then returned to the idling pickup and started up the road.

"Yes, it appears we do," he said.

The pickup stopped in the work yard. Elliott watched the driver stride toward the house.

"I'll handle this," he told Ms. Crighton.

"Of course," she said.

The driver followed the footpath into the garden. He was tall with dark hair neatly combed back off his forehead. He was wearing a blue polo shirt and pleated chinos.

"Hello," he said. "Do you mind if I ask what you're doing here?"

"We're selling encyclopedias," Elliott said.

The driver smiled through a rack of bright white teeth.

"No kidding."

"It seems no one is home," Elliott said.

But the driver wasn't going to play along.

"I guess you didn't see the sign on the gate," he said.

"What sign is that?"

"The sign that says this is private property. The sign that says you're trespassing."

"I guess we missed it," Elliott said.

The driver wasn't amused.

"Come on," he said, shrugging toward the trellis. "Let's go."

Elliott stared at him, feeling Ms. Crighton's hand on his arm.

"Let's go, Elliott," she said.

But Elliott wasn't ready to leave. He tugged his arm free of Ms. Crighton's hand, his outrage rising.

"My great-grandfather built this house," he told the driver, stabbing a finger at his chest "This was the first house built in the valley. He built it for my great-grandmother, and look what you clowns have let happen to it!"

"Listen, old-timer…"

"You're the one who should be chased off the property!" Elliott all but shouted at him. "You're the one who should be arrested!"

"Now calm down."

"You calm down! You calm the fuck down!"

But that was all. Elliott was done. He had said his piece. He had nothing else to say. He turned to Ms. Crighton and offered her his arm.

"Shall we, Ms. Crighton?"

"Yes, I think we've seen enough," she said.

They walked past the driver and out of the garden and then started down the gravel road. Elliott could hear the door of the pickup close behind them and then the engine rumble to life, the pickup's tires crunching the loose gravel. But as they approached the gate, Ms. Crighton abruptly stopped. Elliott turned to her, standing in the middle of the road with her back to the pickup.

"Is something wrong?" he asked.

Ms. Crighton didn't answer. She was fiddling with her belt, and suddenly Elliott realized what she was about to do, his mouth falling open as she dropped her khakis and bent forward, exposing her bare buttocks to the driver sitting in his pickup. Elliott had never seen such a thing. He was appalled, or at least knew he should be.

She held her pose for a long moment before pulling her khakis back up.

"I thought a good mooning might help make your point," she said. "I mean, what could it hurt?"

THEY RETURNED to Boonville, passing quietly through town, then started back to the city. As they drove through the densely forested hills, the darkness all but overwhelmed the BMW's headlights, even as Elliott tapped on the high beams, the field of light in front of the car barely illuminating the trunks of the pines along the side of the road. Squinting through the windshield, searching for the broken white line painted down the center of the roadway, he drove no more than forty miles per hour, riding the brakes through every turn, raising his right hand to shield his eyes from the blinding headlights of the oncoming vehicles. It seemed to take hours to reach Cloverdale.

"Elliott?"

"Yes, Ms. Crighton."

"Do you mind if I take a nap?"

"Of course not."

"I think the jet lag is catching up with me," she said.

"Don't worry," Elliott said. "I'll wake you when we get back to the city."

After driving through Cloverdale, Elliott pulled back onto the highway. At no more than forty-five miles per hour, he guided the car into the right lane, allowing the vehicles coming up from behind to pull around and pass, then following their taillights until they vanished in the distance. The traffic thickened as they passed through Santa Rosa. At one point, they were nearly forced off the highway by a white delivery van that veered in front of them and then raced up an off-ramp. But Elliott held his course, and as the miles fell away, and they drew nearer the city, he allowed himself to relax, at least to the extent that he permitted himself to sit back in the seat.

But just south of Petaluma, he heard what sounded like a gunshot. Before he realized what had happened, he felt the back of the BMW drop away, and suddenly they were skidding along the shoulder of the highway. He stomped on the brakes and jerked the wheel hard to the left. In the deafening blare of car horns, the car spun across both lanes of southbound traffic, headlights slashing at them from every direction. Ms. Crighton screamed. Elliott clung to the steering wheel, powerless to do anything but close his eyes and steel himself against the inevitable collision – and then with a sudden sharp jolt, a quick shattering of glass, it was over.

In the abrupt stillness, Elliott could feel his heart thumping in his chest. Only then did he allow himself to take a breath. Through the windshield, through the drifting dust, he could see the BMW had come to rest down the shallow embankment along the side of the road.

"Are you all right?" he asked Ms. Crighton.

"What happened?" she asked.

"I don't know."

He peered into the side view mirror, into the headlights of the approaching cars, then pushed the door open and pulled himself up to stand. As he made his way back to the rear of the car, he could smell the scorched rubber, and then he saw the smoke rising from beneath the right rear wheel well, the shredded tire clinging to the rim. When he walked up to the front of the car, he saw that the right headlight had shattered when the BMW slid down the embankment and struck one of the wooden fence posts running along the highway, the right front fender buckling back to the passenger side door. But that seemed to be the extent of the damage. He knew the outcome could have been far worse.

He opened the trunk and pulled out the tools he had brought to clean up the graves in the cemetery, then reached in for the spare tire and heaved it onto the ground. Although he hadn't changed a flat in years, he remembered to loosen the lug nuts before he jacked up the back of the car. He knelt down and pried off the hubcap and fit the tire iron socket onto the lug nut on the bottom. But the nut held fast when he tried to loosen it, so he repositioned himself to lean on the tire iron. Still, the lug nut refused to turn. So he took a deep breath and tried again, this time bringing all his weight to bear on the tire iron – and suddenly the lug nut came loose. As the tire iron slipped off, he lurched forward, his forehead slamming into the rear fender.

In a daze, he dropped the tire iron and rocked back onto his heels. He reached up above his right eye. When he brought his hand down, he saw a smear of blood on his fingertips.

Ms. Crighton rolled her window down and stuck her head out.

"Elliott, are you all right?"

Without responding, he placed the tire iron socket on the next lug nut.

"Is there anything I can do to help?" she asked.

He paused for a moment.

"You could roll the window back up," he said.

And, God bless her, she did.

Eventually, he managed to loosen all the lug nuts. He jacked up the back of the car and pulled off the shredded tire. After two tries, he managed to mount the spare on the protruding bolts. He cranked the car back down, then tossed the jack and tire iron back into the trunk. He piled the tools on top of them, then slammed the lid and walked back up to the door. Gingerly, he lowered himself into the seat behind the wheel. He pressed his handkerchief to the abrasion above his eye.

"Are you sure you're all right?" Ms. Crighton asked.

"Let's just see if we can make it back to the city without getting killed," he said.

He started the engine and slipped the BMW into reverse, backing away from the fence post, then he guided the car up the embankment, nosing up to the shoulder of the highway. He glanced down at the side view mirror, into the approaching headlights, waiting for the opportunity to pull back onto the highway. The number of vehicles on the highway seemed to have increased, and they seemed to be traveling faster than they had been, the headlights quickly growing larger as they drew near. He waited, reminding himself to be patient, leaning back as a diesel rig thundered past. Two cars were behind the diesel rig, but then he saw the opportunity he had been waiting for.

After waiting for the second car to pass, he stepped down hard on the accelerator. The BMW lunged forward, the rear end fishtailing across the shoulder before he was able to steer the front end onto the pavement, the tires barking on the asphalt as the car leapt forward. He glanced up into the rearview mirror. The headlights behind them were as small and distant as stars. Gradually, they gained speed, and he peered ahead, into the light cast by the lone headlamp. They were traveling at nearly forty-five miles an hour again. That was fast enough.

Elliott glanced over to Ms. Crighton.

"It won't be long," he told her.

THE TRAFFIC WAS LIGHTER than he feared it might be as they passed through San Rafael. The normal backup on the long grade leading up to the Waldo Tunnel failed to materialize, and as they emerged from the tunnel and coasted down to the Golden Gate Bridge, Elliott looked out across the bay to the glistening lights of the city, never so glad to be home.

They drove across the bridge and returned to North Beach. He double-parked in front of the inn and climbed out of the car, his back so tight he couldn't fully straighten up as he made his way around to Ms. Crighton's door. She took his arm, and they stepped up onto the sidewalk. As they stood beneath the canvas awning, she looked at the welt above his eye, the crust of blood on the abrasion.

"You poor man," she said. "Would you like to come in so I can clean you up?"

"I'll be fine," he said.

"Will I see you tomorrow?" she asked. "I have one more day before I have to fly home."

Elliott hadn't given tomorrow a moment's thought.

"Do you know what I would really like?" she asked.

"What is that, Ms. Crighton?"

"Do you have any photographs of your great-grandparents, any photographs of the ranch in the old days?"

"Of course."

"I would dearly love to see them," she said.

Elliott was too tired to discuss the matter.

"I'll call you tomorrow morning," he said, turning away and walking back to the BMW.

"Thank you again, Elliott. Good night!"

ELLIOTT DROVE back to Russian Hill. As he turned onto his block, he could see the lights were on in the garage, which, of course, meant The Sores were practicing. He pulled onto the sidewalk and pressed the button on the remote. As the garage door rolled up, Nigel and Jeremy stepped back out of the way. After parking beside the workbench, Elliott doused the headlights and turned off the engine. Leaning forward, resting his forehead on the steering wheel, he gathered himself for a moment, then pushed the car door open. As he got out, Alissa slid off her stool and walked out from behind her drum kit, her eyes growing large when she saw the shattered right headlight, the damage to the right front fender.

"What the hell?"

And then she saw the welt, the abrasion above his right eye.

"My God, you're bleeding!"

"No, not anymore," Elliott said.

"What happened?"

"We had a little mishap on the drive back," he said.

Alissa turned to Nigel and Jeremy, looking on with their guitars.

"We're done for the night," she told them.

Without a word, they turned off their amplifiers and propped their guitars against their speakers.

"I'll see you tomorrow," she said.

As they walked out of the garage, Alissa pressed the button on the wall and closed the garage door behind them.

"Let's get you inside," she said.

Leaning stiffly forward, Elliott stepped out from behind the BMW. With her arm around his waist, Alissa led him out of the garage, along the side of the building and up the back stairs, pausing for a moment on the landing before she eased him into the kitchen. As he took off his coat and sat at the table, she noticed the scratch on his forearm from the blackberry vines at the cemetery, the tear on the back of his shirt where he got caught slipping through the barbed wire fence, the hole in the right knee of his trousers, torn when he replaced the blown tire.

"Just look at you," she said.

"I'm fine," he said.

She walked out of the kitchen, returning a moment later with rolls of gauze and adhesive tape, a box of Band-Aids and a washcloth. He watched as she moistened the cloth and cleaned his wounds. She placed a Band-Aid on his arm, then tended to his eye, placing a small pad of gauze over the abrasion and securing it with two strips of tape.

"I knew I shouldn't have let you drive that woman up to Anderson Valley," she said.

She stepped back to inspect her work.

"I'm worried about you," she said.

"There's nothing to worry about," Elliott said.

"I'm serious."

Elliott rose unsteadily to his feet, still bent slightly forward, spasms shooting through the muscles at the small of his back.

"You can barely stand up," she said.

"All I need is a good night's sleep," he assured her, even if he wasn't necessarily so sure himself.

"I don't like this," she said. "I don't like where this is going."

He started toward the door, pausing to grab the doorframe and turn back to her.

"Thanks for patching me up," he said.

He made his way down the hall to the bathroom, then turned on the light and stood before the pedestal sink to examine himself in the mirror on the medicine chest. He raised his right hand and touched the pad of gauze above his eye, then opened the medicine chest and reached for the bottle of aspirin. He shook four tablets into the palm of his hand, then popped them into his mouth and washed them down with a swallow of water, hoping they would suppress his aches and pains, at least to the extent that he could sleep. He had never felt so old in his life. He felt every hour of his seventy-eight years. And it was Ms. Crighton's fault. She was entirely to blame. None of this would have happened, if not for her.

CHAPTER FOURTEEN

ELLIOTT REACHED under the shade and turned on the standing lamp in his study, then sat at his desk and opened the bottom drawer. In the drawer was a manila envelope with a handful of photographs taken at the ranch over the years, images he had tracked down from various sources, beginning, of course, with Lila at the historical society. He lifted the envelope out of the drawer and withdrew the photographs and quickly flipped through them. At a glance, he didn't see Benjamin Harrigan, but he would let Ms. Crighton examine them more closely.

He returned the photographs to the envelope and slipped it into his satchel, then he rose from the desk and carried the satchel into the living room. Sitting at his great-grandmother's secretary, he opened the upper right drawer and reached in for an old leather-bound family album. He placed the album on the fold-down desktop and looked through the old photographs, secured on the heavy pages with black corners. Most of the photographs were of family members sitting for formal portraits, or at holiday celebrations at the ranch, or on vacation at the coast or in the Sierra, their names written in neat script below. There were several photographs of his great-grandparents, quite a few, actually, of his great-grandmother, but, again, he saw no photographs of Harrigan.

After closing the album, he rose from the secretary and stepped up to the fireplace. He took down the daguerreotypes and carefully wrapped them in pages from the morning *Chronicle*, protecting the partially torn, leather hinges that bound the two portraits together before placing them in his satchel. He was sure Ms. Crighton would want to see the daguerreotypes. They were certainly the best photographs of his great-grandparents, taken in the prime of their lives for precisely this kind of occasion, a formal introduction.

Those were all the photographs he had of his great-grandparents and the early years at the ranch, so he picked up the satchel and album and started down the stairs. As he let himself out of the building and started up the sidewalk, his legs were heavy and his back stiff, a pulsing headache beneath the pad of gauze above his eye. He couldn't help but wonder how long it was going to take to recover from the effects of yesterday's trip to Anderson Valley.

He made his way over the hill and down to Washington Square, and as he crossed the street and approached the inn, he was startled to glimpse Ms. Crighton sitting in the high-backed chair in the front window, waiting for him. He was fully prepared to have to wait for her to come down from her room, late, as always, by her own admission.

She opened the door for him, stepping aside as he entered the lobby.

"Good morning, Elliott."

"Good morning, Ms. Crighton."

She noticed the pad of gauze taped over the welt above his eye.

"Oh, look at you, you poor thing," she said. "Would you care for a cup of coffee?"

"Thank you, but no, I'm fine," he said.

She led him over to the sofa in front of the fireplace, where a large coffee table was positioned in front of the hearth. Elliott placed the album on the table and his satchel on the hardwood floor, then folded his coat over the back of the sofa before sitting down.

"I'm so excited," Ms. Crighton said, sitting down beside him, pressing her hip against his.

Elliott opened the satchel and reached in for the daguerreotypes.

"Why don't we start with these," he said, gently unwrapping the sheets of newspaper and arranging the portraits on the table.

"Oh, my God," Ms. Crighton said, her voice falling to a hush.

"They were taken in San Francisco in 1863," he told her.

"She's beautiful, Elliott."

"She was twenty-seven years old."

"And your great-grandfather! He looks so aristocratic. He looks like a senator or a governor."

Elliott had to smile. He was sure his great-grandfather would appreciate her kind observation.

"Yes, he does have an aristocratic bearing, doesn't he?"

"I've tried to imagine what your great-grandparents looked like ever since I read Benjamin's letters," she said.

"I trust they haven't disappointed you."

"Oh, no – just look at them."

And so he did, one more time. Over the years, he had spent hours studying these two photographs of his great-grandparents, trying to read their faces as they were caught in the sudden bursts of flash powder. He saw them slightly differently every time he looked at them, as if always in a new light.

"You are so lucky to have known your great-grandmother," Ms. Crighton said. "I wish I had known Benjamin, even if just for one day."

He gave Ms. Crighton a moment more to look at the daguerreotypes, then he reached for the leather-bound album. The first photograph he wanted her to see was one taken of the house at the ranch not long after it was built, a photograph of the house as his great-grandfather had built it for his great-grandmother. He slid the album over to her. His great-grandparents were seated beside each other on the broad front porch, his great-grandfather in a black frock coat and a white shirt, his great-grandmother in a long dark dress, her son Matthew cradled in her arms. Standing beside his great-grandmother, her brother Zachary was wearing a white long-sleeve shirt and a buttoned-up vest. At his left arm, his wife Charlotte wore a simple high-collar blouse and a ruffled bonnet. Their two children were sitting on the steps in front of them, the older boy, Ames, prodding one of the sheepdogs lying on the ground with a stick.

"This is the earliest photograph I have of the house at the ranch," he told her. "I don't know the exact year it was taken, but my grandfather, Matthew, was born in 1858, so the photograph must have been taken not long after that."

Ms. Crighton smiled as she gazed down at the photograph.

"In better times," she said.

She looked over to him.

"It was a wonderful house, Elliott. I can see why you were so upset when you saw what's become of it."

He turned the page carefully, making sure none of the photographs peeled off the yellowed paper, the glue on the black corners dry and brittle after so many years. He turned back to the photographs of his grandparents, sitting portraits taken in a studio in Ukiah in 1900. Thirty-two years old, his grandfather was wearing a dark suit, his hair cropped short and parted straight down the middle, his eyes perfectly centered within his round wire-rim glasses.

"He looks so serious, so intelligent. He looks like a young engineer, or maybe a scientist, a chemist," she said.

"My great-grandfather wanted him to go to private school in the city. He wanted him to become a lawyer, like he had been. But my grandfather had no interest in school and even less in the law. All he ever wanted was to work on the ranch. He had little more than a grade school education, I'm afraid."

Ms. Crighton studied the portrait for a moment more.

"He looks like you, Elliott."

That Elliott had never heard before. He leaned closer and looked at his grandfather's portrait, and he supposed he did see a slight resemblance.

"Or should I say you look like him?"

"I take that as a compliment."

Ms. Crighton looked over to him.

"I wish I had known you when you were a young man," she said.

"You're fifty years too late," he said.

She laughed.

"Fifty years ago, I was six years old," she said.

That gave Elliott pause, naturally, but he quickly returned his attention to the album.

"This is my grandmother," he said, tapping the portrait with the tip of his index finger.

She looked to be a proper woman, frail and slight with a narrow face and piercing eyes, her dark hair coiled on the top of her head.

"Her name was Sara Ellison," he said. "She was the daughter of another rancher in the valley."

Elliott gave Ms. Crighton a moment, then turned several pages, unable to resist a smile as he looked down at a photograph of his father nattily attired in a gray pin-striped suit, a silver watch chain looping down from his vest pocket, his thick black hair combed straight back.

"My father was an attorney here in the city, a partner at a firm downtown," Elliott said. "He grew up in Boonville and then went to Cal and then to law school at Hastings. Once he lived in San Francisco and got a taste of life here, there was no returning to the ranch."

On the following page was a photograph of his mother, sitting in the living room in their flat on Vallejo Street. She was an elegant woman with long dark hair that she wore up on formal occasions, slender and composed in a dark sweater with a string of pearls around her neck.

"Look at her," Ms. Crighton said.

"She died of lung cancer when she was fifty-eight," Elliott said.

Ms. Crighton looked up.

"That's so young."

"She smoked," Elliott said. "It was an act of defiance, her personal rebellion against the conservative values of the day."

"And it killed her."

"I'm afraid so," he said.

But that was enough. Elliott closed the album and set it aside before Ms. Crighton could glimpse the photographs of him as a young boy: images of him dressed in short pants with matching socks and sweaters; or as a young teen at the helm of his father's sailboat; or standing stiffly erect in a tuxedo, on his way to the high school prom. He leaned down and withdrew the manila envelope from his satchel.

"Here are a few photographs taken, I believe, on our ranch. A few of them include some of the men who worked for us."

"Where did you get them?" Ms. Crighton asked, watching as he placed the photographs on the table.

"I got this one from Lila," he said.

The photograph had been taken during the apple harvest. In the orchard, two men were high in the trees, standing on the stilted three-legged ladders that enabled them to reach the uppermost branches, picking apples and slipping them into the long canvas sacks resting on their hips. The photograph was undated. The men were not identified.

"I don't suppose either of these men look like Harrigan," he said.

"No," she said.

He placed a second photograph on the table, this one taken

in the hills at the back of the ranch, where sheep were grazing in the meadow grass, wandering through the white oak and live oak. Three men on horseback were watching over the sheep, but they were some distance away.

"I found this one at the California Historical Society," he said.

Ms. Crighton leaned down and inspected the photograph.

"No, I don't think so," she said as she straightened back up.

"And these two at the public library."

The first photograph was of one of the shearing crews that worked on the ranch every spring. A half-dozen young men were posing for the photographer, two of them kneeling in front, the other four standing in a row behind them, clutching the hand shears they sharpened on a grinding wheel every night, their overalls stained dark from the lanolin in the wool. The second photograph was of the wool wagons lined up in front of the barn, the long sacks of fleece roped down in the wagon beds, looming above the teams of horses waiting to begin the long haul to Petaluma. Two men were standing in front of the horses.

Ms. Crighton studied the two photographs, then slowly shook her head.

"I always knew it was a long shot," she said.

And that was true. Elliott was glad she understood. He hoped she was not excessively disappointed.

"I'm afraid that's all I have to show you," he said.

But he could see that Ms. Crighton was thinking. As he returned the photographs to the envelope, she turned to him.

"Do you know if the public library is open today?"

AS THE CAB PULLED UP in front of the inn, Elliott reached down and opened the back door, so Ms. Crighton could climb in and slide across the back seat. He joined her and tugged the door closed, appreciating only then the pungent aroma of marijuana that suffused the cab. The driver looked back over the seat, his lank gray hair falling to his shoulders, his large dark eyes filled with veins.

"The Civic Center," Elliott told him. "The Main Library."

The driver tapped the meter, then pulled away from the curb, doubling back to Union Street and starting up the hill, casually rolling through the stop signs at each intersection. At the crest of the hill, the driver turned onto Hyde, and they drove through the canopy of ficus trees lining the street, over Nob Hill before descending into the Tenderloin and passing through the rundown residence hotels and liquor stores barricaded behind steel grates, the rescue missions and padlocked churches. As Elliott looked out at a group of men passing around a quart of malt liquor, he wasn't entirely sure what Ms. Crighton's expectations were, but he hoped they weren't excessively unrealistic. It was highly unlikely that they would find a photograph of her great-grandmother's uncle in the library's archives. But if she wanted to have a look, he was certainly willing to accompany her on this last day of her visit.

"Elliott, may I make a request?" Ms. Crighton asked.

"Of course," he said.

"Do you think you might call me Phoebe, instead of Ms. Crighton? We do know each other now, wouldn't you say?"

And yes, that was true. After their trip to Anderson Valley, they did indeed know each other. Elliott knew more about Phoebe than he ever could have anticipated, that he couldn't deny. He was amenable to her request. It seemed a modest concession to their new familiarity.

"As you wish, Phoebe," he said as the cab pulled up in front of the library's Grove Street entrance.

After paying the driver, Elliott pushed the door open and got out of the cab, a stab of pain in his lower back as he held the door for Phoebe. They walked past the book return bin on the sidewalk and passed through the glass doors, making their way past the uniformed security guard sitting beside the metal detector and then through the brightly lit atrium. Waiting, they stood in front of the bank of elevators. When the door to the elevator on the right opened, they stepped inside, and Elliott pushed the button for the sixth floor. As he turned to Phoebe, she was smiling in anticipation, disclosing an optimism he couldn't bring himself to share.

"Cross your fingers," she said as the elevator began to rise.

They stepped out of the elevator and walked over to the library's Historical Collections department. Elliott opened the heavy glass door and followed Phoebe into the large hushed room filled with rows of long tables, the walls covered with bookshelves lined with musty histories of the city and biographies of the men and women who had shaped its past. A woman with a blue scarf was sitting at the far end of one of the tables, looking through a folder of photographs, while an elderly couple was seated beside each other in the back of the room, whispering as they thumbed through one of the thick leather-bound histories.

Elliott and Phoebe walked over to the main counter and signed in, then approached the photograph desk, where a librarian with narrow black eyes was staring at his computer screen.

"Good afternoon," Elliott said. "We'd like to look at your historical photographs from Mendocino County."

"You'll need to fill out a request form," the librarian told them.

"Of course," Elliott said.

He leaned down and grabbed a pencil and quickly filled out one of the forms, then pushed it across the desk to the librarian. As he rose to retrieve the photographs, Elliott and Phoebe walked over to sit at the first table, pulling out the heavy wooden chairs. But Phoebe bounced back up almost immediately, walking around the end of the table to stand in front of him, reaching into her bag for her camera.

"Good God," Elliott said, as she raised the camera to take his photograph. "Is this absolutely necessary – Phoebe?"

She lowered the camera.

"You remembered," she said.

"If you absolutely have to do this, would you at least do it quickly?"

"On the count of three – smile!"

She took the shot, then dropped the camera back into her bag as the librarian emerged from the archives with a file folder of photographs. Elliott took his library card from his wallet and gave it to the librarian, who then slid the folder across the desk, along with two pairs of white cotton gloves.

"Please wear these while you look at the photographs."

"Of course," Elliott said.

He picked up the folder and the gloves, and he and Phoebe returned to the table. He gave Phoebe one of the pairs and then attempted to put on his. The gloves were far too small for his hands, but he managed to pull them over his fingertips. His struggle seemed to amuse Phoebe, who had notably less difficulty with her pair.

Elliott nodded at the folder.

"Go ahead," he said.

The file was thick, each of the photographs protected by a sheet of blank white paper. Many of the photographs were of the nineteenth-century logging operations, the mills with their log ponds and stacks of cut lumber, but they hoped they might glimpse Harrigan among the photographs of the crews working in the forest, felling the huge redwoods and then chaining the downed trees to teams of dray horses to drag them out of the woods.

"Benjamin only worked on the logging crews for a few months," Phoebe said, as if to explain his absence.

"But it's worth looking," Elliott assured her. "You never know what you might find."

They flipped through the folder, inspecting the photographs of men peeling sheets of bark from the trunks of the tanoaks and then rolling up the sheets and loading them onto teams of mules to be transported to the tanneries; photographs of the early vineyards planted in the valley, the workers stooped over, harvesting the heavy clusters of grapes and then loading the baskets into wagons to be delivered to the winemakers; photographs of hunting parties returning from the forest, men kneeling down beside the bucks they'd taken, lifting their heads to display their racks of antlers. But Elliott knew the odds of finding Harrigan in any of the photographs were long.

"It's hard to even know where these photographs were taken," he said.

They continued searching through the folder, inspecting the images of the men working with the sheep, grazing among the oaks in the winter mist, and of the men working in the apple orchards and at the wood-fired dryers, where the apples were peeled, cored, and sliced and then placed on racks to be dried. But ultimately they were disappointed.

"No, I don't see him," Phoebe said.

"But it was worth looking," Elliott said.

She closed the folder and took off her gloves.

"We might have better luck at the historical society," he told her.

"Would you mind?" she asked.

"Of course not," he said.

WITH HER HAND through his arm, they walked out of the library and down to Market Street. When the streetlight turned green, they crossed the broad boulevard and stepped up onto the boarding island to wait for a bus. Delivery vans and bobtail trucks streamed past them, the drivers pounding their horns at the bicyclists in fluorescent green jackets swarming down the street. A yellow cab streaked past, pedestrians in the crosswalk leaping out of its path, seeking the safety of the brick sidewalk. Elliott looked up Market and could see a bus approaching. He could see that it was the 6 Haight-Parnassus.

"We can take this one," he told her.

They waited until the bus pulled up in front of them, until the doors folded back to permit them to climb aboard. Elliott dug a handful of coins from his trouser pocket and fed them into the fare meter. After taking their paper transfers from the driver, they made their way down the aisle as the bus lurched forward, then dropped into a pair of seats across from the back doors. Elliott sat beside the window and looked out at the grim mid-Market malaise, the adult novelty shops and long-closed theaters, the discount stores and tobacco shops, the addicts and homeless slumped back against the grimy storefronts. He hoped Phoebe understood that the likelihood of their finding a photograph of her great-grandmother's uncle in the historical society's archives was no greater than at the public library.

Soon, the bus rolled past the fashionable retail emporiums in the shadow of Union Square, the sidewalks crowded with well-dressed women carrying bags filled with merchandise from upscale clothing stores, street merchants selling cheap bracelets and necklaces displayed on card tables, bare-chested drummers pounding out rhythms on upturned plastic buckets. They rose from their seats as the bus arrived in the Financial District, the high-rises clad in tinted glass, polished metal and precast stone as they ascended into the faint blue sky.

When the bus stopped at Third Street, they stepped down onto the boarding island, her hand again through his arm as they walked past the venerable brick and granite office buildings, the sleek modern hotels and condominium towers. At Mission Street, they made their way down to the Historical Society, which occupied a remodeled hardware store built in the 1920s. As Elliott reached down to open the door for Phoebe, he saw she was rummaging through her bag again.

"Not another," he said.

"Just stand right there," she said, raising the camera to her eye.

"One, two, three…"

After taking the photograph, she returned the camera to her bag and stepped up to the door.

"Now, that wasn't so bad, was it?"

He followed her into the lobby, past the bookstore and gift shop to the receptionist sitting at a desk in front of a large partition, a young man with a black beard trimmed around the rim of his jaw.

"We're here to look at your collection of historical photographs," Elliott said.

"The library is in the back," the receptionist said.

They walked past the receptionist, around the partition into the main exhibition hall. The walls were covered with blown-up photographic panoramas of San Francisco, taken from hilltops before the great earthquake and fire laid the city to waste, the wooden floor creaking beneath them as they moved through the glass display cases, past the roped-off staircase that led up to the research archives and reading room on the second floor. Quietly, they entered the library and found one of the librarians seated at the reference desk.

She was a middle-age woman with a blue sweater over her shoulders, her hair streaked with gray and pulled back into a tight bun. She looked up as they stood before her.

"We'd like to look at your photographs of Mendocino County," Elliott said.

"Of course," the librarian said. "I'll have them brought up.

They crossed the room and sat at one of the large glass-top worktables, surrounded by walls lined with bookshelves. Only two other patrons were working in the quiet room, two men in tweed jackets seated at a table near the door, examining an antiquated map of the bay. In the corner of the room stood the old card catalog cabinets, now quaintly obsolete.

It took only a few minutes for the photographs to be brought up from the archives, the librarian wheeling a small cart into the room. On the cart was a stout gray box with metal corners. The librarian placed it on the table, then gave them each a pair of white gloves.

"If you have any questions, please don't hesitate to ask," she said.

As she returned to the reference desk, Elliott put his gloves on as best he could, then reached for the box and carefully raised the lid. There were several file folders in the box. He lifted out the first folder and placed it on the table in front of Phoebe.

"Let's hope we have better luck this time," he said.

They began thumbing through the photographs in clear plastic sleeves, again most of them taken of the logging industry, photographs of crews felling the giant redwoods, teams of mules and horses dragging the fallen trees down skids carved into the mountains, horse-drawn freight wagons loaded with stacks of railroad ties and steam trains with flat cars bearing huge redwood rounds. In the second folder were a number of photographs taken in the small towns and settlements that had sprung up in the valley: women in bonnets and ankle-length dresses working in the hops fields near Philo, a man in overalls standing on the porch at the post office in Yorkville, clouds of steam drifting through the houses of the men who worked at the mill complex in Wendling, now Navarro.

In the third folder, they found several photographs that had been taken in Boonville, images that Elliott recalled seeing during the course of his research: a wedding party on the lawn in front of the Methodist Church, two men in frock coats standing beside the door of the Boonville Hotel, a group of young boys sitting on the plank sidewalk in front of J.T. Farrer's general store.

Elliott tapped the photograph of the general store with his gloved fingertip.

"My great-grandmother brought me here on my birthday," he told her. "She bought me a pair of black stitched-leather boots and a black cowboy hat. I wore them every day, all that summer at the ranch."

But Phoebe was already looking at a photograph that Elliott had never seen. On the main road as it passed through Boonville, dozens of men and women were standing shoulder to shoulder, as if everyone in town had been summoned to be photographed for posterity.

"Look at this," she said.

As Elliott looked down at the photograph, he had to wonder if they had found what they were searching for – Harrigan might very well be among the men and women standing in the road. They leaned down to inspect the image carefully, the solemn figures in their long coats and hats and hand-sewn dresses, staring intently at the camera. But the men and women were difficult, if not impossible, to identify. The photograph had simply been taken from too far away, their faces obscured by the distance.

"He's here, I can feel it," Phoebe said.

And Elliott did not necessarily disagree. He rose from the table and walked over to the librarian at her desk.

"Would you happen to have a magnifying glass?" he asked.

"Of course," she said.

She opened the top drawer of her desk and withdrew a large round magnifying glass with a short handle.

"Perfect," Elliott said as she handed it to him.

He returned to the table and sat down beside Phoebe, watching as she slowly passed the thick lens over the photograph. But even enlarged, the faces of the men and women standing in the road were largely unidentifiable.

Phoebe sat back in her chair.

"I know he's here," she said.

"You might very well be right."

"But we'll never know, will we?"

Elliott was loath to disappoint her, but he was not going to deny the obvious.

"No," he said quietly. "I don't suppose we ever will."

She turned the photograph over to look at the next image in the folder, but there were no more photographs to look at.

"I'm sorry," Elliott said. "We tried."

"Yes, we did," she said, closing the folder. "Thank you for indulging me."

AFTER THANKING THE LIBRARIAN, they left the historical society and walked back to Third Street and caught a cab. The driver was a Russian with a flushed pink face and a large purple mouth, grunting to himself as they drove up Kearny, skirting the edge of Chinatown before turning onto Columbus and heading into North Beach. Elliott glanced over to Phoebe, who was looking out the window as the city flashed past. He could see she was disappointed, and he certainly knew how she felt. They had come so close to finding a photograph of her great-grandmother's uncle, and perhaps they actually had. It was entirely possible that Harrigan was one of the men and women standing there on the road through Boonville, but no, they would never know.

And yet it must also be said that they had given it their best effort, and they could take some satisfaction in that. And in the years to come, he would look for any information he might find about Harrigan, and he knew that Lila would do the same at the historical society. Perhaps they would get lucky. Perhaps one day they would learn all they ever wanted to know. All they could do was hope.

When the cab pulled up in front of the Washington Square Inn, Elliott tossed a twenty-dollar bill over the seat and pushed the door open. They climbed out of the cab and were buzzed into the lobby, Elliott proceeding directly to the desk in the back.

Jeffrey rose from his chair, his shirt today featuring white hibiscus blossoms against a dark blue background.

"I've come for my satchel and album," Elliott said.

"Of course," Jeffrey said.

He retrieved them from the office and brought them back out

to the desk.

"Thanks for holding them for me," Elliott said.

"However we may be of service," Jeffrey said.

With the satchel in his left hand, the album tucked under his arm, Elliott returned to Phoebe, standing behind the sofa in front of the fireplace. He wished he could have been more help to her. He wished they'd found a photograph of Harrigan at the library or at the historical society. He knew all too well the frustration of a fruitless search, the disappointment when a promising avenue of inquiry ultimately leads nowhere. But an idea had occurred to him, a modest gesture of consolation.

"Ms. Crighton…"

But she stopped him, raising her hand.

"Yes, of course," Elliott said, hastening to correct himself. "Phoebe, I'm sorry we didn't have better luck today. But since this is your last night here, perhaps you'll allow me to take you out to dinner?"

He was pleased to see the thought seemed to lift her spirits.

"That would be lovely, Elliott."

CHAPTER FIFTEEN

EXPECTING HANK to be waiting for him, Elliott climbed the stairs leading up to his flat, but the dog, curiously, wasn't there. As he walked down the hall, he caught a faint whiff of one of Alissa's clove cigarettes, and it was then that he noticed the door to the back porch was slightly ajar. That puzzled him, but only momentarily. When he crossed the porch to close the door, he saw that Alissa was down in the yard, scooping up Hank's prolific deposits. Elliott couldn't remember the last time his granddaughter had cleaned up after her dog. He wondered what had inspired her to take up the task now.

He moved into the kitchen and set his satchel and the album on the table. As he removed his coat, he could hear Alissa climbing the stairs, Hank scrambling up the plank steps ahead of her, bursting through the door as if to break the momentous news that Alissa had disposed of his leavings. She appeared in the doorway a moment later, wearing her ragged blue jeans and a black undershirt, peering out from beneath her dyed green hair.

"Where have you been?" she asked.

"All over the city, it feels like," he said.

"With this woman?"

"Phoebe," he said, as if to remind himself.

"That's such a strange name," she said.

Elliott shrugged. He didn't necessarily disagree.

"Maybe a little old-fashioned," he conceded.

"You still haven't told me anything about her."

"What would you like to know?"

"What I'd like to know is who she is."

That didn't seem unreasonable to Elliott, though he wasn't entirely sure where to begin, other than with the obvious.

"She's an artist," he said. "A painter, to be more precise."

"Is she married?" Alissa asked, which, he supposed, is what his granddaughter really wanted to know.

"She was, years ago."

"And she believes some relative of hers worked on our ranch in Anderson Valley?"

"Actually, there seems to be very little doubt about it," Elliott said.

Alissa studied him carefully, her arms crossed over her chest.

"What else would you like to know?" he asked.

"Where is she now?"

"She's at the Washington Square Inn," he said. "I'm taking her out to dinner this evening, if that's all right with you."

Alissa shook her head, feigning disgust.

"This is so weird," she said.

"It is a little odd," Elliott admitted. "I won't argue with you about that."

He picked up the satchel and album and walked into the living room, where he carefully propped up the daguerreotypes on the fireplace mantel. After returning the album to his great-grandmother's secretary, he made his way down the hall to his study. He sat at his desk and slipped the manila envelope back into the bottom drawer.

"So is this getting serious?"

He turned to find Alissa standing in the doorway behind him, Hank squatting on his haunches at her feet.

"What are you talking about?" he asked. "Of course not."

"I mean you're not exactly a spring chicken."

"And I thank you for reminding me," Elliott said. "I'd gone all day without thinking about my age."

"You know what I mean."

"Yes, I do," he said, rising from the chair. "I know exactly what you mean. Now, if you'll excuse me, this old rooster is going to take a shower."

AFTER TAKING OFF his clothes, he moved into the bathroom and swept aside the shower curtain, then leaned down and turned on the water. He gave the water a moment to warm up, then stepped into the tub and drew the shower curtain closed. With the water drilling the back of his shoulders, he couldn't help but think about what Alissa had just said. She was right, of course – he was not a young man anymore. His body ached, his legs were weak, spasms of pain routinely lit up the small of his back. He felt every day of his seventy-eight years. And yet, it must also be said that he felt better than he had in years, better than he had in longer than he could remember. The truth was, Phoebe's visit had not been as disruptive as he had feared. She was quirky, yes; eccentric, to be sure. But despite his initial apprehension, he had enjoyed meeting Phoebe. He had enjoyed learning about her great-grandmother's uncle. And he looked forward, frankly, to taking her out to dinner to commemorate her visit to San Francisco.

After drying off, he reached for his flannel robe and eased his feet into a pair of slippers. He wiped the steam from the mirror and brushed his hair and taped another small pad of gauze over the welt above his eye, then he returned to the kitchen and made himself a cup of coffee. When he heard his cell phone ringing in the pocket of his coat, draped over one of the chairs at the table, he thought for a moment that it might be Phoebe, calling to cancel on him. But as he looked at the phone, he saw that it was his daughter.

"Hello, Claire."

"Finally," she said, her voice thick with exasperation.

"Finally what?" he asked.

"I've been calling all afternoon."

"I'm sorry," he said. "I've had my phone turned off. I was at the library and then at the historical society downtown."

But that was not what his daughter had called to discuss.

"So what's going on up there?" she wanted to know.

"What do you mean?"

"Who is this woman you've started seeing?"

Elliott could have laughed. Of course. He understood now.

"I gather you've been talking to Alissa."

"She called this morning," Claire said. "And I'm glad she did."

"I told you she'd call, if you gave her a little time."

"She called because she's concerned about you – and so am I, to tell you the truth."

"I can assure you, there's nothing to be concerned about," he said.

"She told me you drove this woman up to Anderson Valley yesterday."

"Yes, that's true."

"And she told me you crashed the BMW on the way back."

"Well, not exactly."

"She said you have a nasty lump on your head and scratches all over your arms."

"That's a bit of an exaggeration."

"And you weren't going to tell me about this?" she asked indignantly, anointing herself the aggrieved party.

"Of course I was."

"When?"

He didn't have an answer for that, not a specific date or time.

"I really don't understand why you're so worked up about this," he said.

"Worked up? You're damn right I'm worked up. Some woman you don't know flies out from New York City to see you – and you don't even tell me?"

"There's really not a lot to tell you, other than I'm taking her out to dinner."

"Good lord," his daughter groaned.

"And then she's flying home tomorrow."

He heard Claire take a breath, as if pulling herself together.

"And that's it?"

"That's it," he confirmed.

And that seemed to appease her, at least for the moment.

"Is there anything else?" he asked.

"All right, all right," she relented. "Just call me the next time you decide to run off with some floozy."

The thought made Elliott want to laugh.

"I promise. I give you my word," he said. "But I have no reason to believe there will be a next time. This is it."

And for a moment, Claire was silent, as if trying to decide whether to believe him.

"All right," she said. "I'll talk to you later."

As Elliott turned off his phone and started back down the hall, he realized what he had just told his daughter, suddenly feeling its full weight. Phoebe was indeed leaving to return to New York City tomorrow, and it was also true that there was no reason to believe that he would ever hear from her again. He had fulfilled his obligation to help her learn what she could about her great-grandmother's uncle. He could return now to his own work with no more distractions. And yet, as he took off his robe and stepped into a pair of trousers, he had to admit that at least a part of him was going to be sorry to see Phoebe go.

AFTER SLIPPING ON his coat, Elliott walked out of the bedroom. The instant he started down the hall, he saw that Alissa was waiting for him at the top of the stairs, leaning back against the railing with her arms folded across her chest, wagging her head at him as he approached.

"You're really going to go through with this, aren't you?" she asked, as if there might have been some doubt.

"I am, indeed."

"What time will you be getting home?"

Elliott smiled, appreciating the irony, even if she didn't.

"I don't know," he said.

She shook her head at him again, watching as he began descending the stairs.

"Just don't do anything stupid," she called down after him. "And if you can't help yourself, at least wear a condom!"

Elliott let himself out of the building and started up the sidewalk. He appreciated his granddaughter's counsel, even if it was presumptuous in the extreme and displayed little knowledge of the functional limitations of a seventy-eight-year-old male. He knew she had his best interests at heart, and yet her concern amused him. She had never expressed this concern before. As far as Elliott could tell, her compassionate instincts, to the extent that she had any at all, were directed exclusively at Hank. It made him smile to think that Phoebe's visit had discombobulated his granddaughter as much as it had discombobulated him.

He walked over the hill and down to the Washington Square Inn. When the door buzzed, he reached down and stepped into the lobby and then made his way back to the desk.

"Good evening, Jeffrey. Would you let Phoebe know that Elliott

Madison is here?"

"With pleasure," he said.

Elliott crossed the lobby and sat in the chair in the front window. He looked out at the square and saw a woman sitting on a bench with a white feather boa around her neck, a man in a long navy peacoat playing a saxophone beneath the pines. Standing on the sidewalk, a uniformed beat cop was smoking a cigarette, idly blowing smoke rings into the warm evening air.

When he heard someone coming down the carpeted stairs behind him, he rose from the chair.

"Good evening, Elliott."

In a simple blue dress with a white collar, a thin white belt around her waist, Phoebe walked across the lobby to him, a dark blue sweater wrapped around her shoulders, the arms loosely knotted across her chest.

"Good evening, Phoebe. I hope you're hungry."

"Ravenous," she said. "I just woke up from a wonderful nap. I feel revived, rejuvenated!"

"I thought we might walk down the block to La Felce. I trust you enjoy Italian food?"

She threw her arms wide as if to embrace him.

"I love Italian food," she said.

They walked out of the inn and down the sidewalk, her hand, as always, slipped through his arm. At the corner, they waited for a delivery van to pass before they crossed the street and approached the door of the restaurant, standing to the side as a middle-age man with gin blossoms on his cheeks staggered through the door. As the door swung closed behind him, Elliott caught the edge and held it open for Phoebe, then he trailed her into the softly lit bar, the dark red walls covered with autographed black-and-white photographs of the long-forgotten celebrities who had patronized the establishment over the years.

Standing behind the mahogany bar in his gray vest and white

shirt, the bartender greeted Elliott warmly.

"Elliott! Come in! It's good to see you!"

"Hello, Jimmy."

In a black tuxedo with a red bow tie, the maître d' emerged from behind the heavy red curtain draped over the door to the dining room.

"Good evening, Mr. Madison."

"The two of us for dinner, Edgar."

He nodded, then drew the curtain aside and led them into the dining room, ushering them to one of the tables in the back. The room was loud, filled with the raucous cheers of men in dark suits and silk ties, peals of laughter from women with hives of white hair and faces caked with makeup. Edgar held Phoebe's chair for her, then helped her move closer to the table. As Elliott sat down across from her, she glanced around the dining room, at the mirrors in gilded frames mounted on the sand-gray walls.

"Your waiter will be here in a moment," Edgar said.

As he walked away, Phoebe leaned across the table.

"Oh, Elliott, I love it," she whispered. "I feel like we're back in the 1950s. I feel like ordering a martini."

"I think that's a splendid idea," Elliott said.

He looked up as Dante, their waiter, approached the table.

"Two martinis, very dry, " Elliott told him.

"Very well."

"But wait," Phoebe said. "Would you mind taking a photograph of us?"

"Of course not," Dante said.

Phoebe fumbled through her handbag for her camera, then gave it to Dante and summoned a broad smile. Elliott knew he was obligated to do the same.

"Ready?" Dante asked.

He leaned down and snapped the photograph.

"Thank you so much," Phoebe said.

As he left for the bar, she reached for her bag and began digging through it once more.

"I brought something for you," she said.

It took her a moment, but she eventually placed a photograph on the tablecloth and pushed it toward him.

"I asked Jeffrey to have my pictures developed while I took my nap," she said.

When Elliott leaned forward, he saw it was the photograph that Lila had taken of them in front of the old schoolhouse.

"Don't you think it's a nice photograph of us?" she asked.

Elliott took a closer look. Phoebe was beaming for the camera. Standing beside her, he had managed a smile, too, though it lacked the enthusiasm Phoebe had marshalled.

"I think we make a very handsome couple," she said.

"If you say so, Phoebe."

"It's for you, Elliott. You can keep it – a souvenir of our trip to Anderson Valley."

"That's very kind," he said.

When Dante returned with their martinis, Elliott leaned back out of the way, looking on as the waiter placed the thin-stemmed glasses on the table.

"Are we ready to order?" he asked.

They hadn't consulted their menus, but Elliott knew what he wanted, what he always ordered at the restaurant, one of the house specialties.

"Perhaps you'll allow me, Phoebe?"

"Of course," she said.

Elliott looked up at Dante.

"We'll each have the veal piccata."

But before Dante could write their order down, Phoebe emitted a soft sigh.

"Oh, Elliott."

"What?" he asked.

"Veal? Don't you know what they do to those poor calves?"

Elliott felt himself smile. Phoebe's views on veal did not surprise him. He might very well have guessed she was an animal rights activist.

"May I ask how you feel about chicken cacciatore?"

She didn't say anything. She didn't have to. Elliott looked up at Dante.

"We'll each have the fettuccine alfredo," he said.

As Dante departed for the kitchen, Elliott picked up his martini, pinching the stem of the glass between his thumb and forefinger.

"A toast to Benjamin Harrigan," he said.

"What a lovely thought," Phoebe said, raising her glass and clinking it against his. "And to your great-grandparents – William and Amelia Madison."

Elliott watched her take a sip of her martini. With her blue eyes and wide ineluctable smile, shallow dimples on her cheeks, Phoebe was not, he was prepared to admit, wholly unattractive.

"Delicious," she said.

DANTE BROUGHT two simple salads with iceberg lettuce, sliced tomatoes and kidney beans, as well as a basket of warm buttery garlic bread wrapped in a white cloth. A moment later, he delivered the huge plates of creamy fettuccine, speckled with cracked black pepper. They ate slowly, as if lingering over their last meal together, twisting the long ribbons of pasta around the tines of their forks before lifting them to their mouths. It was more than either of them could eat, but they did manage to finish a bottle of Chardonnay. It seemed a proper reward after a long day running around the city, searching through the photographic archives at the public library and the historical society.

Placing his cloth napkin on the table, Elliott leaned back as Dante took their plates.

"Would you care to look at the dessert menu?" he asked.

Elliott looked across the table to Phoebe. When she shook her head, he turned back to Dante.

"Just coffee," he said.

As Dante walked away, Phoebe began searching through her handbag again.

"Now don't be mad that I didn't show this to you sooner," she said.

Elliott had no idea what she was talking about.

"It's a letter," she said, producing a clear plastic baggie. "It's a letter your great-grandmother wrote to Benjamin's niece, telling her that Benjamin had died."

"What?"

When she handed the baggie to him, he saw that it did indeed contain a small creased envelope. In utter disbelief, he stared down at it in his hands.

"You can read it," she said, as if the thought had yet to occur to him.

He glanced across the table to her, as if to make sure this wasn't some elaborate prank, but no, it clearly wasn't, and he turned his attention back to the baggie. He unsealed it and carefully withdrew the envelope, addressed to Dorothea Smiley in East Fishkill, New York, immediately recognizing his great-grandmother's handwriting. He lifted the envelope flap and took out the letter, holding it gently as if it might disintegrate in his hands. Slowly, he unfolded it, observing the faint brown ink on the soft paper, fibers raised by the nib of his great-grandmother's cherished fountain pen, still residing in the upper drawer of her secretary.

September 18, 1898

Dear Dorothea,

I write to you with the heaviest of hearts, delivering, as I must, word of the death of your beloved uncle. It grieves me to tell you that he died of a sudden heart attack while out hunting. Benjamin was a lovely man, a kind and decent soul, and I shall always be grateful for the years he worked on our ranch and for the pleasure of his companionship. I shall miss him dearly. Please know that he spoke fondly of you and was deeply grateful for your care during his recuperation after the war. We gave Benjamin a proper burial yesterday, and in the years to come, you may take comfort in the knowledge that I shall personally see to the maintenance of his grave.

Yours in deepest sorrow,

Amelia Madison

Elliott looked up.

"Isn't it beautiful?" Phoebe asked.

"I don't understand," he said. "Why didn't you tell me you had this?"

"Because I didn't know you, Elliott, because I didn't know who you were."

But that hardly satisfied him.

"I want you to have it," she said.

"What?"

"Don't you see, Elliott – I told Lila about this letter. And when she told me about your project, about your great-grandfather's journals and your great-grandmother's letters, when she told me that you intend to donate them to the historical society, I knew that's where this letter belonged, too, with your great-grandmother's other letters. That's why I'm here. I needed to meet you. I couldn't just send the letter off to someone I didn't know. I couldn't just drop it in the mail and take the risk it might get lost or damaged."

It was more than Elliott could immediately digest. He still couldn't quite believe that his great-grandmother had written a letter to Harrigan's niece. It didn't seem possible that he was holding that letter in his hands.

"It's such a lovely letter," Phoebe said.

Elliott carefully slipped it back into the envelope, then returned it to the baggie.

"Your great-grandmother obviously cared about Benjamin," Phoebe said. "She obviously cared a great deal."

"It seems so," he said.

"And I think Benjamin must have cared a great deal about your great-grandmother."

"What do you mean?" he asked.

Phoebe shrugged.

"It's just a feeling," she conceded. "But I felt it the moment I read the letter. There's something there, Elliott. There's something between them. Don't you feel it, too?"

He looked at her, as if there had to be more.

"Don't you ever wonder why your great-grandmother never remarried?" Phoebe asked. "Don't you ever wonder if there was anyone else in her life, after your great-grandfather passed away?"

"She had her son Matthew," he said. "She had her brother Zachary and Charlotte."

"But when did your great-grandfather die?"

Elliott had to think for a moment.

"He died in 1864."

"And your great-grandmother?"

"1933."

"Elliott, that's nearly seventy years."

Which was true, of course. He did not quarrel with the math.

"Haven't you ever wondered if she got lonely?"

The question stopped him. No, actually – the thought had never occurred to him. He had never really thought about his great-grandmother being alone for so many years. He had never asked himself why she hadn't found someone else, or why she had chosen to live alone after his great-grandfather passed away. Always, he had viewed her as the valley's enduring matriarch, a woman larger than life. He had never seen her as a grieving widow, a woman who tragically lost her husband, the father of her only child. Now it seemed so obvious. He felt like a fool, ashamed. He felt as if he had never really known his great-grandmother at all.

He looked back down at the letter in the baggie.

"Are you sure you want me to have this?" he asked.

"Yes, absolutely," Phoebe said.

"I don't know what to say."

"There's nothing to say, Elliott."

"I thank you, of course. I'm deeply grateful."

She reached over and placed her hand on his forearm.

"I know you are," she said.

AFTER HELPING PHOEBE rise from the table, Elliott led her through the dining room, through the heavy curtain into the bar and then out onto the sidewalk. Darkness had fallen, the illuminated spires of Sts. Peter and Paul rising up into the cloudless night. A yellow cab quietly idled along the curb. As Phoebe slipped her hand through his arm, they crossed the street and walked back to the inn. He pressed the button beside the door, and they entered the lobby and walked over to sit on the sofa in front of the fireplace. Phoebe moved closer, taking his arm and drawing herself toward him.

"Thank you for a wonderful dinner, for a wonderful day," she said. "Thank you for two wonderful days, actually."

"It's been my pleasure," Elliott said.

"I'd invite you up to my room to express my gratitude," she said. "But I'm not the frisky sex kitten I used to be."

Elliott turned to her, permitting himself a bewildered smile. She batted her eyes at him. He had no idea what to make of her.

"When do you leave?" he asked.

"My flight departs at 10:30."

"May I drive you to the airport?"

"I was hoping you would offer," she said.

AS ELLIOTT WALKED down Vallejo Street, he could see the light leaking out from beneath the door of the garage. Nearly a block away, he could hear the hideous din Alissa and her bandmates were generating. It grew only louder as he approached the building. He unlocked the gate and opened the door leading down to the garage, then made his way down the stairs as if descending into hell itself.

Nigel spotted him first. When he abruptly stopped playing his bass, Alissa lifted her head from her drums and sat back on her stool, perspiration gleaming on her forehead as she rested her drumsticks across her thighs. Jeremy was the last to notice him, lost in the excruciating currents of feedback he was extorting from his guitar. Finally, he turned down his amplifier, a merciful silence settling upon the garage.

"I just wanted to let you know I'm home," Elliott said to Alissa.

"We won't be playing much longer," she said.

"Play as long as you'd like," he said.

With his ears ringing, he left them to resume their practice and made his way up to his flat. After letting Hank out to attend to his business, he walked down the hall to his study, then reached into his coat pocket and carefully withdrew the letter Phoebe had given him. He placed it on the writing pad on his desk, then took off his coat and kicked off his shoes, stretching his aching back before slipping on his sweater and sitting down. He still couldn't believe that Phoebe had given him this letter written by his great-grandmother. It was an extraordinary act of generosity, the gift of a priceless family heirloom. Never could he have imagined this letter might even exist, much less that he would come to possess it.

He took the envelope out of the baggie and withdrew the letter, unfolding it on the writing pad and gently smoothing it out with his fingertips. He read the letter one more time. It was indeed a moving expression of condolence, offered with genuine sorrow. There could be no doubt that his great-grandmother was devastated when she learned that one of her ranch hands had died while out hunting, that she felt a profound sense of loss upon Harrigan's death. And it didn't surprise Elliott that Phoebe was convinced their relationship had moved beyond the daily operation of the ranch, beyond the realm of the platonic. She didn't want to think that her great-grandmother's uncle had gone to his grave without knowing love, and Elliott certainly didn't fault her for that. But she possessed not an ounce of evidence to support this wishful thinking. It was based solely on her intuition, what she had divined between the lines. And that was fine. Phoebe needed no evidence. She was free to believe whatever she wanted to believe. She was free to go wherever the wild flights of her imagination took her.

As he sat back in the chair, he understood that was simply who Phoebe was – a frisky sex kitten batting her blue eyes at him. He couldn't help but smile as he reached for the photograph that Lila had taken of them in front of the old schoolhouse. He propped it against the dictionary on the right side of his desk. It was a very fine photograph. He was glad Phoebe had asked Lila to take it, and he was grateful to Phoebe for making a copy for him. Perhaps he would buy a simple frame, so he could position the photograph here on his desk, a reminder of the day they spent in Anderson Valley, of Phoebe's visit to San Francisco. And, yes, it was true – he and Phoebe were indeed a handsome couple. Those were Phoebe's words, her exact words, and he did not intend to dispute her.

WHEN HE NOTICED the night had fallen silent, he realized The Sores had stopped practicing. He could hear Alissa walking up the back stairs and opening the porch door. He heard her opening a can of dog food and slopping it into Hank's bowl, then setting the bowl on the kitchen floor. And then he could hear her walking down the hall, her footfall on the hardwood floor.

As he turned around, she appeared in the doorway to his study.

"How was your dinner?" she asked.

"Very nice."

"Where did you take her?"

"La Felce."

"Old school," she said.

"Yes, as am I," he said.

"And then you took her back to the inn?"

"Yes, I did," he said. "And you'll be relieved to know that I managed to resist the temptation to do anything stupid."

"Thank God," she said

She leaned against the doorframe.

"She's still leaving tomorrow?"

"I'm taking her to the airport," he said.

"And she's not planning on coming back?"

"I don't know why she would."

"So that will be the end of all this?"

"Yes, I'm afraid it will be," he said.

She seemed to think about that for a moment, as if wondering what else she might want to know, what else she should ask him. He didn't understand his granddaughter's concern about Phoebe, or his daughter's concern, either. At least they had finally spoken on the phone.

"Just don't tell me you're going to miss her," Alissa said. "I don't want you mooning around the flat, feeling sorry for yourself like some lovesick fool."

"You have my word," Elliott said.

CHAPTER SIXTEEN

TAPPING THE BRAKES, Elliott turned into the gas station on Van Ness, intending to fill up the BMW before driving Phoebe to the airport. He pulled alongside the pumps, then shut down the engine and climbed out of the car. As he twisted off the gas cap, he couldn't help but notice the wrinkled right front fender, the spare tire without its hubcap. The trip to Anderson Valley seemed a lifetime ago, and despite his righteous outrage when confronted with the condition of his great-grandparents' house, he nonetheless liked to think it had been a productive day, meeting with Lila at the historical society and locating Harrigan's grave, even if the journey had left him and the BMW a little worse for the wear.

He fed a credit card into the pump, then lifted the hose and inserted the nozzle into the sleeve leading down to the tank. As he grabbed the squeegee and began scrubbing the windshield, he found it hard to believe that Phoebe had been here for just two days – it felt so much longer than that. He felt as if he had known Phoebe for years, and, to be perfectly candid, he was sorry that her visit to San Francisco was coming to an end. He couldn't help but feel that he had been a poor ambassador for the city he had lived in all his life, that he had failed to present the city to her properly, and suddenly it occurred to him that he might ask Phoebe if she'd like to stay for another day or two. The thought stopped him. It seemed so easy, so simple. It was certainly an idea worth presenting to her.

After returning the hose to the pump, he drove back over the hill to North Beach and double-parked in front of the inn, turning on his emergency lights before walking up to the front door. Jeffrey buzzed him into the lobby, his shirt today featuring lush green ferns against a white background.

"Good morning, Jeffrey. Would you mind letting Phoebe know that her ride to the airport is here?"

"With pleasure," he said.

Elliott watched as Jeffrey dialed her room. It seemed to take an inordinate amount of time for Phoebe to answer, but finally she did.

"She told me to tell you to go on up," Jeffrey said.

Elliott was not in the habit of visiting women in their private rooms, of course, but if that's what Phoebe wanted, he would go up to her room as if it were a matter of accepted practice. He started up the carpeted stairs and made his way down the hall. He knocked lightly on her door.

"Come in!" she called out to him.

And so he would. He reached down and turned the doorknob, then slowly pushed the door into the room and followed it inside. The room was in total disarray – the bed unmade with blankets flung to the floor, a suitcase lying open beneath a pile of clothes at the foot of the bed, a gauzy nightgown tossed over the back of the antique chair in the corner. Through the open door, he could see Phoebe in the bathroom, her reflection in the mirror as she brushed her black hair, pulling it back and securing it with an elastic band.

"I'm running a little late, no surprise there," she said. "I overslept.

My God, I slept like a baby."

In black slacks and a light blue blouse, she emerged from the bathroom, smiling guiltily.

"It won't take me a minute to pack up," she said.

"Of course," he said.

He watched as she began gathering her clothes, sweeping them up in her arms and then dumping them on the pile in the suitcase. She tried to close the suitcase, tucking in the stray garments and pressing down on the lid, but she needed to hike her hip up onto the lid to press it closed. As she glanced over to Elliott, he saw that the effort had brought a flush to her cheeks.

"I'll put on my shoes, and we can go," she said.

As she picked up a pair of sandals and carried them over to the chair, it seemed the moment to tell her what he had been thinking at the gas station. It only made sense to present her with the idea now, before they started for the airport, before, frankly, he lost his nerve.

"I had a thought," he told her.

She looked up at him.

"It just seems like we've been so busy, driving up to Anderson Valley and searching through the archives at the library and the historical society – I thought if you were interested in staying a day or two longer, I'd love to show you a little more of the city."

She sat back in the chair, her hands on the padded arms.

"I thought perhaps you could extend your stay here," he said, as if to explain his thinking. "Or, if you prefer, you could stay with me on Russian Hill. We have an extra bedroom, my study, actually."

"Are you serious?"

And suddenly Elliott wondered if he was serious, if he had any idea what he was suggesting. A surge of panic gripped him – he realized he might very well be making a terrible mistake, thoroughly misconstruing Phoebe's flirty remarks, her hand always slipped through his arm, the frisky sex kitten playfully batting her eyes at him. The suggestion was absurd. He had no idea why he'd thought she might delay her return to New York, why she might want to spend another day or so with him, with a feeble seventy-eight-year-old man, no less. And now, good Christ, he had utterly humiliated himself.

He could feel his face blooming red.

"It was merely a thought…" he hastened to say.

But she needed to hear no more.

"Elliott, I'd love to stay. I'd love to see your flat."

He stared at her, momentarily confounded.

"You would?"

"I would, yes."

He took a cautious breath, nodding to himself, still absorbing her ready acceptance of his offer. Yes, she would. She had just said that. He had heard it, every word. She would like to stay a little longer.

"Well, let's go, then," he said. "Whenever you're ready."

WHILE PHOEBE TOOK a last glance around the room to see if she'd forgotten anything, Elliott picked up her suitcase and lugged it over to the door, then he started down the hall, down the stairs to the lobby. He carried the suitcase out to the BMW, wincing as he hoisted it into the trunk, then leaned back against the side of the car to wait for her.

A moment later, she emerged from the inn.

"Ready?" he asked.

She smiled, extending her arms and then letting them flap down to her thighs.

"I most certainly am," she said.

Elliott helped her into the passenger seat, then walked around the rear of the car and slipped behind the wheel. He started the engine, and as they drove past Sts. Peter and Paul and then headed up the hill, he couldn't help but wonder what Alissa was going to say about him bringing Phoebe home, what she might say about his arranging for her to spend the night. He'd told her he was taking Phoebe to the airport, so she could catch her flight back to New York City; he'd told her he had no reason to believe that he would ever see her again. As he braked and turned onto Vallejo, he knew his granddaughter was not going to be amused by this sudden change in plans. The only material question was how she might choose to express her disapproval. Her options, unfortunately, were many.

He pulled up in front of the garage and pressed the remote to open the door, then guided the BMW into the back corner. As he got out of the car and opened the trunk, Phoebe walked over to stand in front of Alissa's drum set and her bandmates' guitars and amplifiers.

"My granddaughter plays the drums," he told her. "She plays in a heavy metal power trio. They call themselves The Sores."

"That's quite the name," Phoebe said.

"It is, indeed."

"Have you heard them play?"

Elliott laughed to himself. Phoebe didn't need to hear about his evening at the Anarchists Club.

"They're loud, they're intense – I'll give them that," he said.

He lifted the suitcase out of the trunk and then carried it out of the garage and along the side of the building, Phoebe following him up the back stairs, the heavy bag banging against his leg with every step. As Elliott opened the porch door, they were greeted by Hank, sitting on his haunches and staring up at them, his head cocked to the left and his tongue lolling out the side of his mouth.

"This is Hank, my granddaughter's dog," Elliott said.

"And what a handsome dog he is," Phoebe said, kneeling down to scratch him behind the ears.

Elliott started down the hall, all but dragging the suitcase into his study. As he dropped it beside the desk, Phoebe entered the room behind him. She immediately noticed the map he had pieced together and pinned to the wall above his desk, tracing his great-grandmother's journey across the continent. She crossed the room to examine it.

"So this is your study?" she asked. "This is where you work on your manuscript?"

"It is," Elliott said.

"How long have you been working on it?"

"Ever since I retired, not quite fifteen years ago," he said.

She turned to him, as if surprised by the duration of his project.

"That's such a long time," she said.

Elliott did not disagree.

"The time does go by, doesn't it?"

He gestured toward the sofa pushed up against the opposite wall.

"This folds out into a double bed," he told her. "My daughter Claire tells me it's very comfortable. She sleeps on it when she comes up for a visit."

"I'm sure it will be fine," Phoebe said.

"Would you care for a cup of coffee before we venture out?"

"That sounds wonderful," she said.

They walked back down the hall to the kitchen, where the morning sunlight streamed through the window above the sink. Elliott filled the teakettle with water and placed it on the stove. As he rinsed out the glass pot, Phoebe pulled out a chair and sat at the table.

"It's a lovely flat, Elliott."

"It's all my granddaughter and I need," he said.

And, as if on cue, Alissa appeared in the kitchen doorway, her eyes bruised with sleep, her green hair pressed flat against the side of her head. In her loose white robe, she stood there barefoot, her toenails painted a glossy black. Elliott wondered if the toenail polish was new, or if he simply hadn't noticed this most recent of his granddaughter's menacing affectations.

"Good morning, Alissa," he said. "May I introduce Phoebe Crighton?"

He gave Alissa a moment to respond. She declined the opportunity.

"And Phoebe, this is Alissa, my granddaughter."

"A pleasure," Phoebe said.

He watched as Alissa fished a pack of clove cigarettes from the pocket of her robe, then shook one out of the pack and took it in her teeth.

"Alissa, you'll be pleased to know that I've persuaded Phoebe to spend another day or so here in the city."

She struck a match and lit the cigarette, then took a long drag and exhaled through both nostrils.

"In fact, she'll be spending the night with us," he said.

Through the ribbon of smoke rising from her cigarette, Alissa stared at him, her eyes bloodshot beneath their sagging lids.

"How nice," she said flatly.

"But don't worry," Elliott said. "We'll be leaving as soon as we have a cup of coffee."

Still glaring at him, Alissa took another drag on her cigarette, then turned and started back down the hall to her bedroom. Elliott smiled after her. She had made her point – and point taken. And he was relieved, surprised, actually, that her performance hadn't been more dramatic. And yet he was sorry his granddaughter disapproved of his relationship with Phoebe, if it could even be called a relationship. He had to believe that Claire would disapprove as well. But that was too bad, he told himself. He had invited a woman he had come to know over the last few days to extend her visit for another day or so. And now he intended to show her around the city. He hadn't done anything untoward or inappropriate. He had absolutely nothing to apologize for, certainly not yet.

HE KNEW EXACTLY where he wanted to take her. They climbed into the BMW and drove down the hill and headed south on Van Ness, traffic thickening as they approached the Civic Center, stoplight to stoplight past the gilded dome of City Hall and the white granite keys of Symphony Hall. They turned up Market Street and drove through the teeming Castro, the city's central thoroughfare narrowing as it swept up and across the face of Twin Peaks. Elliott braked and doubled back onto the street leading up to the tops of the peaks, slowly winding through the pastel houses and terraced apartment buildings until he eased the car over to the retaining wall and shut down the engine.

"Are you ready for a little exercise?" he asked.

"Lead on," she said. "Take me where you will."

Across the street, they started up the open trail to Noe Peak, slipping on the loose rock and plodding up the steps carved into the slope, halting several times to gather themselves as they made their way up to the summit. But this was the view of the city that Elliott wanted Phoebe to see – the sun-washed metropolis on the hills above the blue-black bay, the distant tinsel glare of the downtown financial towers and the subtle aggregation of its districts and neighborhoods, its constituent spires, steeples and turrets and its sinuous streets and avenues, the quiet refuge of its greenswards and parks.

"Oh, Elliot, I love it!" she exclaimed. "Stand right there. Don't move."

As he turned to her, she was lifting her camera from her handbag. He squared his shoulders and rose to his fullest height, as if to measure up to the city behind him.

"One more," she said, still peering through the viewfinder.

But that was enough for Elliott. That would have to do. He watched as she took several more photographs, as if committing the city to memory, then returned the camera to her bag.

"It's such a beautiful city," she said. "San Francisco may be the most beautiful city I've ever seen."

And yet Elliott couldn't look out upon the city without thinking about the remote windswept settlement his great-grandfather found here on his way to the gold fields – the hotels, saloons and gambling halls thrown up along the marshy shoreline and flanking the public square, the ragged tents and ramshackle huts scattered among the barren hills and sand dunes, the fleet of ghost ships abandoned beyond the wharves. And now to see what the city had become, its glorious transformation.

"And what a day!" Phoebe said, looking up at the golden sky.

"We call it earthquake weather," he said.

She turned to him, reaching up to gather her hair.

"It comes every autumn, usually in October," he said. "It reminds us of the last one, the last big one."

"The last earthquake?"

"Loma Prieta, 1989 – magnitude 6.9 on the Richter scale."

She looked at him as if she wasn't quite sure whether to believe him, the corner of her mouth curling up in a wary smile, as if this might be a tale reserved for unsuspecting visitors.

"You're making me nervous, Elliott."

He laughed. No, that was not his intent. He wanted Phoebe to appreciate the beauty of the city. That was precisely the reason he had brought her here. But she should also understand how fragile and tenuous that beauty was. She should understand that it all might vanish in an instant.

"This weather makes us all a little nervous," he said. "It makes us all a little crazy."

He gestured back down the trail.

"Come on, let's go," he said.

THEY RETURNED TO THE BMW and drove down to Golden Gate Park, the wind-sculpted pines swaying above as they rolled past the

Botanical Gardens, bicyclists weaving through the clotted traffic, the sidewalks crowded with nannies pushing strollers and tourists consulting their maps. As they approached the entrance to the Academy of Sciences, Elliott slowed to allow a class of schoolchildren to file across the street, then he drove on until they reached the single-lane road leading to Stow Lake. He turned up the hill, and when he spotted a place to park along the unpaved shoulder, he immediately pulled into it.

"It's not entirely legal," he told Phoebe. "But it's the best we're likely to do."

They climbed out of the car and crossed the grass to the asphalt path and then made their way down to the old stone bridge that arched over the gray-green water, walking past the old men sitting on canvas folding chairs as they sketched the lake on their drawing pads, through dog walkers doling out treats as they trailed their leashed packs, lovers strolling arm in arm, whispering to each other in languages Elliott couldn't identify. Soon they approached the old boathouse, the rustic low-slung building above a wooden dock lined with white, fiberglass pedal boats. Beyond the frantic young mothers and their shrieking children, swarming over the picnic tables and green plank benches, a group of people stood in front of the steps leading up to the open concession stand.

"I'll be right back," Elliott said.

He walked up to the concession stand and took his place in line behind a woman in a peasant blouse and blue jeans, ordering hot dogs for her three young sons. As she tucked her change into her pocket, Elliott stepped up to the counter.

"I'd like to rent one of the pedal boats," he told the concessionaire in his red-and-white-striped shirt.

He slid a credit card across the counter, then picked up his receipt and carried it down the steps to one of the dock hands, who led them over to a pedal boat tied up beneath the long arm of the overhead lift.

"Perfect," Elliott said.

He stepped down onto the shallow platform at the stern, steadying himself with his left hand on the top of the seat.

"Oh, Elliott, don't move," Phoebe said.

As she fumbled through her bag for her camera, Elliott released the seat and straightened up, summoning yet another pose for her. But just as Phoebe took the photograph, a ripple across the surface of the lake caused the boat to bump the dock. For a panicked moment, Elliott feared he might topple into the water, but he lunged for the seat and caught himself, narrowly averting catastrophe.

"Are you all right, Pops?" the dock hand asked.

Smiling through his teeth, Elliott said, "Fine."

He reached out and took Phoebe's hand as she stepped down onto the boat, then helped her into the seat on the left while he lowered himself into the seat on the right.

"Shall we?" he asked.

"By all means, Admiral. Full steam ahead."

They lifted their feet onto the pedals, then leaned back and began pumping their legs, and slowly the boat pulled away from the dock. They pedaled along the shore of the wooded island in the middle of the lake, past the pintails and mallards feeding in the rushes, past the turtles floating amid the twisted crags, their nostrils piercing the murky waterline. After passing beneath the Roman Bridge, they plowed across the jade-green lake until they could see the waterfall cascading down the side of Strawberry Hill.

"This feels like one of those long-lost worlds we used to see in Saturday afternoon matinees," she said.

The thought pleased Elliott. He remembered well the long afternoons he'd spent as a boy in the city's great movie houses.

"I used to bring my daughter Claire here, when she was a young girl," he said. "I used to bring Alissa here, too, years later. This, of course, was before she took up the drums."

"Of course," Phoebe said.

"She loved the pink popcorn – they both did, actually."

Phoebe turned to Elliott as if in alarm.

"Pink popcorn?"

"I'm afraid so, yes," he said. "You can buy it at the concession stand. It comes in a brick."

"It sounds perfectly awful."

"Oh, it is, absolutely," he said.

She laughed as they drifted toward the Chinese pavilion at the base of the falls, lifting her face to the sun.

"So tell me, Elliott – tell me about your manuscript."

"What would you like to know?"

"How close are you to finishing it?"

"I like to think I'm nearly done," he said. "I have to believe I know as much as I'm ever going to know."

"What will you do with your manuscript next?"

"There are a few publishers in the Bay Area that specialize in local history. I suppose I'll contact them."

"That sounds wonderful."

"There's no guarantee they'll be interested," he said.

"Will you send a copy to Lila?"

"I will, of course," he said. "I couldn't have written it without her help."

"I'm sure she'll love it."

"We'll see," he said. "Lila can be a little persnickety herself."

Phoebe had to smile, knowing exactly what he meant.

"What about me?" she asked.

Elliott hadn't thought about giving a copy to Phoebe, but she certainly had a vested interest in learning what she could about his great-grandparents.

"I'd be glad to send you a copy," he said.

"Of course, you still have to write a chapter about the torrid love affair between Benjamin and your great-grandmother."

Elliott laughed.

"Yes, I'll get started on that right away," he said.

But Phoebe was serious.

"Don't you want it to be true?" she asked him. "I do – I want it to be true. I want to believe your great-grandmother was the love of Benjamin's life."

"Yes, I understand," he said.

"And you can't tell me I'm wrong."

And that was true. He had no proof that Harrigan and his great-grandmother were not lovers. Phoebe was right about that. He could not prove the negative.

"I'm right, and you know it, don't you?" she said, once again batting her eyes at him.

Elliott could only smile. There was nothing he could say to that.

AFTER RETURNING the pedal boat, they drove west across the city, along the southern edge of the park. Phoebe had come this far, more than three thousand miles – he would take her out to the edge of the continent to watch the sunset, as if to complete her journey. At Ocean Beach, they left the BMW in the parking lot and walked over to stand at the sea wall. They leaned onto the concrete and looked out at the long expanse of open shoreline – the last few clusters of people on towels quilting the sand, couples with their pant legs rolled up to their knees as they dashed in and out of the surf, surfers in their wetsuits sitting astride their boards as they waited to catch one last wave for the day. With seagulls wheeling overhead, they watched the sun slowly fall through the western sky, the bands of molten light as it sank through the horizon.

"The sun never sets on the Atlantic," he said.

"No, not like this, not in New York City," she said.

They returned to Russian Hill and walked up to Frascati on Hyde Street, a neighborhood restaurant just around the corner from his building. As a rule, Elliott didn't care for dining in the front windows of restaurants; he disliked feeling as if he was on display for anyone walking past to inspect or observe. But when he and Phoebe were ushered into the alcove beside the door, he raised no objection. He was relieved to be sitting down, and he had to believe that Phoebe felt the same way. They ate as if they hadn't seen a proper meal in weeks – the grilled pork chop with a glass of Chenin blanc for him, the pan-seared salmon and the Chardonnay for her. He sat back in his chair as their waiter cleared the table.

"Elliott, may I run an idea past you?"

"An idea about what?"

"About your great-grandparents' house in Anderson Valley."

"What about it?"

She took a sip of water, smiling across the top of the glass at him.

"Have you ever thought about restoring it?"

"What do you mean?" he asked.

"I mean fix it up, as good as new."

"Are you serious?"

"I am," she said. "Absolutely serious."

"Now how would I do that?" he asked. "It's not ours. We don't own it anymore. We haven't owned it for years."

"I know. I understand," she said. "But maybe you could work something out with the current owners."

"Like what?"

"I don't know," she said. "But they obviously don't have any use for it."

Elliott had no idea what Phoebe was talking about. He suspected she hadn't given it much thought, either.

"It's just such a beautiful house," she said. "Or at least it used to be."

"I don't think so, Phoebe."

"But have you ever really thought about it?" she asked.

He reached for his glass of water.

"No, I can't say that I have," he conceded.

"Don't you think you should?"

"Should what?"

"Have you ever thought about buying the house back?"

Elliott could have laughed. No, he'd never thought about buying the house back. Nor had he ever had cause.

"As far as I know, the house is not up for sale," he said.

"But that doesn't mean you can't make an offer," she said.

"Beeman and his son aren't going to sell the house back to me," he said.

"Well, maybe some kind of lease, then, a long-term lease."

"And why would they do that?"

"Why wouldn't they?"

Elliott laughed at the absurdity of it all.

"What have they got to lose?" she asked. "And you don't have anything to lose, either, not by just talking to them."

Elliott had no idea what might have prompted Phoebe's inspired thinking. But as appealing as the thought of restoring his great-grandparents' house might be, it was utterly unrealistic, the obstacles bluntly obvious. He saw no point in pursuing the conversation further.

"I'll give it some thought," he said, as if to put the matter to rest.

"Do you promise?"

"I promise," he said.

He placed his napkin on the table.

"Shall we?"

She didn't resist him.

"Of course," she said.

They rose from the table and stepped out onto the sidewalk. As they stood beneath the ficus trees planted along the sidewalk, a thickset man in a white shirt and red suspenders stepped out of the canine grooming parlor up the block, trailing his smartly coiffured Pomeranian. Elliott and Phoebe moved over to the curb to let the man and his dog pass by, nodding as they walked past the restaurant.

"Can't you just imagine it, though?" Phoebe asked.

Elliott looked over to her.

"Imagine what?"

"The house, Elliott – brand new, like it had just been built."

Elliott was at a loss. He didn't know what else to tell her.

"Think about your great-grandparents," she said. "Think about what they would think."

And that did give him pause. He knew exactly what his great-grandparents' would think if they could see their house in its current state.

"And who knows," Phoebe said. "I might just come back and help you."

THEY CROSSED CLAY STREET and entered the market on the corner, slipping past the rack of cut flowers beside the door, then making their way past the checkout counter and the narrow aisles of dry goods to the wall of cold cases in the back. Elliott opened the clouded glass door on the left and reached in for a bottle of champagne.

"I believe this will do," he said, showing the bottle to Phoebe.

"Champagne will always do," she said.

He carried the bottle back to the counter, where the owner of the market stood beside the cash register in his green grocer's apron.

"Do you have any glasses, or cups?" Elliott asked.

The owner leaned down behind the counter and produced two clear plastic cups.

"Excellent," Elliott said.

He paid for the champagne, and they left the market and started down the block, walking past the three-story apartment buildings that fronted the street, the bay windows above filled with light. They could hear scales being played on a piano, a child practicing, perhaps. As they passed the Nob Hill Cafe, they could smell the marinara sauce simmering on the stove in the open kitchen, the patrons seated at tables on the sidewalk, leaning over slices of thin-crust pizza and sipping glasses of red wine. The night was warm, perfectly still.

They walked down to Huntington Park, a quiet refuge at the crest of the hill, across from the gray Gothic monolith of Grace Cathedral. They climbed the stairs leading into the park, passing through the neatly trimmed hedge and the acacias that enclosed the modest brick square. There was a fountain in the middle of the square, a whimsical work of art featuring four lithe young men standing on the backs of dolphins as they reached up for the tortoises crawling out of a shallow marble bowl.

Elliott led Phoebe across the square to one of the benches facing the fountain, water splashing softly into its polished, rose marble basins.

"It's like a private garden," she said.

Elliott withdrew the bottle of champagne from the bag and placed it on the bench between his thighs, then carefully twisted off the wires securing the cork. Using his thumbs, he pushed out the cork. It released with a pop, shooting across the square, a torrent of foam surging out the mouth of the bottle as Elliott lifted it up and held it at arm's length, waiting for the foam to subside.

Phoebe steadied the plastic cups on the bench as Elliott filled them with champagne. He set the bottle down, and they raised the cups in a toast.

"To today," Elliott said.

"And the days to come," Phoebe said.

They sipped the champagne and sat back and looked up at the twin towers of the cathedral, sheathed in white light. Phoebe scooted toward him, her hip pressing against his.

"Are you sure you have to leave in the morning?" Elliott asked. "Are you sure you can't stay another day or two?"

"I wish I could," she said.

"You know you're welcome to stay at my place as long as you'd like."

"I know, I do," Phoebe said. "But I do have to get back."

Not at all seriously, Elliott said, "I hope you've got a good reason."

"I have a couple paintings in a show, actually."

"What?" he asked, turning to her.

"It's a group show, an artist's collective that I belong to," she explained. "It opens on Thursday night."

"That sounds very exciting," he said.

Phoebe allowed herself a laugh.

"I don't know how exciting it will be, but it's not like I get to show my work very often."

"I'm still impressed," Elliott said.

"My oldest daughter Laura is flying up from Texas," Phoebe said. "She teaches English in Brownsville."

"And your younger daughter?"

"No," she said. "Sandra won't be there. She's in Egypt. She's working on an archaeological site there, photographing the ruins."

"They sound like two very accomplished young women."

The thought seemed to settle over Phoebe.

"I miss them," she said. "I miss them every day."

Elliott had no difficulty understanding that.

"At least you'll be able to see Laura," he said.

"Yes, I'm grateful for that."

Elliott picked up the bottle of champagne and poured a splash into Phoebe's cup and then his own.

"I'd love to see your work some day," he said.

"You can always come visit me in New York."

The thought amused Elliott. He hadn't been to New York in years. For that matter, it had been years since he left the city.

"Yes, I suppose I could."

"I'm serious, Elliott."

"I know you are, and I thank you," he said. "I would love to fly back to New York some day. But these days, I feel like I need to stay around here."

"Alissa?" she asked, as if to be sure.

"I like to think she needs me, even if she doesn't know it," he said.

"She knows it, Elliott. Deep down, she knows it."

And Elliott liked that. He liked hearing that. And he did believe it was true. There was a way forward for Alissa. There was always a way forward. And as a man of his advanced age, he was old enough to know that it would reveal itself in good time.

AFTER DRINKING a second glass of champagne, Elliott rose from the bench and carried the half-full bottle over to the man in a camouflage jacket sleeping on a bench on the opposite side of the fountain. He set the bottle down in front of the bench, then he and Phoebe left the park and walked back to Russian Hill. As they turned onto Vallejo, he was relieved to see no light leaking out from beneath the garage door, relieved that Alissa and her bandmates were not practicing tonight. He opened the grate for Phoebe and then stepped up into the porch and unlocked the door to his flat. Hank was waiting for them at the top of the stairs, and after letting him out, they moved into the kitchen.

"Would you care for a nightcap?" he asked. "A shot of brandy, perhaps?"

He opened the cabinet above the refrigerator.

"No, I'm fine," she said. "I'm afraid the wine at dinner and the champagne in the park were more than enough for me."

Elliott reached for the bottle of brandy only to discover it was nearly empty.

Closing the cabinet door, he said, "That's probably enough for me, too."

"I think the trip has worn me out," she said.

"Shall we make up your bed?"

"I'm afraid I am a little tired."

They walked down the hall to his study. After turning on the lamp beside his desk, he lifted the cushions from the sofa and stacked them on the seat of the chair, then he leaned down and unfolded the sofa, the springs groaning as he pulled the mattress into position. He walked down to the hall closet for a pair of sheets and a comforter. Together, they made up the bed.

"We should probably leave here around nine to make your flight," he said.

"That sounds fine."

"Is there anything else?" he asked. "I'll leave a clean towel in the bathroom."

She reached up and touched the side of his face, her fingertips on his cheek.

"Thank you, Elliott. Thank you for today. You've been so kind."

The gesture caught him entirely by surprise, a warm rush of blood to his face. As she withdrew her hand, he took a step back.

"If you need anything, I'm just down the hall," he said.

"Good night, Elliott."

"Yes, good night," he said.

He turned and walked out of his study, down the hall to his bedroom, not at all sure what had just happened, what might have just happened. As he unbuttoned his shirt, he couldn't help but feel a vague sense of regret, perhaps even loss, as if a moment might have just slipped away from him. And yet, he couldn't be sure. And he certainly didn't mean to presume. Very likely, it was only his imagination, the indiscriminate stirring of a long-dormant impulse, a thought to be dismissed as swiftly as it arose. He took a deep breath and stepped out of his trousers and sat on the edge of the bed. It was only then that he realized how tired he was, too. It had been a fine day, a very fine day, but it had also been a long day.

As he stretched out on the mattress, it pleased him to know that Phoebe had enjoyed her extended stay in the city – the view of the city from Twin Peaks, the sunset at Ocean Beach, circling Stow Lake in one of the pedal boats. The thought made him smile, remembering her asking about his manuscript, her suggestion that he add a new chapter about the relationship between Harrigan and his great-grandmother. She was a dreamer, to be sure. And perhaps she was right. Perhaps Harrigan and his great-grandmother had been lovers. It was possible. He didn't deny it. But there was no way to know for sure, and he certainly didn't intend to speculate about the nature of their relationship in his manuscript.

And yet, as he stared up at the ceiling, he couldn't help but hope that Phoebe's baseless speculation might just contain an element of truth. He didn't like to think that his great-grandmother had lived alone all those years after his great-grandfather passed away. For her, and for Harrigan, as well, he hoped Phoebe was right.

And he was intrigued, increasingly, by her idea to restore his great-grandparents' house. The thought of returning the house to its original prominence had never occurred to him. It still astonished him that it had occurred to Phoebe. And yet what she had suggested was more than an idle thought, more than a mere idea – it was nothing less than a vision, an inspiration. She had seen the house in its abject disrepair, abandoned and all but forgotten, and she had envisioned what it might become again, recalling the photograph he had shown her of the house shortly after it was built. Of course, a project like that would not be as simple as she seemed to believe. The restoration would surely take months, if not years, to complete. And he didn't even want to think about how much it might cost. But in her enthusiasm, she was right to urge him to think about his great-grandparents, to imagine what they would think if he were to undertake such a project. It felt like an awakening. It felt like a calling.

Of course, he had no idea what she meant when she suggested

that she might be willing to come back and help him.

"Elliott?"

Startled, he pushed up onto his elbows. She was standing in the door of the room, a silhouette against the light down the hall.

"Is everything all right?" he asked.

"I wondered if I might join you."

"Of course," he said.

She moved into the darkened room, the mattress sinking as she sat beside him.

"Are you sure you don't mind?"

"No, of course not."

"I just thought that since this is our last night, we might spend it together."

"Certainly," he said.

He lifted the blanket for her to lie down beside him, but she leaned over and kissed him, pulling away slowly, the faint taste of the champagne still on her lips.

"Are you sure this is all right?" she asked.

"I'm sure," he said, his heart quickening in his chest. "I'm quite sure, actually."

As she stretched out alongside him, he drew the blanket up to her shoulder, and then he moved toward her, lifting his right arm so that he might drape it over her, fitting his knees into the backs of hers – but then he stopped. He drew his arm back and pulled away, abruptly fearing imminent humiliation, the shame and embarrassment of intimate failure, the inability to summon all that she might want or need from him. But surely she understood the limits of his affection, certainly on a moment's notice, before he might have prepared himself for the occasion. Of course, she did, he assured himself. Of course, she understood that he was no spring chicken, a weary old rooster, indeed.

He drew her toward him, fitting himself into her warmth, his arm across her chest and his hand beneath her breasts. At the back of her neck, he breathed in the scent of her skin. When he closed his eyes, he could hear the soft hiss of each breath passing through her lips. It seemed an eternity since he'd last held a woman, since his wife had walked out on their marriage. His half-hearted flirtations with Ms. Holbrook aside, he had all but reconciled himself to the likelihood that he would never enjoy this elemental pleasure again. And yet here Phoebe Crighton was, this curious woman from New York City, inexplicably in his arms.

Still, he had to know.

"Did you mean it when you said you might come back, if I decide to restore the house at the ranch?"

She didn't immediately answer, as if she needed a moment to ask the question of herself.

"I think so," she said. "I think I do."

"Well, I think it's only fair to tell you that I'm giving the idea serious consideration."

CHAPTER SEVENTEEN

IN HIS TAN KHAKIS and red-and-black flannel shirt, Elliott walked out the back door and down the plank stairs. Gripping the railing with his right hand, he was painfully aware that his balance was not what it used to be. He'd never fully regained the strength in his left leg after hip replacement surgery seven years ago, and a severe ear infection last winter had left him vulnerable to the occasional bout of vertigo. It was only last week that he'd tripped while helping Phoebe carry groceries into the house, stubbing his toe on the threshold and stumbling to his hands and knees, landing hard on his right shoulder. And despite the heating pad he applied every evening, his shoulder was still sore and cranky, not at all unlike his mood whenever he recalled himself sprawled out in the foyer.

At the foot of the stairs, he started across the vegetable garden, walking slowly along the rows of dry corn stalks, treading softly on the gravel path. After letting himself out the back gate, he walked over to the last of the fruit trees planted by his great-grandmother nearly a century ago. Although the apple orchard had been torn out shortly after his father sold the ranch, one last apple tree had survived behind the garden – an ancient Northern Spy. Most of its craggy black limbs had died off over the years, but several branches were still alive, propped up with wooden poles, their leaves trembling in the warm breeze moving down the valley. Elliott reached up and twisted off one of the green red-striped apples. He needed eight of them. Alissa was driving up to the ranch for a visit, and, in honor of the occasion, Phoebe had promised to bake a pie.

When he finished picking the apples, he carried them into the house, where Phoebe was rolling out the pie crust on the kitchen counter. She looked over to him as he closed the door. Threaded with gray, her black hair was casually clipped back off her face. Her blue jeans were dusted with flour handprints, the sleeves of her white shirt folded up above her wrists.

"Well?"

"They look good," he told her. "They'll be fine."

He placed the apples on the table, then walked into the pantry and retrieved his great-grandmother's cast-iron apple peeler. It was a crude device, heavy and awkward, and he struggled to tighten the clamp to secure it to the edge of the table. And yet, as primitive as the peeler was, it was also highly efficient. He pressed one of the apples onto the two horizontal spikes and began cranking the wooden handle, and as the apple rotated, the blade removed the peel in a long thin strip. He pulled the apple from the spikes and pushed out the core with his fingertip.

"Perfect," he said, as if to congratulate himself.

When he finished peeling and coring the apples, he cut them into slices and placed them in a large bowl beside the spice bottles – cinnamon, nutmeg and cardamom. After returning the peeler to the pantry, he stood beside Phoebe and watched as she carefully wrapped the pie crust around the rolling pin, then unwrapped the crust onto the glass pie plate.

"Well done," he said.

"This ain't my first picnic, sonny."

Elliott allowed himself a laugh, then walked out of the kitchen, down the narrow hall to the front door. He stepped out onto the porch, pausing for a moment as a scrub jay swooped down from one of the sycamores, then walked down to the wicker chairs at the end of the porch. As he sat down and leaned back in the chair, the thatched cane groaning beneath him, he found himself thinking about the summer he'd spent here with his great-grandmother, sitting here on the porch in the evening, listening to the big bands on the radio, the up-tempo jazz that should have lifted her spirits but instead always seemed to sadden her. He liked to think he understood a little more about the source of that melancholia now, the hardship and heartbreak she had endured over the course of her life. Now, he had to believe that music simply reminded her of what might have been, of all she might have had.

She died that fall, only a few short months after his visit, her funeral held on a late autumn afternoon very much like this. He remembered arriving at the Methodist Church with his father and mother, walking through the mourners standing on the front lawn, feeling their eyes upon them as they climbed the steps leading up to the church doors. The pews inside were filled, the walls lined with mourners who had no place to sit. In front of the pulpit, the oak casket was covered with white Calla lilies. He could still hear the low murmur of voices, the muffled sobbing as the pastor stood before them in his white clerical robe, leading the assembled as they rose to their feet and sang the chosen hymns. He would never forget watching his father break down while delivering the eulogy, recalling the life of a woman who seemed to belong to them all.

When the service was over, they walked out of the church, trailing the pallbearers as they carried the casket out to the idling hearse. In his father's Hudson, they drove to the cemetery, where the pallbearers carried the casket through the sunlight boring down through the mingled limbs of the oaks. Beneath a white cloth canopy, he sat between his father and mother in folding chairs positioned beside the excavated grave, the silence broken only by the footsteps of the mourners gathering for the burial. At the head of the grave, the pastor bid his great-grandmother farewell, then quietly looked on as her casket was lowered into the ground. His father rose from his chair and tossed the lilies onto the casket, his voice breaking as he invited everyone out to the ranch for a celebration of Amelia Snyder Madison's remarkable life.

Standing here on the front porch, his father waited for the mourners walking up the gravel road. He shook the hands of the men and embraced the women, thanking them for coming and ushering them into the house. Elliott would never forget wandering through the gathering that afternoon, through the dining room where a great feast had been arranged on the long walnut table, through the gallery of photographs in the parlor, tracing the long arc of his great-grandmother's life. He still remembered the stories about her kindness and generosity, the ranchers she helped and the men she hired, her role in the founding of the town and her broader vision for the valley itself. Even then, even as a young boy, he'd understood that his great-grandmother was larger than all those who had come to mourn her passing, that her death marked not merely the loss of a great woman, but the close of an era, the end of a way of life. What he would give for another hour with her now, now that he knew what he wanted to ask, now that he understood all that he didn't know.

SURELY, SHE WOULD BE PLEASED with the restoration of the house, though it must be said that it had not been easy. When Elliott initially approached the owners of the ranch, Beeman and his son dismissed the idea out of hand. Elliott understood that it was an unusual proposal. He understood why they might be hesitant to even consider it. But he pressed them by letter and by phone, ultimately persuading Beeman's son to meet for lunch at the Boonville Hotel. Over that lunch, Elliott told him about his great-grandfather's voyage around Cape Horn and the year he spent on the West Branch, his great-grandmother crossing the continent on the California Trail. He told him about those first difficult years on the original homestead, the sheep they raised and the apple orchard they planted. And he told him what the house meant in the fullest context of the valley's history. His proposal was simple: he would pay all the costs of the restoration if they would lease the house to him for twenty-five years. Finally, a deal was struck, secured by a handshake across the table. Still, it took nearly a year for the Beemans' lawyers and the lawyers Elliott hired from his father's old firm to finalize a lease.

With the signed lease in hand, Elliott boarded a flight to New York City. He had been keeping Phoebe abreast of the negotiations, of course, but he hadn't told her that he intended to fly back East to celebrate when the arrangement was settled. He landed at JFK at nine o'clock at night. By the time he collected his bag and caught a cab into Manhattan, it was nearly eleven o'clock. From the sidewalk in front of her apartment building, he called her on her cell phone. She shrieked with delight and rushed down to let him in. They spent the next two weeks drawing up plans for the restoration of the house – and penciling out plans for themselves as well. When Elliott returned to San Francisco, he contacted a realtor in Boonville, who helped him rent a cottage in town where they would live during the restoration. Phoebe joined him there three months later.

As Elliott sat on the porch, breathing in the divine aroma of Phoebe's pie in the oven, he had to laugh at the sheer improbability of it all. It was absurd, insane, irrational in the extreme. It still amazed him how little he and Phoebe knew about each other when they decided to embark on this project. It was small wonder that Claire and Alissa thought he'd lost his mind, objecting to their plan in the strongest possible terms. Phoebe's two daughters were just as appalled. And true, it was a gamble, an uncalculated risk. But what, really, did they have to lose, and now here they were, nearly ten years later.

Their first order of business had been to hire a contractor to conduct a thorough inspection of the house. It was immediately determined that the old stone foundation needed to be replaced, and it wasn't until the new concrete foundation was poured that the restoration began in earnest. Scaffolding was erected around the perimeter of the house, so the disintegrating wooden shakes could be stripped off the roof and the damaged shiplap siding replaced with new siding custom-milled in Santa Rosa. While the broken-out windows were removed and new double-pane windows installed, a carpenter from town repaired the intricate woodwork that adorned the eaves, and a team of stonemasons repaired the fireplace. Finally, they brought in a colorist to oversee the crew of painters who returned the house to its original blue-gray with white trim.

Meanwhile, they gutted the interior of the house and brought it up to contemporary standards. While preserving the original wainscoting, the walls were properly insulated and the plumbing and electrical lines upgraded. The original hardwood floors were stripped and sanded, the water-damaged sections replaced before the floors were stained and lacquered. They purchased a new stove and refrigerator for the kitchen, then installed a dishwasher beneath the black granite counter tops. In the dining room, the built-in hutch was meticulously refurbished, including replacing the beveled-glass cabinet doors. The colorist also directed the painting of the interior – the kitchen a buttery yellow, the dining room silver-gray, the parlor and the library cabernet red, the bedrooms upstairs sky blue.

He and Phoebe drove out to the house nearly every day to consult with the contractor and observe the work being done, and as far as Elliott was concerned, the project was worth every penny he paid out over the course of nearly twenty months. The house at the ranch was not only the oldest house in the valley, it was now, in Elliott's opinion, the one of the finest houses in the valley, resplendent in its restoration, a fitting monument to the vision and determination of his great-grandparents. It had been a process of renewal and rebirth, and when he and Phoebe moved in, he couldn't help but feel as if he had been born anew as well. He had to believe that Phoebe felt that way, too.

He could hear her inside the house, the shrill whistle of the teakettle on the stove. She had convinced him to give up coffee and was preparing a cup of tea for him instead – the hibiscus and cinnamon tea that in her view provided any number of beneficial medicinal effects, from lowering blood pressure and reducing cholesterol to boosting energy and cleaning out the toxins that invaded the body cells. She liked to add a small strip of dried orange peel, believing it contained anti-inflammatory, antioxidant and anti-cancer properties.

She brought the tea out to him, setting the mug on the cedar table beside his chair.

"Do we know when Alissa will arrive?" she asked.

"She said they hoped to arrive early this afternoon, but who knows," he said.

"I can't wait to see your great-granddaughter," Phoebe said. "They grow up so quickly."

"Why don't you bring your tea out and sit with me?" he said.

She smiled, placing her hand on his right shoulder.

"I've still got a few things to do in the kitchen," she said.

AS HE TOOK A SIP of the tea, he looked out across the yard, through the grown-over trellis and down the gravel road to the gate leading into the ranch. It would not be long before he would see Alissa turning in through the gate in her blue Honda Civic. And he was indeed anxious to see her. Nearly three months had passed since he last held his great-granddaughter, and it seemed so much longer than that. Phoebe was certainly right when she said children grow up quickly. He had witnessed that swift metamorphosis with his daughter Claire, and Alissa had been no different – one day a perfectly delightful, inquisitive child, suddenly a sullen teenager in open conflict with her mother, now, miraculously, a mother in her own right.

With a laugh, he wondered if she had ever read the book he had given her. To be perfectly honest, he doubted it, and that was fine. It was her decision, and he had no intention of asking her about it in the future. He had published the book himself, after approaching several Bay Area publishers. While they all praised his manuscript, specifically the quality of his writing and the thoroughness of his research, they all, ultimately, declined to publish it. He then wrote to a number of agents to ask if they might be interested in representing his manuscript, but the few he heard back from didn't view the project as commercially viable. So he hired a former colleague at the *Chronicle* to edit the manuscript and proofread the pages, another from the art department to design the front and back covers. The initial press run was two hundred copies, which he knew might be excessively ambitious. But it was better to be optimistic than not, he told himself.

Shortly after receiving the first shipment of books, he drove down to the city with several copies in his leather satchel. He parked in the Civic Center garage, then walked over to the Main Library, the automatic doors silently parting for him as he passed through the entrance. He crossed through the atrium and climbed the stairs up to the third floor, where he found Stanley dead asleep and slumped onto his desk, his head on one of his yellow legal pads. He thought about waking Stanley to present him with a copy of his book, but he was snoring so robustly that Elliott declined to disrupt him and simply placed the book on the table, where he would find it when he woke.

When he emerged from the stacks behind the reference desk, he saw that Doris was working at the Page Desk. He hadn't seen or heard from her since he moved to Anderson Valley. As he approached the desk, she looked up, peering at him over the red rims of her reading glasses, a thin smile of recognition forming on her gray lips.

"Well, hello, Elliott. How may I help you?"

"Actually," he said with a casual flourish, "I brought you something."

She sat back in her chair, her limp brown hair falling to the sweater wrapped around her shoulders, looking on as he reached into the satchel.

"A copy of my book," he said.

With a bow, he presented the book to her,.

"Why, thank you, Elliott," she said, gazing down at the book, studying the cover for a moment, then turning it over in her hands.

"It's signed," he said. "There's an inscription on the title page."

She opened the book and turned to the title page and read the inscription aloud:

"For Doris, Thanks for all your help, thanks for everything, Elliott."

She looked back up at him.

"That's very kind."

"It's my pleasure," he said. "And I brought along two extra copies. I thought perhaps the library might want a copy or two."

"A book by a local author, a former editor at the *Chronicle* – I'd be glad to deliver these to the acquisitions department for their consideration."

"I'd be most grateful."

He watched as she picked up her tissue and dabbed her nostrils.

"Will there be anything else?" she asked.

Elliott had to smile, the night they met for dinner and a movie now all but forgotten.

"No, that's all," he said. "There's nothing else."

AND, OF COURSE, he had given an inscribed copy to Lila, along with a brief note thanking her for her assistance with his research, as well as their many broader discussions about the history of the valley. She had a few minor comments about his book, naturally, but her remarks were largely positive, and she consented to allow him to sell copies in the museum. She insisted, however, that all profits from the sale of those books be divided equally between him and the historical society. Elliott had no objection.

He sold fifteen to twenty books per year at the museum, most of them to casual visitors to the old schoolhouse. But he also sold copies to the scattered descendants of some of the oldest families in the valley, alerted to the publication of his book by the occasional reference in the historical society newsletter. Every now and then, he would receive a letter from one of those descendants, typically sent to the historical society and subsequently forwarded by Lila, and it was a delight to hear from them, to hear about their ancestors, the stories of their lives in the valley and their relationships with his great-grandparents. It felt like a validation of all his research, of all the hours he had spent at the library and in his study. Their letters made him feel as if his primary mission had been accomplished, that his great-grandparents lived on in the hearts and minds of all those who read his book.

Several years ago, one of those readers contacted Lila to ask if she might be interested in seeing a brief memoir her great-grandmother had written about life on a ranch outside Boonville. Naturally, Lila was intrigued and wrote back to say that she would very much like to read the memoir. Titled "Memories of Life in Anderson Valley," it was a slim typewritten volume of fifty-three pages, and Lila read through it the morning it arrived in the mail.

She immediately called Elliott.

"I think you might want to see this," she told him.

He and Phoebe drove over to the historical society that afternoon, parking in front of the old schoolhouse and then letting themselves in through the balky front door. They passed through the museum and found Lila in her office, sitting at her desk, her white hair loosely pinned up.

"Hello, Lila," Elliott said as he positioned a pair of folding chairs in front of the desk.

She waited for them to sit down, the early map of the upper valley on the wall behind her.

"Do you remember the Whitman family?" she asked him.

Elliott recognized the name.

"They owned a ranch just down the valley from us, I believe."

"Several weeks ago, I received a letter from a woman named Marilyn Byrnes, who asked if I'd be interested in seeing a copy of a memoir written by her great-grandmother – Lucinda Whitman."

"I'm not familiar with Lucinda Whitman, specifically," Elliott said.

"She and her three sisters arrived in the valley with their parents, James and Eleanor Whitman, in 1867," Lila said. "She lived in the valley until 1904, when she moved to Cloverdale to live with her oldest daughter. She knew your great-grandmother quite well, as you might assume. She had many kind things to say about her."

"That's always nice to hear," Elliott said.

Lila looked to Phoebe.

"She also knew your great-grandmother's uncle, Mr. Harrigan."

Phoebe smiled nervously.

"What does she say about Benjamin?" she asked.

At the sound of Harrigan's given name, Lila seemed to soften slightly, a copy of the memoir on the desk in front of her, several pages tagged with yellow post-its.

"She describes Mr. Harrigan as a sweet man, a quiet man who largely kept to himself, a bit of a loner, it sounds like."

"That wouldn't surprise me," Elliott said, as if to confirm the observation.

"No," Phoebe quietly said.

But Elliott knew that wasn't why Lila had called. And he was sure Phoebe knew that, too. He watched as Lila picked up the memoir and turned back to the pages she had tagged.

"I'm afraid Mr. Harrigan was also known to disappear every once in a while, often for days at a time," she said. "No one would have any idea where he'd gotten off to until word eventually arrived that he'd turned up in Ukiah or Manchester or Fort Bragg, typically in a state of extreme inebriation."

"Dear God," Phoebe said.

Lila lifted the first of the pages she had tagged, looking down as if to make sure she wasn't misspeaking.

"There was some speculation, apparently, that these episodes might have derived from Mr. Harrigan's experiences during the war."

"That wouldn't surprise me, either," Elliott said.

"No," Lila said, lowering the page. "That certainly seems possible."

She lifted her eyes to Phoebe.

"It also seems there was concern these episodes might result in substantial harm to Mr. Harrigan's wellbeing."

"Oh, Benjamin," Phoebe sighed.

Lila turned to Elliott.

"And so your great-grandmother would go fetch him and bring him back to the ranch and nurse him back to health. And then, apparently, life would go on as before, as if nothing had happened, nothing at all."

Elliott could only nod.

"I see," he said.

He watched Lila peel the post-its from the pages, then straighten up the memoir.

"I'm sure that's not what you were expecting to hear," she said.

"I don't know that we had any expectations, not specifically," he said.

She handed the copy of the memoir to him.

"I'm sorry," Lila said.

They drove back to the ranch and sat at the table in the dining room and read through the slender volume. It was largely devoted to life on the Whitman family ranch, of course, their struggle to survive those first years in the valley, and Ms. Whitman's observations about Harrigan were not long, nor many. And yet from those brief passages, there was every reason to believe that he was a tormented soul, profoundly troubled by what he had seen and experienced during the war and in the prison camp. It was easy to believe those disturbing experiences might explain why Harrigan migrated west after his recuperation in East Fishkill, as if he meant to leave the war behind, as well as why he never returned to see the niece who adored him. Clearly, he had found sanctuary on Elliott's family's ranch. He had also found a woman willing to care for him when those haunting memories returned, a woman who was heartbroken when he died.

"This explains so much," Phoebe said.

"We certainly know more than we did, more than I thought we ever would," Elliott said.

"They were lovers, I believe that now more than ever," Phoebe said.

But that was further than Elliott would permit himself to go. The paragraphs in the Whitman memoir were a revelation, certainly, but not, in his view, a confirmation.

Still, he was not going to dispute her.

"It's certainly possible," he said. "I'm not going to tell you you're wrong."

WHEN HE SAW Alissa's Honda turn in through the gate, he pushed up from the wicker chair and started down the front steps, steadying himself with his right hand on the railing. He crossed the yard and passed through the trellis as Alissa parked the Honda in the shade of one of the chestnuts. As he approached the car, he could see his great-granddaughter strapped into the baby carrier in the back seat. With his forepaws on the base of the window, Hank stood on the seat beside the carrier, his tongue hanging out the side of his mouth.

Alissa pushed her door open and climbed out of the car. She was wearing a white peasant blouse and a pair of blue jeans with a beaded belt. Her hair was no longer a mass of dyed-green spikes but had grown out soft and brown and curled around the sides of her face. And she had forsaken the green eye shadow and dark mascara that used to crudely define her eyes, though a few of the stars tattooed on her neck were still visible above the collar of her shirt. She was in her early thirties now, the mother of a baby girl, no longer the angry drummer in a heavy metal power trio. As Elliott had discretely noted to Phoebe, The Sores had healed.

"Hello," he greeted her. "You made it."

"I'm sorry we're late," she said.

"You're here now – that's all that matters."

He took her in his arms, kissing the top of her head as she slipped her arms around his waist.

"It's so good to see you," he said.

He held the door of the Honda for her as she released the baby carrier and then lifted it out of the car. The baby was crying softly, a string of saliva leaking down her chubby chin.

"How is she doing?" he asked.

"She's heavy, is what she is," Alissa said. "She weighs almost twenty pounds."

As she started toward the trellis, Elliott waited for Hank. Old and arthritic, the dog slowly climbed down from the seat and then stiffly followed Alissa into the interior yard, walking as if each step was an exercise in pain. Elliott had no trouble imagining how Hank felt.

When they reached the front steps, Phoebe emerged from the house.

"Welcome!" she said, spreading her arms. "Come in, come in."

She stood aside as Alissa lugged the baby carrier up the steps and then into the parlor, where she placed the carrier on the sofa and dropped down onto the cushion beside it.

"She's beautiful," Phoebe cooed. "My, how she's grown."

When the baby began to whimper, Alissa lifted her out of the carrier and cradled her in her arms.

"She's just hungry," Alissa said. "I fed her before we left, but that was three hours ago."

Elliott walked down the hall to the kitchen. He took a stainless steel mixing bowl from the cabinet and filled it with water and then returned to the parlor, where he placed the bowl in front of the hearth for Hank. As he straightened up, he saw that Alissa had lifted her blouse to nurse the baby. The sight of her swollen breast startled him for a moment, the baby greedily suckling her left nipple. He discretely turned away and crossed the room and sat in the armchair in the front window.

He still could not quite believe how motherhood had changed his granddaughter, transforming her into the person he liked to think she was always destined to become. He recalled his initial alarm when she told him that she was pregnant and that Nigel was moving into the flat on Vallejo. Now he knew he should have trusted her. For the past several years, Nigel had been working the night shift at the public parking garage in North Beach, and Alissa intended to return to her job at Tower Records as soon as she could. They had found a way to make their lives work, and Elliott would be the first to say the building he had inherited from his father looked no worse for their occupancy, although the last time he and

Phoebe had visited them, he had noticed an unfortunate abundance of Hank's droppings in the back yard.

"How have you been?" he asked her.

The question seemed to soften her, her shoulders slumping as if finally relaxing from the drive.

"I'm exhausted, mostly," she said. "Cassandra's still not a very good sleeper. I'm up at least two or three times a night."

Elliott felt himself smile again, remembering when Alissa was considering changing her name to Cassandra, as if she wanted to become someone else, someone other than herself. That seemed so long ago.

"Your mother was like that," he told her, remembering his ex-wife Evelyn getting up in the middle of the night to attend to Claire. "It will pass."

"That's what they tell me in my mother's group," she said. "We meet three mornings a week in Washington Square."

"You might call your own mother, from time to time, for a little maternal advice," Elliott suggested.

"She calls almost every day," Alissa said.

"She was a fine mother," he said. "She was absolutely devoted to you."

"So she likes to tell me."

When Cassandra finished nursing, Alissa tugged down her blouse and wiped off the baby's wrinkled mouth. With the baby in her arms, she rose from the sofa and crossed the room to him.

"Would you like to hold her?" she asked.

"You know I would," Elliott said.

He reached out and took Cassandra from her, gently cupping the back of the baby's head in his hand as he drew her to him. She did, indeed, seem heavy, certainly heavier than when he last held her. He had to believe that was a sign of good health.

"Hello, little one," he said.

He looked down into her faint blue eyes. She stared up at him as if in astonishment, her cheeks round and pink, downy brown hair clinging to her scalp.

"How are you?" he asked.

She wiggled again, thrusting out her tiny feet, then burped up the milk, sluicing out the corners of her tiny mouth.

"Goodness," Elliott said, lifting her up to rest against his left shoulder.

As he gently patted her back, she burped up a little more.

"Oh, dear," Alissa said, quickly digging through her bag for a burp cloth.

"It's fine, perfectly fine," Elliott said. "What else are great-grandfathers for?"

THEY PREPARED A LATE LUNCH – spaghetti with a sauce Phoebe had made with plum tomatoes she'd grown in the garden behind the house. Having been raised in New York City, she was not a natural gardener, but she took to it quickly after they moved out to the ranch. In the spring, they cut fresh spears of her asparagus and harvested her artichokes. Every summer, she grew long rows of tomatoes, corn, green peppers, and eggplant. They expected her blueberry bushes to begin producing next year. Elliott loved to sit on the back porch and watch her work in the garden, wearing her straw hat with its floppy brim, as well as the kneepads and cloth gloves he'd purchased for her birthday. As he took the plates down from the hutch, he knew his great-grandmother would be delighted to see that Phoebe had revived the garden that had lain fallow ever since she died.

After Elliott tossed a green salad and Phoebe ladled the sauce onto the spaghetti, they carried the bowls into the dining room. Alissa was already sitting at the table.

"Please, help yourself," Phoebe told her as she placed the bowl of spaghetti in front of her.

"I thought I might open a bottle of wine," Elliott said. "This certainly qualifies as a special occasion."

"A fine idea," Phoebe said.

As she and Alissa lifted the spaghetti onto their plates, Elliott opened a bottle of pinot noir. He filled their glasses, then sat at the head of the table and raised his glass in a toast.

"To Cassandra," he said.

"Oh, yes," Phoebe said. "To your lovely baby girl."

Elliott looked over to the baby in her carrier in a chair beside the table. Teething on a plastic ring, she was wearing a Cream onesie featuring the likenesses of Eric Clapton, Jack Bruce and Ginger Baker, the seminal power trio still one of Alissa's favorite bands. Hank lay on the floor beneath her, as if on sentry duty, his muzzle gray now, nearly white.

"It won't be long before she's walking," he said.

"She's already trying to stand," Alissa said.

"And then she'll begin talking," Phoebe said. "I remember when my oldest daughter started talking. There wasn't a moment of peace in the house from that day on."

Elliott reached for the bowl of spaghetti.

"When will she begin daycare?" he asked.

"Not for another year or so," Alissa said. "I've already started putting her name on lists. It's a pain in the ass."

"Parenting is so much harder now than it used to be," Elliott said. "It's too hard, in my humble opinion."

Alissa took a sip of her wine.

"We'll be fine," she said.

"Actually, I have no doubt," he said.

They ate slowly, a quiet communion among themselves, a celebration of the family they had become, absent, of course, Claire, who complained that Alissa hadn't told her about the gathering until it was too late for her join them, and Nigel, who had enrolled at City College and was taking courses in law enforcement with the goal of finding employment in the more lucrative private security industry. But they were there in spirit, certainly, members in good standing of their singular clan.

When they finished lunch, Elliott rose to clear the table.

"Can I interest anyone in some apple pie?"

"I would love a piece," Alissa said.

"Then you shall have one," he said.

He walked into the kitchen for the pie, the glass plate still so hot from the oven that he had to use a dish towel to pick it up. He carried the pie into the dining room, then returned to the kitchen for the salted caramel ice cream.

"Phoebe made the pie," he said.

"It's beautiful," Alissa said. "And it smells wonderful, too."

"Elliott picked the apples," Phoebe said.

"It's true," Elliott said. "I did."

"And he peeled and cored them on your great-great-great grandmother's apple peeler," Phoebe said. "It's quite the contraption."

"The apples are Northern Spys," Elliott said. "My great-grandmother said they were her favorite apples for pie. She liked them because they're so sweet and tart."

He looked on as Phoebe gave Alissa a slice of the pie with a spoonful of the ice cream, as Alissa cut a piece and raised it to her mouth.

"Oh, my God," she said, closing her eyes as if to dissolve into the very moment.

And that was all Elliott needed to see – the pleasure she found in a simple slice of pie, the transcendent joy she found in the fruit of the last apple tree on the ranch, bequeathed through the generations. As Elliott picked up his fork, it felt like all that mattered.

WHEN THEY FINISHED, Elliott carried the pie and ice cream back into the kitchen. Before he returned the ice cream to the freezer, he pried up the container lid for one last spoonful, then he cut himself a final slice of the pie before wrapping it up and sliding it into the refrigerator. There was still enough pie for tomorrow, perhaps even for breakfast. He loved eating pie for breakfast. It seemed so decadent, especially with ice cream.

After rinsing off the plates and running the dishwasher, he walked down the hall to the parlor, where Phoebe and Alissa were sitting beside the baby carrier.

"She's sleeping," Phoebe whispered.

He looked down at the baby, swaddled in a soft white blanket as she lay on her back, her head turned slightly to the left. He remembered the hours he'd spent looking down at Claire as she slept in her bassinet, the overwhelming gratitude he felt upon the occasion of his daughter's birth. He had to believe that Alissa felt the same way when she looked down at Cassandra.

"Come sit with me before she wakes up," he said to her.

They moved out onto the porch, the screen door rattling closed as they walked over to the wicker chairs. The afternoon sun slanted down through the sycamores, elms and chestnuts, bathing the porch in its failing light. It was still warm, even this late in the fall, but he knew a chill would arrive with nightfall. He thought perhaps he would build a fire tonight, the ritual first fire of the year.

"I started reading your book," Alissa said.

Elliott turned to her.

"Is that true?"

"Your great-grandfather is on a ship called the *Cordelia*. They've sailed across the Atlantic and then down to Rio de Janeiro. But that's as far as I've read."

"It's about to get exciting," he said.

"What do you mean?"

But he was not going to tell her. He had worked too hard on the book to give the story away.

"You'll find out," he said.

She smiled, taking him at his word.

"I try to read it while Cassandra is taking her naps," she said.

Elliott looked back out to the shadows lengthening in front of the house. His granddaughter had no idea how that pleased him.

"I'd love to know what you think when you finish reading it," he said.

But before she could respond, he felt an odd burning sensation above his stomach. He placed his hand on his chest. He supposed it was the last scoop of ice cream, the last slice of pie. He supposed he'd overindulged.

"Are you all right?" Alissa asked.

"A little indigestion, that's all," he said.

"Shall I get you a glass of water?"

"No, no," he hastened to say. "I'll get it. I'll be right back."

But as he pushed up to stand, he felt light-headed, the porch slowly revolving around him. He reached down and gripped the arm of the chair, afraid for a moment that he might lose his balance. He lowered himself onto a knee.

"What's wrong?" Alissa asked, quickly moving over to steady him.

"Nothing, nothing – I'm fine," he assured her.

And he was fine. He just needed a moment, that was all.

"Phoebe!" Alissa called into the house.

It occurred to him that he might feel better if he sat back down. He raised his right arm for Alissa. She took it and helped him up, his legs wobbling as if they might give out beneath him as he lurched back into the chair.

"Phoebe! " she called out again. "Could you come out here?"

And, yes, that was better. He took a deep breath and let himself settle into a simple rhythm, breathing in, breathing out as Phoebe emerged from the house and hurried over to him.

"Elliott?"

She sank down onto her knees in front of him, her hands on his thighs.

"Elliott, are you all right?"

He wanted to laugh. Of course, he was all right, though he could use a glass of water. That would help.

"Absolutely," he said.

She took his hands, lying forgotten in his lap.

"I want you to look at me," she said.

But he was still looking down at his hands, remembering them, recalling how he loved taking hers on their morning walks through the vineyard, or when they drove into town for dinner at the hotel, on their visits to the cemetery, where they stood in the hushed grove of oaks and paid their respects to all those who had come to reside there.

It brought to mind the day they had driven up from the city to look for Harrigan's grave, the day they found the headstone that had toppled over. He would never forget lifting it up and scrubbing the dirt from its face, that glorious moment of discovery when they saw Harrigan's name scored into the smooth granite. The memory of her unexpected visit, those three sublime days, always brought him pleasure. Hapless romantic that he was, susceptible to moments of misty sentimentality, he liked to remind himself that in searching for Harrigan's grave, he and Phoebe had found each other.

And yet, she seemed to be crying. He didn't understand. He tried to lift his arms, so he could reach for her and comfort her, but a strange gravity weighed him down.

"Elliott, can you hear me?"

And that was better, the sound of her voice. He felt himself relax, the quiet rise and fall of his chest. He could hear the leaves rustling high in the trees. Yes, it was certainly that time of year. And suddenly he felt himself smile, overcome by an incandescent burst of joy. What a splendid autumn day it had been! What a wonderful afternoon! What a lucky man he was!

And when Phoebe called out his name, he wished he could tell her how much he was going to miss her, so much more than she would ever know. He closed his eyes and tipped his head back. He took a deep breath, filling his lungs with the sweet liquid air, and yes, it was true – he could feel the warm blush of the sun on his face.

ACKNOWLEDGEMENTS

While writing this novel, I relied upon the extraordinary body of literature that has been written about the nation's westward migration and the California Gold Rush from George Stewart's seminal "The California Trail" to J. S. Holliday's "The World Rushed In: The California Gold Rush Experience." I found two publications particularly helpful: "The Overland Journal," published by the Oregon-California Trail Association, and the "Dogtown Territorial Quarterly," later the "California Territorial Quarterly," published and edited by Bill and Penny Anderson. I also relied on the two-volume "History of Butte County," by Joseph F. McGie.

When writing about early San Francisco, my primary source of information was "The Annals of San Francisco," a history of the city between 1845 and 1855, by Frank Soule, John H. Gihon, M.D., and James Nisbet.

The Anderson Valley Historical Society was an invaluable source of information about the history of the region. I found "Sketches of Anderson Valley," published by the society in 1989 and 1990, to be most useful. I also drew from "Down to Earth: A Mendocino County Life," by Maurice W. Tindall.

There is a wealth of literature about the Civil War battles and campaigns in which the 128th New York Voluntary Infantry Regiment was engaged. I was introduced to the regiment by "Full Measure of Devotion: The Columbia Companies of the One Hundred and Twenty-eighth New York, A Narrative," by Bud Miller. I was also able to locate two books published by members of the regiment: "Diary of an Enlisted Man," by Lawrence Alstyne, and "History of the One Hundred and Twenty-Eighth Regiment, New York Volunteers (U.S. Infantry) in the Late Civil War," by D.H. Hanaburgh.

I will always be in debt to friends who read my manuscript and offered their invaluable insights: David Auld, Susan Browne, Joe Kane, Katie Kleinsasser, Meredith May, Regan McMahon, Joan Ryan, and Gary Thompson. My deepest apologies for such dreadful early drafts.

I'd also like to note that while I worked on this manuscript, three close friends passed away, each of them a great source of support and encouragement over the years: Jeff Gillenkirk (1949-2016), Bryce Conrad (1951-2017), and Michael Blumlein (1948-2019). This novel was written in their memory.

Finally, I could not have written *Westbound* without the love and patience of my wife, Christine. As always, this is for her.

www.ingramcontent.com/pod-product-compliance
Lightning Source LLC
Chambersburg PA
CBHW030824310726
48980CB00006B/622/J
9780985631222